Sacred Ground

A NOVEL

By Charles E. Miller

iUniverse, Inc.
New York   Bloomington

Sacred Ground

iUniverse books may be ordered through booksellers or by contacting:

iUniverse
1663 Liberty Drive
Bloomington, IN 47403
www.iuniverse.com
1-800-Authors (1-800-288-4677)

ISBN: 978-1-4401-0327-8 (pbk)
ISBN: 978-1-4401-0328-5 (ebk)

Printed in the United States of America

iUniverse rev. date: 1/26/2009

FLAKES OF GOLD

WARNING!

THE SEARCH FOR AND THE ACQUISITION AND
POSSESSION OF GOLD ARE AT ONCE MAN'S
GREATEST FOLLY AND HIS MATERIAL SALVATION.
GOLD CONTAINS THE MYSTERY OF WORTH, THE
THREAT OF LOSS, THE PROMISE OF UTILITY. IT IS
AN ICON THAT RESISTS DESTRUCTION YET LURES
BARBARIC AS WELL AS CIVILIZED MAN TO ACT IN
WAYS CONSISTENT WITH HIS GREED YET INIMICAL
TO HIS FINEST INSTINCTS. THINK ON THIS.

PREFACE

This story is not an historical account. It does not try to define any particular event except the panopoly event of gold prospecting. The story presents the violence, the adventure, the risks of the early West. Wild dogs did exist. Indian memorialization of their sacred burial sites is a reality that expanding modern civilization continues to encounter.

The Early west was harsh, violent, sacrificial, traumatic, and filled with surprises for the immigrant into the gold fields, adventurers sometimes called Argonauts, other times Panners, Prospectors, Hard Rockers, Sourdoughs.

Hundreds if not thousands of towns much like Mystery, failed because the Miners had no intention of staying once they had discovered their fortunes in gold and could then return home. Many, if not most, returned impoverished. Some adventurers never made it. Their story is far from over....

NOTES OF MYSTERY

Dense smoke from the crowd of late night diners lay like horizon fog across the room. Shafts of colored light from powerful spotlights flooded pools of brilliant amber, blue and red across the wooden stage. The light enveloped the perfoming arena in the sea of smoke mist. The ceaseless clatter of dinnerware and silver plate spangled the silence as the three maharachi trumpeters in brass blared their raucous melody with flitting fingers and petulant, explosive cheeks of shiny gold. Their notes rasped like tinder-light over the diners' tables. Dining guests seated t the dozens of round, candlelit tables hooted and clapped while busboys and waiters scurried among the tables like driven mice, anxious because of the money…and an occasional generous tip…to serve the customers at *El Tripoli Restaurant*. It was a hot summer night. Soldiers from nearby Fort Funston were in town, their ranks swelling the café's Saturday night crowd in their khaki, the flinty brass of their uniform bluttons glinting occasionally.

A solitary man dressed in a tuxedo, seated at a side table delayed responding to the waiter's tab, hesitating as if undecided over a matter. He then paid his check without ostentation, retrieving a thin mauve wallet from his vest from which he extracted the necessary money for his check. He continued to sit and watch the musicians. His casual manner was that of a regular to *El Tripoli*, a cavalier who gave the impression of an enchanting and handsome vagabond, with which most night club cafes are furnished. His wide black moustache matched the black of his tuxedo. He sported an ample waist, impeccably groomed, stringy black hair and a lolling sort of manner in the way he sat in his chair. He pressed his money into the palm of Dimitri Avron including, beneath the check, a sizeable greenback. The waiter looked pleased and nodded discreetly. The luxurious gentleman arose, flattened his tuxedo lapels, cast a glance at the maharachi musicians. He then left the restaurant. The waiter cleared the table, returning to reset it, this time examining the note that was handed to him by the departing stranger *Senor*.

Dimitri Avron understood discretion. He also understood the grand twenty dollar bill, the tip from the discreet gentleman in black. But he kept all this to himself. He did not want to scan the note except to hand it to the trumpet player whom the tuxedoed gentleman had had surreptitiously pointed to. The horn player happened to be Juan de Jose con Murrillo Valdez—a long pedigreed Latin name for so small and so humble a man. But the note taker did not blink when he read the scribbled words given to him by Avron.

"He is too generous," Vladez said to the waiter.

"I do not know this. Who is he?"

"He is a man of much wealth and power—he runs a factory on the East side. They make electrical parts and they sell them to the government. It is a very rich company."

"Yes, the government pays like God. So he wants you to play for some…special occasion?" Avron asked. He had handed the note to trumpeter Valdez, unread.

The two of these in conversation were not exactly friends, but they did share in a practical way the life of *El Tripoli*—some good and some bad times—at the café and off work. The trumpeteer, Juan Valdez, lived in the apartment above Dimitri Avron's modest quarters. They had met when the waiter could not sleep for the trumpet playing directly above his bed. It was when he rapped on the musician's door that they met. Valedez played four nights a week and still he had to practice. What a weevil of energy!

"He wants to see me and…Frankl," Valdez said to the waiter, indicating one of the other three trumpeteers, pointing them the same mysterious figure in a tuxedo who loitered in shadows beneath the imitation palm tree. .

Well, then, he must like your music," said Avron.

"We are to serenade him and his lady."

"He is alone."

Juan Valdez's laughter had a magic in it, yet it drew suspicion to its intonation, like a dark insinuation only without words.

"He wishes...yes...he says so right here in his note...." He pointed to the words with his trumpet mouth piece. The three trumpeteers of the restaurant band—the second trumpeter was Simon Frankl—a modest man with a college degree. Jorge La Manche was the third of their *Trio In Brass*—as the sidewalk billboard described them. All were now privy to the note. They installed their trumpets in their purple-velvet-lined cases and prepared to depart for the night *El Tripolie Restaurant*. From here on there played soft background music—not very genteel but practical for the management. The spotlights that glistened off the brass of the horns and that flashed from the trombone and clarinet keys were turned off, leaving a dim amber light to warm th stage and table candles to create ambience for the room.

"He wants to see me because...listen closely...to search for real music...the music he loved in old Madrid..he says so...and if we can play it for him he says to me he will *give that musician much money....much dinero.* Valdez stuffed the note into his bandcoat pocket.

"How do you know all this?" Dimitri Avron asked.

Valdez's glance at the waiter messenger spoke the one word—*incredulous!* He tapped his forehead as if he had prescience of the future stored in his skull. The invitation was at least a mystery to him, too, and yet, inside his beggar's soul he felt that this visitor, this well-dressed gentleman, was prepared to ransom his past for whatever reason...and for whatever memories floated up through the nostalgsic songs from his beloved Madrid. He must be an aficionado—more than a lover of art, Avron speculated.

"Oh, you are going?"

"*Porque non?* Why not? I shall meet him…and I still have his… written invitation." Valdez stuck one hand into his pocket and smiled. The meeting did not mean travel or an excursion or cost to him with his meager wages. He had only to cross the crowded restaurant floor. What could be simpler? Then again, if the man in the tuxedo was honest and brave and had a good intention, he would not be absent the next night.

"I imagine there is not reason you should not go…no reason," said Avron. What did it matter to Simon Frankl? They were only casual restalurant employee acquaintances without any personal commitments.

Avron walked away to return to his duties of clearing and resetting tables after the last diners had departed. Almosttwo hours hd elapsed since the man in the tuxedo had issued his invitation. He was still there. Avron waited impatiently for a lingering couple to leave for the night, or rather the morning. He wondered what all this was about. The note, the request seemed simple enough. Yet the matter was none of his business. He kept glancing at the lonely figure, departed for the night, who had requested authentic music from old Madrid. What could be more romantic…or possible? He fought the temptation to intervene and find out things for himself.

He did not lack talent although he had to wait on people. That was his job at the restaurant. People came to *El Tripoli Restaurant* to dine and to dance and enjoy themselves. This, by itself, made him jealous of the trumpeter Valdez, even Frankl and La Manche…while at the same time suspicious of the man in the black tuxedo. Why had no one ever said anything? He, Dimitri Avron had taken on this work at the *Tripoli* hoping that the management would ask him to sing. He had involved himself with other musical ventures, a minstrel at the railroad station between trains, a singer of operatic tunes at a San Francisco bistro. But neither Valdez nor his friend, Frankl…what did they understand about fine music? He decided that he must also make himself available to the stranger in the tuxedo. Perhaps he could introduce himself as the agent of Juan de Jose con Murrillo Valdez. Or at least as a struggling bistro singer.

After the doors to *El Triploli* had closed for the night..although it was early morning…he said to Valdez and Frankl –La Manche had gone home—as they sat in a booth of an all-night coffee shop.

"You must surely get an agent," Avron said to his friend. They were alone in the coffee shop. "Nobdy in this world finds work without an agent…an artist, I mean."

"Well, perhaps, But the stranger gentleman already wants us to play for him. What is the matter with you, Dimitri? We do not need an agent. The man in the tuxedo will love our music when we play it for him."

"That is good…work is good for the soul, but you, Juan Valdez…you are an artist, and artists need agents."

Avron drew two coffees from an urn and returned to their table. Valdez paid for the both of them. Avron said, "I don't know what you are talking about. After all, he simply invited us to play grand old music from Madrid. Soo…we will come play it for him. I am what I am."

"You are that, my friend Juan…and much more. But about his villa…he must be a very rich man," said Dimitri

"How do you know this—that he has a villa? Foolish idea. There are no villas around here," said Valdez.

"not many very rich gentlemen either," the waiter responded. "An agent will give you a face. He will say, 'my client plays the trumpet in the *Tripoli*. But he can do many things with his music when he does not work in the alley shadows."

"Besides..if he wants maharachi, I will come also," said Frankl.

"Alley?...shadows! What are you talking about? You cannot fool me, my friend. After all, you sleep in the same building as I do and on the floor below mine. If you die in a fire, I die in the same fire."

I have his address…right here…my pocket…: He withdrew the scrap paper, on *Villa Consciennesi Corte. La!* There!"

"He lives in a court…that is elegant. Then perhaps I shall change my mind," said Valdez. "If he likes my old music, then perhaps I can…dedicate my music in *la restaurant* to him when he comes to sit alone."

"Do not forget my friend, that I too like old music and that I have a very fine voice and I can sing may of the old songs of ancient Spain."

"You are too...marvelous, Dimitri Avron...far beyond bus-waiting on the customers."

"He sings like...like Caruso...not like pidgeons cooing," Frankl added.

"Yes, I know many songs.....The Man just sat and watched. He smiled many times. He listened for two hours tonight. He will know the old songs."

I will say to this very fine gentleman that I shall play with Simon Frankl here, who comprehends the daring sweet notes of the music. We will weave the harmony."

One is not *bastante*..sufficient, it takes two for the harmony and I shall sing more than a few bars of the *Rigoletto Song* and other opera songs. We shall watch his face and he will smoke..."

"He wants to see me...because...he *suspects*." Valdez held the word until Frankl, the thin, one with spidery arms and fat lips, looked him in the eyes. "You are a dreamer Avron. I for one shall bring my finest music to play, the *Maharachis* grow like sunflowers by the sides of the road in Madrid."

"You can sing what you like to sing," said Frankl.

The earliest light of predawn had come and they arose from the table and gathered their instrument cases, Avron his hand satchel where he kept any tips from his night's work. They shared a little handshake of convivial agreement before heading for the apartment where, like a captain going to his quarters and a corporal of the guard to his, they parted company for the night. It was good to dream, Avron thought.

Then it was dance night at *El Tripoli Restaurant*. This would allow the three of them, Jorge La Manche inluded as the third of the famed **Brass,** to go over to the stranger's table to regale him with the music he loved. They stood there, Frankl with his treble cornetto horn, and Valdez and La Manche with their trumpets while Avron prepared himself with words to three old Spanish songs. *My Love, when the Night*

Was Young and *My Conchita. Bessa Me Mucho,* as a popular Mexican song, he felt the stranger might like. Valdez began the conversation after the introductions and much vigorous and mutual handshaking around. The Man at at a table to on side of the heaviest diner traffic.

They had already discussed among themselves during the after-hours coffee reprise how they would present their request for compensation for this special music. While the dancers and the three other members of the band played the smooth, gliding rhythms, the folur of them gathered in the corner to alternate with the several old Madrid songs that Juan had found for them to play before the solitary patron in the black tuxedo.

"I'm sorry I have taken so long to introduce myself," the man greeted then. He announced that his name was Vasili Kastinov Muscovich, that he was Russian by birth but having lived as an importe-exporter for years in Madrid, he had fallen in love with Spanish music. His manner toward them was that of aa Benedictine Monk blessing the pilgrims who had made the journey to his redoubt. He waved about in his left hand a carved ivory pipe. When he spoke he conveyed with his words a cryptic sense of mystery. They contained an inner force that put his guests on their guard. His blue eyes sparkled in their deep sockets as he gestured and changed the expressions on his face. He was anything but somber or reclusive...or even secretive. That had been Avron's first impression of the man. It was after they had performed for their special guests, and the rest of the diners had applauded with great animation, that he spoke. He addressed them, wlith a stiff cordiality, in this manner:

"Now that you know my name is Muscovich, you still don't know who I am...but that's the curse of wealth and power. Take your choice. My *moxie* is that I work for a living." He laughed. "To be brief, my friends...I own a factory. I manufacture electrical parts for the government." These details Avron had already learned. The maharachi brass sat awkwardly in chair before their guest, impatient ctually to return to the vbandstand. Was this some kind of joke nonsense, a rebrellion aglinst their manager. Afterall, they played their insruments for *el dinero*....

"You understand, gentlemen, that not all I do is...legitimate... dealing in electrical parts."

"No, we did not know that," Avron said.

"Just as well...or you might not be interested in my...musical hobby."

"My friends here will plays the music you like, old Madrid stuff. We did not know what else," Avron said.

"Just as well that you try...or you might not go on with what I have to say."

Avron got up and returned moments later with drinks on a plater to go round. The musicians had not even tried out their intruments on *When the Night Was Young*. "The other members of your band are good. I have heard them. They will pick up on the melody." So that before the corner table they all, the entire *Trio In Brass*, serenaded the stranger.

"They're good," said Muscovich while the music played. "They can get along without you in their midst." He drank a deep draught from his tequila.

"We are a *brave three*, I call them," said Frankl, a morose one, as if he had just buried his father. Somebody in the room began to pound the table with a wine bottle. It stopped. A tub of dishes and silverware crashed to the floor. The other members of the band, strings and piano band began to play a tango. A cork popped, a shout went up.

The man name Musovich appeared was ready get down to his business. His audience werekept mystified about what was to happen next. He had established his authenticy as a diner. "The long and the short of it, gentlemen is that I need couriers."

"Couriers! For what!" Valdez exclaimed.

"For what?..Frankl simply asked, his sour nature coming to the fore.

As if dispatching orders in combat, the *Tuxedo-Man*—for so they had referred to him—then said; "Couriers to run small items to interested customers." He chose his words carefully. He fummoned the barwaiter to fill replenish the drinks of his four guests...for such they were—guests of a guest—who sat at his corner table. He was meticulous, professional in his somber and deliberate manner.

Avron, the oldest of the four spoke: "You think we are interested in the electric business. We make enterttainment, Senor Muscovich," he said.

"Hell, I know that. I want you to play here...for me... for my other guests..." This reference astounded Valdez. The man was preposterous. He was proposing that he hire them; they were independent contractors for sure. Yet, too, they were all paying patrons of *El Tripoli Restaurant*.

"Do you like tequila made in the old way...with cactus?" The Man was trying to divert their attention from the single thought of... illegal trade. They had, all three of them, band musicians, run abruptly into the same idea, simultaneously. Dimitri Avon had arrived there first.

Valdez picked up on the ruse. "*Si*, made the old way, in the small villas of Mexico. You like it?"

"Yes, it is good!" the Tuxedo-Man replied. They leaned forward in anticipation of some strange, unwelcome news.

"I would like you to be my contacts with...sellers in Begota." Muscovich waited for a reaction. None came. The next round of tequila arived. They all fared becoming too drunk to play. The night was not over. Avron spilled some of his. The Man went on.

"The best way...or one of the best ways to...transfer the stuff is through night-club entertailnment. You could be great...all of you. You won't need to be drummers. You can be...horn players...all of you... like Mister Valdez here...a *trumpeter extraordinair*! Frankl started to get up and leave. "Don't go just yet, gentlement." They had no intention of doing so.

"We do not use drugs," said Avron, the singer. A dark and troubled frown appeared on his countenance. "We play music. We entertain the diners at the *Tripoli* here. What do we want with this... this arrangement? We will all be in jail and our music is gone."

"I understand your feelings," said Muscovich. He appeared astonished by their response, and he was exasperated as if renegades had rejected his offer. They were wrong. "For money...!" He pinched his fingers. "For profit..," he said in a soft voice poisonous with its seductive undertone.

"We…my friend here, Frankl…we are only musicians," Valdez repeated. "I can play my trumpet in *any* night-club band, but that is all I do. *Bien?*" He looked at Frankl, master of the Cornetto, who nodded in agreement.

"That's not quite all, Mister Valdez. Listen to me. I am prepared to offer you a *nice*…salary…with bonuses…for being my agents."

"…For playing the Maharachi in a night-club in Begota and dealing with…." Dimitri Avron shruggd, and then he shook his shead in refusals of the offer. He had spoken for all thee of them.

"Drug Lords? Hardly…you would be…respectable traders…as in old times, and they have an earned and well-deserved respect. After all, we Americans traded with the Indians. We smuggled guns from the French in the Revolution. We sold our oil to Hitler and scrap-metal to Tojo. What does it matter the content? A deal is a deal. It's the… integrity of the trade- action that counts."

Valdez started to get up from the table. Muscovich put a hand on his arm. "Our lives won't be worth the spit from a brass horn," said Frankl.

"Oh, but it will! Sit still…everybody you meet will be my friend. It can be almost…too cozy…too easy. Fiv thousand dollars every time you make a hit…*ahem*…," he excused himself "…a contact."

"No," said Valdez in a flat tone. La Manche simply nodded. He listened and said nothing.

The tuxedoed stranger was adamant and went on. "Soon you will say, 'let's go…*vamanos*' to the key distributors and…so…the shipment goes through and you are paid without a question."

"Five thousand…?" queried Avron. "Incredible!"

"And more with the bonuses…for just a few little words like…*a whisper of love*…in the middle of your music….like…a secret code to the buyer in the audience," Muscovich said; he was almost ecstatic. The quartet of *Tripoli* employees cast questioning glances among themselves then back at Muscovich. He started to refilltheir glasses from a third bottle of tequila. Each covered his glass with his hand.

From one pocket of his coat the Tuxedoed Man, the leg man for Begota drug lords, withdrew a small black leather case. Plying it open, he showed them four gemstones, saphires of glowing blue. Take my offer, gentlemen, and I shall give you these to wear around your necks or on your belt buckles...tokens of my trust and my favor. You will be welcome anywhere south of the border. These will get you through."

The offer of the man in the black tuxedo stunned the musician comrades. "It is dangerous wherever you go lnowadays. But you, my friends are *muy grande*...you show exquisite taste in your music. You obviously admire my...hospitality or you would not be sitting here with me, discussing...matters. You will be matchless, sought after wherever you go. Take my word for it," Muscovich finished.

"So we give you our ansxwer...." Valdez said;

"When?" Frankl asked.
"Our...final word...?"
Anger showed on Muscovich's countenance, but he conrtrolled his temper. It will do you no better if you wait a year...ten years. Then y ou will be dead. The time is at the present. You, Mister Valdez can be the interpreter and body-guard as my...selected...trumpet player...representatives...all of you...of Muscovich's Electrical Works."

"It is dangerous," said Avron. muscovich shrugged. "It is dangerous to be alive in these times," he said. "Ah, but then, luck comes to your door." He stopped talking for a long minute and regarded the trio with a smile. He turned to Valdez. "I shall give you the script of what to say. All of your...activities can be accomplished between nine in the evening and one in the morning...while you play your trumpet and horn. And you...Avron...give them your...support?"
"I dont think so," Frankl burst out.
"A rebel in spirit! I love that, sir," said Muscovich. "We of the poorer classed must exercise our right to rebel...must we not? Is that not so, Mister Avron?"
"Your...set up is...easy. What if...what if we should report you to the police?" Valdez was beginning to slur his words. The rest of the band—a trombone, an alto sax and a guitar—had ended its moking break and had resumed with a waltz.

"If you go to the police, you could just…die," said their host. The poilice in Begota are…filth, drit! The are know nothing, hear notling, see nothing. They could easily be bribed…but then…you would have to run…like chickens in front of a car!" Muscovich drained his tequila glass and half-filled it again. He called for another bottle from a waiter. It was settled noislessly into the bucket of ice. "Naturally, you could… stay here in this city and blow your trumpets for the rest of your lives and…clear tables for the lovely ladies who care not a fig you're your music…or… you can come my way…play this innocent little game with me. Like I say, gentlemen…a business deal is a business deal. The cargo is of little importance…in the long run." He drank from his glass, his eyes observing them over the tumbler. "I will give you protection….You can count on that! If I change contracts why…then maybe you can drop out. I am looking for…*winners*, gentlemen." He sipped cautiously, regarding them with perceptive, cunning eyes that drafted suspicion into every corner of their thoughts "If you wish to… play in cafes in Paris or…Cairo or in…Rio de Janero or Liverpool… consider yourselves…*diplomats*. The world is a big place, my friends. There are always convenient ways of resolving difficulties and rewarding by, let us say, *contrilbutions*. You could retire, you know, Mister Valdez. You are not getting any younger.

"Some day."

"Ah, just as I thought…..More tequila?" Valdez refused. "Why don't we…why don't you all…? He summoned a waiter "…come into a more private room here at the restaurant….for lovers, eh? Would you bring your instrument cases and follow me?" He knew the layout of the *Tripoli* as well as Dimitri Avron. "We go to where it is not so much noise. I have more details. I see each of you is not convinced of the value of my splendid offer…or the propriety of my help for you."

"We are not convince you brought us here to listen to our music," said Valdez.

"Oh, damn me, that's right!" Muscovich got up from his chair, rather tipsy and unstable, and he walked to the bandstand stage where the band was just finishing the rhumba. He grabbed the microphone and introduced Valdez, Frankl and La Manche to the crowd, who knew them by sight. He begged them listen to some of Mexico's finest

Maharachi music, as played by three experts from south of the border. Polite applause followed this lttfle speech. The band sat back relaxed yet ready to accompany the trio. Dimitri would sing the words to the song, the **Trio in Brass** agreeing upon *Lisbon Dreams*. They invited three other band instruments to join them. They began their brassy music while the crowd listened, enthralled by the traditional sounds and the rhythm. When they finished, the crowd shouted for more. They chose *Bella Noche*. They drew in Avron to sing the words; he, of course, was elated and sang his very best this night.

But Muscovich was getting impatient. When they had finished playing their second number, the audience did not cease to applaid, until Muscovich raised his hand. The band took up their instruments again. The duo, Valdez, Frankl and La Manche put theirs back into their cases and together with Avron, the waiter, followed the tuxedoed stranger crom the bandstand. They would return momentarily. Frankl told the remaining instruments to play dance tunes. The four recruits followed the Muscovich to a quiet room for amorous play, off the main salon in the restaurant. While all this activity was coming off so smoothly, the Manager Gary Jackson, a *Gringo*, was nowhere to be seen.

The music and sounds of the crowded restaurant came muted through the doors. Valdez, least of his companions, thought he might be trapped into dealing in illegal drugs...so long, however, as he did not have to touch the *stuff* or finger Muscovich's profits, only accepting the five thousand dollars he would receive on each delivery when approached for a sale. He felt that he would be safe both from the police and from suppliers and drug lords whom the man lin the black tuxedo dealt with. They would be only the couriers, according to the agreement. He could not be too concerned. Avron was less persuaded of the...practicality of the arrangement, although he, too, was looking at the money. What about Frankl, the doubter? What about LaManche, the silent one who had kept his distance from the entire recruitment. He grasped the fact that *Muscovich's Electrical Works* was a front for a drug dealing operation. He and his friends were to be the intermediaries for heroin, flown in high altitude aircraft for easy border crossing, the heroin chiefly from Central and South America, the marijuana from Mexico. Airdrop at night would be the means of delivery.

After Muscovich had explaied his plan, he urged on them that they remember their humble station in life.

"It does not do you good to be too proud. I know. I once was a very proud man but…now…look at me. I talk to you like a brother. Is that not so?"

"We are only afraid, Senor Muscovich," said Valdez, a bit more sober then when he sat at the table in the main restaurant.

"Fear…fear…fear. Bless me, gentlemen, are you not men! Do you not have a man's courage? Are you nannies who must feed pap bottles to infants? Eh? Do you not take the world by the tail and spin it around and let the cowards run to the police. Muscovich was temporarily overcome by his own eloquence. He paused to remove a thin flask from his valise. He poured a jigger of brandy for himself, offering it to the others. They refused. From the valise, which they had scarely noticed, he took a contract and placed it in front of lthem. He tried to smile but was too drunk. I know you will put all those old woman's fears behind you. I know you will sign, and become rich…overnight."

Captivated by the size of their bonanza and fascinated by the ease with which they had fallen into their new wealth, the four recruits put their signatures to the agreement, to act as agent-facilitators for the *Muscovich Electrical Works*. Their act of signing bestowed immense relief upon their co-partner host. He promptly let them out of lhe small private discretion room and into the restaurant patio. He breathed in the night air and told them do so likewise…the mark of freedom. He then led them back to the bandstand and there, again, he introduced them directly and intimately to the gay crowd. Breaking protocol, he requested that the band allow Senor Valdez, an eminent trumpeter to play one of his *Triploli* favorite pieces—a trumpet solo that always brought back sweet memories to him of his days in Madrid. The crowd was swayed, an *ooh*, an *ahh*, sounded from within as they faced the bandstand. Their drinking, their intimacis, their indifference and joy of life for the night allowed them to accept the Man's ovettures. The number, *Fling Torreador*, a fanciful piece, filled with cadenzas and trills an sprang from the melody. The story of the three musicians, an attentive waiter and their *confidante* was about over.

In the manner just told them was the musician Juan Valdez and his two musician friends, the German Frankl amd Frenchie La Manche—let us not forget Dimitri, the singing waiter busboy—Dimitri Avron—were subverted to use their music and services for the man in the black tuxedo. His largesse promoted the trade in drug traffic between sovereign nations. Valdez, like a man in bondage to the mad warlicks of cartel drugs, disappeared altogether from public life. Muscovich was shot. Frankl was murdered for a failed delivery of opium probably. La Manche returned to his native Le Mans, France, and Avron went insane. Their dissatisfaction with creating joy through their muic took over their lives. Dimitri Avron's yen to be an a great restaurant and cabaret singer by way of drugs destroyed him in the end.

He had tried to bring his friends along with him but had failed.

AT THE CUTTING EDGE

Grotteau raptured again and again, down in **The Scorpion's** basement morgue, place of spiders, once a sidewinder cooling off from desert sands…anyway the repository of the village history for seventy five years. This was a land of simple structures, a fresh one newly built here and there, yet a land that remained almost soley in possession of snakes, scorpions, s the vultures, an occasional redtailed hawk, gray rabbits and, most unwelcome, white men who came to dig their fortunes from mother earth. The morgue contained the lives of deceased miners of the village..Grotteau researched his morgue files to find useful stories of the past. Another side to Grotteau's mind lay in wait for opportunity. His lust for power was fated to be the poisonous asp that would strike the heel of hones prospectors, give him control, small men to become indentured…as they were already. Like most men in power, he was learning how to manipulate the forces of power for personal gains. His was the lust that animates the demons of hell and ultimately yearns for supernatural power. Reiner Grotteau kept this phantom of power chained to his imagination, and quiet to all.

He lived among men whose sole ends and means in life were to stay alive, to share bacchus and nilght howls of thle wily coyote amid the solace of wine and petty good fortune, These were like carcasses of town life and ill fortune, without which existence became petty and drab. The affections of the miners gathered not around survivors of cave-ins, rockslides and disease, but around those who sought luck, chanced risk, and endured on an almost daily basis a sense of threatening danger and the semi barbaric style of life in a gold camp.

The miners waited for fortune's merciful handouts, which now came in the form of land deeds in exchange for what all miners possessed, their personal weapons. Some thought the deal madness but kept silent. Others, as we've seen, complied. Grotteau drew others into his orbit by his rough charm and devil possession. Even after *De Vancha* had lost the *Continental Hotel* to Grotteau, I saw then that he would never be content to stop there, nay, not until he owned all of *Mystery*. That ambition, that nyielding lust made him dangerous to deal with. That was his charisma, the fascination of the viper to certailn prey.

Being French the phantom lure of gold had struck his brain like the lure of furs to early trappers in the great Northwest. Grotteau was not a man without virtues: he wrote poetry, sometimes publishsing it in **The Scrorpion**, and he could sing a sweet baritone voice to the lines he had written. He once was seen pulling home a Russian Cannon from *Triangle*, like a caisson, He placed the thing in front of the hotel. Wagoned from Fort Ross for a sale of its bronze. it represented to de Vancha, hotel owner, the glory of conquest. Like a compact wilth th devil, the placement of the cannon enobled the Spaniard hotel. Such was the man Grotteau.

He coveted the original Kittrick nugget, if he could find it. He still coveted the *Continental Hotel*, built by the Randal Brothers, as a stage stop, after which a Wagon Works, saddlery and General Merchandise Store sprang up. Often the main street of a village paralleled the tracks, but in this case, the Stage connected *Mystery* to the station. The *General Merchandist Store* carried everything from a horse collar to barrels of salted crackers, fish, pickled hams and canned goods and things like nails, ammunition, coffee and sugar staples and...gossip. Miners equipment, canteen bottles, picks, pans, shovels were always available. The store was the only apparent coiner of gold in the village. Early Chinese in tlhe gold country were shrewd to catch onto that enterprise.

Reiner Grotteau had found what he was looking for iln a newcomer named Ludheim. He set the story to type for the next edition of *The Scorpion,* a sheet that was formerl hand- written with the banner *The Ore Rocker.*

Mystery, 1836 –
Prospector Cannister Kittrick
exited at Assayer Almayers office'
at six o'clock last night

He vilrtually scrambled in
to report that he had stumbled
uponm—founda nugget of
considerable size below lthe
Indian Head Rock where the
creek once flowed.

As a result of Kittrick's find the
assayer James Alamyer, well known
to the miners hereabouts, for his
assay skill, awarded the claim to
Kittrick.

It is only a matter of time
before thousands of gold
seekers flock into *Mystery* and
the surrounding stream banks.

Residents are warned to lay in
a goodly supply of provisions
before suppliers at Ormsbys
General Marchandise Store, which
are adequate for lthe villagers of
Mystery. But supplies can be
hastily and recklesslyconsumed
by hordes of newcomers and
city gold-prospectors.

Through his newspaper, **The Scorpion**, Grotteau had come to represent to the miners the doctrine of faith for either heathen or desperado. He would make them partner and confidante to his vision of the future of the scattering of shacks, tent cabins and open camp sites, and he would do so by sharing his grasp of opportunity. He was already the Oracle of the village. The icon of the Kittrick nugget was held up before them like the Cross of Christ to the Christian, the Gold of the Earth for the miner. The nugget was like a foreign ambassador of deliverance. It would come into their lives and occupy their souls like a religious faith, by which they would find new worth and human value.

In his office, Grotteau held the article up to view and cried, "This is the miracle I have waited for, Ludheim!"

Tenderly he replaced the precious clipping in an envelope. "This is the proof of the richess of the land." He did not know that if a man pushes too hard, the tiger of suspicion will be let loose from its cage, and it will devour all you can feed it.

Ludheim turned to him from his compositor's bench. "I believe in evidence. As a former lawyer, I must. But as to the character of that evidence…that's another story."

"You are too pessimistc, Ludheim."

There is just one nugget. Find me a dozen more and I will believe your story."

"There may not be enough to go around," said Grotteau.

"There may be more nuggets than we suppose, said Ludheim. They both laughed. Luck—you saw how I played my luck at the poker table, did you not, Grotteau?"

"*De Vancha* had the hotel, and you…you hoved your law books.. You are not contented."

"Contentment!" exclaimed Ludheim, "is a state of mind.

"Conditioned by a man's faith."

"Oh, your damned philosophy. Only I, *mi amigo*, can find my treasures…by myself. Who else can I count on? Even you show signs of…of defectilng.

"I speaks the truth, Ludheim."

"Truth is what you can touch," said the lawyer. "you can't eat, touch or barter speculation."

"Hope is truth…the miner's hope.

"But if it fails, truth fails with it. Is that not so?"

"Hope renews itself," said Ludheim.

"Damned pontification!:" Grotteau exclaimed.

"Once the gold is gone, it is gone, *pfft*—like that, into the dust of the winds." Luhdheim was upset.

Then let it vanish. But is will not vanish for me. You will see. Gold is magical. It inspires, lures, it is seductive, it entices, it is cruel and will inflict punishment on any who abuse it. Is that not worthy of worship, Ludheim?

"But gold will not forgive."

"Not the gold…only…God, who talks about forgiveness way out here? No, blood speaks frosm the past," said Grotteau. "Blood will never forgive. You're right, Max." He walked toward his grungy office that fronted the plank sidewalk outside where his sign ***The Scorpion Pres,*** *newpaper of choice*, swung idly in a breeze. He had never seen the grim, lugubrious irony of that sign. Nor did he comprehend the transience of the idol he sang shis praises to. He was constructing a cult of wrath under the heavens. . Ludheim went into the pressroom. Grotteau sat in the front office like a pagan idol in fat imperturbility, contemplating the mad self-admiring participats in his scheme, as if worshippers at the shrine he was building. He did not ask to be anointed but only admired. To himself, he might have seemed a mad, absurd inquisitor into human motives for power, into an inordinate love for what to all appearances seemed most abundant in this distant winderness—gold, both visible and screted by nature in the rocks. The power that he had to charm with a sutle cruelty, he was soon to discover. How savage is gold as an antagonist to the non-believer!. Grotteau and the miners' ignorance of his latent power—those were the true illiterates. That was their misfortune.

From his front office, looked out over the landscape. Shack dwellers they ere, the white miners who scratched a out they ellow dust like rats in a clapboard shack. Freezing in winter and broiuling in summer on the stream banks and under corrugated roofs,--he had been there for two years—he saw that the townsfolks had endured the scouring winds that swept across the landscape from the north cast, winds that flailed the flesh likestnng demons of retribution for their daring even to squat on the land. They had endured without respite or complaint. Heavy snows assaulted them one winter, a blizzard that piled up snow to the height of shack roofs. Their tenancy on the land was marked by the rusting iron of an abandoned plow…for what crop?…by broken clay pot shards, by the wood scraps and iron springs and axles of an abandoned wagon, and by those emblems of hope, the few abandoned cabins that had not been devoured last winter by the landscape's the scouring winds.

Poor devils, Ludheim had said, not knowing that Grotteau did not share that womanish sympathy for the sourdoughs. Some haddied of pneumonia. Cholera was always a waiting spectre. Fazakerly's fresh creek water, delivered in dewn wineskins, was a preventative…all lendered for that pinch of gold in creek water that was not potable for drinking. These hardluck habitluees proected their claims, their gold from thieves or claims jumpers with weapons…before the Great Gathering. As some called them-"grungy" shacks—several that remained perched on the local hillside like carbuncles of rock extrusions on otherwise barren slopes. A room, the main room, in a shack could be the entrance to a *gopher* mine shaft..a tunnel behind the shack. That diggin' could be discerned by tailings outside the shack. The shack and its tailings resembled spilled blood from a ugly gash on the hillside when the copper-red sun struck the mountain. It was among these hrdy, desperate folk and their *creations* that Grotteau sought his oconverts to a communal gold mine enterprise. He was wily. He possessed in his heart no compassion for them. They had the will to dig, he had the plan as to where…and he was furthder impressed with its spotential abundance by old scraps of news from **The Ore Rocker.**

Un his contemplation Grotteau silently declared himself to be crazy to have overlookd the instant wealth beneath the footpaths, the main street *Dog Street*, and dykes bneath shop floorboards of the village, its boardwalks and the few stores that lined the street, fronting the plains of sand. His vision took in the *Hard rock Saloon*, the *Contisnental*

Hotel, the smithy forge and anvil, the *Wagon Works,* Hornsbys *General Merchandise Store,* the barbershop and the office of *The Cruthfield Stageline.* These properties were situated on gold-bearing sands. But they were not permanent. Fire had provd that. The exploitation by the law would reinforce the proof: in his thoughts this idea ecame increasingly solitary, loathsome and potential. It fored him to put Ludheim and *De Vancha* aside.

Grotteau needed more intimate details about the prospects of the village. Where could he put his hands on letters? That was it! A brilliant move to unearth the richess of the past for skeptics like Ludheim and others. He foundwhat he was searching for in an abandoned, room at the hotel. Their source was a mystery, but their content told much about the village. He opened one and began to read.

"I thought it would all work our, Marlee,
But I can only cry for you and live time away.

Another read: "Why I came out here I don
figer out. They aint one crum a gold and I
been diggiln fer two solid mos. I'm gonna sil
my shovel and pan and ketch a stage out hyer fer
no gold, cause it haint all they said it was hell
or China, whichever coms first. So long, and
kep them drays in good shape, cause they's
more money in haulin stuff in Kansas City
er was out here in them derned gold fields.

Ludheim was aware of Grotteau's ambition and monstrous ego, his unquenchable disdain for any competition. Since he was superstitious, he believed that the simple act of reading those private letters—and there were others—would give success to his mission. He was troubled aboutl his legacy. Did they expect him to perform signs and wonders. Would he be the ruler of men's passions? I saw this mestastasis in him as a dereliction of his humanity; when a man tries to cotrol the soul of his brother, he ends up controlling not the man but the spirit of destruction and corruption iln the surrounding community, especially if he is avant guarde of elements of savagery amongst them. That desertion and demise were inevitable. There was nothing Reiner Grotteau or Ludheim could do to stop trouble. Julius shot…murdered. Hammond just last week at their diggings. Korinth put bullets into his sidekick, his gold digging partner at Hammit, just last Saturday. Harvey Trumen got into a drunken quarrel with Jasper Peters at the **Hard Rock Saloon** He drew a pistol and shot Peters in the head…for nothing. These incidents were one good reason Grotteau felt justified in his mission to give up weapons of murder for the prospect of gold.

"Peace spirits are missing in this here village," he said to Ludheim. He set out each night for weeks on his mission. Moving amid good men, so-calloed solid citizens, disillusioned yet abiding by crude laws of the township that related to ownership, property rights and habitation. He almost literally pushed his way into doorways. He dropped down beside campfires and invaded panners' sites. He left no stone unturned. He was determined to recruit the village into his scheme.

Adamant and deterfmined, in the immense silence of the high desert night, Grotteau impaled his mining-town posters on cactus thorns. He dropped some along known trails. He stuffed several cracks along the board sidewalk. He knew that svtluck is seldom the companion to diligence. He encouragfed the dark wings of freed and the sour stonch of old lusts, vultures screached over the land. He knew what the shimmering of gold does to a man's soul, how it tarnishes pride and other possessions, and what men will give up to possess it, stolen from the gold in due time to surrender all to the purpose of pride. They had known the sale and declaration of defeat, death to the morrow that awaited them around the capfires of their claims. They stood on common ground. Hunkering down before their fires, their vaniyy sought consolation from the winds of chance or solace from the lips of others like them. They always listened to beleaguered tales, and like children. they listened to the ancient harms of others who had barely missed conquesests or were hiding lies about gold taken from the ground, torn from shattered rocks of fate. The stamping mill in Frost was redolent with such lies, fibs, if you will, only become lately tales of success.

Such men are likely to drive a hard bargain or to give up a chance encounter with a new promise of richess. Grotteau knew their kind. He sought out their passion for gold to magnify his own pride. He would advise them by the trick of their greed and also their propensity to fail. He stopped at Clayton Hornsby's *General Merchandise Store*. There, shovels were selling for two hundred dollars apziece, wheelbarrows for somewhat less. Honsby was making much gold from the miners They would pay him in small sacks of dust whch he carefully measured on a counter scales, and did so with a conscience for fairness. Picks, a good one, sold for two hundred and fifty dollars, blasting caps and dynamite went for twenty five dollars a stick. Food supplies, canned good were more reasonable—a can of beans for six-fifty. These crippling, outrageous sprices were readily accepted by the miners, since they knew that the rocks held much more wealth than they were capale of spending. Hornsby made sure to ride with his day's take, at night, over to the depository of Wells Faro in Frost. He rode alone, by wagon. Some nights he went by horseback. With the gold kept under his counter he replenishled his supplies, returning to Mystery early the nexrt morning. One winter he was lost in a blizzard. Only because his animals knew trhe way did he return safely to the village. It was now spring, the creek was running strong and the miners could not complain that they lacked water.

Back at his press office. A day or so after his find of the letters, the Mayor *De Vancha* called on Reiner Grotteau. he sat in his front office of ***The Scorpion***. The big Mexican came in thundering.

"Town here belongs to the miners," he said, his voice and manner almost threatening the editor.

"They protect themmselves."

Withj what...yuouve destroyed their protection.

"Yes, they do that, *bueno, Senor. Pero*...they are *los hombres de violencia!*...men of violence! They're men of violence." he repeated. "They cause trouvble. Violence is a curse to the the *hombre* who digs alone," said *De Vancha*.

"*Bien*, peace spirits is missing in this here *violencia*. We get peace only by doing away with weapons."

"Now they will start to dig on their land claims, inside the village. How do you plan to open those claims?"

"lI will make rounds. they will restore their honor when they find gold. I'm sure that it is out there."

Damn that Ludheim. He aint the law out here. You expect to perform a miracle, Mister Grotteau? It's got to be a struggle between man and the and.

"Remember *De Vancha*...that gold has no owners...except to those who touch it and hallow it

"Like a pretty woman."

"Fickle? Gold aint fickle, Mister Grotteau."

The Mexican saw into the wanton mindset of possession, as a quixotic truth in the schooling of Mammon that posession is love, and he would just as soon own the whole town as he would sell his own soul. There lay, there lurked in his obsession and refusal to acquire, another perspective the sleeping truth that as a man sows, so he shall he reap. Corruption breeds corruption. Grotteau would work his wicked will on the miners. Grotteau espied a fortune in gold. Ludheim, the lawyer and innoculous compositor for the paper, watched **the Scorpion** Editor transgress almost every structure and pathway in Mystery, even the hotel with his map lines for possible sites, the saloon, the boardwalks, the **Wagon Works**. At last he seemed to have his will with Ludheim's precautions.

"You got only one thing to do Mister Ludheim and that is to set type and run that press in there. Right now, I am the law around here." Ludheim almost expired at this draconian pronouncement. His eyes merely widened a little. He kept still. "Here's what I want you to say in a poster you set up..."

> *Dog on tje streets. wake up to find*
> *you're walked on, spat on, very unkind*
> *Put your shovel in and dredge up a purse.*
> *you'll never again call on bad lucks curse.*

Invcest in Mystery, buy a new diggin
Theres gold under Mystery Gods riggin.
You've walked o'er it, neighbor, far too long
It'll cost you your firearm trade for a song

Now, pistol, shotgun or rifle doth stifle
Only varmints to fear, costs but a trifle
Form a new company brave souls bold
Surrener what;'s useless, gailn yeller gold.

To Ludheim this sounded like a mantra for the town's destruction, ominous and foreboding. this proclamation was a formula for self-annihilation of the town of Mystery bu citizens stricken blind by their lust for the precious metal. Wjo ever heard of sluch a bondage, of cistpdu by a general will of the townsfolk? Who but an idiot would surrender his gun. But, the irony was that it had been done before lin wartime acts of sllurrender. Yet the townsmen of Mystery were not at war...or were they? . this proclamation of ransome was to give credibility and make authentic the bonfire destuction of weapons that was certailn to take place in the town square, wherever that was, in front of the **Continental Hotel** quite possibly. Who but a confirmed mad man would give up his means for protection, rusty or clean bright new? The style, make or condition of his firearm did not matter. Some miners had bought along to their diggins weapons thley had recently purchases for such libe and limb emergencies. After all, the town of Myastery still lay in the open territory known as the Wild West. They had not yet bought into Grotteau's scheme. they were young men, farm hands, often, professionals and artesans who had come in pursuit of the illusory gold. They were not greenhorn strangers to firearms. Many had been game hunters from the Mountains of Appalachia, the desolate stretches sof the Ohio River Valley, the swamps and reaches of the South East and even parts of the Northwest still little inhabited. How...or better, why, whould they even consider such a hairbrained scheme? Why, ind33d, n3ed they indenture themselves to a idiot named Grotteau iln the name of civic protection for the pursuit of the illusive metal? But the gold would evaporate, vanish by this means. Had the miners not left greater things behind than their guns? .

"Now sign that!" Teiner Grotteau, the editor shosuted from his desk to Ludheim.

"You'll be owner of the whole village!" Ludheim shouted back. Reiner took his words as a complement.

"Let then think I do. that's almost as good. A man'll believe whatever he wants to believe." Reiner Grotteau would not be dissuaded from his arrogant presumption that any bunch of miners will greet such an offer with shouts and timbrels of rejoicing. Gold was at hand, Digging would prove almost effortless. But the process had begun, for two nights. The priest, miners recognized and unknown, had already brought their weapons to the bonfire and thrown them into the flames. the poster authenticated their sacrifice. It was what the law would look at...a public agreement. This was a fantasy of communal delusion, a tgravesty on the law, Ludheim instantly realized. yet, he elected to do nothing to stop this action of mercy...so it was called...agailnst those who had already been maimed by a firearm or would certainly to be killed or injured in the future. The whole thing was a mosntrous act of determined surremder to vulnerability and defeat. He lacked the courage to speak out, this Ludheim fellow. Grotteau had estimated his man aright, je who prided himself on his **Vault** of iconic display before the ignorant and the illiterates of the law, as if he were the leopard of the law, the fanged avenger for the town's misdeeds.

Grotteau clung to his code of retribsution against the miners. He would have the Indians to fight next, for by his clever scheme of land sales he had wrought the whirlwind of rage and defiance as by the Indans for the desecration of their burial ground. They, too, understosod the indebitures of slavery, under the Conquistadores. Grotteaus plan would involve the act of a fierce, protracted and bloody retribution.

No white man had a clear idea of the location of the Indian graves, but Almayer knew that the town had been built atop the bones of tribal departed spirits. No one had said anything about the reality of the desecration. Mulheim knew that the Indians were within their rights. The Whites had planted the village they later called *Mystery* in its present location because of the proximity of an upper spring, some sheltered offered from the scorching desert sun by a rock cliff face to the West and North, adjoining which were hills, small defiles and ravines were miners had established their claims. The **Sheshone** Tribe had one representative in Almayer's wife. Yet they knew that the White man's laws forbade revenge attacks. There were other ways for the Indians to deal with the desecration.

Falling Waters proposed that they not ravage the village but, instead, appeal to the law at the court in Triangle for a redress of their grievance. The court would refuse to grant their request for a stay of the digging plan simply and arrogantly, the court felt, on the grounds that prospectilng for gold offended the memories of the local Indians. Grotteau's plan was now well known among the *Sheshone*. What measures could they use to stop the diggings? After all, the whole town landscape was siltuated on Indian graves that went back centuries. Also he Indians had learned of the trade of weapons for land-deeds for gold exploration. The Indians were not to be fooled. They also knew that a pack of feral dogs had once invaded the village and bitten many of its residents. They had come through the town on a night of celebration on the founding of *Mystery*. And the smells of the barbeque had attracted the feral dog pack. The townsfolk would know better next time; but they would have to prepare against the assault by the ferocious animals, with pikes, boards, pitchforks and other tools in the hands of the terrorized and enraged citizens.

Grotteau's father, a Colonel Elias Grotteau, had lived by the philosophy that one must "occupy the enemy's land" to gain the envied instrument of power, the land. He had also become an agent of the government, while he saw his son Reiner Grotteau as but a dreamer and hardly wohy of respect. However; Grotteau had known about the Spanish land grants and of the *Diego de Vanchas* connection, translated into lthe Mayorship of the small village. It was largely a position of honor, with hardly any official duties, but there it was.

Mayor de Vancha could do nothing to forestall trouble with the Indians. He distrusted them, as had his Spanish forebearers. The Indians met upon Coyote Butte. *Big Thunder* spoke. "The white man will celebrate their find of gold. We will help them." Chants followed this pronouncement of a doom, in the circle of Indians who had Shoshone by birth with White man's blood in his veins, from his mothers side. He was very religious and respected by the thirty or so Indians from outlying hogans in the hills. They had gathered as the Tribe did of old to air their grievances and to explore their options for action against the White invaders and maurauders of vgrave sites. They had done nothing for almost forty years. They had stood idly by and watched the White man build his structures over their ancestors' graves, insulting their forebearers. Triangle was another town, 30 miles to the West of Frost. It contained its Indian malcontents, restless, anxious to achieve some small vindication for their loss of the land and the erdication of their culture. thus they met here atop the butt upon Almayer's invitation. He wished to present to them a problem of great dimensions that would not bear waiting. The white man Reiner Grotteau and his cohorts, had a plan to dig up portions of the village of *Mystery* to find gold. It would be a sacrilegious and monstrous thing to do, and would make the white man forever their enemies. they had met and they were chewing upon mescaline buttons.

They chanted amongst themselves, swaying in the firelight. *Big Thunder* was speaking from the center of their ring.

"We show them the worth of our Indian graves. Those spirits they will put to dath a second time."

"Big Thunder speaks the truth, my friends. We will join with them to celebrate. The wild beasts will cover their blood in the streets."

"*Sand Cobra* has spoken well," said a small peevish man, wearing a flatbrim black hat like a tribesman at a dance. "We mus;t not let them desecrate our forebearer graves. It is already too late."

We cannot...and we will not," said Almayer, the instigator of this small coterie of Indian tribesmen, the majority of whom had never lived farther away than they were this night. As in a trajedy chorus, they all agreed upon a plan to seek some sort of rebribution for the desecration, even gunfire.

"But the White man, lhe has no guns any more," said Almayer. the Indians were astounded and regarded him with questioning and suspicious looks. "They have given upl their arms, their rifles, their pistols for a piece of the land with a piece of paper that promises it is their land to keep."

Big Thunder enquired: "How do they expect to hunt...if they do not kill us."

"the Great Father in Washington will help them." there came silence after these words.

"The gods of our foreathers will bless us and curse them," said a young wildeyed Indian, who wore fringe jacket and sported two feathers in his hair.

"They will die with their yellow gain," Almayer shirlled.

A chant like some distant dirge broke out but without full partticipation.

"They will die wilth their yellow gain," Almalyer repeated.

"They will for their gain," said *Big Thunder.*

"They will fail in their search for the yellow dust," said the Indian with lthe two feathers. There came a shrill, almost screech like voices, but there was no drum amongst them ti keep up the frenzied beat. The swaying in front of the campfire light continued. They were all perspiring heavily. Their feet scuffed upon the dirt. A bone bracelet here, a turquoist breastplate there shown in the unsteady firelight. Who could understand their troubled souls but others who worshipped the land their their primitive kachina spirits. Almayer, it had become apparent, was their unsolicited yet acknowledged leader, their contrct with the White man, for it was in the village that the depredation would occur. Pride ruled their hearts and the intentions. Almayer understood their fury and their capacity for bringing trouble down upon the miners, and of adding to their plight of helplessness. Let the White miners in *Mystery* prepare to receive the angry spirits of the grave that would arise to seek revenge against such unhallowed and pitiless spirit disinternments, the spirits of the Whsite man that were sure to polute the open graves.

The doctrine of Christian Indian converts was simply stated: *what is visible is real.* The maurauders swept down upon the town in the smiddle of the night and by force occupied Grotteau's **Continental Hotel.** It suddenly became their fort, from which they began to fire upon the villagers who, this stime, could not return flire. They had turned in their weapons in exchange for a piece of yellow sand. they came down upon the town with the intent not to kill but to occupy. Then let the White man remove them from the villge. That was the plan of *Big Thunder*. There was also the chance that they might steal some of the townsmen's horses, if they could be found.

APPROPRIATE
INTRODUCTIONS

It was very soon well known at the town saloon, that the Crutchfield Stage had been robbed so often they had put two sotguns on the rack. The man in conversation with the bartender, Cannister Kittrick, was a well-dressed fellow named Max Ludheim, a man relatively unknown at the time. He was wanted for murder, he said, and so openly that a listener would at once have doubted his guilt. The two men talked about the murder in the **Hard Rock Saloon** moot court. The law had not found him; Ludheim said that he had killed another man in self-defense. Being a retired lawyer and three-year resident in the small Sierran town of *Mystery*, he mentioned that the motive for most most murders was...gold.

"I—they will find me and hang me. they will not see you. String out. You can fling a small handful of dust into the diggings of every miner. Salt their diggins. Make them shout Eureka! I've found it—pay dirt!" He finished his tumbler of wine at the bar. He said something about the vault; Cannister did not catch it. From a coat pockt he took out a note pad that shaped like a panther's tongue and he began to sketch, as if doodling. At the top he put *DeVancha*.

"You know who he is?"

Cannister confessed that he did not.

"He's the future mayor of this here village—a hundred percent Mexican mayor of *Mystery*, fascinated like the blower snake by his power and glory and prestige."

"A lothario...?" Ludheim shrugged and gave a faint smile. "I aint seen a woman since I left El Paso."

There was a snippet of the Machievellian in the Ludheim's prophesy. "What about those villagers who do not dig for gold? What does power to them?" Cannister asked.

"Unite...as one...the power of consensus."

"Backed by gold...?" He served a jigger of whiskey to a miner, who, boots muddied, trousers and shirt unwashed and hair tangled, as he shifted his black, muddied hat. He was typical of the panners. Cannister went on: "This De Vancha...he's not a bandit is he?"

"He is...or was...a bold bastard who will appoint—not elect—his deputies...decide boundaries...well, need I tell you more?"

"Why are you telling me these things?" the bartender asked.

"Self worship...it goes with the power and the gold."

Both men knew the dream was Arcadian, magnificent in its potency of self-worship. It eluded the stranger...or did it?..that there was an occultic power to gold mining of any sort...like the worship of a demon god. "the man...the newcomer to *Mystery*...and wanted? Cannister did not know. Had he come to town to worship at the shrinequest of gold?

"Keep a sharp eye out for the handsome Mexican," Cannister said as Ludheim exited the saloon. "He will tell them where to dig, dig, here, don't dig there. He will make up their minds for them." He drank from a bottle of beer. "And, oh, I almost forgot, that Grotteau feller...'s editor of the paper...he won the Continental Hotel from DeVancha in a card hand. May be some excitement over that."

"I'll keep it in mind," said the lawyer...when already he had watched DeVancha sign over his *bonanza* to the man they called Grotteau. The hotel had become his through a gambler's flip of a card in a game of faro.

The parties to the contract met in a dugout beneath the hotel, a gloomy, dry and hot place Ludheim called ***The Vault.*** Here is how that transcendental scene of property transfer went. Its Western typicality is worthy of notice. Simplicity and cunning marked its character.

Ludheim was speaking to de Vamcha. "You are quite right, quite right, Senor de Vancha. He was referring to DeVancha's praise of the handsome woodwork in the hotel. Ludheim took out a large yellow cigar case and offered an *El Tropico* red, short cigar to each of the men. Reiner Grotteau was the receiver of the property and, or couse, was naturally present to sign the title of repossession. Ludheim lit up and exhaled a drift of still white smoke into the airless and stuffy room.

He became perfunctory again. Tediously grinding the freshly lit cigar between his teeth, the lawyer rolled up themap with the delicacy and respect of a visiting dignitary. He handed it to Grotteau, then drew out from his attaché case a document which at the top read; ***Deed of Title Transfer.*** Beneath these words were more words, scripted in a generous bold hand:

> *The Continental Hotel,*
> *including the land on which*
> *it sited, its accoutrements*
> *and appurtneances, except*
> *for those which cannot be*
> *removed, and all other rights*
> *and privileges of ownership*
> *without esception, that attach*
> *to the aforesaid hotel are by this*
> *deed-paper transferred into the*
> *of Reiner Grotteau, this day of*
> *May 12, 1830.*

Ludheim thrust this document under the nose of DeVancha. "Hail Mary's will do you no good, *Amigo.*" The other two men found drollery in this remark; On the lower left side of the sheet were lines to accommodate signatores to the deed.

"I do not say the rosarys before I sign there." Ludheim summoned a brief, forced laugh.

"It is not a religious document, Senor DeVancha. It is the deed of transfer of this hyer building from you to Mister Grotteau there. *Comprende? This* is not a trick," he ended. He saw the Mexican waver slightly with misgivings.

"*Porque—donde is la justicia? Where is justice?* I do not agree with the cards."

"The law makes this paper necessary. *Es necessario* or the title will not be his after all."

"I do not trust these paper—your paper."

"Senor de Vancha, we must conduct this matter according to the law."

"Where iss the law when the soldiers kill *mes parentes grandes, de mi esposa* Alejandra? The soldiers on their horses—*hacen el cuidado de lost vivos?* I do not think that is true."

"I'm sorry to hear about that...about their deaths. But the shooting back then...for whatever reason...is not relevant to our little agreement, *acqui.*"

"The murder of my blood—that is different..."

Failing to comprehend fully, the lawyer shrugged his shoulders. "We'll work something out," Ludheim replied with a vague indifference to the Mexican's half-articulated anguish and smouldering anger. There appeared also a distinct distrust for the White Man Grotteau, the gambler, especially since such a prize as the Continental Hotel was slipping from his grasp into the worthless an soft hands of **The Scorpion's** newspaper editor. His was the shame of defeat without the eloquence of speech or the marvel of any satisfactory explanation for his loss and the settlement that had just ended.

"I can understand you...your hurt, Grotteau proffered the entangled DeVancha. He chose his sly words carefully, adroitly and with a certain artfulness that betrayed the double meang of hidden intent...*to transfer.*

"I...I..." The lawyer was embarrassed nonetheless. He appeared at a loss for words. "We...Mister Grotteau, it will not be necessary for you to find some ink and pen. I am prepared for this moment, said

Ludheim. I shall furnish myself and our *companero* here with the… necessary tools."

He withdrew a small terra cotta jar from one drawer of the desk, together with a damaged quill for a pen. He examined the point with care. Removing a small cork stopper from the top of the jar, he dipped the point of the feather pen in the fluid, a compound of charcoal and turpentine He handed the pen to DeVancha who scratched his name to the document, where the lawyer's manicured little finger pointed with an exquisite delicacy. The signature was hardly discernable as DeVancha, but there it was, beside itt a large blob of spilled black ink.

Grotteau sighed, scrawled his name with a grand flourish and sat straight upright, an ineffable smile crossing his face. The transfer of ownership was complete. Including the preliminary discussion, the entire process had taken no more than half and hour. DeVancha looked quite dejected and dispossessed, as indeed he was. The deed was done, on paper, accomplished in Ludheim's Gothic Vault office

The suave, ambitious Ludheim related this story to the bartender, Kittrick, his motive at this point being the illumination of the truth—that Reiner Grotteau was the hotel's latest owner—by way of a rather exotic and far-fetched tale. The barkeep lit the tapers on his walls. The village was still a virtual settlement with no electricity.

Max Ludheim knew little about the history of the West. He did not know, for example: that having corrupted the Indians with hard liquor, prostitution, hostility and disease, the Spaniards left the field of California to the Russians, whose wooden battlements at Fort Ross reaped a rich harvest of the skins of millions of seals, beaver and deer. This DeVancha, Ludheim imagined, was a Spaniard in temperament, maybe an American in action, but…untrustworthy. He remembered how the Mexican had hesitated at the signing of the document of property-title.

Explorer Francisco Vasquez Coronado, who despaired of finding no more than a little gold for the Spanish crown, catapulted

King Ferdinand, in the first half ot the 16th century, into awarding grants of vast areas of the southwest to his sycophantic mercenary soldiers, thereby claiming and holding the land as Spanish Territory. The Indians would prove an inexhaustible source of slave labsor. Ludheim had sensed that DeVancha dwelt among these Grantee emissaries, in his imagination.

Two hundred years later a missionary Friar named Father Junipera Serra was setting up Christian missions with slave-labor Indian help, while fewer than one hundred years later, swarms of malcontents…for many of those first Argonauts were leaving a better life for a worse one, trickled at first then flooded into the golden land. DeVancha, had already tried to prove his linkage to Senor Sepulveda, one of King Ferdinand's soldier favorites.

As Mayor. *El Alcalde DeVancha*, he could then greet newcomers with open arms…and a pen for their signature, those who could write. He had the mind of an indigent, the spirit of a Conquistadore and the ways of a vagabond. His long black moustaches made him visible on the streets of Mystery. Ludhiem, it appeared, was a promoter for personal gain, a figure consistent with Westward Expansion, erroneous trail maps, golden promises, vast homestead acreages for settlement and use, and the like.

He had a formal way of welcoming them. His welcome was, he said, a rehearsal for great things to come, Diego DeVancha, *Alcalde* Diego de Vancha. At these words spoken by a photographer standing at his elbow, he was jubilant and ecstatic. He removed his fine revolver from its fine holdster and fired three rounds into the air, calling them the blessings of the Holy Trinity. Playing the priest was joyous for this half-mad soldier and outlaw named Diego DeVancha. He was wanted in Arizona Territory for at least four stage holdups and one murder.

Summoning the village by the ringing of a locomotive bell at the newspaper office of ***The Scorpion,*** the construction of an adobe-brick City hall being yet under way, Ludheim announced to the few who ran to find no fire that their new Mayor was Mayor Diego DeVancha and that they must spread the word. This welcoming overture took place before ***The Scorpion,*** on *Dog Street*, the main street in the village. Reiner Grotteau was the editor and owner of said news sheet of two pages.

"I have a grande surprise for you, *Alcalde de Vancha."* He made this promise after Ludheim, with bandolier clips, had placed two epaulets on the new mayor's shoulders. Ludheim had stolen them from a Civil War uniform display in El Paso. He descended to the foot of the wooden steps and called out several Spanish surnames. He used the classic stage approach of the traveling medicine vendor. The expression on DeVancha's face turned somber, then surprised, exultant and finished in an emotional comaraderie of feeling. He embraced the Spaniard indigents, three of whom he called his "sons", who worked in the *Wagon Works*, one a smithy by trade; one in the leather tanner, a bootmaker by trade, the third, labored in the surrounding countryside as a carpenter. "All *piasonos, todos companeros."*

Ludheim, who adopted the role of a politician because of poor health, had retired in *Mystery* to the status of a printer's helper, a sometimes compositor. He smiled. "Just like those damned Mexicans— celebrating before their election to office. You'd better pick up some bodyguards!" Ludheim said to a townsman standing nearby. He need say no more to catch the spirit of the town. No love was lost between Max Ludheim and the Mexican indigents in *Mystery*. They were a minority he could use.

The small crowd standing in the broiling sun before ***The Scorpion*** office, appeared appreciated the gestures of friendship with Mexico. At Max Ludheim's invitation, they all—eighteen of the townsfolk— walked about two hndred yards, down *Dog Street*, to the adobe brick city hall , pride of Ludheim and the newspaper editor Grotteau and, or course, Cannister Kittrick, first finder of the gold nugget and town founder, now the bartender. They drew others along in the stroll of their entrourage. It was not fantasy that almost all townsfolk believed in the goddess of fortune. The story was current still that a prospector had shot a buzzard in flight which black raptor, when it plummeted from the sky, fell at a spot that became the *glory hole*, the shaft hole for a fabulously rich gold mine. Several sourdoughs set out to find the spot but had failed, returning to their panners' sites.

At first a trickle and then a swarm, prospectors for gold came in search of El Dorado, the Arcadian paradise, believers in the goddess of fortune. The Mexicans in the village exchanged looks of incredulous surprise, mingled with disdain. They faked smiles and seemed to exhibit ingratiating genuflexions, a kind of barbaric body language. DeVancha, the self-appointed *Alcalde,* stood on the steps of the clity hall that was only a symbol of the law. He held the aloft what he considered the appropriate token of his majesty's power, a Spanish sword that belonged to Ludheim. Its flash was felt to anoint the townsmen who looked on, members of a relatively small group who stood in patient ceremonial acceptance of the political power in the village. Ludheim, the Gringo Politician, uged them to thank their new *Alcalde* for appointing them. citizens of Mystery, as his deputies, a response measure by fear and uncertainty and with sheepish grins.

Hordes of prospectors, like locusts, were settling upon the Mother Lode country. They were staking out their claims in the foothills of the Sierra Nevada Mountains were, without any proof, they believed there was was located the main "mother" vein of the gold ore, just under the pristine surface of the ground, an indescribably rich vein that simply awaited their picks and shovels.

Their diggings lay, generally, in a north to south direction. Visions and dreams were their birthmark. In their lust to find that gold, men gave up their lives, left families and homes, rewarding jobs and indolence, to search and to prospect. The icons for this influx of manual labor were the miner's simple pan, pick and shovel—only later the *monitor* to wash down the mountain. But at first, the transportable tools ,usually strapped to a burro, announced that a single miner had penetrated deep into the Sierra foothills. He was an authentic gold seeker.

Some of the miners were good men and some were bad. Most were honest yet lacked foresight. They had left their pasts often without remorse, always with ambitious hope, and seldom with regrets, to trek across the plains or skirt the Straits of Cape Horn or cross the steamy malarial jungles of Panama to reach California.

Invited by *El Alcalde Nuevo* to enter the clity hall, miners' shadows were elongated in the gloomy low-vaulted room of the adobe structure. There was a sinister purgatory quality to the small informal ceremony; but then, too, so is the ceremony of the hangman. The lawyer lit a fresh cigar by the torch which DeVancha now held, having replaced the sword. He pulled it down still in de Vancha's hands, to insert the end of the weed into the torch flame. The torch was a tin filled with oil and rags. He pushed it back to an upright position. Power and submission were ordained by that simple act. All were bonded by their investment of time, tools, will and greed to scheme by deception yet to prospect by honest labor at the creeks and streams in the region.

His four *companeros* shook de Vancha's hand. *Jorge*, very dark, black moustache, sombrero that hid his face, gnarled hands, skinny arms and ragged shirt with *Mio* embroidered on it—grinned. *Jesus*, the second slim, tall, long.faced Andaluvian features, almost Caucasion— he too with a moustache and beard, his head balding. He actually bowed as o an emperor. The third, *Tobio*, looked like a wrestler, brawny, ruddy-faced, open smile that showed rotting teeth. He smote one wall with his fist to test its strength. He was a smithy. A fourth, *Jamsie*, was a mall scrubby hangeron, gnarled icon of ferocity buried under a swatch of coal black hair. He coughed ans spat into the dust. They had all gravitated to the Alcalde, to volunteer for his official deputies. They were also desperadoes, in flight from a crime somewhere, fugitives in essence, yet DeVancha's "sons" as he called them.

They were important simply because they underscored the danger of the community, wild revenge, moments of panner envy, retaliation, trespass without enquiry, gross hatred based on culture and a cross-section of the evil that can find tolelerance behind a common goal, to locate and extract the valuable yellow metal. They all owned and some carried firearms.

"I shall make the celebration known all through the town and the diggings."

"*Si, Senor,* a dance to celebrate."

"I had almost forgotten...of couse, a dance...perhaps at the *Wagon Works*. It has the best ground for a dance. It has a wooden floor. There you will be..knighted." They laughed. "Crowned," DeVancha amended. They laughed again.

"I am not a king. I am the Mayor. I can do much worse than a king." There lay a shadowy threat to his words. Even behind jesting and laughter one knew that evil hid its many faces.

He was therefore entitled to be called *El Alcalde,* the Mayor of Mystery, Blood- ancestry DeVancha. Ludheim at this moment rehearsed his knowledge of Spanish history, his research, the power of the family flame, their blood, authority, spirit of fight and resignation...and their obsession with crueltyas tlhe wine-flagon of power.

Of course DeVancha said that he felt honored. The dance would make it known to all, when the miners will be taken by surprise, since the office had not existed before. Max Ludheim advised DeVancha about the Indians, who would also try to lay claim to the land as their own.

"Your *companeros* who work at the *Wagon Works* they will be useful to you, El Alcalde DeVancha." said a townsman. They were conversing at the saloon.

"Also I will introduce you to Senor Grotteau. He will be invited to the dance celebration. Senor Grotteau will give new life to Mystery. He plays the guitar. He also plays at poker in the saloon. And he is also a mans to be feared...Senor Grotteau is a shooter."

"I do not fear him." said DeVancha, "if he choses to come to me with peace in his heart." His words carried a foreboding.

"He may run to the side of the Indians," said Ludheim.

Even a newcomer could see that moments shared by a community of good men do not bond them, that the sacrifices of some men...be they miners, settlers, missionaries or medicine men...bring no lasting justice. Their ultimate sacrifices are not gold or comfort. Their ultimate sacrifices are their honor, their integrity which, trashed or ignored, subjects them to their vulnerability before power—to the chains of one man's zeal for power. Ludheim had reflected on this sort of sacrifice in law courts. In his so-called indenturement to Mister Grotteau, he had simply affirmed the witness of his earlier years—that good can be exchanged for evil if the laurel to be gained is of great value." Thus spoke Ludheim in his frontier wisdom.

As a lawyer still, Ludheim had not abandoned the pursuit of truth. What was important—his use of truth once a man had found it. He identified with the miners' endurance. He was the fatalist son of an improvident father, yet he had learned about lthe conditions of men who toil in hard, unalterable circumstances, men warped by their distrust, by the tragedies of their families and friends and harassed by monstrous debts. His observations of life in the village were the lodestone of his sanity. He wondered, apart from the god of Nihilism, if events that he had encountered later were merely inducements to adopt the cynical mysticism of fatalism. Favored men of the cities and in other governments would call him an Idealogue.

Senor *Alcalde DeVancha*, was, by appointment, the Mayor, *chosen*—the best construction Ludheim could put on the word. Little did he realize what an enterprise he actually headed—which included suppliers of miners goods, steamship lines, grubstakers and promoters who catered to the naïve voyagers coming into the gold field. Even, *El Alcalde* had to laugh at the poster of an Eastern gentleman stooping down to pick up a nugget that lay atop the ground. They may have listened too closly to the flare of Cannister Kittrick, the loquatious first-nugget finder of the village.

There were camps by creeks, on the banks of the Americn Yuba and Sacramento Rivers where he could pitch his tent and begin picking, shoveling and panning. There was then his village of Mystery whose gold seekers were a proud race, yet insecure, avaricious and in muddied boots, dirty torn breeches, shirts and hats, dedicated to their task, their labor of picking the ore having it crushed, or panning the gold flakes and dust from the black sands in which they found it. The mining community was by token authority, let by the Mayor;

he was a flambuoyant visionary. The village, on the other hand, was a community of survivors, adapting to a new place, displaying their ignorance, grappling with new circumstances, fabulous, far-fetched, and accommodating themselves to the rigors of the weatherand their crude outdoor existence.

Since Ludheim was merely a printer's devil, a Medieval insinuation, a distributor of printer's type to the font case once the paper had been published—a necessary task nonetheless—he worked for the man named Reiner Grotteau, already introduced, a strange, enigmatic man who came to town to search for gold like everybody else. They called themselves Argonauts. Gotteau had tried to tell Ludheim where he should site his cabin and build. Ludheim saw then that Grotteau was a controlling sort of man. As a former lawyer, Max Ludheim would not be Reiner's puppet, but he might be of service in other modest ways—like also setting type for his Chalmers treadle-operated press... to publish *The Scorpion* newpaper.

Ludheim was the idealist, Grotteau the reformer who hated violence, though he perpetuated it by his enmity toward claim jumpers, shooters and conspirators. *The Scorpion* had fast become, in its two years, an instrument for bribery, threats and intimidation, for personal power and, generally, for the editor's manipulation of the townfolks in the village of Mystery. Ludheim thought of him at first as a humanitarian, a samaritan who cared for the troubled and the suffering of other men...but particularly for those who could maximize his power. Ludheim knew that he and Grotteau would eventually clash on matters of power and control.

We had had talks in the **Hard Rock Saloon.** I had already met the Mayor there. The main drag was called *Dog Street.* The Continental Hotel of eight rooms was fronted by *Dog Street.* Also, the smithy, a barber shop and a corral, and the Wagon Works operated by the four desperdoes, the "sons" of El Alcalde. Along *Dog Street* there came to be located and opened for business a saddlery, a gunsmith, and Salem Horsby's *General Merchandise Store.* That was the town, except for the Crutchfield Stagecoach line that kept a small office at the hotel.

Coming down from Oregon to Mystery, the route next went through Frost, then Triangle, fifteen miles to the East, trekking over a southern Sierra Pass into Nevada, from whence it turned south to Santa Fe New Mexico. It served its purpose well, to advance the spread of Manifest Destiny and bring settlers from San Francisco into the gold country.

A little more about Diego DeVancha, the Mayor, a former highwayman who had been reformed by whisksy, religion and a woman. He had wanted to pose as a regenerate soul. He had been owner of the Continental Hotel, who had insisted on having prostitutes live in two back upstairs room. The Stage rolling out of San Francisco through the small river town of Sacramento and into Mystery had been his favorite targets. He could not endure the loss of income from his stage robberies and so had intalled his ladies of the night in two upstairs rooms of his hotel, won at a poker table in the **Hard Rock Saloon,** a royal flush beating a straight set. He collided with Crutchfield who, being a religious man, was too devout to endorse DeVancha's profit-making scheme. He did not wish to suffer that his stage patrons should have to have to mingle with brothel clients in order to get a night's rest. But he persisted when Alcalde DeVancha offered to give any one or couple of his passeners a free room for one night if they were traveling through. They need not use the Continental's special service. Grotteau kept the arrangement when he acquired the hotel from DeVancha in a faro game, authenticated on legal paper by Lawyer Ludheim in the *Vault.*

So it was. the mingling of tradition, customs, prejudices and antagonisms in a brew of diversity. Even ***The Scorpion*** was a purchase from an Easterner named Oglethorpe, called ***The Rocker,*** hand-written and therefore hardly a mirror-likeness transaction. Grotteau had had the Chalmers Press and type-font cases shipped down to gold country from San Francisco.

Just a word about the paper, apart from its corrupt aspect. A pig with feet of gold—said so—adorned the masthead; the press was a platten roller type with a 16 by 20 inch chase, treadle operated. It turned out a two-page paper. The motto was ***Beware of Richess Like the Scorpion Sting.*** It carried boiler-plate advertisements for Kerosene

Lanterns, patent medicines, Wagon Works repairs, horse collars and the like.

The village paper also carried Grotteau's inflamatory articles on mining claims in defaut, on land possession and general avarice among miners who could not satisfy themselves with small gains of gold dust. It tended to be hortatory, blaming miners for their own losses, yet pigging up miners who had struck it rich. It announced failures in bold type, to admonish and advise others. And it transgressed feelings by pointing out dudes who gambled all their winnings away then coveted with grand envy the successes of their neighbors. it singled out card cheats and defied their exposure. It mangled facts with fiction to exploit bullies in the village. *The Scorpion* controlled the villagers by threats of publishing their various sins of assault, gun play at the saloon, theft of tools, claims jumpers and solitary abandonment of claims. *The Scorpion* made reprehensible all violence and threats of violence, boasting that it had a plan to remedy the defect in character. Thus the paper was reformist, boldly and blatantly so. Ludheim saw and waited. Grotteau had long hid an ambition to turn Mystery into a company town over which he had complete control His newspaer would be his *instrument of seizure*: Ludlt had fast become Grotteau's engine provsocateur by which he dnagled threats to annihilate miners disloyal to prospecting, citizens suspectsed of gross crimes sof rape, one or two cu-throat murders and claim-jumping. Reiner Grotteau lacked the character to resist slander and inflamatory accusations of wrongdoing.

The Scorpion's humble appearance reminded the injudicious miners that the king's land grantees had fought the mission fathers, endured squatters, speculators, and at last gold-seekers, who in no way were enobled by charging them with gluttony. The *Land Act of 1851* had affirmed the title of the miners to their claims. The paper transformed from a handwritten single sheet to a two page newssheet, set in moveable type and produced amid the bloodshed, avarice, prejudices and violence, written up by a tabloid dedicated to the elimination of these vices. It did so by intimidation...a form of public extortion...and by bribery of the miners to submit to his "requests," to help support

Roads, Fire prevention, which was a joke, and official guests from the Capitol—all to their, the miners', advantage. He would publish the names of generous doners, yet excoriate by name those who scorned his *enlightened* appeals.

Ludheim found from history that Diego DeVancha could claim ancestors in the de Cassiones Family who, on a Conquistidores misssion, had gone inland and settled with the local Indians tribes; that his mother had been a ful-blooded Spanish lady of wealth and station in Madrid, his father the patrone of the Spanish soldier king. History disappeared, but DeVancha was, indeed, related by blood to the recipient of an ancient land Grantee named Senor Jose Sepulveda, and he was pressing his good fortune when he entered the echelons of gold discoverers, their fractious society, the exclusivity of their single purpose. Despite his violent past, or perhaps because of it, DeVancha was the man to reside over them—Max Ludheim decided.

A first danger that begged for a solution were the squatters, dangeous in readiness to jump the claims of others in the owners' absence. Their breed was one of drifters and figutives who promoted fear and murder, as by choking or stabbing to death a sleeping miner... and other nefarious crimes to gain access to the gold. The Tong Wars and the Dutch Colonist conflagrations were the lodestones for these drifters, despite Frenchmen barracades against them. Bloodshed and violence uppermost, these battles *du monde* all made news for **The Scorpion**

Ludheim opined that " if they come in...all at once...in droves, they will become afrightening, they will create terror," he said of the drifter squatters.

"So, we will chase them out, make them run in front of us like scattered chickens," said Kittrick, the barkeep.

"Our horses will make the noise of terror for them," said Ludheim. Like the night is falling down." He was talking to Reiner Grotteau, the editor in the **Hard Rock Saloon**

"That is right, make claim-jumping...squatting a bad disease... we are impatient to get wealth, but not by dishonest means," said Reiner Grotteau in a moment of unnatural piety. He became the village moral conscience—only when he opposed a claim-jumper. Otherwise, when it came to greed to find the gold, he was silent. Cyrus Crutchfield had once said to Ludheim , at his station stop.."when I had come out here to inspect the town, from Boston. I thought then...everyone will be purged with fire, and every sacrifice will be seasoned with salt. Take care Mister Ludheim!"

That wisdom stuck with the lawyer. Right from the start he distrusted Reiner Grotteau for the power he wielded. That power was more than salt. And likewise, he held in disrespect the Mayor because he perceived his grasp of power through the authority of ancestry, which belonged to time and history and not to his special talents. Ludheim knew *El Alcalde* was good at cards and with a gun....

Ludheim made a colossal mistake when one day he showed DeVancha a title deed, a document that noted the vast desert acreage on which the lawyer had made a circle with an "X" to locate Mystery, this document being an acquired item of treasure of his victorious life in the law. They were talking in the Vault; Ludheim had invited the Mexican down into his refuge for a little chat, so that, as the lawyer put it, "they could get better acquainted." He thought, *know your foe*. The panther-skull lantern in Ludheim's Vault office mocked at life. The flame in its eye sockets and jaw caught the ink gloss and parchment quality of the document. Ludheim remembered an old Spanish proverb. **Give glory to god and to gold—one is impossible without the other."** DeVancha remembered how that feverishly he had wanted to keep his hotel and had shown a royal flush, Grotteau a pair of duces. It rankled him still. He, Diego DeVancha des los Carciniones de Jose Sepulveda would get his *chance* some day....

"You really did ot want to keep that old hotel. Confess it, DeVancha. Just think—now you can pimp for your two ladies of the night."

DeVancha did not brighten with these words; he scorned Ludheim to begin with. He found it necessary to hate the man for his being an intruder Gringo into the history of his proud ancestors. In a word, he despised Ludheim, a bad attitude since the retired lawyer was not unaware of DeVancha's bloody past as a rogue, a murderer and highwayman. The feelings were mutual. However, he would, for appearances, render the El Alcalde a token respect. He broke open a bottle of wine, lit another lantern whose flame began to burn in the skull of a jaguar. He walked over to an armored skeleton and rattled the face mask to see if the knight was listening. "*Quien sabe, mi amigo soldato?*" he addressed the mask, turning back to the Mayor who sat dumfounded by this mad show of...wisdom, power? De Vancha could not fix a tag to the illusion. They drank for several minutes without speaking.

"You are a...permanent Mayor here In Mystery," the lawyer said, "Does that not please you?"

"Mucho, Senor Ludheim. I can help Senor Grotteau with his plans. He will ask the gringos for homage...des homage...for their sites.

"Oh, and I had not heard that! A...percentage of the gold profits mined."

"Si, si. They will pay their...fee

"Like reny for their claims."

"Si, si."

"That was your idea...?"

"My sons have the idea—rent the land, pay a ...just a small piece of gold for big pieces of gold.

"I...I hardly think that will go over, DeVancha."

"They will not fight. They will agree. That is the way to peace in fhe villa."

"You just may be right," said Ludheim. From a case, while DeVancha looked on, the lawyer removed several knives and placing them on his desk, he began to sharpen them, to hone thir edges on the rough sandy-tongue of a leopard separately mounted in a block of wood on his desk. He did this, smiling a smile at his guest but keeping silent until the Mayor, unable to bear the sight any longer stood and announced.

"I have much to do in the City hall, he said.

"Yes, I suppose so. Keep your loyalties separatted," siad Ludheim. "Here, here, take one of these. A token of my respect. But that is to protrect you from…threats? Keep it hidden. Its handle is made of finest pearl." He smiled a forced smile land handed the Mayor a sharpened Bowie knife. He stood as DeVancha, now somewhat discombobulated, did not know exactly what to do. Ludhein put out his hand, DeVancha shook it, and without a word passed out of the vault and into ltlhe upstairs world. Ludheim llneeded the figure of the Mlayor as a safeguard against general revillion among the townsmenl when they discovered that the would be takes cor the use of…al legitimalte Grantee's land

Ludheim had become a Sage in the village. He had witnessed the obsession of *panner envy* and territorial hostilility betweeen prospectors…such as he never knew existed between starving coyotes who eat anything, dead or alive, yet share. Ludheim had seen the senseless and insensible come to the surface in men's hearts and concluded that brotherhood among men was a lie, a corruption fostered by posession of gold, actually a compromise in hatred that deferred murder as a resolution. 1 Perhaps, Lulheim felt, he did not deserve to tell this tale, but then he must. He had to confront his own fears and resolve to remain an inhabitant of the village.

Men here were divided by covetousness, driven betweeen one goal and another, undecided, like a swallow hunting a place to build its nest. The lawyer had learned, also, that beggars are often times impulsive givers. Reiner Grotteau was not a malevolent man, creatured by a vulgar, profane society of gold-seekers. Instead, he was a convert to the philosophy of acquisition for triumph—benign at first blush but treacherous in the breech. If and when his own survival depended on animal cunning, he would survive regardless of the consequences to himself or to other men. He let Mulheim publish a small poem of his in **The Scorpion** that signified this transmutation of the human soul into the demonic image. Indulge him, if you would:

THE APOTHECARY

Across the valley a bell tolls grace
to immgrant tents that join increase.
They clot the sands, spring hasty
/apace
their honor fed by wind's caprice.

The village Apothecary drug culture
/lacks
to find within th desolate stones
Mystery's gold where the viper tracks,
th' cxoyote whines, gnaws old bones.

Made wise by his quintessential cries,
Man seeks by will thel and to keep
Yet vanquished by his necessary ties,
he withers, dissovles in pride to sleep.

Fitting the description of the Apothecary, Cyrus Crutchfield, a man with a voracious appetite for profits but stingy with his risks, certainly was not a visionary as was Mister Grotteau. A free room to Stagecoach guests is hardly the symptom of a yen to explore rather to exploit. The Continental Hotel was first owned by DeVancha by the turn of a card. Yet he had neither the intelligence nor the will for conducting a successful business except that practiced at the muzzle of his six gun. By accolades, the turn of a faro card and, ultimately, by the legal maneuvering of Max Ludhiem he, **The Scorpion** editor, was now the hotel's owner.

Bartender Cannister Kittrick, at the **Hardrock Saloon** knew the story well, with embellishments, the tale of the transfer of the ownership of the hotel. We've witnessed the document signing. Whereas the bartender was a better instant source of news than was **The Scorpion.** the news had reached the City by the Golden Gate as evidenced by a clipping that fell into Grotteau's hands about a week after the event. It came from San Francisco's **Alta Californian.** It read.

Alta Californian: 6-7-71—We have assurances from Haggarty and Haggarty in this City that an old hotel in the gold country known as the Continental Hotel has een "sold" for the value of the turn of a card in a poker game—in that village of Mystery. Such is the lot of losers in this country.

It has a small saloon on the ground floor and boasts of rooms for rent on the first and second floors, some ten in all. It was a meritorious acquisition, and a fair investment for any man who desires not to have to put up with the smells of whisky, tobacco smoke and Chinese egg fu yong as exists in certain of this City's less preferential hotels.

*We are told that the **accoutrements** of The Continental are most tasteful and reassuring of traveler comfort that will impart a special delight to the traveler's journey.*

Sucn a 'way out" hotel cam be both profitablel and a lodestone that will not attract drifters and others who abound in that godforsaken country of the mines.

We wish the new owner success. We are informed that the salubrious and accommodating stagecoach, owned by the D. & O. Cyrus Crutchfield lines, Mssrs, passes through and makes a stop at the Hotel. Not all is lost in such an arduous desert passage.

We already know his *companeros*, and that they employed their skills at the Wagon Works shed. One was a smithy who fabricated gate hinges, horse shoes, wagon springs pick heads for the winers, some of which items he sold at Clalyton Hornsby's General Merchandise Store on *Dog Street*.

Not everyone in Mystery had met the real Max Ludheim, former lawyher in San Francoisco and compositor for Reiner Grotteau editor and , owner of **The Scorpion**.

"I will lay upon you the sword of…honor and public approval. Thse words were Ludheim's. s[oken to DeVancha down in his office called **The Vault**, a palce where he did not have to confront rats and spiders or the smells of Chinese cookery. It was underground. He was sitting in a wovenbasked and ironwood chair, he referred to one wall where there hung an array of ancient swords. This was De Vancha's second visit, by invitationl from Ludheim himself. He took down a huge sword—it looked like a Claymore sword—that measured some six feet in lngth and at least four inches broad.

"This will do admirably," he said. "For Your Exellency, De Vancha…You may think, your honor, that I am going to chop off heads in the village, but instead, I shall place the end of this word on your shoulder, Senor de Vancha…there…and say to the good folks out there…Ladies and…sorry, we've got no ladies, yet…gentlemen of the soil, rich and prosperous miners and sourdoughs in your humble attire.. this good man here, a natire of the surroundiing hills..wishes to help promote order and happiness in Mystery. As the lawyer in residence—I am called—I hereby knight…once it was called appoint, in the absence of any noble election Senor de Bancha to the enviable position of *El Alcalde*…for you of Mystery to cherish, to oversee the general welfare of your village." This rhetoric amused Ludheim as it would the crowd at the eremony. But, the crowd would realize the pretense, and that the display of a public knighting of affirmation d was all bushwhacker language, *lingo*.

He turned to de Vancha who had come to review the procedings as they would happen. "If you think I am giving you some kind of authority over their digfgins, their lives, think again, said Ludheim, "I will say: He will see to it that all mining claims are observed. He will prosecute as Alcalde all claim-jumpers, he will arbitrate, consider, any feuds between miners, creditors, etcetera. Then, said Ludheim to de Vancha,, "they will aplauds, make no mistake about that Senor de Vancha."

"I do not, si, Senor. *Que tal?* What then happens, what's next?"

"You show my artillery and my armor to…all the people." The ceremony would not be empty charade, for in the Vault there reposed…how he had managed to truck them there almost, as it were, unseen boggled the imagination. Yet there was a Napoleonic canon and caisson, the suit of armor already referred to, various types of daggers, swords and pistols and derringers and, most important by the lawyer's own choice, an immense scales, on wheels, upon which at each platform there was affixed a chair to accommodate a person.. "My secret divice for getting at the truth;," Ludheim explained and laughed

52

at his show of this bizarre artifact. As an afficianado of warefare and weaponry, he had also collcted a shield, several smaller swords, a chain and balls for decapitation, and a miniaturized rack-and-pinyon. He held these artifacts as a sort of repository of memories, gloating over his collectors's treaslure. pieces of ancient warfare art kept in his Vault.

"The sword—Que hace…what do I do with it after I am…. touched?"

"Knghted…You applaud with the people and I cry **Bravissimo! Senor de Vancha"**. You keep the broadsword of your new office…in your quarters at the city hall…until someone replaces you."

"That can never happy, Senor Ludheim…it must never happen."

"I have written out a paper you will read, Senor Alcalde." He handed a documnt to the newly appointed mayor,who then began to read with a halting, stumbling voice.

Senor Diego de Vancha hereby agree to cause to be made a township by certain metes and bounds of the village of Mystery… which shall be posted and that my by auhority is…

"…committed…"

"committed to its limits. l Go on, read? Ludehim nodded. "By this paper, I declare a treaty with hostile Indians."

Ludheim handed DeVancha a pen made from a vulture's qulll. "You DeVancha put your *Senor DeVancha* on the document." After he had done so, "Excellent, my friend, said Ludheim. You are a very wise man. You know how to recoup your losses like a gentleman…no blood spilled, no anger shared…*nada de nada*."

DeVancha started to arise from his chair. " More wine?" Ludheim asked.

"Si, Senor Ludheim." He gulped down another tumbler

"Good…I shall turn in this story to *The Scropion,* " Ludheim promised, which was one of the few he ever kept, proof of which was the story lin full typecast print at the end of the week. He, Ludheim, could now look forward to the celebratory ceremony.

Grotteau, the editor of ***The Scorpion***, was tolerant of his own outrages, his promise, without sproof, that the miners could ever find another Kittrick Nuggett, the largest chunk of gold ever discovered in the Mother lode. He only pretended to honor slquatters rigts. Ludheim well knew and I knew that they had no rights.

After this meeting Ludheim looked upon these hills with their morning mists gathered and swarmed like smoke clouds and lazy-whisped into dripping stillness, as rains downshed from the pines that rose absove Mystery at a distance. The hills, the scrub pines stood silence before the hundreds who had traveled here to Mystery via the Crutchfield, by lsteamship, by horseback and burro.

Manhy would disembark in front of the Continental Hotel steps, the place where my story begins. Reiner Grotteau examnined these emigrants with la certaisn fascination, they who had crossed the plains by wagon and trekked throug the jungles of Cntral America and sailed around the Straits of Horn. He watched them with pitiless eyes some men came to realie, was his nature.

Ludheim had a prescience that he coud and would alttempt to mitigate their dissatisfaction as prospectors. He was of a *nature*, as Grotteau's, who could set traps and seduce the unwary voyager. He had informed himself as to where lay the open, unproductive ravines, the redrock crevices of promise, the quartz veins that scintllaged gold dust. These place, all of them, could be staked. I imagined with good cause that ***The Scorpion*** editor would try to set up a mining company of sorts.

The trail for Ludheim began at Almayer's assay shack over near the creek, just off *Dog Street*, a shack where men's lust for gold led them inevitably to appraise the value of their discovery. Mister Reiner Grotteau was about to transcend time with a few miserable scraps of paper. I knew that it might spell trouble if the townsfolk ever found out the true nature of the man who directed and controlled their thoughs with his newspaper. There was in his life the potential for those acts and destinies of evil that at times mock humaneness and the soul of compassion. For Ludheim had learned in his practice of the law in San Francisco that power and kindness do not reasonably yoke together. Power had to be the benefactor of cruelty wherin other men did not have a choice.

A handful of miners were working the creek near to Reiner Grotteaus shack. They had not foundany nuggets, yes, but several had filed a frenzy of mining claims for both sides of the Bear Creek. Their shacks were shantys tied down to the hillsides, made of scrap boards wagoned in, timber cut from trees above Mystery, pole logs and heavier foundation timbers shaped with a double-bitted axe. Some of the miners had trucked in ,by mule train, lumber from the mill in Frost.. The shanties and tent-houses with their lower walls and floorboards presented a certain ugliness amid the beauty of the hills and the red pumice-like sandstone that capsulated the village. Only about 300 souls lived there at that time of our story.

De Vancha's "sons" lived in several of these shanty's, riveted to the hillsides. All four of them had been in and out of the jails at Triangle; they worked at the Wagon Works where they had built several crude wagons for ranchers over at Frost. These "sons" also ran a shrewd game of craps at th **Hard Rock Saloon.** One of them devised a roulette wheel from a discarded wagon wheel, but that venture was comic to more intelligent minds. They quietly grew rich, as is sometimes the case when outlaw talent is put to lawful use.

> This verse appared one day in **The Scorpion:**
> What message does the sentry bring
> That challenges the bandit tottering
> Before his fall from honor's golden
> ring? Why 'tis his luck its solace doddring
> That steals his gold with craven sting.

All gold-seekers competed with the remorseless opportunism familiar to Reiner Grotteau. He reveled in raw competition. Ice water ran in his veins, as the old saying goes. For his friend Max Ludheim, the end justified the means They were a pair, the latter a loner Greotteau was a quarter Indian…he said…, the grain of his inner soul visible to those who knew him. And among a company camp of miners, he shared not just gold prospecting as a fever, but as a fatal disease.

The ides of weather had kept the scrub pines, and wild grasses and chaparral green, high above the village. Upon a closer inspection ofl the rocky hillsides, Ludheim had found quartz flecks and intrusions of prehistoric volcanic activity. It would be up to the prospectors and panners to discover what these rocks held. Ludheim had lived in Mystery for almost eight years, Grotteau for about six. Before them, the great space of the Western desert greeted newcomers. Why the stage line had built its trail through Mystery was founded mostly on the whims and distant home of Mister Crutchfield, the owner. Nonetheless, there it lay, a village of tent shacks, shantys of nondescript wood, accessible by horse and wagon andf the Crutchfield stagecoach. .

Growth of the primitive West was as capricious as flocks of restless birds wheeling about for a place to land. Grotteau knew the passion of their gold lust, daring to risk their lives and futures in the quest. Ludheim had met another stranger to the desert, an Essene Priest of lthe desert. He could be regarded as a religious anchorite, which he was not, yet a man who had exiled himself to his isolated hell, a man acquainted with other men's dark deeds, their advocate of the devils creed. This same Priest flew like the wind into Grotteau's newspaper office one day and asked simply for a drink of wlater, then queried Grotteau on the whereabouts of the sinners' camp. This question sounded the tone of their relationship from them on. Grotteau was without any moral base or ethical cdompass. even ethics. The Priest was bound by his Essene oath search for his unique vision of a Nirvana of the West.

One of the hard rock miners said to Ludheim as he settled into his own tent shanty: "See dig a hole…a tunnel, one hundred feet into the side of that redrock mountain."

"Yes, that is right…have you looked for gold in the stones?"

"For good…maybe for water. There's maybe a spring around here..and to store tools, shovels, picks and dynamite."

"We work for ourselves. The Mayor Senor DeVanca rides herd."

"That's his idea."

"Mexicans work harder than the White Gringo...."

"For the glory of wealth and...De Vancha. Diego de Vancha." Ludheim sensed that the Mayor was attempting to take command, not because of his native talent, but because of his Conquistadores ancestors.

"Timber...timber to shore up the mine...from Frost mills and dynamite from Triangle...ore carts if we need them. Bags...bags of gold dust...lots of it. To pay for the costs."

"It maybe is good..to get a lend of money."

"He wants to set up a company, *el Alcalde*. He is out of his mind—to make Mystery his land company. you listen."

"Let the Chinese pick through the tailings."

"That is right."

DeVancha was not an experienced miner. He did not comprehend the method of extraction, the thump-thump crushing of ore at the stamping mill, placer extraction by the roar of the monitor. A shortage of water at Mystery was a drawback. They would need a flume from the upper Tuwolome River...a long flume.

He will stake the claim of the whole town in the name of his Ancestors. Ludheim laughed with the miner...**Grotteau's Mining Company**. *Nada, de nada.* From nothing. Ludheim...and the miner... knew that, he, Ludheim would have to engineer the arrangement, call it that. DeVancha trusted the German to come up with any... necessary...papers, provisng ownerhip of the property claims the town sat on. Disputes would arise. The lawyer would reolve them in favor of the *El Alcalde*, he would devise papers that proved ownership where there was none, and he would fabricate disputes as to where claims had been staked out. The Mayor would resolve them to the glory of his office. This was Ludheim's promise. The strategy for total ownership rested in Ludheim's hands.

An unknown miner entered Max Ludheim's vault to see about my own claim. He did not distrust the lawyer...at this time. Ludheim was proud of his vault. Wooden statuary carved like totem figures, the eagle beak with feathers at the top of one, a bear at the top of the other, Kachina icons. Down these poles were carved the faces of coyotes, a badger, a brace of snorting horses, vulures protruding at intervals and stones of rich white goldquartz inset like diamonds wrought the totem's magnificence as each sparkled in the stray light.

"They will protect you," said Ludheim. "Their spirits will hover over you…rescue you from perilous troubles." A knight in armor stood at one side of the vault. It appeared to be a knight in waiting, clasping a torch instead of a sword. Other artifacts of warfare were on display in the Vault, as already noted. At his desk Ludheim wrote out a document of a claim and had me sign. That was all. I scarcely knew what I was doing, exept that I trusted the German lawyer Max Ludheim. My boots clattered and ground into the stone steps as I made my way up and into the night.

The two men, DeVancha, Grotteau and Ludheim in the shadows, were co-conspirators. They wanted the entire town for themselves, to declare their ownership, to make the miners indebted to them!

"It will take time, Diego…a miner who buys stakes a claim up here, puts up a tent-cabin, or throws up a shack…is entitled to what his shack stands on—no more Mineral rights under his claim…only surface rights."

"That is very good, excellent!" said DeVancha, as if a Conquistidore for the land and the king bargaining with an Indian instead of a shrewd lawyer, experinced in land titles. Only he was rablid to take power over the town. The lawyer had hinted about his ambition DeVancha, "You will get used to your inheritance. I'I give you that paper…a deed. The land but not the mineral rights belonged to your ancestors.…

"And to us, Senor," said the Mayor to the lawyer. Grotteau had only to print their agreement to become a party to the pact.

"Senor Grotteau is making a big mistake. He thinks he owns rights to the gold. But he does not own the land where the gold comes from," Ludheim said to the *Alcalde*. This time they were seated in the **Hard Rock Saloon.**

There was about this found conspiracy a charade of untruth; supposition had replaced truth of the proprietorship. ***It is my land,*** Proclaimed the cursae of indenturement for the miners, thougfh they did not comprehend. This is my land. Ours, Senor de Vancha— Ludheim had to keep reminding the Conquistidore, as he came to be called. It suited his nature, his ancestry, his desires.

"We don't know what mineral rights there are…" Gold may not be all. DeVancha was silent and thoughtful.

Ludheim new that the entire notion of conquest rested on the premise of no resistance, either by lthe White miners or the Indians. And if a battle should break out horse soldiers might have to settle matters. Grotteau, through his newspaper, raised the flag of personal virtue. He declared that he was the owner of sage, cactus, jackrabbits and sand on which the village sat. He would prove his proproietorlship and title with a deed. Max Ludheim would be the co adjudicator of the Seizure. A blind blacksmith hammering at his anvil could not be more absurd. "All that not true Klaleb Hammer, a panner and our press operator. told me when I stood alongside his ore rocker, watching him pick out flakes of gold where they showed through the black sand

"Do one thing, Max," the miner said to him "Take samples to Almayer. "He's reliable and honest. He will record your visit and his analysis."

"That is good in a court of law, Jack." They shook hands. Neither man wanted to see the ohter cheated. That was the classic sort of agreement. They shook hands.…

HIS APPOINTED ROUNDS

Grotteau bellowed out the name "Grant Harrimon, you here? Oh, Grant Harrimon!" He received no answer. Grant was a guest by the new policy of Crutchfield to inspire over night stops at the village, room free of charge at the **Continental**. The desk register showed that the hotel had two guests for its ten rooms. Gotteau shouted Harrimon's name again. A man suddenly appeared on the staircase landing, looking as if he had gone through the battles of some hazardous fight for life, visible with a torn shirt, scrambled red hair, dingy trousers and bootless wilthblood on his face.

"You Harriman?"

"I am that, sir. What can I do for you?"

"Go put on yer boots and come down here, if you would. I"m selling mining claims to some of the richest gold ore in the territory… right here in this town of Mystery."

"Don't say."

Within minutes, the disheveled Harrimon reappeared, blood removed and looking neater than he had before. "Pardon, sir…what's this you're trying to tell me?"

"I'm setting up a claims office here in the **Continenta**l. I'll be selling claims for another gold strike…small investment…you a shooter?"

"Pardon, sir?"

"Guns. You own a gun?"

"Nary a one."

"No mind. Fer a small charge you, too, can own a piece of gold country."

"I come out here…I'm a furrier headed for San Francisco."

"Not got much in the way of furs, but, stick around. We got a few wild dogs and some desert jackrabbits." The man smiled.

"With jes a small investment—a twenty dollar gold piece holds a claim—you can have acces to all the gold that's under the ground, and, sir, is is tested and tried and found…copious, plentiful." Grotteau dragged in a few more splendiferous words to brighten his offer.

"I got me a job, Mister Grotteau…but I haint no gold seeker like them other ones."

"Well said, well said, Mister Harrimon. I be assured there's much gold hereabouts—but they's a shortage a miners to dig it up."

"Sir, I'm no digger, fact' is I got a lame hand, hit a feller over a woman oncet, broke my hand. Don't mean to be insultin yer offer, sir but..'see, I cannot dig much…" He held up his lame hand as proof of his words.

"Well, not that's too bad, Mister,…cause I got a claim not twnety yards from here..so rich, you can afford to hire a Mexican to dig it for y' and give him a percent." Harrimon thought, he pondered, then he shook his head.

"I don't think so, fur is my trade."

He went over to the stairs again, and started back up to his room.

"I can find you…I can locate a choice claim for you, just for you…a capital piece of gold-bearing real estate that'll make your fur business look mighty small." Silence greeted this overture. "Give it a thought, mister Harrimon."

"Well said, and I'll do jus that.," said the hotel guest and he climbed back up the stairs to hisroom. Wind and the rain and blowing sand did not depress his scheme to posess the gold town, lock, stock and barrel.

The *Entrepreneur* editor of **The Scorpion** went next to the *Hard Rock Saloon* and walked immediately to one of two busy card tables. He was interested because he had habitually dealt many a hand as a former card-table gambler in New Jersey.

"Social visit?" one of the players asked out of suspicion

"You nailed it, Mister Clanton."

"Too bad your fancytalk don't say, 'cut me in'."

"It just might. Fact is it will. I got a proposition. sir, that'll make yer hair curl." The gambler named Clanton regarded Grotteau with a skeptical eye. He chortled in disrespect and doubt.

"It's you I'm thinking about, Mister Clanton. You being the king's gambler and all that sort of rot."

"What're you getting at, Grotteau, Cain't you see I'm busy?"

Grotteau kept silent and watched the game come to an end. Clanton loset his gamet...to the tune of several hundred dollars.. Grotteau invited him over to the bar, treated him to a drink and began to work on the angry gambler with a passion. Right here, under this here saloon, Mister Clanton, there's gold. I read your mind. I got a geologist friend—Almayer—who says the same thing."

"Look, sir, this here's a town full of squatters, that all. I play from saloon to saloon. That's how I make my money. Frost, Triangle... .I ain't interested in no gold digging."

"What if I tell you I own this town, Mister Clanton?"

"Impossible...Say! How'd you know my ;name?"

"Irish name...I'm part Iirish...and you purt near wrecked that bank up in Indian Camp with those sticks a dynamite.."

"How...how'd you know...l" The culprit was dismayed by Grotteau's knowledge. "I did'nt take a dollar, Mister., and that's a fact. Bank was adobe. They can rebuild when the rains come."

"I got a whispering diary called the morgue...tells me a lot of interesting things. Also, did you know yer wife plans to come out West to look fer you?"

The man was totally bewildered as to how Grotteau could come upon such intimate information. "Just follow the bouncing ball, Mister Clanton, and you'll come out all right. Meantime, why don't you turn in that double barrel shot gun for a piece of gold territory."

"You seem awful sure."

"I am sure of myself...I got the best gold assayer in the world."

"Mebe so, mebe so. But I don't aim to turn thet shotgun over to any body but my son when he comes a age." Grotteau showed the gambler his preprinted title deed of ownership of the lands of *Mystery*…a mining claim inexchange for any old hunting piece. ***"Fair exhchange"*** the handout said. The printing was finely styled and blqckbold, from ***The Scorpion*** press. "I don't know what your talking about, mister. Go your way and leave me alone. I'll be obliged to go finish my poker game."

"Suit yourself," said the editor of ***The Scorpion.*** The miner returned to his poker table. The editor left the saloon, frustrated on his second try of the day to win buyers into his scheme. But that was not the last of their meeting, for no sooner had Grotteau settled down at ***The Scorpion*** to plan the next edition than Clanton, bottle in one hand and shot glass inthe other, came wobbling down the street to pay Grotteau a social call at the newspaper office.

"What you jes tole me back there in the saloon caint be real," said Clanton.

"'Tis so, my friend. Why, theys Pawnee Indian goings on… Smithy Jorgensen, member him? Well—he's a sure-fire relic from connistoga days—he's going to give us some privileged entertainsment from the back of his buckboard…down in the village…fer folks who's interested in latching onter a mining claim. He's already found gold. His testimony, y'know. Why, thunderation! Let'm tell you." Grotteau was about to beginanother sales pitch when his client interrupted.

"Sir, I think your offer is humbug…fake."

"Oh, come now Clanton…no more 'n you were back in the saloon." The mention of Clanton's trick hand unnerved him and so he poured for himself another shot , setting the bottle on the edlitor's desk. "I don't know what I ought to do with you," Clanton said, his voice ominous.

As a crimianl trial lawyer Ludheim had given Grotteau this enlighntenment, He. Max Ludheim, had perceived that in the most extremem moments of rage a long quiescent conscience can lead a potential killer not to forgive but to postpone the violent act, waiting for a change of mind, a vision, a chance event to intervene and so grace his , the criminal's, as well as the vicim's life There is , however, a forgiveness of spirit, a conditional acceptance that can equal the motive of vengeance if the feeling is real. But if it is fictive, as in Clanton's case, that murderous spirit can be transferred to another person, the victim, the witness, the recipient of the dark deed spawned by a malignity of the soul.

At that precise moment of Clanton's threat, Grotteau felt he had absorbed a portion of that malevolence that inspired murder. "You sure'n hell aren't going to shoot me and run away to hide, like you did him." He did not mention Clanton's victim—if there was one. Instead, Grotteau struck the man's conscience. "You're a fugitive Clanton, but…my being a newspaper editor, I'm probably the only one knows it. Folks fergot what they read in *The Scorpion*, oir they're too busy to care. Comes to the same thing."

Grotteau removed a long barreled 45 from his desk drawer. "I know the drift of your thoughts, Mister Clanton. I knew a lawyer once who was acquainted with desperados, and knew one when he saw him." He paused to light a cigar, watching the revolver on his desk like cat a mouse. "Me? I'm not tolerant of liars…got a living hatred fer liars, 's matter of fact," his shaggy red beard shook, his freckled face reddened.

"Go on."

Grotteau fingered his revolver. "I'm giving away the land. Almayer—he's the assayer, official like—says there's a vein runs under this hyer village….he gave me a map thatg shows the location. You be here to that celebration—it's a wingdinger to drum up trade. You just be there, y'hear?"

Clanton remained silent. The facts in Grotteu's mind had gagged the other man's tongue. For Clanton had run from the law for five or six years, yet while he stayed in in *Mystery* he considered himself to be safe. Grotteau put his revolver back into the desk drawer. "See you there…killer!"

Grotteau heard the anguished retort as Clanton smashed the half-full bottle of whiskey over the iron wood stove . "I got a good thing going," Grotteau shouted after him. "Map's true and correct… old Kittrick's. You know I wouldn't peddle counterfeit claims, Mister Clanton . Why I'd be hung at sunup if I did." He raised his voice. "You got to believe! You got to believe!"

"Take yer gold 'n run with it to hell then, Scorpion!"—his last words 'of contempt. *I should have put to more push into the sale of the land, damn their hides!"* he thought. Clanton did not stop to listen to Grotteau's last spoken words. He stomped out of ***The Scorpion*** office.

Smoking his red cigar down to finger size, Grotteau snuffed it out on the stove, among the broken bottle shards. He felt intrigued by this sense of renwewed power which knowledge of Clanton's past gave him. That was in itself a kind of gold, exchangeable for the real item…in due time, in due time. Flipping the cigar butt into the wood stove, he mounted his mule and headed out toward the shack of Jimmy Tyler.

Now Jimmy Tyler was a small man of five-feet six, coal black hair, a sallow complexion who seemed to mumble with a twitching of the lips. He carried a sheathed bowie knife under one arm. He was a watchdog for his mining claim. He was not especially glad to see Grotteau. Nor had he entirely retired from mining—a delayed fuse had blown off most of the fingers of one hand. but he carried on as a panner along the creek. He troubled little about the future of *Mystery*, the village, as he tried to pan for a little of the yellow dust. For some inexplicable reason—perhaps good luck—he kept a clutch Mexian centavos in one coat pocket. He also seemed always to be in a stage of asphyxiation, a kind of asthma.

His pale skin was mottled by old scars, mottled by burns gotten during his powder-monkey days. His voice possessed the twang of a struck bowstring. His favorite phrase was that he "allowed as how," this or that had occurred. There was about the man a manner of avoidance, both in his shifty eyes and his hands—what should he do with them— perhaps an embarrassment over incaution that cost him the loss of his fingers. He could not hide the defect. Grotteau had run an add for him in his paper to sell off some old barrels of keg horse shoes, the which he had come into possession in a way nobody could guess. But their sale purchased for him gold panning equipment, and he became like one of the other wet, clucebox gold miners from Dutch Flat to Triangle.

Jimmy Tyler lived in a shack. Grotteau called on him in the morning. When the editor-drummer had knocked on his shack door, there could be heard a stumbling about inside.

"Well, greetings…and who are you?" To Grotteau's utter amazement a woman came to the door. "I"m Jimmy's wife, Verta," she announced. Grotteau, for all his news leads, had not known that any woman lived in Mystery…ever, except perhaps the one prostitute, Hetty, who had ensconced herself in an upstairs back room at the *Contibental Hotel.*

"Is Jimmy in?"

"He is…"

Not much of an introduction for a powder-monkey who had lost most of the fingers on one hand in a mining accident. Jimmy had heard of Grotteau's plan through Hornsby, the hadware man who sold miners equipment, drygoods and foodstuffs at the Genral Store. Tyler pushed past the woman brusquely and without introduction. "What'er is it you want with me?"

This challenge brought Grotteau up sharp. He was accustomed to a more cordial welcome; and he had assumed that Tyler was an almost inert character in the town. Grotteau had, in his mind, shaped him into a an iron peg, an intractable, invisible villager.

"I'm here to visit with you a mite, Mister Tyler…and maybe talk you into..joining my mining company."

"Yer….? Well., I'll be goldarned and go to hell!"

"You'll suffer less is you hear what I have to offer." After Grotteau had finished his presentation…and he had the gift for rhetoric…Tyler's reply was:

"Plain damned foolishsness. Ant no such gold neath the streets of this hyer town!"

"I've got a official map…shows just where the vein runs, north by northeast by south…plain metes and bounds to find it. But…only problem is it runs under one or two shacks, down *Dog Street*, under the hotel and Hornsby's Hardware store, then out across the desert into the red hills. There's a spot brings the vein up from the sand from the creek, as I contemplate it, Mister Tyler."

"Don't say."

"I do say. Oh, I won say a word about those two hangings of your two friends—five years ago...the Indian and the White Man...traders who cut you out of that lumber deal...I read all about it. I just might rereun the whole story. It was a fine one."

"You do that and...goddamn your hide..."

The sourdough slowly walked toward Grotteau, a miner's small pick that he kept inside the door clutched hard in his right hand. "Damn yer soul. I put in my time, y'hyer me...ye hyer me!" He raised his pick, and then his voice broke. He raised the pick higher. Grotteau stood petrifid not fivd paces from Tyler. He carried no—gun; that was the way he always walked about the countryside. Also, he carried no knife. Even Father Exavier, a stranger in the village, carried a small skinning knife under his vestments. I had heard him sayso oncet at the **Hard Rock**. Tyler spat at Grotteau. "You don' come up hyer and start accusin' me all over agin, Mister Scorpion. He was ready and so angry he wanted to drive Grotteau off his claim property. Grotteau was not a claim-jumper , it seemed to him. He took another step toward Grotteau, drew back his arm as if to strike his accuser. Grotteau slowly backed away, neither man dared to turn his back. Tyler lowered the pick, then flung it behind lhim . He kept Tyler in mind for one of his "deputies" ,his knights, to see to the correct operation of his plan He mustered his courage and confrontded his threatening attacker .

"Yes, Mister Tyler. You won't have to bend the knee to any sharper traders from here on...just...hand over your gun and lI'll write you out a deed for the best piece a real estate you ever grabbed aholt of."

"Which is where...."

"Your word, sir," Grotteau insisted.

"Caint. Don' know nothing...'sides, I keep my *bessy* close by...coyotes and sech like Now..." He had dropped the miner's pick a short distance behind him and he now approached his advesary.

"On second thought, I'll run a big banner headline, **Tommy Tylers past comes alive,** *he committedexcuseable murder when cutthroats tried to negotiate a deal.*

"Damn your hide! Damn, damn!"

Grotteau looked closely at his victim. *I should put more push into the sale of the land, damn their hides!* "Well, we're having a big bonfire in the middle of Dog Street. Brnig your gun and pitch it. 'S easy and simple and then you'll be in the money with a fresh, brand new land title that'll make you like Rockefller. Ain't no cause fer a gun here in Mystery…snake now ana agin…but then you gotta find anfd fetch it…"

"I don't know who or what yer talking about…?".

"Were trying to do away with violence in *Mystery*, Mister Tyler.

"Then I'll have to consider you…consider you…a enemy."

Gomg inside agaim, from behind a door he drew out a 12-gauge shotgun, not believing a word of what Grotteau was saying, but supinely, like a tearful yet trusting child, he handed over the weapon to the editor of **The Scorpion**. Grotteau hrard the trigger snap. He blroke the gun and removed one unchambered shell.

"I got more important things to do today, Jimmy Tyler than be your hunting dog…you bastard! You wanted to kill me1" Grotteau responded. He pled the memory of misery of the town's suffering—wholly a iction on his part—he recalled glory days when picks glinted in the sun and shovels rang shiny and bright wih new gold ore dug up. There was…he invited Tyler, a windfall of new-day's promise to be found in Almayer's old map. Grotteau spread out the map on the porch; few shacks had porches. This one did because a porch gave stature and status to the shack owner. He could call himself one of the newly rich who drank rotgfut whiskey at tlhe **Hard Rocl Saloon**. They sat down for a spell to chat in rocking chairs.

Tyler allowed as to how his idea was a grass-roots good one. Grotteau had the charm and boldness to play on the man's mewing sympathieshe who lived with a woman his wife and a prowling gray tomcat. He heard Grotteau expound on the bounty of hidden gold dust and pebbles of gold when water ran through and over Mystery long ago and left not just flakes and dust but an overlay upon probably gold lode ore, undiscovered by human effort, *smarts* or ambition..Why, the tidal gold would sweep across the glistening desert and mingle with smoke from a thousand miners' fires and escort in that civic joy and laughter that had accompanied the new hope of a renewed gold strike. The promise was an ecstatic one, Grotteau prompted theTyler. He ought to be gratified that it was brought up smart to his door without his having to prospect in the silence of the desert, alone.

As the rhetoric went on, Tyler grinned in satisfaction. Grotteau; mixed his poetry with remembrances of the old burro-chasing days, of battles against bliaazrd snow and hordes of Indians...they were still around—and the catastrophes of other crucible miners who were made almost paralytic by their hunger for gold. They had been greenhorns who had taken the first train West to Frost to find what Cannister Kittrick had found, nuggets big as fists. What a camaraderie it had proved that men might share in their lust to gamble with diehards who shouted, "Gold for All! Gold is God!. Rejoice ye saints in the new brotherood!"

Grotteau thus droned on, touching Tyler's nerves of lust for gold, a clever cajoler who was showing the old and clrippled miner that glory of a gold strike could be his again. The woman stood back in the shadows of the shack room, absorbing every word.

"Do not lament, Jimmy Tyler. Your missin fingers will grow back with this new gold. They will be proof that the strengthn is in your will to use the pick and shovel again. That's the magic of yer will, Jimmy, me man."

"You make it sound honest—and bountiful."

"And full of mercy, Tyler. Mercy that becometh the prophets of old." This last piece of claptraq was common to Grotteau around the pressroom. It was a part of Grotteau's stock and trade for mind manipulation. If an appeal to the ancient Prophets did not work ilts magic, then like a mystic conjurer, he would invite the spirts of religiousity to invade his client's conscience.

"I got me no pan or shovel, man," Tyler blurted.

"Hornsby will furnish you the tools to work your lode, Tyler... out of the his rich treasure of the necessary tools," he raved, trying out a little eloquence. "We cannot be strangers to your desperate—and luntimely needs." Grotteau must have smiled as he looked off into the distant desert mirage. His prospect hardly comprehended the eloquence of his words, much less their significance.

"I've alone—'cepting for her—she keeps my house."

69

"I truly understand, Mistger Tyles. You're a sourdough with a purpose," Grotteau layed it on. "There's Columbine, the cat. She keeps track of desert rats for me. Had a pan or two broughten off by one of them desert pack rats just last winter." Grotteau was used to this sort ot sentimentality among often lonely miners.

"So sorry to hear," said Grotteau. "Well, then let me…let us all join hands, Tyler. Let the lightning gash in the West and the thunder of ore hammers pound ore into dust in Frost!"

They got out of their rockers , and he spread out his map further. He jotted down Tylers name on a corner of foolscap, paper from the pressroom. He would comprise a list of his disciples. On the map he had scribbled Tyler's name by the bridge at the dry creek. "You will dig here " He entered his convert's name by the bridge at the dry creek. "There—dig here! There is gold!. Take my word for it…old creek-gold. Water washed it down years ago. Here…look at this." Grotteau withdrew a large gold nugget from his pocket and held it up to the Tyler's eager eyes.

"Has a shine, don't it?"

"Sure do."

Grotteau waved the stone before Tyler's eyes as if charming , past the man's face several times as ilf to mesmerize him. It cast a proper hypnotic spell. Grotteau's mantra had quickly disarmed the crippled old miner. "Of course there must always be percentage entailedl..,.say twemty percent. How does that sound to you, Tyler?" The old miner could not say for certain, yet if the earth was as rich as Grotteau said it was, why twenty percent couldn't be too much out of the claim. The fear of lifelong debt would vanish for Tyler, if he put his whole back into mining his claim "…like so many others," Grotteau reminded him.

"Ah, but then I do not compel you, Mister Tyler. Go…go to your cool shack…but think on these things. When you come into town and see my signs—I shall have a tent erected—and the bonfire outside, warming sustennce, pitch your shotgun into the flames. Contribute…." He could hve shot the old powder-monkey when he raised his pick to strike. But a murder even in self-defense was a crime that often feeds on another crime, cannibalizing such a bloody victory as *justice.* For Reiner Gotteau, there needed to be only the catalyst of anger to make a murder both lethal and excuseable before the law…a crime of passion.

An acceptable event often breeds a perverse sympathy. Grotteau had not wandered from his ploy. He would prevail....Grotteau knew that some things never needed to reach print. The hangman's noose was just a short walk between outrage and the death of truth by its denial.

"We have not the price of a loaf of bread right now."

"Credit, sir. Credit I lend you. Bring that old shotgun...for you've not the price of shells anyway, and there's no hunting around here...except for Columbine chasin' the rats."

Grotteau laughed at his sardonic humor—a part of his dark side. He was fully capable of laughing at the misery of other men without a trace of shame in him. "Just pitch it into the flame of the fire."

Upon this salutary greeting, met by the promise from the old sourdough of his genuine gift of a rusting shotgun, a sacrifice for his years, the old miner stood a ways off. He had shot game with it for starving miners up on Starvation Flat, rightly named...but then, his conscience was fallible. They would make out. He watched Grotteau refold his map. the conspicuous camaraderie on Tyler's face summoned a grin of feigned consent; the two then shook hands. Grotteau mounted his mule with a grunt, set his back toward the shack and his convert and ambled, rocking in the saddle, back along the trail. His next apostle would be the man Franklyn Kirsten, a seldom seen in the village. He was an early-commer, a son of a panner's black gold sludge...down to his boot straps. He was also, a village carpenter. Yet he had insight into the meaning of the land...the land...the *land*...proud possession of the *Conquistadores*, still ?

Kirsten had served his time and the sanguine sentence of a platitudinous judge who knew even less about the law then he did hummn nature. Kirsten had abandoned his wife of thirty years to seek escape as a vagabond, here in *Mystery*. Having drawn all the family's savings from the bank, he had absconded and his wife sought him on a warrant of arrest. She wanted him in jail. He once threatened her with a gun; that was sufficient cause. Grotteau, wishing to force Kirsten to enter his scheme, threatened the man with running a story in **The Scorpion**, libelous on the surface yet true underneath, that his wife had threatened to poison him for infidelity and he, in turn, had threatened to blow outl her brains for outsmarting him about their money. The marriage was an unhappy one. To avoid the nasty aspects of the union, Franklyn had come west to this small-town mining community, by all comparisons still a village.

And Grotteau would make merry with the man's painful past—in effect he said so when he promised a revelation of complicity. Whatever that meant, it was the courage and strategy of Frankylyn Kirsten to join with the robber baron Grotteau…and that Ludheim fellow. Grotteau was not insensitive to Kirsten's plight. He simply wanted to man's firearm in exchange for a land title, but hopefully, also his coopertation in the mining deal. Reiner Groltteau, the visionary, wanted his victims to tremble in their pain, fear and rage, as when the trapper approaches for the kill in his power trap. Then could they be purged forever of their misery and their guilt. Grotteau played upon these human traits and expectations.

He had no alibi for self-flagillation and scarcely an excuse for his incompetence with money and marriage. A higher power would have to absolve his guilt, but, meanwhile, Grotteau could expect great things from Kirsten…first that he surrender any weapons he might possess, and second, that he go over to Triangle…there was a parish church there…and confess his sin of infidelity. Grotteau found himself as an aide to Father Xacier's foggy, ill kept, and wrongly diagnosed past in the church, he who had promised to supply South Amerilcan reolutionaries with guns.

Spindrifts of hot sand lay against cactus roots and thorny desert firesage where scorpions dwelt. Clopping his hot sun-drenched way toward the shack of Franklyn Kirsten, who would stand in the line of another son of deliverance for Grotteau's coveted enterprise in gold mining. He reined up his mule. He lifted his half-gallon canteen, sewn in buck-skin leather, to hie parched lips and drank heartily, dripping water onto his mule's flanks. He gorged several gulps and patted his mule. He banged the cork back into place, returned the bottle to its hanging strap from the saddlehorn, clucked to his mule "Sally" and resumed his journey. Such rites were familiar along the trails. The mule beat crescent moons into the desert sands with its lanky, angular iron-shod stride.

A cactus wren flew into a Joshua tree. Grotteau spotted the weathered brown ochre shack perched on a shelf on a nearby hill, a misiserly rocky shore of *Mystery*, a mountain that to all eyes but Kirsten's had failed to render up lthe gold promised to dess icated miners and weary prospectors. On another side it was the same mountain where Aleman had hidden his whiskey still.

The editor of *The Scorpion* heard the working of a rope hoist and squeeking pulley as he drew, scrambling amongst loose rock, toward the upslope and the shack. Some shanties appeared to stand on stilts, others, like this one, were anchored into the rocks like a ram's cloven hoof, upheld and made stable by the roots of two great trees.

"Mister Grotteau…" He heard the pulley squeek, the rattle of a tin bucket and the low sound of wind over the rock escarpment as he pausled. He stood abruptly in the domain of Kirsten, proud where he lived and downlooking into the village below. The miner was an early drifter-miner of gold in the land. Grotteau stomped his work boots on the gritty front steps and cracked open the warped, weathered front door. The shack, almost empty of furniture, was mostly in a shambles but durable for a man who lived alone, and had done so for an uncounted number of fierce desert winters.

"Whatchawant?" came a surly voice. "Cant y'see I'm busy?" A foolish question for most men in *Mystery* were busy one way or another—mining, drinking, regretting, dreaming and inspecting the earth. The drummer of mining stock opened up his scheme in the same terse, unforgiving way he had done so at Jimmuy Tylers place, as he had done at the grand *Continental Hofel*, which belonged to him by a trick of the law, and at the **Hard Rock Saloon**, sheer lluck of a cpoker hand at a beastly hangout for those waiting to for a turn in their luck.

"Can I come in? Got some news for you, Malloy."

"Damn it to hell!!. What air you standing out there in th cold fer?"

"Grotteau took the threat of the question for an unsavory invitation to enter and he did so. At the rear of the small, squalorous room there opened a door into a sacred tunnel of gold ore—or so Malloy believed. By this means of accommodation he had both proteted his shaft from claim jumpers and could work out of the sandstorms and unrelenting snows of winer. Meanwhile, in the brisk air of the morning, he had built a warming fire at the tunnel entrance, whose smoke and heat, by means of an extended flu system, went up the chimney to his shack. The arrangementl was both cheerful and satisfactory. Any miners could tell you the same…that Reiner Grotteau was bent on disarming all the miners because funs were a threat to the administration of his power. The village was to be his kingdom without challengel or coup. The presence of guns, generally, among the miners, should they revolt, was a foolishness that would make his zeal for power ring hollow. One surrender, one gun, one collapse of initiative was the way to secret tyranny over the village.

A grimy miner in coveralls stained with sweat and the dark earth, half bent over by the low cut out of the tunnel rock, emergfed from the darkness, his lantern in his face. He looked like an animal emerging from a disturbed hibernation, in his hand an ancient 20-gauge shotgun. His scowling frightened face, black whiskers and hollow eyes confronted his unwelcome visitor like the visage of a long-interred anchorite summoned from his exile. He set down the lantern before the lowering makeshift-hearth blaze and leaned his shotgun against a rock outcropping that formed part of the shack's rear wall.

"Where you say that…nugget a gold be?" He had heard by word of mouth those two magic words in the small community, They flew on the wind so that few of its inhabitants could ever tell the real source. All picked up the strains sooner or later.

" 'S 'long the ridge line, above yer property here, Malloy. I got to tell you, it's a mighty promising location for a gold digging. You lived here almost since *Mystery* begun."

"Don't make much…got to build a *arastere* to crush your rock. Not much profit. But I do what I think's right, Grotteau."

"Religious?"

"Begone! Fool! You keep away from me, Grotteau, y' hyer? Unless you care to join me."

"I aint no miner, Malloy. Just a...drummer for a gold stock thing I've a mind to start."

To Grotteau's utter amazement, Malloy reached behind a Celtic Cross carved from deadwood taken off the desert floor. He withdrew a small Psalter.

"You are a...a man of faith," Grotteau muttered in total astonishment.

'Bette'n a short-gun. I think on sech things. Got time to think whilest 'm picking and shoveling in there."

"That's so." Grotteau sat spellbound for a long moment. Now chu come traipsying up here to...interrupt my workings...and viting yerself into my ruminations, take a listen here. It says hyer, a man's life don't consist in what he owns. Says so here. Not my bucket er this shack er my lantern here. But in things of...." He squinted as if he had not seen the word before "...Spirit....says so right here." He proffered the small volume to Grotteau but the editor of **The Scorpion** refused the offer.

"Then why do you go on...digging...searching for gold, Malloy?"

"Got nothin' better to do. We wuz put here to 'njoy life. Now as few digging fer gold...well, there could be lots a worse things a man could use up his time adoin'."

"You believe in God...course you do."

These hyer words come from...from...." He could not cite their source. In confusion and embarrassment he sneaked the volume back to its hiding place behind the wooden Celtic cross.

"Well you larnt a thing or two about Tommy Malloy. I hope yer muchly gratified now, Mister Grotteau."

"How'd you know my name?"

"Oh, I got ways," he said mysteriously. "If you'll be on yer way. I got more rumination to do...and a load of ore to crush in my arestere way below."

"Wouldn't want to take a look at my map would you, 'fore I go?"

The bent-over miner could say little more, his face piqued by skepticism.

"What makes youl think theres any gold up hyer?"

"This here map...drawed up by your friend and my friend, Mister Almayer, the assayer. You can see there the smudge marks. Grottau had spread the map out on the eating table. I see 'm, but they mightnt be dirt marks 'stead of gold cropppings...

"Trust the assay, Kirsten. Look here."

He trook out his snugget again from his pocket. "This here I found down by the ol' Indianhead outcrop by the wash. There's many a nugget still hereabouts. This whole area used to be under water...running creek wash...and that means gold laid down, don't it Malloy?"

"I got enough work t'keep me busy up here," he growled, "besides abundance a richess won't ne'r be mine."

"Caint never tell. You can have more gold with less work... ifn you give this here mining company a chance. God don't prohibit enjoying life, does He? Why just look at the good times He set up for Adam and Eve." The face of the old anchorite miner quickened.

"They weren't no choice for them back then." He looked around as if for a way of escape. "Sides, I haint got money to buy a claim, and...they's only one claim fer ever'miner hereabouts."

"Look again at the map...." He studied the miner's face. "You got three little uns—two girls and a boy. Run off and left them and your darlin' wife without a track or notion as to here you went."

"I'll be goin' back, you nosey polecat!"

"But why not with yer pockets filled with gold, Malloy?"

"You haint no prospector either. Almáyer makes mistakes. So put yer map up, Grotteau."

In the morgue he had learned may things, not exactly a crystal ball. He confronted the miner. "I hope you'll not regret my savvy for a good investment...'nd gold to yer little family who cry out for you to come home. They will be waiting long to hear from their papa and feel your arms 'round 'em."

"Crap!" exclaimed the fully undone Malloy, his face the image of bewilderment and incredulity and disbelief.

"I can write your wife and tell her your whereabouts, if you want."

"You do that and Ill kill you, Grotteau, so help me God."

"You do believe in God."

"I would not murder a man…but you take my senses away."

"Get rid of old hate. That shotgun won't start a fire but it will…it will bring you closer to God, Malloy." The old miner sat mute with the homily.

Grotteau grinned and left the perplexed Malloysitting in silent anger, looking down at the floor like a defeated man. The cold draft of the shaft bearing its dank earthy smell crossed the room. The drummer walked out of the shack without another word and moments later was a mere memory to Tommy Malloy. His long isolation had not taught him how to cope with such persuasion as Grotteau had just opened to him. It had taught him that a man must bear his own thoughts without recourse except to a god made of flesh or made of wood. Father Boniface Xavier could use the weapons for his Central American, Gratamalian revolutionary movement. He did not need to be reminded of the impropriety of retribution among the saints, and of insolent accusations likely to come from the Revolutionaries…even possibly from God. Grotteau could only wonder at the course thlat events had taken.

He sp urred his mule, clucked in its long ears and, reminiscent of mule swagging days in Arkansas, hurrid along the broken trail to the diggins around the nose of the hill, down into the shallow hollow. There in another ten minutes or so he hailed Daamon Jackson from his panning labors…he had diverted the upper Spring Keseys spring, named for a mule skinner before *Mystery* whose life was saved by the presence of spring water. *Jackson possessed gold arms*, a village wagonner once said to him, who had trucked his ore to Frost. But clay hands and feet had ventured into copper smelting that the hot desert sands would possess him forever. Sometimes on his return trip he would bring in a load mesquite wood, if it could be found, to confront the winter snows in shack stoves or at the sites of diggings in the high desert.

The editor of **The Scorpion** was quick to knuckle down to business of his damning call, that "when you set fire to your sawmill you didn't burn down your memories, mill-man. You set that fire for the sake of another man's dark angels?" After his visit to the anchorite he thought that on this visit he would work a little religious lore into his presentation... "You only destroyed the mill for the cheap insurance? Wasn't it? Wages it would bring?" by moving closer to Daamon, Grotteau tried to show a certain sympathy; for the man. "I sort of take to arsonists...Daamon. Used to be one myself...luck and capacity to endure heat...the only regrets."

"You must figure your some sort of bastard sheriff...that right? You're the editor, coroner or what not of that there...sh...sheet in town, rightly enough."

Now that you put itso kindly, I'll have to admit to my failings, Jackson. And you to yours...?

The miner kept silent. It was clear that he mightily resented this intrusion both into his mining claim and into his past life. He had been found, without invitation, hammering rivets into his cart wheels, in the sje;ter of his shanty off a quarter of a mile from *Mystery.*

H looked wildly about him as if searching for some sort of weapon and then turned to confront the intruder. "Just what are you mouthign off at me?"

"You once owned a fine working saw mill...but bad timber management cut the supply of logs...and other things...a half-ass goverment bureaucracy don't know much about logging, only about money."

"You got that right, mister. So why you com here bothering me? Caint you see I'm busy?" Same old question, same answers.

If I was to run a article about your...well, your mill you lost... unexplained fire, that sort of thing...." Grotteau did not finish.

"Damn your black soul," the miner cringed in deep distress and volatile anger. Seen you acomin'...up t'ere...the road...it always gives off a red smoke and a hissin sound like when you rides, Mister Grotteau."

"Oh, another religious fellow. These hills are peppered with the drought . I'll have to make a note of that, Daamon. But my sould is in safe keeping...up here," he said, pointing to his forehead.

"I don't know who you are...editor or something like that. lemmme tell you...."

"I'm Reiner Grotteau."

"Lemmme; tell you something, Grotteau, a logger fired my mill. Said I held back value for his logs."

"That so? Wasn't proved, was it?" the miner held his tongue. "Anyway, I put your story in my paper...oh, some time ago. Folks got short memories. They forgotten by now...no bad recollections... or anything like that."

"So now you...you fool, you think you're going to black-mail me."

"I haven't even tol' you about my plan."

"Scheme?" The **Scorpion** editor nodded assent to the point.

"Your problem at the mill...lots of others too...all buried six feet deep, Jackson. Trust me."

"I wish to hell I could!"

"Try me." Grotteau was talking to a cork-booted, choker-setter, hardened logger, tall, bulging shoulders and gray massive face with gray sideburns, eyes thart moved about nervously as if estimating a present danger.

He regarded the dying flames of his campfire, his campsite with its rocker with shovel lain aside, tailings scattered around the rim of the fire and all over the slope. He punched one hand into the other like al man waiting for calamity or trying to stay warm. Jackson licked his lips, moved about cautiously, gathering small splinmters sof wood to feed the fire, alwalys on the alert as if in the presence of a deadly enemy. His anger was the anger of a hardy man cornered by a preditor with a different, a deadly sting. He hardly looked at his accuser. The miner was slow of speech, but his words were spat out like wooddust before the teeth of a sharp and whining saw....effective and deadly. He was not the sort of man Grotteau delighted to encounter, for he had sized up Daamon Jackson when he first saw him bent over his sluice box riffles, peering down for flakes of gold. Grotteau hauled out his lodestone, flashed it before the face of Jacksons and returned it to his pocket. Jackson snuffed in disdain and a measure of disbelief. He had seen real nuggets before...at the assyers office, on the bank scales in Frost and maybe one or two miner friends down in *Mystery*.

"Sticking around Grotteau? You got all you come here for?"

"Not just yet."

"You don't appear to be a man who's safe to be around, Grotteau." The editor looked wideeyed at his antagonist and smiled his grim and deceptive mile of knowing the wrong in a man's past others did not know.

"As safe as others in this here camp, Jackson."

"I know who you are...mister boreworm from that asp they call *The Scorpion*."

"Tsk, tsk...no compliments this smorning, Mister Jackson. It's too early."

"then what in thuneration it is you want outa me? I got work to do."

"I'm bartering off mining stock in a gold mining company, Daamon."

The lminers expressioin brightened, as if he had stumbled upon a real strike in the rock. "I heard aboutl that. News gets around. Saloon news its called...whiskey news, there's Indians under *Mystery*. They let lus go on about our business. Like innocent squatters. We're jumping their burial grounds. Let me be ironringing clear, Grotteau.. We be corrupting their burial grounds with yer damned gold mining—inside town limits."

"I got all lthat worked out, Daamon. They'll be no shooting either. The assayer Almayer's said there's gold under the streets, wagon trails, mayvbe under a few shacks.. th' hotel, saloon. Hwll, who knowswjhere e;se/ But, well, give the project a try, Daamon. Give it a try. The *Mystery Gold Mining Company*, stocks for sale and barter... cheap We'll bring in the wate, never fea."r.

Jacksons face had turned lived, then ashen. He could not believe what he was hearing, even a sinple man such as himself...to tear up the land under Mystery!

Grotteau had his gold nugget as a sort of proof token of hidden gold, awaiting the miner's pick an shove...and he possessed his map as reliable proof, as trustworthy as Almayer's word. After all, he was the assayer.

"Let me telll you, one thing," Grotteau cautioned, by his acitons making ready to leave. "I got a map here shows where the lode is under the town…almayers map. As for the Indians, why we'll conuct a proper burial ceremony for them."

"A proper ceremony, mister? Jackson queried. "With a Priest, I suppose." The question astonished Grotteau; the words were unfamiliar to men like Daamon."

"Well try.

"You can't baptize bones," Jackson said.

"We can bless all the same."

The miner turned away as if choking on the idea. "Insult the Indians again…?

"I figure we can just lay the bones to one side and go on digging…the ceremony ll take care of everything."

Jackson spoke not a word for a long minute or two, then busied himself at his morning campfire, pouring a cup of tepid coffee for himself alone over the few burning sticks and ashes sthat that smouldered. He kept a neat site, no animal, horse or burrow in sight, his tunnel boarded up during the night as he worked outside at his rocker box. He was a thorough man. His tent was rolled up for the late rising sun. Jackson was a petty but a neat and diligent miner, traits used as a mill owqner and operator. The monkey on his back was the suspicion that he had fired his own sawmill for the insurance money. No one had offered contrary evidence. Grotteau, like a ravenous dog, hung onto the bone. Jackson removed a skinning knife from his belt and began to sharpen it on a whet stone, as he had often done at his sawmill. Keeping the saws sharp saved time and money. While whetting his knife, he watched the face of Grotteau. The two men were alone in the hollow.

"You know, Mister Jackson, you could've grubstaked yourself from the sale of the mill and been free of any suspicions of crime."

"That so?" said Jackson with bitter skeptcism in lhis voice, hard and ready.

"That's so. Demons must've taken over your soul…your whereabouts."

"I keep my peace with everone. That includes the devil. I turned my logging trucks into gold. I live here, mister boreworm. This is my place in the desert. I'm a nomad." He laughed a bitter, sardonic laugh.

"How come you know so much?" Grotteau said nothing. "Fazakerly brings me water. I dig…right there. He motioned to the tunnel with his head. Always on the look for lost gold. I bring the ore outside… stuff glints in th' sun…glint disappears after noon unless you look real close. There's my sluce."

"Can't hide from the law in that there tunnel, Daamon. You keep a shotgun behind that tunnel door?"

"Wal, no I don't…just this hyer knife."

"You're lying Daamon. I saw you put it there when I rode up. Won't do you any good. If wolves attack, that there hid shotgun won't do you a bit of good. Heres my map…should you wonder where there's gold in town. Under boots, under wagon wheels…."

He spread open the map upon the uneven ground, touched with patches of dry desert dew. Structures and trails and the few streets were lined in by Grotteau. Jackson glanced at it and turned away, kicking at the scree with a mocking laughter in his voice. He scoffed at such get-rich-quick ventures.

"Insurance company and sheriff may still be looking for the real arsonist. Get smart. Fight'm with gold!"

Abruptly the big miner and former mill-owner turned to his antagonist, who sensing a fight hastily folded his map and stuffed it into a saddle bag. Jackson set the boards to one side that stood at the mine entrance. Picking up his shovel at his rocker sluce box he disappeared into lthe maw of tunnel darkness. Grotteau shrugges, though to himself, *he thinks he can shake gold from hard rock…and that with no water! Man don't know much about prospecting.* He mounted his burro and set off toward the diggings of others outside of Mystery. He was etermined to build a fire in the soulds of those met along his *Recruitment* road.

"Think it over, Daamon!" he shouted toward the tunnel entrance.

As he rode down the draw choked with thorn bushesl and lined with redstone strata, Grotteau took alternative pleasure in the red rocks and the shimmer of its of mica and the smells of the warm stones and trail sands and the clean smelling rawbark air. He hardly expected what or whom he would next encounter, though not a stranger to a compass though a visitor to the hills, he did not anticipate malevolent litter of the tongu, the gouch dress or unaccommodating manners of the isolated miner who next appeard like a vision from the solemn desert crags. Such men as would have riddn beslide him are often jaded. Grotteau for all his bland skepticism and bitterness and unabashed suspiciousness of characrer, was not a jaded man in his complex character. He did not look to find someone who had abandoned his profession to look for gold. Why should he? They were as plentifully sprinkled amongst the miners as iron pyrite I black river sands. Such men as they are easily tortured by loss and quickly jaded by failure to find gold; for desire rarely matchs their lust. Ennue becomes the accomplice to faded ambition. Grotteau was, however, not so well informed that he could tutor himself by other mens lives in the gold fields.

The miner he next met with on his power venture and Machievelllian manipulation, had been a professor of science at Pavlov University. He had taught science to the young, attempted to reconcile their ignorance to the demands of society. But in this he counted himself a miserable failure. He had long adopted the pracxice of treaching his students with proverbs, as many philosophical ones as religious from Scripture. *When power ecomes unbridled, it turns ruthless by man's inner nature"* that was one. He had indulged himself in the ways of justice to redeem the innocent and convict the guilty. Science had answered for him many of the pleadings of the powerful and the mighty, such as those of St. Thomas Acquinas that God's heaven was imaginary, pain an illusion of the flesh. *Voila!* There stood triumphant Herodotus' fictive sway, that a king's power belonged to the dead, or St. Paul's dicum that by his words doth a man make his nature known.

He was by his own concession a devout Darwinian, for in the university classroom as well as in the gold fields, survival of the adaptable was the *sine qua non* for life and and mere existence. He dwelt on honor and courage before both his students and his peers, and on the question of respect that sons owed their fathers for their years. When he began to lose the power of his voice, due to some hidden affliction, he began to dwell in th shadows of the lost, the ethic confusion of the damned of civilizations past, the lore of hell, believing himself, as he did so, to be among the weakest of human species. He had fallen into disgrace for some insignificant words and for nought he was summarily discharged from service to society. In suffering this humiliation he had in fact proved himself most adaptable; for the preditor often has only power and pupose to accomplish hts quarrys destruction, in this case the warrants of officials of academia. In his natural diligence, mining for gold met his temperament.

This morning he imagined that he saw nother man on horseback, another specimen of his kind. At this instance, however, he was mistaken, for Grotteau, although he wrote tolerably good English for his newpaper, was not actually the epitome of the rascal, the abomnination of decent men and the renegade to gold-prospecting opportunity whenever it was most invulnerable. And beside, he was astride a mule. He was, instead, an adventurer. He could not have cared less for the graves of the Indians, or for that matter for Douglass Merriman of the mines. Though amused by his jaunts into the hills, he cared about the dead more as a curiosity of the landscape. Actually, he abhorred desecration of any sort. He considered life to be framed by the the *de ja vu* of all satanic needs. In his assessment he was not adept. Another such as Max Ludheim. The ex-lawyer, had to evaluate this amazedly tortured and complex man who seemed the walking image of unabashed naivete.

When Grotteau meandered among dry, windbroken sage, sand ripples still evident, he had always somehow seemed at home in his element. In the defile where ancient waters still seeped, he heard a voice like a distant thunder clap call out his name. Could this be the voice of a warning?

"Hey there! Scorpion!"—an appellative Grotteau had conjured upon hiself, who then looked upward toward a corrugated brow of the nearfby low hill. Upon a slant of ground, a cabin was situated, half hidden, whilest standing as if a fallen piece of windblown deadwood, there stood Merryman waving his hat as if at a vanishing past. Minutes later, Grotteau had drawn up and dismounted. Together they lit a cigar furnished by Grotteau from his saddlebag. They smoked, puffing valiantly for a long while, the smoke drifting into hillside shade and tainting the immediate air with the aroma of conviviality. Merryman was stout, like a boxer, thin lipped, with almost childlike apect in his eye, his smile under the white straw beard. His hands were calolused and fractured by the nature of mining, lines of dirt, seams, some of which showed on his fce. He walked like a cavalryman, stiff, upright, determined, like a man with disciplined mind and sensibilities. Merryman's mind saw intuitively the mark of death upon the **Scorpions** errand.

"I call you a scorfpion. Ha, ahhha, I hope you have no sting."

"None whatsoever," a puff to greet this ode, "but I"m a ready spirit...shall I say...to shock my enemy wherever I meet him."

"Spoken well, sir. Well, then what is it to be this time, Mister Grotteau...host to the vultures of an errant goat with the sins of us sinners on its back?"

"You flatter me, sir. The incidental is not always the accidental."

"that should have been my pithy comment...I have said so quite often. I know you don't come up here without a wager, and on a woebegone donkey at that...."

"Mule, sir. It's a mule...quite sterile."

"Oh...therefore woebegone...to discuss rhinish wines in the morning rocks. Have you invited the snakes to come out of their holes like the Irish Priest Saint Patrick...under my cabin?" His suspicion had been adroitly conealed by flattery. Grotteau had said so to himself.

"You acquit yourself well, Mister Merryman. You've done a service to society. Though condemned for it. You can recover much of your old grandeur...permit me, sir...if you will juin with other gold seekers...."

"What! On a tribute journey to death."

"To life, Merryman. You cannot inhabit the past...you can only expunge it or salvage the debris of past wrecks."

"I do not get the drift of your words, Mister editor."

"You can become a bonifide part of the West by opening up a new gold claim."

"Oh, and how do you come by this high talking magic?"

"Not magic, sir...the truth."

The **Scorpion** editor plucked his false nugget—this time from a shirt pocket and showe it pinched it between his thumb and forefinger, held it until, revolving it about, it glistened dully in the morning light as if a burnished gemstone. "Come. I solicit not your incredulity but your trust, Mister Merryman. After a spell you can return to your classroom and regale your students withs stories about life in the gold fields of California. Tell them you recovered from bites of the fatal Scorpion and desert sidewinder…you even had the scorpion gold plated…that you parleyed with bandits from Mexico, you fought a real gun duel from behind desert rocks to save your treasure, maybe… let's say…you wandered lost only to find a miraculous desert spring, which brought you back to life. There are many twists and wonders you might relate."

"I see. And do you realiae how much of the truth of my life you've just related. God, to catch and eat that scorpion withou being stung was a feat but I saved my life…and do you know, Moses must have struck that rock to bring forth a trickle of water…oh, yes, that gun duel to save my small bag of fold dust…I still bear the scar of the bullet on my right forearm. That's the tattooed one…"

That was all Merryman had to say. His expressive face darkened. It suddenly became fierce and black and boiling if within there stirred an anguish and wretchedness that threatened to escape from his compressed lips. He turned his head away to survey the shadow across the motionless, sunlit desert floor.

"That was disease…the rebellion of the children, the futility of the parents was as endemic as their hostility. Grotteau raised his eyesbrows. "Pervasive, sir. Everywhere…as if the wine or ignorance were preferred to the storm of an informed intelligence. And so it was. You know yourself, sir, lives of some men produce little character. They destroy the future. They consume it in the flames of self-adulation." He paused to watch Merriman's solemn and strongly-featured face "You were serious to teach your students."

"Yes, and as must be so, the parents as well. They were nowt grown, or course. But neither wished to learn. Then the stalemate of shared learning became a debacle. Education went down in the roar, dust and consummate end of the desrruction brought upon by themselves."

Merriman swept his full head of white hair back over his head. He drew heavily on the shortening cigar furnished by his guest. The long face, deliate nostrils and lined cheeks marked the woven years of his life. On his forehead, darkened by the time , Grotteau perceived the look of a man who was enjoying his last pleasure before his abandonment by life.

"You...perhaps...lacked an...infinity."

"An infinity! God God, I told them what I knew as the truth about history and such things...and there was the end of my knowledge."

"...The he infinity of practical wisdom when undiseased by price."

"You have hit it...their unyielding pride. I had no answer. I am a fatalist, sir."

"Fatalist?" Grotteaus wonderment increased marvelously, for lhe too shared something of that impervious philsoophy that led men to their deaths or to glorious triumphs over circumstances of dread and death. "Fate has brouht you here?" Grotteau enquired.

"Has let me off from whence I came, the source...closed down like an old and abandoned well."

"But fate has many surprises in store for her children."

"Perhaps...yet she is also an indifferent goddess...or possibly the vengeful God. Yes, I am a pagan. I believe in fate, not in what Christians call *providence*. In order to believe in providence one must believe in and acept the existence of God, or a god, at least with the power to deliver a destiny or a circumsrtance or a calamity".

"True...but providence is only an actioin. It augures, it implies a design. Are you not a scientist who sees the designs in nature?" Grotteau aske;d.

"Ahaha...there you have hit a fine point, sir. Nature's designs did not come from an infinite mind but from the evolution of the creature in his natural habitat, confronting his possiblities of change? Since man has the power to alter design, he has the power to create it if he choses to do so."

"Darwin could not prove his thesis."

"I have proved it, sir. I am here. I have adapted. I lost a wife, son in the war against England. A beautiful ranch in Alabama…verdantadorned with powerful, sleek horses…but also…I sustained many unpleasant, yes, even calamitous events in my life. I refused to use the word *suffer*…,"

"They might have come about by a higher power…God, let us say."

"You said it, sir. I'll have nothing to do with God…I'm proof of evolutionary adaption. I do not have to prove the existence of God. I have lost too much ever to believe in his mercy.".."

"tautaulogical evidence proves He exists."

"Fabrications, Grotteau…fabrications of the theologans, whose words, nay…whose beliefs I could never share."

"Well, sir, though I am myself an agnostic, a doubted like Saint Thomas, if you will, I think there is a power that directs, that governs."

"So you say, but then we can never claim fto lhave our wills free.ree will."

"But you just said animals adapt. They must have to exercise a will of some sort. even if it's called instinct."

"By finishing to smoke this cigar, I express pleasure. By throwing it away, I show disgust or displeasure…or a form of uselessness. So it is in nature. All of life is both an adaptation and a purgation."

"I think, Merriman, that you are now getting beyond me. While you say that fate brought me here to visit your diggings today, will fate decide for you what credence you give to my proposal?"

"Which is…?"

"I almost forgot…to buy into my stock company, as it were. I can locate claims for certain that will produce gold."

"For this…indoctrination you want…?"

Grotteau thought with meditation, patted his mule and quietly said, "As you have guessed, a small percentage of the find, a bagatelle. Let me show you my map."

"I want no maps from you, Grotteau." He flipped his cigar into the sage and like a dog scuffing its paws after defecation, to mark an ancient animal rite of territory, he simply turned and delivered his last words, as ifthleywere a pleasant eulogy to his visitor. "Your nugget may be promissory…and there may be others. quite possibly there are. I won't trust fate to find them for me."

"If you succeed, sir, you can live like a true pioneer here in these hills…if you chose to do so…in abundance and comfort." Merriman paused, reckoning many things in his astute and elaborately trained intelligence. Grotteau remembered the broadside he had printed up for him on the treadle press several nights ago it was. Going to his mule, he reched into a saddlebag and wilthdrew tlhe handbill. Grotteau held out his missive and invited him to read what Ludheim had printed.

"A lonely old man is vulnerable to many temptations, Grotteau." He began to read.

"Aloud if you please," said Grotteau.

ATTENTION GOLD BUGS

You dreamed of gold. You thought of gold
a most admirable pursusit of all dreamers
and you would have dressed in gold like
the veritable princes of all Asia and
Europe had you found its rich and
lavish pockets lain down by a generaout Nature.
Now you can again fondle gold and pour it
into your pockets and entrust your futures
to its veritable value. The phantoms of fate
Have brought you here to indulge your
fondest dreams with expectations of reality.
It will be yours for either amodest percentage
of your diggings, or the modest sacrifice of
an old, yet worthless firearm of any sort.

Just under your feet, where you sit and
ride along the streets, where you walk and
ride in your weatherbeaton wagons, in
deed, where your burros trod only yesterday
you can find more gold than even the Con-
Quistadores envisioned for El Dorado.
There, beneath the floorboards, the

*decks, basements and porches of your
cherished edifices…you can dig up this
vast storehouse beneath the streets and
corruptible structures, you can explore
this fate of your glorious future.*

*An old mining claim filed over twenety
years ago set out a site by the rock outcropping where the present stock corral
stands. It was entered into without full
nspection. Our noteworthy inspector
Assayer Gregor Almayer affirms that the
aforesaid vein traverses this town of Mystery
in a northwesterly direction , its metes
and vounds constitute largely the present
corporate limits of our beloved village.
It is a vein of gold lain down by ancient
waters. And, glory be, it is accessible to all!*

*You will not have to forage for gold in the
streets, as starving animls forage for food.
On this next week following our July cele-
brations, I, Reiner Grotteau, editor and pub
lisher oft The Scorpion, will activate papers
filed with the court in our neighboring town
of Triangle. In the professional opinion of Mr.
Almayer, which none dare contest without
contrary evidence each and every site will
surrender to your diligent labor at least 5
grams of gold dust, for which Mr. Grotteau
sell share options of stock in the aforementioned mine field. One share entitles
the holder thereof to dig in a space one
hundred feet square for as long as he can
find to his utmost satisfaction the promised
existence of gold therein.*

*o this prospect and venture I humbly affix
my honorable signature with great expecta
tions that if not all, then most, of the citizenry
of Mystery will lend their fervent efforts of
exciting participation.*

*Signed this 12ᵗʰ day of June, 1848,
at the town of Triangle, in the California
Province of His Majesty the, illustrious
King of Spain.*

When Merriman had finished reading this missive of utmost importance at least to his caller, the intinerant abandoner of academia, raising his white eyebrows and seeming to smile with benign rejoicing, simply turned once again toward his shack upon the ledge of red rock and sighed.

"Well, Mister Grotteau, if you think fate has delivered you of this...significant document...and your map logo imprint seems to bear some resemblance to the sword of *Excalibur,* whose presence in the stone only King Arthur could remove...may I congratulate you on your...your...how shall I say it?..your audacity and your...plain damned foolishmess!"

"I cannot expect that you would believe. After all, Merriman, it took three long years for the Lord to convince his disciples He was worthy. I have only just begun."

"You cannot deliver me from my malaise of rejetion, sir, try as hard as you may."

"I am not a healer, Merriman. I'm an expositor of the word. For nought...pitch your relic firearms into my judicious pyre. Let us rid the village of the scourge of violence...and one full claim shall be yours."

The itinerant schoolmaster, an evacuee of the University of Pavlov, smiled an enigmatic smile and left the field to his visitor, certain that no crime could be charged against him, but according to Reiner Grotteau, equally certain that he owed no debt to sociey that he had not already paid with his professional life.

Grotteau headed downtrail, weaving through the debris of rock fall and into the desert's crawling shadows and limpid heat. The miner's resistance was a hallowed force since it was fully charged mercenary labor. He knew that Merriman would show up even if only to gratify his curiosity. That was the scientist in him, which, in itself, is often the target for brigands and confidence men.

Grotteau rode into the overzenith, into the mythical mists, he rode across the hot sands, uneasy about the quandries of his obsession. His enemy was, in the great openness of desert skies, his own avarice. The freedom he found in the limitlessness of the desert helped fabricate his dark spectre within his own soul. Nature's bounties can feel Man's ambition. In his future he would see the consequence of his articulated greed. Men such as he contructed their own scaffold. Yet, try not to as he might, enamored of his own will, he would show some men the way, emblazoned by his counterfeit gold nugget that thus far charmed the slow-witted and the avaricious. If only the miner, a stranger to desolation, would reach down alongside his boot, where that nugget shone in the sun, and pluck it from the blazing sand, he would survive.

It'll be my poison, he had thought, *my treasure to seduce the miners, and others, to liquate their lives, to take up shack living for all the gold in hell. Let their own consciences be the argument*

A dog barked.

"Not here…in Mystery," said Grant Colby. "Not right here." The hair in his brows parted in a pretended smile. Gottteau had accosted the hunted man at his claim site, hidden among the rocks like a bandititos' hideout. For of a certainty, Colby was a wanted man. Colby and Grotteeau were facing one another in the shade of the miner's desert shack. Old sardine and bean tins, a bottomless pail, some tangles of boards and a bottle thrown away—all lay scattered about the place. Grotteau had caught the man as he returned to his abode from the outhouse. The editor had run the half-page ad and posted copies here and there in the village. When Grotteau had ridden over the brow of lthe hill and into the small ravine, pausing just long enough to see if others were there in Colby's hideout, he knew of the man's past because *The Scorpion,* his paper, had published a story about the escapee and his clever breakout from a federal prison in Kansas, seizing on the sensation but ignorant of the fugitive's whereabouts. Miners liked such news; it befriended them and gave a tang and sanction to their mission which, as all knew, was to discover more and more gold. They could take it—that some men searched with dark dishonesty in their hearts. It was a soul release to a criminal that he could forgive another his crime.

Colby rubbed one hand across the back of his neck. He touched the houndog's head with the other hand to reconcile his presence with the reality of the hunter and the hunted. His swarthy hatchet face, bearig the visage of fear, glistened in the sun, his bright blue eye were cold and almost lifeless. He had killed a man at some time yet he was better known as a stagecoach robber. Like *Billy the Kid,* he had also robbed a bank or two...perhaps several. Now he stood alone by his camp site, fear and suspicion on his face directed toward his visitor.

"I can't hold the opportunity open much longer." Grotteau. said.

"Tha's a fact, tha's a fact then," Colby remarked. "You and me, we got a lot in common—wha's yer name, did you say?"

"Grotteau..."

"Sounds French..."

"A mite of Polish."

The squinting, hatchet-faced man extended his hand. Grotteau shook it. They both looked as if they felt obliged to share some sort of confidence.

"Sssure...sure...I heard tell yer that feller runs a newspaper. Big News...I run stage coaches...off the road." He laughed. His humore was sly and stupid. Grotteau was not searching for brilliant minds, only accomplices in his mining venture.

"I been in Bolivia, Grotteau. I'm...I'm what tey call a...a revolutionary."

"That so...a revolutionary. What, let me ask you, sir, are you revolting against?"

"Woulda believe it?...injustice."

"Injustice! You don't say."

"I do say…injustice. Little guys like me got tér watch out we dont get stomped on."

"Admirable self-pity, Colby. Admirable…." Grotteau looked the man up and down. "Who is going to do the stompinng?"

"Wal, now…if yer that newspaper feller, maybe y ou."

"Yer words sound ominous." Grotteau did not carry a side-arm, did not believe in them as useful argument. The very crux of his crusade, in part, was to rid Mystery of all firearms of any sort and therefore all violence…of a sort."

"I hert you…fact is, you've just admitted it…you rob stage coaches."

I used to…not much profit in it any-more…sometimes I got to kill a man…don't really like to..but got to do what you got to do."

"I see…that is….get at the gold."

"Dead right, Grotteau."

"We do have something in common. I'm hereat inviting you to share stock in my gold mining company." The hatchetfaced man with the cold blue eyes preened his blonde moustache. He was working on an iron wheel rim. He layed his hand maul aside and sat down on a nearvy rock, crossing his legs and taking out a sack of Bull Durham to roll a cigarettes. He did this with skill and calm and silence. He turned his attention back to Grotteau.

"If yer gonna sit there all day on thet mule, why we won't have much to talk about. Why don'cha get down off it and come jine me with a little palaver? What say…newspaperman?"

Grotteau dismounted at the invitation. He figured he would get a quick convert; Grotteau always did have that optimism when it came to money, in his case land sales. "That's more like it. When my old lady sobers up…she's there in that shack…why she'll have a real story to listen to." Grotteau was flabbergasted for he thought the man was here alone, a fugitive. But there was a female companion here with him. *Well, no mind*, he thought.

"You got lota bottles, Colby," said Grotteau, observing that one wall of the shack was constructed entirely of all sorts of bottles, cemented together side by side.

Yup, sure do. Wife's notion. Purple ones spruce up the place."
Silent, Colby scanned his visitor with a squinteyed expression, then
made a deduction with a squint on his face. "I kin tell you come to no
good up hyer with bad news."

"Bad news, Colby. Why, whatever made you say that?"

"Devil did, I'd say. I ant feard a reading yer snakeyed counts
about gold in the town streets, I ant so dumb, y know."

"Some folks call it opportunity."

"You come down here with the devils bad-luck scheme on yer
back. I call thet punity."

"Well, whatever you call it, sir, mining's never anythin' less
than hard work." said Grotteau. Colby spat into sand so hot the spittle
vanished as soon as it hit. "You and your moletunnel sort'll be digging
for gold in these hills 'till they flatten down," he finished.

"Stealin's a mite, a whul lot easier. Let. 'm dig fer you."

"Shavefaced, skinflint jackass," Grotteau muttered as he ground
his teeth an looked down His miner-friend's patience was gone and, by
the tenor of Colby's words, his luck as well. He was mighty ready to
listen to any new scheme.

"I got a scheme rightly enough, Mister Colby, you nailed
it—that'll make you rich in no time—almos' like as if you'd robbed a
stage." The slim sourdough straightened up, spat again, hitched up his
suspeneners and looked hard at the red hills where his kind had dug
away, serpent like, for almost ten years.

"Aint nothing quick bout borin a tunnel inter thet there
mountn side looking fer gold. I ant so damn clever without yer having
to say so, Mister Grotteau."

"You don't trust me, I see. Well, I an't a Indian."

"Yer newsypaper's named fer a big landcrab with a stinger.
Pois'nous t' boot. A scorpion's got no trust but 's got claws to catchm his
grub…and kill it to eat. Your newsypaper's good for nothing mostwise
but paddin' a snake den or growing a worm farm. And I ant yet been
told a any good fishin here'bouts."

Working on an iron rim when Grotteau rode up, Colby, puffing
hard on his tailormade cigarette, picked up his maul and struck a blow

or two with his hand maul on the rim that was braced between two sawhorses. "M' ore cart, y' see…use it to carry rocks over to Frost."

"Build a little fire, why dontcha. Heat up that rim to expand it then let it strink down cool onto the wheel?"

"You got lota a good ideas, mister. They ant no fire wood nearby…see any fer a fire? Do them peppercorn eyes a yourn see any wood hereabouts to build a fire? Might jes have to start burnin my shack floorin' to keep me and my old lady warm when the winter sets in."

"Glad you got a opinion, Colby. We know where we stand. You're right. Trust is not for animals or buzzards. Trust comes by… well, by practice."

Colby's hammering momentarily squelched talk. He mumbled to himself as his heavy caloused hands labored. Then he said, "You'll die on them words, Grotteau. Nothin' but blood'll ever come from palaver gold." Grotteau surmised he meant by talk that was trickery.

Colby, the sourdough, regarded his visitor with meticulous scrutiny, almost with a disdain, inspecting Grotteau's small, shriveled countenance for the true intentions of the man behind the face, for the honest reason for his visit. Colby turned his attention again to his riveting, listening but not looking up.

Colby, he noticed, had evidently once dressed well, almost debonair, a highwayman without pity. The miner wore a well tailored shirt, his cuffs were once fastened with links. It was torn in one place and dirt grimed, was of a good, almost fashionable cut. His black fashioned boots showed an early polish and style. They bore carvings filigreed by hand that were n ow obscured by mud and rock abrasions that were. . His black, flat-brimmed hat, quite soiled, a ripped spot, disclosed fine design and early blocking. On his right hand he wore an emerald set in silver, on his left a small garnet in gold, the rings his yet purloined in some former stage robery. He wore no wedding band. There was a man who did what he had to do…as he said…which was to kill any passenger who opposed his holdup. For another cigarette, his fingers wrapped the tissues of the *zigzag* paper around the tobacco with a delicacy akin to that of a professional gambler, or of a musician, say, a guitarist…even a surgeon adjusting a suture.

"Tried to jine the army," he said "Couldn't stand my thiefing. I steal...still do when I can...for the fun of it. Cleptomania. Like catching fish and trowing em back inta the water."

Then Grotteau pulled a story from the morgue of his memory. I know you seed hard times, Colby old man. Remember when you was in prison for stealing a man's horse and wagon over at Haymow? Then years for that dastardly mistake...judge called it a crime. But wasn't so until you killed him...accidentally."

Colby stood as if chiseled from stone, starting open mouthed at Grotteau. It was all a...*happenin.* he said stiffly. Thats all it were...a happenin." His voice failed him. "I didn' want thet wagon ter roll over him...buit he wasnt dead. It was a accident, I tell y'."

"You were in a rage..."

"But he werent dead! The muscles in Colby's face tightened as he starred at his accuser. "The law wouldn't believe me."

"No, it was the law aworking. Made you a good...a good revolutionary," said Grotteau, changing the subject..

"Best they is. Yessir. In Bolivia, I was butler for *El Presidente*...I speak some Spanish...*hasta la vista*...weren't a quiet moment on the job. I sold off his silver...to help the cause. We wuz going to rape the government, take over...from the French...contraband come to us... we trained in the woods. I learnt to dress elegant for the *El Presidente*. I stole some official papers not much use to us revolutionaries...but the poor folks down there...they was getting stomped on by the right high-class...drug...drug cartels ripped the heart out of the people. You can un'erstand my position."

"Fully, Colby. So why did you leave..."

"Them friggin sheriffs...they put me in jail....suspicioning things....and they was right. I escaped...bribed the jailor with Mexican drug money...got out...come nort' again. The stage coaches was...all the tin' you know...mong some of us robbin' stage coaches because the gold...oh, there was lots of it...was being shipped out round the Horn instead of 'cross country, to Carson City, Kansas. Pleaces like that there..."

"You're quite a adventurer," Grotteau said.

"Yup...never back down from...from things."

"And... you're still a practicing revolutionary?"

"Just time to time...when I sees some sort of injustice."

Colby's braggadocio amused Grotteau. He ascribed the man's glib account to a practiced habit of throwing others off balance, of distracting them with wondrous tales of righteous zeal, fighting for justice among the oppressed. Colby was posturing but Grotteau did not attempt to strip the man's mask from his face but, instead, only to use him in his own profitable design.

"Mebe I can use you, Colby...you got the grit to get others here in Mystery to come along...with us."

"If they's any money in it, I'm listening."

"I need somebody with brass to push the botodraggers into line with my plan."

"I'm still listening."

"I need a deputy or two. You can share a little of the extra gold...slush droppings.....t' help me move the project."

"I'm yer deputy...put my life at risk...."

Grotteau stopped him. "No guns, no guns after a time, a weapon in exchange for a title deed for a tract whereof to dig. That's simple as I can make it, Colby. You don't even need to show yer face... just tell 'em...that I willl...I got a deputy or two will help you decide. You unerstand?"

"I gotcha, Mister Grotteau."

"Good...and here's a twenty dollar gold piece to begin with, they're minting 'm in Denver...."

Grotteau and Colby were facing one another beside the of the miners desert shack. "When your wife wakes up...."

"She an't my wife.

"When she come to, you tell her you can dig gold out of th grond like hog chittlins and cook them out to pure yellow. That'll buy the little lady some new iron pans."

"And some other goodies, too, if you know what I mean."

"I see there you're in need of a new water pail."

"Oh, that...she throwed that at me one night."

"Oppression all over again." Colby did not appear to like Grotteau's humor. "Tell you what, Colby...you come visit my diggings in the hotel in town next week. If you join with me , your revolutionary fervor will turn into gold fever. I can g'arantee that."

"Gold always;s did 'tract me somehow, Grotteau."

"Send some of it to your revolutionary friends in Bolivia."

"I jes might do that…yesssir. I jes might…Got to have a trade, you know. Diggin' for gold 's as good as any other."

"I like your spirit, Colby.

"Same. Care to roll one?" The figutive miner offered his Bull Durham pouch and papers to the editor, but *The Scorpion* ediltor refused.

"Put temptation out a yer way also, Colby. Throw away any old guns you got hanging around here. You don't need'm."

Colby refused the offer with a gale of laughter that surprised Grotteau, for he thought the man humorless, cold, ignorant and distant. "Jus you remember one thing, *Scorpion*…I'm 's good a man as you any day."

Grotteau started to back off, for neither shame nor guilt nor any sort of enligntened perception shone in the robber-miner's features, except that his moustache ends moved as he seemed to gnaw on one lip nervuosly. He threw away his cigarette. It seemed to Grotteau—he had recited this fact later on to Ludheim, the lawyer…that the man Colby's face was that of a man dispossessed of honor, no longer capable of flight or struggle or of combat. He was just the sort of man he could use to…promote…acceptance by others here in the village.

Colby stood up from the rock where he had sat. He put his maul down to listen, he went up to his shack where he kicked a pot of dead flowers away from the door, clicked the latch and opened the screen. A woman half=drunken, pressed herself against the screen. Grotteau could tell nothing about her except that she seemed to fill the entire screen frame. The hound waited patienltly for the screen door to open.

"Hey y' old bitch, you hear what the man said…our own claim…gold!"Silence followed. Grotteau stood stonily still, aghast at the man's disrespect for the woman.

"Y' see?...the bloomin door closed." The woman went back into the shadows of the shack. "Deceit's the devil's spy!" Colby shouted. A sudden flash of insight told Grotteau that the fugitive had another side to him. He mounted up on his mule, swung the rein to turn around, ready to go.

His newspaper morgue story had told about the mask, the fake gun, the commotion staged and the shots into the air that had fooled everyone in Haymow. Colby had spent the stolen ten thousand on an ore cart, a mule and some miner's tools, staching the remainder in his mine shaft. Then he had come into *Mystery* to hide as a panner, a fugitive in failure.

As he rode away Grotteau dropped deliberately one of his broadsides., its garish sketch and exotic lype fonts Ludheim had worsked on for weeks—a masterpiece that would catchl the robber's eye. He could use Colby, the revolutionary to gather the guns of the violent men of Mystery, the shooters, former murderers and robbers of one sort or lanother. He needed then only to connect with the priest, Father Xavier, who was an itinerant revolutionary from Bolivia. He need not hurry.

The desert sun was going down like a twenty dollar gold piece dropped into loose and. The venturer snaked his way through fields of carbonized rock, greasewood sage and sandsmells of the heated desert. In the skies glowed the faintest onset of dusk in hich the brightest stars would begin to show themselves.

The campsite of Jerome Gottleib was distant from Colby's dismal venue of old wood shanties and a stubborn hatred for public notice and recognition. Clouds this day threatened a hard driving desert rain; cyclonic winds often accompanied them, but Grotteau was determined to visit one or two more mining sites. As he approached Gottlieb's shack he heard the man playing a harmonica. He was seated on his porch steps. Fatigue had overcome him and he took his time in the late afternoon sun. The harmonica wailed. Gottlieb was a retired railroad man, a layer of rails come to the village of *Mystery* to hunt for gold and a station at the end of his line. When he saw Grotteau moseying toward his shack, he stopped playing his harmonica. As the unexpected visitor approached the shanty, the miner invited the younger man to "disengage yourself from thet there mule, and come sit a spell…a stack of scrubpine firewood is all I got for a company chair."

Gottleib's voice was hard and metalic like a struck piece of iron rod, a face like that of a well-off lawyer, maybe similar to Ludheim's countenance, a cultivated personality and mind. His eyes continually batted as if from an affliction. His hands shook with a minor palsy, he possessed a thin, almost shrunken frame that showed boney shoulders and hands. He had had a hard work life. He pocketed his harmonica just as Grotteau seated himself in a wicker chair that cracked under his weight. The solitary miner had recently painted lt white.

Grotteau knew that the man had a wife; he had seen them together down in the village—the thought crossed his mind that she was the third woman in *Mystery*, including the prostitute at the **Contenental.** But they were pretty much alien to one another. Grotteau began his pleading like this. He had found the colloqual tongue most effective, so dissimilar to his journalistic prose.

"Yer wife can read. She'll take to this right smart."

"My wife 's' most blind in one eye…keeps t'other trained on me like a bird dog. She watches pennies. More'n that…she watches to where pennies is hid.. so's she can track'm down when they 's missing."

"Thrifty woman, Jerome." There stirred the clatter of pans and pots inside the shack.

"Gottlieb," Grotteau began right off, "a little more than expected gold in a vein runs under the village. Almayer says so himself." The editor got up, went to his mule and removed his map from the saddlebag. Gotlieb has come outdoors. Grotteau spread out his map on the ground, at the foot of the steps.

"I got a mine already," said Gotlieb.

"Expand your holdings, Jerome…cheap."

"Caint—allowed only one claim in this here territory."

"I can make exceptions. I know all about the agreement. Two claims will bring in more to the governmint."

"Gov'ment! By God, we haint had a gov'ment round here since Hector was a pup! An what's more…we don't want no damn gov'mnt snooping 'round our places hyer, looking to axe us for a tad of our hard earned money. Go to, sir, with yer gov'ment." He took out his harmonica and gave a blast or two to clear the tines. He stopped suddenly. "We hant got no govmint here in *Mysatery*. You know that, mister…."

"Mister Gottleib, sir." Grotteau readied his inner self. "Novbody is going to put you in jail…jes yet. I ran a story. Remember that time you hijacked the locomotive in the Triangle switch yards?"

Gottlieb stood up, astonished, flushed and angry at the same time and appeared as if he wanted to kick booth the map and his visitor into kingdom come. But he kept his temper. "Soo? We all make mistakes."

"I'm thinking you can give yer gold to yer grandchildren.."

"I han't got no grandchildren." Gottlieb muttered an untelligible oath.

"Make extra…brand new digging. Right down in town. You can have some creature comforts…."

"What'n hell does that mean—one of them damn flush toilets…?"

"Fresh water…new well, Mister Gottlieb."

"Critter comforts…I'll be goldarned! If that don't take Jenny's hen house….!" He tapped his harmonica and blew into it. "Why you hant got much sense, Grotteau!"

"Le'me show you." Grotteau's boots scuffed up the dust as he got up from the a clhopping stump. Gottlieb's coarse grayblack beard circled his sweaty face. A black brimmed hat shaded his eyes. He also stood. When they entered his house, a woman's plump figure slid behind a door like a shadow as Jerome opened another portico door to his mine tunnel.

"…Just like Jimmy Tyler's digging," Grotteau muttered. Gottlieb lit a lantern and led Grotteau into the tunnel's depths. He swung the lantern around, held it close to the rock, then up to the ceiling. There sparkled dust grains of gold. so tiny that when the lantern struck them they flashed with a powdery scintillation. This spectacle was all still miraculous to Jerome Gottlieb. He was contented; Grotteu saw the pleasure on his countenance. They returned to the front entrance to the tunnel, which existed within Gottlieb's two-room shack.

"Far be it for me to try to get you to buy stock—not when you're rich already with gold ore...right here...!"

"I knew you'd see things my way, Grotteau. But then...you never kin tell."

"No y' jes caint," Grotteau replied. Grotteau went out to his mule and in a few minuts returned, handing Gottlieb one of his landbills."

"Am I wanted fer something? You sure haint th' law."

"I remind you yer a wealthy man, Gotleib."

"this off your newfangled print press down in town."

"I hear you carry gold around with you," said Gottlieb. "A nugget, maybe." But the miner evinced little interest in the stone. "Wha'd I do a thing like that.fer....and be robbed?"

"You take no chances. I don't m'self." Out once more promptly olut came the nugget charm. fished up from a breeches pocket. He rolled it over and over between his thumb and forefinger, before Gotlieb's staring eyes. "You kin almost always pick up pieces as big as this 'n—twicet as heavy—right under your feet."

"I seed one afore."

"Big nugget...but I didn't cheat or embezzle a man to find this." The words caused the old sourdough to sneeeze. He stood up, immobile, his mouth shut, his hands clenched at his sides. "You won't need to rob banks...ever agin, Gottlieb". All the geniality in the miner's actions was gone, the blood drained from his face. The sourdoughs were a strong breed of men, a grim, forbidding environment shared by a wife at times, his hardships, possibly a washer woman, vitually invisible to the rest of the settlement in her humble labor. Grotteau knew of this way of life, and of vagabond roads that led to it.

"Bank heist, a scandal. Word gets around, Gottlieb. You're here like everybody else...for a reason. Gold? Sure, then what? Bad health? A convenient excuse—a pretty stoic place to settle down in." Whlen

Grotteau had published the man's story, that Gotlieb had committred the crime of embezzlement, had broken his parole and fled as a fugitive to these hills when his courage had failed, he wanted to meet the man. Well, here was the fugitive sitting before his very eyes. He resumed his professional pose. "Go down into town, Gottlieb...when you can.. and we can talk over old times...and the possiilities for fabulous wealth with your new mining claim."

The old man deftly and without the slightest hint of what was to come, pulled a knive from his boot and leveled it at Grotteau. The editor appeared to have scarcely noticed it...or at least pretrended not to see it in the old man's quivering hand. The sudden presence of the knife marked the end of their meeting. Grotteau arose and walked out to his mule. He pushed a stick under the cantle of his saddle and lit his a small night lanters. He hung it on the end as as on a boom. He turned and slowly rode away. Gottlieb began to hone the edge of a shovel with a whetstone to make easier his digging. Gottlieb's tired face had shown chagrin, defeat in the clouded eyes—a civilized renegade who had not quailed before Grotteau's insinuations. Grotteau was well aware that he had not just his printing press for a weapon but his bonded promise and his lying finesse. A lie could be turned into a profit. Fear in the Gottlieb household of two had shown itself in the woman's act of flight and terror in her elusiveness, whether this was his wife or not.

The saddle lantern colleced an cast its pale yellowgust as a finger of light into the oncoming twilight. Grotteu wended into the rising sand dust, sharp whiffs of agate smells, his mule's hooves clacking on a stone now and then, the crunch of his animal's weight digging divots into the shdowy sand. From afaar there came the smell of cooking, invisible drifts of smoke from a campfire that joined to the silcnce gave the unremitting shifting echoes the deadness of natures gathering night.

The Scorpion guided his mule down a slight incline, into a dip that butte up sharply into a rockydefile wsame spring use by Fazakerly to bring water to the village fed the methusal rock and brushed over rare fernstons. Thin springs of water flashed in the light of the campfire of Terence McAllister. The probing eyes of Grortteau saw what that he had another man with him. They were finihed work, it appeared, and were making ready their supper as twilight closed in and the sun's warmth left the desert like a chill set aside from the hazy flame of day.

He ground his teeth, swore to himself. He had made a convert of two, perhaps more, as the night would bring others sinto his camp. His hand could write on the rock faces, like the petrogliphs of old, his hunt for game, the quarry that would feed the tribe of the village and make him into a huntmaster to lead them. He sensed the thrust and risk of his own power in this journey.

Smells of coffe and flamecooking beef strips and the pungeance of greasewood burning hot ladened the cooling night air of the hillside redoubt, the rertreat of McAllister and one other man. His partner raised his eyes from the fire ring, shifted his torn hat and looked into the desert night to obvserve Grotteau's approach, the saddle lantern dangling woefully, swinging freely from its cantle-lashed stickpole. The mesquite fire blaze reflected off the sweaty lfaces of noth men, who had withdrawn for the night from their work of panning for gold.

The riffling sound of the creek lay in the background. It was apparent to Grotteau that they were using sluceboxes in tandem and had damned a small reservoir of spring water above the camp site. As it filled, they would release the water it into the baffles of their sluces, loaded with shovelsfull of ore, expecting the fresh-dug ore to drop any gold along the way.

McAllister joined his partner in inspecting the darkness. Grotteau halted his mule beyond the ring of direct firelight, his lantern's swing suddenly ceasing, lighting upward the ears and forhead of the mule and the stature of the man astride it.

"I see...Terence McAllister, you've not foregotten how to make camp. Army teaches a man some good things, don it?"

Looking up from here he squartted, hardly daring to answer. McAllister then stood bold upright, a cooking fork of wood in his hand. His pal disappeared into lthe murk undoubvedly to fetch up a gun of some sort...a shotgun more than likely or an army rifle.

'Well, what is it. We do All right. You see who we are…what were about," said the companion fellow, squat, small, black moustaches, in the pale light the obvious torture of suspicion an readiness on his swarthy face. He was a Mexican but spoke English like a native. Grotteau examined the two of them, his eyes never leaving them as they stood solemn and still like figurees in a night diorma.

"I spect soldiering was not your destiny," said Grotteau. McAllister broke the fork stick in his hands and tossed the parts into the fire where the gease flamed readily in the heat . He peered into the coffree pot to se if it had come to a boil.

"Captain, didn't like me…I don't' like him…still don't. Same stretch a rop…"

"No reason to go over the hill though…or was it?" The disenfranchised soldier held his silence. The younger of the two men, the Mexican, like his camarade, stood tall and up straight, both of them. In the hands of the latter there was gripped a double-barrel 12 gauge shotgun.

"Cant hunt rabbits with that," said Grotteau.

"Who's hunting rabbits?" said McAllister. "My friend here knows how to set traps."

"Does he now. Thats good. Wal, I meant no harm by asking. Course if you're turned outlaw, that might be another story."

"Were gold prospectors, pure and simple," said McAllister.

"I hope both of 'm is true," said Grotteau. "Actually I'm not looking for deserters." The Mexican lowered the shorun. The implication in Grotteaus mind was that they were desperate for one reason or another, if not as deserters from the Army at Foret Hall, then what…? There was no clothing on or about the site to indicate military presence; they had burned or vureied whatevewr evidence would be visible.

After a long silence during which Grotteau dismounted from his mule and set his lantern on the ground, McAllister ventured a remark:

"I…we mine a little…panners." He waved his hand broadly at the sluceboxes near the campsite. We make out…not too rich, not too poor."

An idler's answer, thought Grotteau, a remnant from his far distant seminary days. "I think mebe I ken help you out." The two men, McAllister and his Mexican pal, looked at each other to discern between them selves, by looks, by appearances only, the meaning of Grotteau's words. The Scorpion went on. "Any man cuts loose from soldiering without official leave is mighty entitled…mighty entitled… to stand tall." This affirmation appeared to relax the two miners as McAllister, with a gesture, invited their guest to share in a cup of coffe and a slice of beef, long done "But my questions is, how did you boys get away with stealing two of the army's finest horses to make your getaway?" McAllister did not raise his eyes from the tipped pot of coffee as he poured Grotteaus tin cup full.

"We only.,..rented 'm." McAllister replied.

"Oh, godamighty7…I've heard 'm all." Grotteu exclaimed, his profanity echoing against the rocks. "So you two boys rented twos of the armys finest ponies…what what did youl do with em…well tell me… ant yet t got caught.

"We turned 'm loose," aid the Mexican.

"Into the desert…!" Grotteau stood, alarmed, bitter words cutting a sharp edge into the onversation "Don't you two bits of desert flotsam…don't you renegades, you simpleminded bastards knowl horses ant wild steers or desert brush wolves. They can't survive…alone out there, without help!"

"They can find their way to the nearest town."

Grotteau went into a spasm of apoplexy. He lrode a mule only because a horse is not a gentle desert animal. "A horse eats grass. It does not hunt down wild game…idiots!"

"Wal, they're either in somebodys corral with army brands on 'm…or they be dead and bleached ones in the desert." He sipped his coffeee, an expression of incredulity on his face. To destroy that way two perfectly good animals was, to Grotteau, a more heinous crime than desertion and he did not mind saying so. yet the two deserters seemed relieved that their guest had fastened on animal theft and cruelty than upon their own escapadeof escape. Grotteau abruptly noticed another thing: the Mexican walked with a slight limp. He was crippled by what cause, for what reason, by what force or violence. The cause would come out if he stuck around. A crippled leg was a minor matter.

Strange how sinformation, facts about a mans life, what he was thinking, tended to float to the surface in ordinary talk.

"I used to be a pacifist, myself," said Grotteau

"We ant no pacifists," said McAllister. "We believe you go to shoot the enemy or he'll shoot you."

"Not all that bad is it?" Grotteau asked.

"Whatcha going to do…beg him to surrender?"

"Thy hant no war th's really necessary. War is manufacturement in hell, boys. Not for certain it is. War is the devil's tool, boy, his supply wagon, his cannons to kill them he don't like."

"Can't tell us they a'nt no good wars."

"I not only can, but I am. Ghandi, Christ, Schweitzer, Nobel—all them was peace-lovers."

"But they warn't no cowards. Some things they would fight fer--specially that Christ feller."

"Desecration," said Grotteau, dimly remembering from seminary the story of Christ in the temple, merchants defiling his father's house. "How you boys feel about killing your brothers?"

"If they kill us first, they hant no cause fer argument." This answer by McAllister prompted instant silence. "But if they practice violence with guns or swords or bayonets or any such things against them who is innocent, what then do you think?" Gotteau asked.

"You kill yer enemy—that's a act of mercy."

"But did not the Scriptures say " forgive your enemy…?"

"Providng he is willing to be forgiven. Rope stretches both ways, sir."

"So then we beg, or do we plead for mercy…mercy caint be forced er its kindness. There's a big difference when it means peace," said the Mexican.

"You got a shotgun hid over by that srock," said Grotteau.

"We got a right to pertect oursefes. Not the same as goin out and shootin a total stranger."

"But ant all men brothers in God's eyes?" Grotteau asked.

"In God's," said McAllister, "but we hant God, no ways, and so we cannot se 'm as our brothers."

"Then God's law about killing…the fourth commandment… don't hold water for your boys."

"God looks the t'other way sometimes," McAllister said.

"I reckon he does," said the Mexican.

"He abandoned his people more than once. Kilt, too, a' times—the flood, Sodom and Ghemorrah…fire and brimstone… and all thet sort of thing." Grotteau reached out for his own past for answers, but he felt that they were inadequate. He had a cause that was more immediate.

"Don know much about that," said McAllister. "But if you'll have this peace of beef on a stick, I'll pour you another cup of steam-engine black coffee." This small operation began…Groteeau had worked up lan appetite…they seemed to want to settle down into more conversation. Only Grotteau had one more move to make.

He watched McAllister eye, like the sparkle of grapeshot in the gatherin darkenss of the flamelight, powerfully strong, though sinuous and agile, his bearded blonde skin radiating the yellow of the campfire, he stood ready and tall, a pot of coffee clutched in his strong fist. Grottau's tin cup hung by one finger in his hand. He accepted the brew, but instantly set his cup down on the bare fround. Its tin was too hot for his lips. He nodded to acknowledge the courtesy of these strange fugitive hosts.

"Don't even know your name," McAllister said.

"Grotteau…Reiner Grotteau. I publish the town's only newspaper, *The Scorpion.*"

"As you were saying…about the gold mining and… soldiering…."

"Sure, I was a soldier, but I put that behind me." He jerked his thumb toward his Mexican counterpart. Grotteau tried to sip from the hot tin cup.

"Like I say, I got plans for Mystery…for the folks in Mystery."

"You come to the wrong place for any news, Mister Grotteau."

"Paper's got a burial ground…a morgue, place where old accounts are kept. Just happened to stumble on yours. From Abelene, long ways from home, McAllister. Well, they won't miss you."

Neither man said a word, precautioning the darkness with mute voices. 'Smatter of fact, I can put gold dust betwixt you 'nd any… unpleasant past history, McAllister."

"Meaning?"

He handed the young miner one of his broadsides. "Right there. Gold under the town of Mystery."

MAllister put down his coffee cup on the bare ground. He stepped over to where Grotteau leaned against a boulder. He confronted the Scorpion editor with a steady, rockeye squint. His thin arms were folded. The shadow of his hat obscured his face.

"Theres always two ways to look at a matter, Mister Growttreau.

"You're talking about your…soldiering. I don't put much stock in such things—a story is a story."

"All that patriontism stuff…pig slop…for amy pay. And no war. Show is all it is, show, sir, no mor'n that and mostly to raise more money sos the politicians can get relected to office agin.

"Radical judgement, McAllister. Still, I didn't drop by to deliver a judgement, Mister McAllister. Oh, sure, I know you deserted at Fort Bishop…or was it Fort Hall…and come West. You mightve made Lieutenant rank…." McAllister turned away, disgust on his face. I see you've done right well here, boys. "I mean…having your own diggings in these hills."

The young soldiers sidekick stepped forward. He gripped in his hand the ever present 12-gauge shotgun. It was lowered; his eyes were steady on Grotteau. His shigh cheekbones and squint conveyed the edge of treachery. He chewed and spat. He played nervous with the shotgun on his hip. A blast of murder would resolve his inner disdain and suspicion. His spirit was fellow to McAllisters contempt for rebuke of the military.

"Were doing pretty good as it is," McAllister repeated, as before. Grotteau could ot tell by his voice if he spoke out of pretense; the voice lay flat, even like hammered tin on a corrupgated roof. Grotteau's perception of the tonalities possible to the human voice was that of a mule skinner or a stage driver…accustomed to shouts to his beasts. His genius lay in his shrewd eclipse of vision, his undeniably clever mind and that certain kind of wisdom endemic to and born out of a mind and soul grown up in the unpeopled wilderness of distances and nature's sounds of the great silence.

Grotteau, undaunted, went on. "You'll dig in a vein that runs smartly under the village, boys. Water coursed through there a long, long time ago. Droped off gold, it did…lots of gold, flakes… one nugget…this…?" He tugged out of one pocket his centerpiece. So there's lots more…maybe not as big. I'm parcelin' off the holdings… one hundred feet square, a grid 'crost the town like a wire screen, boys, for all the folks who want more gold."

McAllister's sidekick stepped forward, his hands still in a death grip on the shotgun, lowered at the redbaking rock, his eyes steady on Reiner.

"This here's dangerous country," said the renegade Mexican. "and is whart gold isallabout. Cant hwn one withoutthe other…not out here."

For the first time Grotteau took close notice of the man…high cheekbones—he'd seen then, a crocked foot…not in the army…hands that appeared claw-like to reach out to grasp…rheumatic maybe…like those of a blind man. He played nervous with that shotgun, off to one side and angered by an inner turbulence. He obviously had fellow rebel in the army deserter and fugitive, McAallister.

"Keep yer claims, Grotteau. We're doing okay as 'tis."
"You dig in a vein that goes just under Mystery. Water…like I say…water layed down gold. Assayer says so. I got Kittrick's big rock in my pocket to prove it. You saw it. Let it be known, gentlemen, that the town of Mystery can be moved. We down there don't never need to keep our village where' tis…that is…you'll pardon me…if 'nough gold is found to warrant the town's dislocation."

The two studied the broadside which Grotteau had first handed them. McAllister only could read, so he read it again, aloud. Grotteau then rolled a cigarette for himself land waited, smoking, rocking slightly with nervous impatience, holding his own court of condemnation and perverse indictment, his silent judgement. While they studied the poster, what Grotteau could not have anticipated was a visit by the Indians of the region to the renegade-soldiers' campsight. Almayer led the reconnaissance party, for that was their apparent pupose. McAllister recognized him from a visit with a small amount of gold dust to the Assayer's shack. The Mexican did not recognzie any member of the visiting party. It became at once apparent that they had come to give the White men a warning. Almayer, now one with his five Indian accomplices, held up a hand in the salute of concord and peace. Almayer spoke, addressing his words to Grotteau. His voice was a monotone of warning, his words short and clipped, the manner of a man delivering an ultimatum to a foreign enemy.

"Mister Grotteau, I know you. You have become evil in my eyes and in the eyes of my brothers."

"Evil…! "

"Do not be surprised." Grotteau moved stiffly to stare up into the face of his accuser. It was almost without expression, inert and devoid of emotion. The features appeared transfixed as if hidden by a full mask of his face. "You know why," the mask continued. "I have warned you not to dig under the village or on its streets. You possess much more gold than is good. You have enough gold. Tthe people will make out without destruction of their dwelling places.

"It is fair to dig. We have freedom to dig in the naked ground."

"Who gave you this right, Mister Grotteau?"

"God…and nature did."

"You do not believe in God. Your wisdom is empty. Your god gave you…the land to enjoy."

"Digging for nature's buried gold is our joy."

"It will destroy you. It will bring catastrophy, Mister Grotteau."

"You are not my prophet, Almayer."

"I warn you this time. If you insist that the earth is yours to steal and to plunder, you will suffer for it. Those who come with you—they, too, will suffer."

"What kind of scare are you trying on me, Almayer?"

"I know the forces of nature better than you do. I know what vengeance nature can bring on those who do not respect her ways."

"Look, Almayer...your job is to analyze, weigh and calculate the value of the gold we find...nothing more."

"You do not tell me my worth. You do not condemn me to one task. I know freedom better than you do. You surrounnd your freedom with protection. This soldier here is that protection. That is not freedom. That is prison to your soul, Mister Grotteau."

His English was school tutored. "I'll have done with you, Almayer."

"You will rape the land of my people...their burial grounds, their sacred resting place for the bones of their ancestors. The White man is not my race..."

"We will lay the bones of your ancestors aside and we will bury them again. We will respect the Indian ancestors. We will do these things." TYhe other Indians on horseback waited impatiently nearby, in the shadows, their horses jingling the bridle links, snorting, washing their tails as if ready for battle.

"You will not expose my people's burial grounds in such a despicable way. These Indians here...and there are many more of them...will bring down their hatred upon you for such violation of all that is sacred to them."

"We will take that chance."

"It is against our god that you do this sacreledge to the memories and the remains of my Indian people."

"I cannot reassure you...."

"Your assurance is a lie. It is to satisfy your greed. I even know your name. I tell you...if you disturb one grave, I shall bring my friends...and many of them remain hidden this night...we shall make war on you and the village of Mystery. That is my promise. I will honor their ancestors. I will not spill any honor on your evil desire. I do not care about your blood."

Speaking thus, this dire, dread promise, Almayer and his five Indian friends, who had remained silent, having ridden up as a ritual token of their anger and love mixed together, tribal clansmen Grotteau assumed, as he must have, then rode away, breaking into a gallop at a distance, the gallop of invisible horses in the dust of the desert night.

"If you listen to them Indians you'll lose good luck," Grotteau warned the ex-soldier and his Mexican companion.
"If we won't listen we will buy into your troubles and who can tell…disaster."
"You're not supersititious, are you, McAllister?"
"Only cautious."
"I see."
"We like it up here."

The Scorpion abruptly mounted his mule , relit his jackpole lantern and, rehanging it on his saddle cantle, he saluted the two miners. He wheeled about and thanked them for their hospitality then rode away into the darkness. They watched, chagrinned, completely astonished and intimidated, as if they had witnessed a ghost of fate visit them at their simple campsite with a message they did not fully comprehend.

He left McAllister and his comrade to stare after him as he headed downtrail. The encounter had proved unusual and intimiating to Grotteau; he only built up higher inside his own heart the flame of his obsession to sequester the town under the codified mantle of his mining company scheme. He could not control his proud land fee by telling himself it ought not to be, or it was evil, or that greed was only a word for retribution against life's hardships.

Grotteau crossed a freshet of water, entered then a narrow defile and down into a sparce grove of scrub pines and mesqusite thorn, through which the light of another campfire silhouetted the black tree tru;nks and wild brambled tracery. He stood at the edge of athicket trying to read the faces of several miners who worried the sticks of a campfire, stirred about and conversed in low voices. A large tent stood off in the shadows, open to show cots within. No other figures were present.

One of the men held a sppon in the air, turning it to inspect it and dropped it into a boiling pot on a gridiron above the flames. Around his thin neck there shone a knotted white kerchief. His sharp Vandyke beard, hidden eyes in deep sockets under knotted eyebrows, his lean torso lin dungarees and leather hide jacket, and the polished reflection on his black boots all matched the hair pomade and slicked backward. His dress and general appearance were not common among the panners. He spoke affably, with intensity and keen excitement. Who the other four men were…one had just emerged from a tunnel into the rock, Grotteau was soon to learn.

When Grotteau rode rode up, all were taken by surprise. "You frlightened my…staff…and my one patient!" the man with the vandyke beard exclaimed.

"Sorry…I'm the editor of **The Scorpion.**

"I'm Doctor Farralones…chief…chief…what in blazes am I chief of…" he chuckled. "Chief of forgery…by God we'll lhave some before long…and …oh, curator of dliseases…I study them and ship them out if contageous. This…." he gestured broadly "….is my field hospital.

Up here…?" Grotteau queried.

"And why not? It's a damn sight better than down there in all that dust and commotion. Call it a…sanitarium, if you please. fine desert air up here. Gnats are a bother at sundown….but no mosquitos. No still water around. A tarantula strays in occasionally…and scorpions.l Your paper's got the same name. Stings to death if a mans susceptible. But we got ways…we got methods. And…if the gods be willing… medicines." He lookedto an tttendant who made the sign of the cross for him, for them.

This introduction chilled Grotteau, for it put his venture completely out of bounds…so he lthought..in this situation—a field hospital…The *dying and the dead*, he thought.

Grotteau swayed out of the gloom into lthe flaked, broken camplight and made his presence known by a remorse-filled laughter. Danger and death were cousins.in his book. Disease and alienation were other kindred. He hated to stir up these sourdoughs with any awful feelings of guilt. Grotteau was proudly compassionate and not a little self-congratulatory about his own wisdom on this matter of disinternment in search of gold.

"I meant no harm." he said, an absurd introduction, he knew. "Of course not…just profitable gain." He raised his hand as he had done to the Indians, onlythis time he was a captain at the head of his column of troops. The doctor stood erect, smiled genially, opened his arml to invite Grottau to dismount and come join them—which the wayfarer, on his rounds of solicitation, promptly did. He extinguished his boom lantern and set it on the ground beside his mule.

"I come here on a errand of good will." His lugubrious words caused the miners to sniff and shuffle. One of them scratched the head of a goat that wandered into the circle. There were, as mentioned, four, including Dr. Farralones. They were present at his campsite for various reasons, not the least of which was to dig for gold. The very opening and size of the tunnel revealed that quest. One of the miners close to the doctor, was a robust, young man, agile and lanky of limb with frostbite marks on his cheeks. His hands were with fingers like a fiddler's. There was about him movement that resembled a caged animal's restless movement, He smiled through his white pokerchip teeth a smile that insinuated disaffection for their visitor.

"I'm Clem," he said and no more.
Another of the doctors helpers wore covertalls and a farmers straw hat. His face was pudgy, almost round, eyes, smartly set wide apart and a body and hands that seemed to belong to another man, as if someone stood behind him operating his own missing extremities."
"Call me ty," he said with an engaging politeness that briefly rattled Grotteau .

A fourth miner scrubbed a pot with dirt to clean the grease. He wore high top logger boots. His hands were almost deformed as if by disease or accident. His face bore marks of combat, a scar over his upper lip, a kind of sidelong smile on his face, which did not change, not a smirk yet not quite the dilsfigurment of a former stroke. The doctor's fourth companion wore glasses. He appeared studious yet somehow ready for battle; by way of his anguslr movements, the swling of his broad shoulders. His small mouth he kept grimiced, as if there burned a cigarette betwen his lips. He was, in fact, whistling to himself. These four men , panners, hard rock miners, depending on the site, were Doctor Farralones' mining companions. Grotteau only noticed, he did not comment. The last man said, "You can call me Lance Scarboro, if it means anything to you." He sounded bellligerant...or diffident, Grotteau could not at once judge.

"Indians used to keep and use a sweat lodge. White man's medicine has pretty much done away with the custom, sorry to say. Young females now go for the gigue to lose weight, not evil spiritls. That there"—pointing to the tent—"is my sweat lodge. No tribal enemies here ...or evil spirits...but plenty of zeal for lthe yellow metal. Observe our tunnel." Grotteau did the same.

"You're a medical doctor, I take it," Grotteau said.

"I am and if there should occur an outbreak of typhoid or diphtheria or, God forbid!...the pox, why, they can, send the patient up here. I have a few remedies...not much you unerstand for as many miners as I've seen along the creek. If I have a really bad case...lets slay...terminal... I bring in an Indian shaman to drive the evil spirts from the sick miner. I use some of the local Indians ways if there's no Medicine Man around." "How is that done, doctor?

With smoke clouds that lift and envelop the sick spirit, then carry it away."

My assistants, the doctor suddenly commented, noticing Grotteau's intense stare and scrutiny of the camps inhaitants, the sick bay tent and the dark tunnel opening. The beggarly ensemble said not a word. It was obious, at least to Grotteau, that they awaited the doctor's formal invitation to speak to a stranger. Grotteau suspected that the tunnel served a double purpose, as a mine for gold and a place for the terinally sick. The entire lair was one of secrecy amid the desert expanse of oncoming night.

"This, then is your medical practice?"

"Medical? Oh, yes, yes," retorted Farralones as he straightened his kerchief, stroked his pointed beard and smiled, or at least tried to make a smile.

"I examine matters…in your case…the presence of gold in the rocks. Lo, the tunnel we have dug. Serves us quite well…for finding gold…got one nugget out of the shovelsfull we disgorged. And so, should I get a felverish patient, lo, I push…I carry him in there to help him cool off. Sort of…refrigerate him." Farralones could not suppress a small laugh. "But…thank God, not dysentery…or snake bites…or paterboil fever cases yet…."

"Maybe you'd consider opening up a second office, Doctor Farralones."

"I told you…Grotteau…" the editor nodded "…I told y ou, this is the one ideal place ofr a field hospsital. Oh, we could do with a few improvements…but for now…this is it."

Grotteau's growl deepened. A silence was cracked by lthe incinerating sapwood in the fire. Grotteau noticed the scratch tracks ofl dry mesquite wood that had been dragged over to the flames, mesquite that surrounded on the scree slopes surrounding the defile encampment.

"I, sir, have enough gold to keep us busy right h ere.I don't neeed to go looking for it." He motioned to the open mouth of the tunnel. Grotteau noticed for the first time Farralones' pale skin, the cut of his cheekbones, sharp and taut above his Vandyke beard. He moved about with almost a slight stoop for his tall frame.

"Are they arterial or venial extrusions? Grotteau asked. The mirth was dry and artless.

"both…theres a vein somewheres…got to be."

"In the village…by my map."

"Curses on yhour damnable map!" Farralones suddenly exploded. Do you think I got no other purpse for being here thans to follow some direction on your map drawn no doubt by a fool?"

"I didnt enquire of the mapmaker, Doctor Farralones, as to whether or not he was a fool."

"Inches close to the top of the ground. Should I go palpitate the ground with my shovel—or my stethoscope?"

"If you want to," said Grotteau. "Either one would be okay." Laughter came from the assistants. It was evident to Grotteau that the Indians and assayer Almayer had already worked their bad medicine on Farralones and the others. He was cool to the notion of digging for gold in Mystery.

The campfire hissed, the wood shifted with a brush. A pocket of sap explsoded.

From lthe vicinity of lthe tent, the logger fellow withl the gnarled hands and high boots and bawny body carried out on twin thin rods…part of some machine…wagon bed, perhaps, two rabbits, skinned, gutted and ready for the fire.

"Care to join us for supper, Mister Grotteau?" the doctor invited.

Don't care if I do." Grotteau sat down on a small barrel that once contained keg nails or shoes… Soon the smell of cooking rabbit meat, invisibly salted the air with an invisible succulence. Grotteau had fetched on of his broad sides from his saddle bag. While the silence continued, but for the fire and boots moving about, Grotteauy, focused on his mission, read his missive to the miners. None looked pleased, none appeared hopeful or downcast or surprised or in the last eager to participate.

Farralones took the poster, glanced at it and then dropped it ino the flames where it curled and caught fire, spontaneously brightening the camp circle for a moment.

"She was brave enough not to charge you with anything but… bad practice…that there was a error in her prescription. How lucky can a man get…Doctor. You see you lost your practice not because of that…animal thing, but because you could not face your own self, sir, for carelessness…a kind of negligence that always carries its own option of care or no care. Goldmining camps are full of folks like you…wanting to own another person's life but not having courage to take over…rape is just a sympton, doctor."

This flip analysis did not perturb the doctor. He dimply smiled from his own inner distance. "Well, we have with us a philosopher… who knows all about medical practice."

"Hardly," Grotteau demurred.

"You know the whole story, dont you? This is my defense , El Inquisitor" he named Grotteau with a nasty tone of voice. Like a man recovering a bullet from his arm, he drew a revolver from a slide holster under his cooking smock, which he had donned to tend the meat and give substance before the eyes of the others in his role. The real purpose for the apron was to conceal the weqpon. His thin face with the charcoal-black eyes fixed on Grotteau. He threw off shis brimmedhat in a grand gesture of sudden defiance and fired one round into the night sky. Thre muz;zle flashed, the report echoed.

"As a doctor I take exception. Surgery is an act of violence. Don't you never forget that, Mister. Violence is one thing, love is another. Sometimes they bond …just like two tissue cells of the body. But they make the operation possiible."

The companion who wore the straw hat, owned the ruddy face and dissociated arms and hands, it so lseemed, wanted to rush at Grotteau to defend the doctor. Instead, he simply hissed a snakelike warning: "I know you…you're a messenger from hell. I feel contempt for you."

At these words, the doctor sus;pect fired another round into the snight air, snipping the reins of Grotteau's mule but not cutlting them.

"I'll be damned!" was Grotteaus response, his expression one of anger and wonder at the nearness of the round to killing his mjle.

"My hand is steady, my aim is damned sure..my resident diagnosis—deadly, sir….Grotteau."

"You've denied the truth all these years, doctor. What is six… elight or ten? I heard about you. If…if you say you I can find gold, then you figure to redeem yourself."

"I paid my debt. I gave up my practice…even as the devil don't give up his soul by sinning."

"But gold, gold, more gold…man That can restore your fortune. It's a curative medicine, doctor. You know that as well as I."

"Let me tell you something you aren't going to like, Grotteau." Before he began the ex-logger removed to rabbit from its spit and cut it into , breast, pieced. He handed a piece around, licking his fingers after havi;ng done so. These iltinerant rouc;h campsite diners ltossed the sizzling meat from hand to hand to cool it before consuming it in nips and bites. The logger, the self-apopinted chef, had made up some biscuit dough and proceeded to pat the cakes and place them on a clean shovel back, like hoe cakes.

"I was at one time an archer…owed a compound bow…shot game for venison and trophies." The doctor was talking. "I also had a yen somewheres in my soul to help people. I helped an old woman flooded out of her house, a young guy caught in a bear trap with rising flood water…hated to hve to cut his foot off. Ye one day, possessed of wanting to help other folks, I went out and caused a great disturbance in the street of my small town by taking my bow and arrow and shooting the horse of a street vendor. Why…because I imagined that that horse was the cause for all that old man's troubles. I did not think ahead. I did not realize that I had snuffed out his means to earning a livelihood…or that he could afford another horse. In my pervertsed imagination, I was the forgiver, the missioner of good will, the priest of compssion who would actually commit paricide to put a child out of its misery. I had this urge to redeem myself bychastening men for their wrongs,l their malevolence, if you will. I was the Great Requiter. Not Christ on the cross but me, myself, l, Heinrich Farralones, a doctor then…a *savior complex*, call it that if you chose…."

"Wrongly directed compassion," Grotteau offered.

"Not even that…compassion? Hear me…a compassionate man will first consider the consequences of his actions. I failed. I never gave shooting that old ventor's horse one thought as to the consequences of my act."

"But by losing his horse, did you not at the same time tell him that he was…was in the wrong trade?"

"Arrogant idea! Arrogant act!" Disgust shone on the doctor's countenance. "How could I do such a thing? How could I? I was not God to forsee another man's future. What could I say to him?

"So the authorlities found you out…".

" confessed to what I had done and offered to reemburse the man for the loss of his animal."

"And did you?"

"I did…twice over…not like Zacharias of thetax man…but I did repay him for the loss of his horse."

"So that should have settled the matter right then and there."

It would have but for the fact that the old man was venial and vengeful and he sued me and had me put in jail."

"After you had paid him for the horse?"

"Exactly…to punishsl me for my killing his animal

"Then your money was not enough.It was your guilt that mattered most."

Not to satisfy his old mind…but it informed me of one thing… that money is the medium of exchange for all human passions…a man's dependence on his horse, his caring for his wife, his disregard for a stranger..his own innocence—all can be settled at the money table."

"Banks…!" Grotteau interjected.

"Banks are where pepople keep their retribution money. The village of Mystery lis a place of danger, sir. Let me forewarn you… in the ground, as you so injudiciously assert, there lies the despicable means to depopulate the entire population of Mystery…retribution money. That's what it is."

"How so?

"By inspiring crime, inciting acts of violence…giving money for the act or receiving the benefits of the act. Works both ways, Scorpion….that's what they call you, I hear…."

"Like a…commercial exchange…almost"

"Against the mores of…of the people, Mister Grotteau. It's the…the commerce of crime as suc;h that is , dark, illicit, evil…" The doctor said little more. He sort of faded linto the shadows of the nilght.

but not the taking of a life, Grotteau thought. Beyond the cluster or rocks Grotteau heard wild, drunken whiskeyboozed laughter, borne on the quiet night air, the sort of raucous gold panning camaderie he had often heard. Grotteau could find no other description for it when he recounted this scene and Farralones campsite.

The man knotted in laugher was the young and lanky fellow with the frostbitten cheeks and the slender fingers of his hands like a fiddler's hand. He had graveled something aboutl "maverick diggings" to another, whose voice it became clear was that of a woman. Grotteau peered intently into the darkness. To his astonishment he saw that the woman was a Chinese woman, youngert than Farralones by years, probably his...lab assistant or something of the sort...like removing bullets from miners' arms and torsos.

"My wife," said the doctor when the woman had made her appearance. "She laughs easily. We have a good relationship. I furnishs her with gold dust, which she sends off to China, and she keeps my clothes clean. Nice arrangement. A little expensive but...."

Grotteau squirmed uneasily. He; moved closer to the campfire light and the lanterns, two of them Farralones and lit and hung, one on a branch of growing mesquite and the other niched in nearby rocks.

"She loves the glint of gold same I do, Mister Grotteau."

"I'm glat to hear that."

"Why should you be glad...?"

"Thats good...and that's bad then. Woman make some times the best stewards of gold...yet they can be most extravagant despoilers of it...its accumulation?

Touching, Grsotteau. Your perception is quite touching...for me...in my...practice here."

"You appear to have all you need."

"Except medicines...I dont require many of those. But Chin Chin here rides bravely over to Triangle to fetch them for me... prescriptions, you understand." Grotteau nodded. " But them..fate..." *again that word*, Grotteau thought "...fate has rought you here. You have a plan to subdivide the village into mining claims" He laughed. "What a marvelous idlea. Everybody now gets la share of...Mystery."

Here he laughed again, uproariously, then "…ah, ha, no doubt you…you realize"…he pinched his fingers in obvious suggestion… "you realize a little take off the top for your delivery of…protection? Your pain and expense? Your…chivalry, Mister Grotteau?"

"I can't claim much chivalry, doctor, but I can lay claim to the deeds from Almayer's office and the office of land management over in Triangle."

"Just so…I knew you were a careful preparer…an astute negotiator. I could depend on you to prep my patient correctly for surgery."

The pair, Chin chin and the slender miner, laughed, this time with the doctor. "Oh, you must not pay any attention to young Clem Jasper. They're enjoying each other's company I…we have such scarce entertainment around her, Mister Grotteau…that even your entrance furnished us with much grist for conversation." The camp was totally quiet at that moment except for the snap of the fire from time to time. A night bird, white under its wings, flew over the site, probably an owl in search of rats of snakes. *All life must eat, must feed*, Grotteau reflected.

"We get so busy around here," Farralones clucked. " I can hardly remember my manners. Gold mining panner sites are not the places for etiquette. Settler…that's Ty…hes my right hand assistant. Not a miner. His work with horses and pigs has taught him the value of food in the life of the animal. Why, just a week ago, we had a gunshot case…wasnt it, Ty?" the man nodded, "shot clean through the breast…well, almost. . Lost a lot of blood. Went home yesterday…to his maker…couldn't help it. But Ty lthere, helpful wlith loving care….gunshots don't take kindly to their victims."

"That was the hearse came through town yesterday."

"Yessir…on the wlay to Triangle. They got the best grave yard hereabouts. **Skyhaven.** Protected from coyotes. Stones on some, board on others…but tidy. Gaw, how those folks in Triangle keep the graveyard tidy! I like tidy places, Grotteau, as you can see. He scanned the field cots in the tent, the shovels, mallets and drilling bits leaning up against the tunnel wall.

"Doctor Farralones, even a fool can be tidy." The doctor was taken aack. "We have as yet had no riots. We have unrest, to be sure. And—hear me, we can expect an Indian raid…"

"Before you continue, remember I do not work for you or your God. I work for the devil himself. Saferthat way. Folks have been convinced they wouldl never need their arms for self defense…but that is not the way of the world, sir."

It was Grotteau's turn to be taken aback. "I see your bewilderment. Strange, yet I confront death. Your…miners up and down the creek confront life with their fear of death. They run from reality."

I am on a crusade, I make known to you and..your…friends here, I intend to collect all weapons, of violence." He let the announcement settle in.

"Violence, sir, is not in the weapon, its in the soul of a man."

"You tire me with your jaded philsoophy. of…guilt," said Grotteau.

"Guilt, to be sure, but guilt with the retribution of tlhe Indian trickster. lI reverses the sentence and sti;ng of death."

"Guns are the cause."

"Gun are the result." Farralones was adamant.

"I will declare the village public domain…no one man can put a hold on it."

"Clever but wanting, Grotteau.l You should advise your miner friends to avoid trouble if they would cure violence. The two are nseparable.

"A man was killed for that reason…He was a moonshiner, an anchorite, a self-exile."

"Just my kind of man…I. too. am an exile. Medical science is dealt a deathblow by those who do notl exile theselves from the ravages of politics…and, of course, money."

"Like lthose …drifters whol try to bivouac at the hotel…exiles from politics."

"Exactly so, Grotteau…the politics of possession which, in its advanced stages, beomes a disease of dispossession."

"I would not play a game of cards on that bet, doctor."

"Nor would I. I am aware that Indians' graves reject the miners shovels, his corrupt intrusions, his cuel disinterment of honored bones of the dead. Remember this, Grotteau;...for your paper, if you prefer... that death invites life only when there is a chance that cuts elither way. That is the glory of the humamn species." They shared a cup of coffee over a long silence.

"That man in coveralls and the farmer's straw hat, pudgy, somewhat obese, his hands and arms seem disjointed somehow... Name's Ty...my right hand assistant. I'm repeating myself, I suppose... it's the hour."

"You've been up here some time...to dig a tunnel like that."

"We have...time I mean and...rocks around here 'r a a challenge, makes gold worth the effort. Hank Willows there...the husky logger looking fellow in cork boots with the deformed hand, seems to wear a smirk all the time...good man. Him and me...we pushed that tunnel back about hundred yuards...isn't it Hamk?" Hank nodded. "You see ,Grotteau, they obey me without my having to buy them out, bribe them, push them, intimidate or terrorize them. They too belong to the devils clique, pardon the expression." . He had vegun to prepare a little desert—French pudding. "Good man, hard working. Oncet hit a man with his axe in a rage, cleft his skull but closed it shut with some tape, put his hat on and threw him back into his bunk. Spent some time on the Rock but there he is. We...I ve got no patients here, Grotteau, only specimens. Im a confirmed anatomist. The body is everything. I let religionists deal with the spirit. Oh, bys the way, hes a hellova good swimmer. Resisted hypothermia by gorging on fats out there, and lung power...crossed through baycurrents by riding one over to Alameda and got off...*just like river swiminng*, he says. Tell me if your pious social constructionsists can beat that with their revolutionary nonsense. Survival! One of God's highest priorities...look at Noah, and a jimmied-up Adam, and that judge and titan Samson who pulled down tlhe temple. Gawamighty, I wish I had that kind of power. My work here is meddling in satan's business. I'm welcome...on his terms."

I'll see you the other side of the mountain, when I make the worship of gold a legitimate religion with icons, destroy or be destroyed..a creed on a field of battle. No, Doctor Farralones, I too greet the great deceiver with awe. I study his plans for deception."

"We think in the same vein, Mister Grotteau. My staff keep me busy sorting out their past lives."

"I think I know your thoughts, sir … gold for pain medication."

"Not for pain, sir...but for escape. We all try to escape pain.. That's the nature of the human animal. but I accept your good will. I like your enthusiam for tricking the devil with his own skill of a double motive." The doctor looked quite pleased by Grotteau's analysis of the medico"s state of mind. Besides, I've got a arrastre to crush out ore...no stampig mill for me and these here slues, with that spring water jes tapped...does jes fine. We do ample, Mister Grotteau. We surely do ample. Betwixt mining for gold and medical work here keps us all humping."

"I should say so,: Grotteau affirmed. Willows emerged like a ghost from the tunnel entrance, lantern in one hand and a small pail of water in the other. He noticed for the first time that the man's beard was red. Farralones kept every man busy to insure gainst clashes b'etween them. Such self-exiles are not readily disciplined; they adopt a way of life to is conducive to angery clashes, occasional, acts of violence unrelated to the presence of gold. Frustration animates their clashes, I knew that.

"My finest assistant...come over here, Scarboro. I'd like for you to met a friend of mine, Grotteau...Grotteau....".

"Reiner."

"Reiner Grotteau. this here is Jess Scarvoro. A little too delicately for these hills and this rough wlay of life. Hes a...a study of history now."

"That so?" Grotsky replied. The miner kept silenct. I'm a student of history also...mister...er...Jess." Farralones smiled.

"I'm certain Joe here won't mind a little...a little recitation. Again the stoney silence. Don't let those glasses fool you, Grotteau. Jess here is a sharpshooter. You're a sharpshsooter, aren't you, Jess?" A smile edged into the corners of his mouth. He trained his eye..."tell 'm how you trained your shooting eye, Jess." No response. "He trained his shooting eye, woudja believe it, shooting pool in Abelene...or was it San Francisco...not important."

"Frisco…lower Market…"

"Lots a practive. Can't read but sure has a dead eye! His hand quivered, his finger iteched to get off a round at the governor. "He's an…*assassinator!*" Farralones said with some pride and a pinch of mirth in his words. "But doggone it, he missed. Not a bad shot… just jostled…and, after all…'s only pracrice." To make a long story short, he took to robbing stages, shot up a stage driver, ran with a gang also took to the mail train. Favorites, you know. Robbed a big church in Abelene…for shame on that one, Jess. Up in Alturea, robbed a bank…wouldja believe it!…by pretending to be a gumshoe with a police dog…let into the vault of the bank, he was…cleaned 'm out… the whole bloody loot…and wouldja believe it!…walked with that damned dog right out the bank door without a soul laying a hand on him." He drank from his coffee. "Then there was the bedlam case… court-appointed doctor…"but why go on? I'm your doctor now, Jess. Agreed?" The miner nodded his head and walked over to the place where the broadside was dropped. Deftly,by one corner like a thing contaminated, he let it fall into the flames.

"There you have it, Grotteau…my assistants. I'll let you in on a little secret of mine, Grotteau. When one of these poor bastards up here dies…by knife, gun, strangulation….ohhh, don'tchu know!…I have a contact in Frisco. I sell him body parts. Dry ice back there. I try to revive the miner. I'm ahead if he dies. I try to resolve pain, but I'm conscious that death and pain are fair contenders fer a dying man." He again drank his coffee. "You begin to get my drift." The doctor's staff stood by like posts, mute, reflecting only the firelight, their faces devoid, totally, of sympathetic expression and intelligent curiosity. Like Zombies. He sells…*body parts of dead miners*, Grotteau reflected with an irresistible shiver.

"My staff don't seem too interested in your scheme, Mister Grotteau;. The Scorpion moved closer to his mule. I'm as much a stranger as you in this godforsaken desert as you, Farralones."

"Get out here!" was the doctor's reply. He raised a revolver into the face of Grotteau who, turning his back to lthe muzzle, mounted his mule. At that precise moment he hard the feathered hiss of an arrors as past his head, followed by the thud of a bodly, the body of

Farralones behind him. An arrow had penetrated all the way through one shoulder. The man's friend Ty hastily ripped open his shirt, broke off the arrows head and deftly jerked out the broken shaft . The doctor lay inert but conscious.

"Goddamn, I didn't know any Indians were still hereabouts." He cursed with a groan. He collapsed into the dirt.

"Cant help you this time, Farralones."

"Get out of here. The doctor threatened,"the gun no longer in his hand. Grotteau again seized his revolver from where it lay onthe ground. He aimed it at his intruder, pain now mixed with anger in his voice.

One of Farralones men. Ty or Clem, it mattered not, shot into the night, chipping a nearby rock and flaking redstone into the enight air, accompanied by the riccochet whine. Grotteau rode away, back hrough the defile and into a hollow, a cape of darkness shroulded his departure from the campfire site...from tlhe doctor and lhis four zombie sourdough friends and the yellow woman. He traveled on. Not bitterness, only contempt filled his heart. He was determined to make his roulette scheme work, so what was the loss of several miners? Evidently the arrow shot into Farralones was a warning, intended for himself more than for the doctor-miner. Grottelau intuitively realized with cold alarm that the intruder had meant the arrow for him, a deaht's arrow.

No tender concern to heal or to mend
Greets the hard hear that malpractice tends.

Lines on a miner's lantern came to mind. l He realized why the vearded one had squinted at him with suspicion; either the Farralones men or the Indian had assumed that he was a claim jumper with a new pitch. He would; appeal to oners, deserters from some previous job or good fortune but like a gambler, seeking even greater wins. He had become convinced that chance, fate, the roulette wheel icon— these things ruled the game of panning and hard rock mining. Human choice, lollowed by accidents in the tunnel, along the creek, a rock fall, a premature powder blast, careless handling of agun, pretended fueuds, a stumble on the rocks...then...silence followed like a spectre of death over all the mining camps…in the hills…in the village. All chance led to death without the favoritism of fate.

Grotteau determined to make one more call before the night deep night came on. He had spent too much time up here at that field hospital damned site. He wanted to make a call on Igor, the Dane. He turned up his lantern, listened to the mule's hooves crunch on the sandy ground, the iron shoe striking a flinty spark from time time on the trail. The slop of the kerosene in the saddle lantern told him he had about an hour or less of time on the trail. Most miners were starting to sack out for the night.

As he headed down trail to the village again, he had hardly begun when a most astonishing spectacle appared from tlhe dark of the desert night: a company of four men, not Indians this time, one astride a horse along th eflanks of which were attached two poles in the maner of an Indian traverse or drag. He pulled off to one side of the trail, beside some rocks but did not stop. In minutes this trail prty came abreast of where he stood. He stared with a fixed and careful scrutiny, mingled with a sense of pity, that the figure of the very man he intended to call upon was Igor (the Dane) Skelund, a lonely man who lived away from tlhe village, a man whose well to do wife had deserted him, left him to work out his destiny in the mines of El Dorado gold fields. An old news story told of how Skelund had involved himself in extortion to assist in his wife expensive tastes. He had recanted, repaid every last cent of what he had stolen and served only minimal time in a correction facility.

He lay inert on the drag, amid much upborne night dust which caused Grotteau to want to follow the party out of curiosity. It seemed to him that the man was either headed for Farralones, and that he had fallen afoul of a knife fight or a gun duel…The one man carryilng the lanterns in hand, and afood, had thrown its light on the victim, walking along beside the drag. From a clump of sage, Grotteau, who had swung around, continued to watch as the man was taken from the traverse and lifted by two of Farralone's staff. He was was carried to a cot inside the tent. The flaps were dropped down. A third man—looiked like Clem—was dispatched to bring water from the tunnel spring to the triage tent. Grotteau had seen enough; anyway, the tent flap was dropped. His thought then was to help the doctor with medicines, but then the mystique of faith healing took over. Farralones talked about pain medicine but practiced a form of tribal ritualism, rare to the White Man, that brought healing. *No…too much charity*, thought Grotteau, *has a weaking effect on the mind and makes a man's conscience flaccid.*

He remembered a conversation with Igor over claim jumpers. He recalled that in a moment of anger the big man had dotten up out of his wicker chair and struck the porch post with the heavy flat of his hand. "Vell, tats my life…hogbuston money bag…I don give a damp vat anybody is tiniking Dats the short off it. You vant me to come play cards in your hotel…" Grotteau had hoped to bring a clientele to the Hotel. When Igor truck the post a second time, he hammered his boots on the wooden porch. "So I prospect…that is not goot for you" I take my golt dust to the Saloon and pfft…it is gone. Maybe I shoult builten vences again. I hav a claim dot I can holpen, Mister Grotteau."

Stubborn old coot…there in that tent, now lain low. Grotteau turned around and this time returned to his abode in town, behind *The Scorpion*. He penned the mule away for the night. He did not elarn until three weeks later that Igor had caught an eight by eight beam that had slipped from its post in the tunnel he had dug and the heavy timber had struck him on his head. That very day, when Grotteau heard of the news of the head wound, a concussion, the very wagon bearing Igors body rumbled through Mystery, Farralones in Sunday dress and one of his aides, Indian Joe Willow, going with the body to the cemetery. Not infrequently some of the dead were children of four or five years, put down by a dystentery fever or killed by a fall lunder a wagon wheel.

It occurred to Grotteau in his near sleep one night that the early settler Kittricks, whose nugget is said to have inspired a gold stlrike, might join his band of townsmen gold prospectors inside town limits. If Alamayer wanted to protrect his oath of honor to his ancestry in the Shosone tribe, he would have to appeal to the White Man's laws. And the tite deeds now in Grotteau possession held that promise for those so deceived. Grotteau had a prescience of trouble that involved the Indians.

He called on the old renegade. He knew Kittrick had not died. He was the bartender at the **Hard Rock Saloon!** He was a man who understood the hardiness of the Indians. Being a half breed, Almayer also understood the Indian's kind of courage…to take a chance. They were natural gamblers. He was certain that Kittrick, whether in his shanty or at his creek diggings, would try to instigate trouble among the sourdough miners. Almayer, he reasoned, would go over to the Indians' side if push came to shove in any kind of showdown over grave sites.

I found them half drunk ant it was not yet noon, in the shade of lthe **Hard Rock Saloon.** "A good assayer has a sharp eye and knows his rock," he said. He knew about Indian nomads, tribal intermixing, long distant cousins who were enemies living in proximity, cliff dwellers with hoganl people. *Almayer can't stop folks from prospecting,* Grotteau thought. .

Hell get high on peyote, talk them into gamvbling. Indians are natural gamblers. Then well see. Kittrick was aloner with a mind for fantasy, some said a visionary, a Zarathrustan oragcle and sagfel. He kept a rain forest parrot on his shoulder. lhe fed it a grape from his pocket. He did the same when he waited bar. The parrot remained on his shoulder.

Grotteau removed the scoll map from his pocket, it showed configurations of miners who had already bought into the scam. Ghost of past battles did not deter nor phase Kittrick, who ad his own ancestry conquestidores. It was said that the century cactus, because the seven-foot tribal giant was silent, fed little children from its sweet flesh, yet slew many White soldiers with its thorns, while coyotes lurked in the shadows, eyes gleaming, fangs dripping and ready.

After Grotteau has presented his plan to the bartender, Kittgrick with the parrot on his shoulder, he removed a bowie knife from under his shirt and stabbed it into the map on the bar. "There is where you dig. Let chance go with you". Kittrick bent over the map to see where on lthe map the point of the dagger pierced the landscape.

"Yer plainsman's map don't show nohing about land grants...

"I know about them grants, Kittrick. I got a lawyer who also knows how to handle them ancient doc'memts."

Whether or not the old miner fell for Grotteau's scheme was almost irrelevant, for the villagers, maps in hand, had already begun to dig into the streets, under dwellings, along roads, under the board walks and wi now commenced thin certain places of business, the hardware store, for one. These diggings were in defiance of any and all Indian claims to the land as burial sites. In the minds of the miners Groteau had concealed , or rather made scarcely obvious, the desecration that went on. Gold once it had blunted the miners' capacity to distinguish right from wrong, set no bounds, caused no delay, obscured doubts and appeased all sense of danger. The miners were not actually engaged in digging up the town, he begged, creating confusion resolved by good luck in their prospecting.. Grotteau published a missive and had his boy from Frost hand them around to the miners, every miner he could find.

You do yourselves great honor this day by searching for more gold. You honor the village of Mystery. You honor your motive for coming here to find gold. You honor your friends and families back home by continuing the struggle. Dig on, comrades. Signed Reiner Grotteau.

It took the villagers three desperate weeks to destroy the appearances of the village...shapes of board walks, the aspect contours of its several streets and wagon ruts, the mapped corners, The possesssors of gold deeds had dug with fury that consumed ltheir passion. Wagons once used to cart legal ore to Frost stamping mills were put to service again carring sacks of contraband ore to the crusher mills. Mystery had deteriorated into one large undefined, cratered, recklessly shoveled and picked gold digging. With a sort of sanctioned savagery, miners had pried up the sidewalks, the old saloon was almost deserted, with floorboards and and boundation stones from it thrown askant, the floor except where the long bar stood was vandalized. Only the hotel did not show marks of the general depredation and abandon. Harri;man, the hotel coowner with de Vancha, had thrown foundation rocks to one side. He had tunneled uner the spaces between the rooms, his own tunnel mineshaft. He had shouted with great alarm that he had found gold coins, nary a nugget yet in his search by lantern light. Here and there a cry went up that gold had been found within the village. Not one cry, not a single voice mentioned Indian graves, bones and relics of the deceaed. The entire nightmarish scene was a wondrous sight of intentional rapacious vandalism to get at the gold. As to the bones of Indian burial sites, none, it appeared, had yet been found—or so one might have assumed from the shouts of discovery and scattered dilapidation of the diggins.

Harriman's shovel clanked on stones, audible in the lobbly of the hotel, to which he had assigned a Chines pit each to the caretaker and clerk. Out on *Dog Street*, wagon lwheels from time to time rocked as they tried to pass through and among piles of dirt excavated into the mainstreet . Wagon mule traffic, such as there was, twisted around the excavations. It was marvelous what energy and diligence had already produced in the way of diggins. A visible, certain carelessness about the hunt lay everywhere; there was no one to oversee the miners' depredations. Grotteau walked among the holes, pits and small tunnels that had egun to show, like so many large gopher craters on lthe village streets. He encouragfed the miners to **keep at it boys.!** He went into tlhe bar, not completely disrupted at the **Hard Rock Saloon** where two skeptics sat at the remaining table, sipping potato beer and cactus whickey refills. He sat in silence, like a visiting ghost, then left. Merryman, the schoolmaster, had come down to his site and as, Grotteau passed, showed a chunk of ore with a sparkle to it. "Clean yellow gold…no two ways about that!" he exclaimed. Villagers here and there had roped off their diggins. Tents now existsed in the streets. Some villagers who lived in shacks *commuted* to their new old diggins. Clayton Hornsby, the hardware man, refused to tear up the floor to his store; he could make lmore moneyl selling mining tools and foodstluffls to the avaraciousminers, and did sol. Miners who had found gold dust in their pans proceeded to unload themselves of their wealth at Hornsbys .

In their burning imaginations, the villagers expected to find their sacrifices reasonable. The miners' astonishing capacity to picture surging personal gold wealth animated their dinging. God would in some mysterious way honor their noble efforts; they would contribute money to missionaries to the poor if God would bless their work of their hands. Beneath the ruts, and stones, the posts and boards, the flooring and structure walls, the dirt wsa sure to show the elusive dust of gold. The town was sure to become a potential quagmire desert rains came. But bad wether did not enter into their fixity of purpose.

In evidence were the picks and shovels, here and there aheelbarrow, to testify to the damning lust for the precious metal as the miners, in possession of reality yet mad with their frenzied search, vandalized the town. They dug with a rapacicity akin to warfare against nature. Prospectors in name, vandals in actuality as they extended their claims. They left llittle space for the errand-bound footprints of villagers, the horses an wagons past their sites, making the village a ghostly replica of past life. The **Hard Rock Saloon** was quiet, as miners worked within, not at poker, but at groping in the dark for the elusive gold beneath its flooroards. They clung to the hope furnished by Grotteau's map. They dug everywhere with the fervor of termites, agents of the devil searching, hunting for a place to escape from life. Field tlents and open-fire soup pots, campfires on the streets, few as they were, became common sights in the next weeks. Alleys of the village glowed in reflecte firelight durinng the long nights. A wealthy man from the East who had spoken kindly of his wife collecion of expensive porcelain and linens, had lain claim to his own spot, by means of Grotteau's map. He had hunkered down to find...gold.

About two hundred of the villagers had by now siezed upon the luck offered by Grotteau. It gave them a sense of belonging, a cure to lostness in the great desert spaces. God as their dedication, their occultic worship. It had given to many of the villagers, roots in Mystery. Not a few of them discovered what they felt was like the ancient Holly Grail, this time gold. Here and there they would exult in a find of richly laden gold ore.

Jeremiah Fazakerly provided a constant trail of water to the miners, some of whom crushed the ore where they dig to washis in frying pans, find find in the slurry what they had dreampt of…god. The water carrier's trade was brisk..two fifty gallon canvas bags brought from up-creek—water to drink that was not muddy. This transport of a vital commodity worried Grottesau, for should the system break down for any reason, the town itself would be imperiled with drought. kept him busy. Fazakerly would at times offer a swig of fresh water to a mliner from a small wicker covered flask, to smarten the hard work. Much superstition prevailed among the miners. They looked for signs to confirm and reinforce their luck. Thy remembered the Indian outrage no more.

Gold fever rose to a caricaturing frenzy. Old men squandered their last years on the luck at finding a nugget, younger men dug by lantern light into the night, the metalic sounds of pick blades striking stones and shovels scraping and caressing the red dirt, all steel blades filled the still air that hung with a certain calm over the village, as if a disaster stood but a short ways off, waiting for a cryptic signal to engulf the vullage in its final gasp of lust for the precious metal. Mystery had become a mining pit, a hole for gophers , a metamorphosed town of hardrock and slurry mining, a collection of random holes and burrow pits where the stubborn and voracious villagers continued at their task like dark and heartless figures upon a plain of vast annihilation. For the village of Mystery was dying.

Important to their survival was the disinterment of the bones of Indians come upon and dug up by accident. Grotteau walked among his miner encampments, finding in numerous places the talked-about stained bones of the Red Man's dead ancestors. He had only a chauvinist's pity for their plea of sacred ground. He could not afford to submit to the Indian shibboleth of the untouchable grave. He had with Ludheim's aid, proclaimed the town his by inference, by deed historically, by document…land entitlements of the diggins sold to the affected mliners.

Grotteau was usually nowhere to be found in the open. He had turned loose the forces the hell. There as about these frenzied labors an awsome mystery...a pathetic and empty madxness, the irrationality of man's lust for gold.

"Can't find all the gold there is here in town...glory holes placed just outside...down there, the street, I know for sure." Every; site with promise was a *glory hole.*

"Seen it in yer dream".

"Been there m'self stranger, Lemme show you." In this like manner, often ran both the conversation and skepticism together, and a faulty optimisn, laced by a hope that verged on the superstitious.

The villagers permeated the air with their campfire smoke, smells of death, and the lingering stench of ancient murders. They searched now for the master of the debacle, which they refused to admit they; ;had conjoined and invited into their lives. The smells ladened the air. Bloof from fights, constant quarrels broke out, and the scent of blood for sensitive noses. They were not the noses, however of humans; thy were the noses of brush wolves, feral animals, dogs, wild, undomesticated packs of dogs that constantly roamed the countryside in search of scant food. Even amongst themselves hunger would do in the weakest and they would feed, cannibalistic-like on one of their own kind. The were drawn to Mystery by the smells both of cooking meat, fresh blood and decay.

At sundown on the seventh day after opening ecelebration when warm desert air had intensified the smells, about twenty of these feral animals, so large a pack as unehard of....led by a vicious, mad coyote—who could say if it was rabid—ran nto the village and began tot attack the villagers. It was the second of such attacks, and the larger of the two. Most of the villagers has no immediate and nearby shelter to run to but faced the snarling, gnashing, yelping—savage dogs, as if relased from hell or by the spirits of the buried Indians allegedly whose graves the miners had opened.

The villagers used what they could find at hand to defend themselves. They seized boards, rocks, shovels and picks to ward off the most vicious of the fanged, snarling pack. The famished animals, excited by smells of cooking and freshblood, bared their fangs, salivating and seizing, thrusting at random, biting many viciously until blood ran on villagers bodies, torn sleeves, pants and bloodied hands. The attack was heinous and unremitting. Dr. Farralones would have many open wounds to stitched closed at his field hospital.

A miner under attack picked up a shovel and swung wildly at the nearest, anohther rained one of the animals, sending it off yelping to die on the street. bests. Carcasses of dead dogs lay about the village streets. Ohers yelped with pain and wounds inflicted by villagers. Yet they the dogs continued their hungry attack. Ahrieks of miners in pain rent the twilight. The dust, the onfusion,the shouts and cries of pain and curses against the cruel animls continued for almost a a full hour. The anlimals kept on attacking because they found no relief for their ravenous hunger. The miners had to defend themselves by improvised means. Here and there a villager would pluck a firebrand from a campfire and, waving it wildly over his head, keep the snarling, yelping, howling beast a bay. These roaming dogs howled with anguish and rage when struck, always baring their fangs. The more courageous villagers with shovels, hay forks from the general store, split boards, bats of timber struck out at whatever they could, loting their weapons above the snapping and voracious canine jaws.

The counter attack began against animals abandoned on purpose, or, their owners having died, they were left to roam. By instinct they joined in packs, of which this was one of the largest. Once divertedand the animals driven off, they found others villagers to attack. In in Mystery the beastial convergence consumed other campfires, other unsusuepcting miners who were not at all used to such feral savagery. Who could have predicted the sudden appearance of the feral dogs, except the Indians. Perhaps they had put a curse on the village and the attack was an answer of the gods who were angry at the desicrationof the graves, especially since they had been warned.

As if by a silent command, the pack inexplicably ran from their bloody assault into the desert, having foraged what foodstuffs that were not protected. Many of the villagers sustained dog bites, some ldeep gashes that would infect causing death. Cactus whiskey, what was left from the celebration, was the only remedy at hand. The village as quickly as the attack had begun, fell into a deathly quiet, except for the moans of those injured by animal fangs. Serveral days after the unexpected attack, without medicine, three of Mystery's residents ould lapse into a coma and painful from rabies. Dr. Farraloned did not see them; he refused to give them false hope. He had no antidotes to administer. Some of the animals had been rabid.

When the dogs ran from the village, they went away almost as quickly and silently as they had come. They disappeared over the desert sands in the direction of Triangle, another mining community. The folks in Frost had guns; the animals instinctively knew this. There was angry cursing that night among the diggins, for now the miners' small pieces of and were their assaulted campfire homes. All of this might not have happened had they not thrown away their weapons of defense at the urging of Grotteau. A great thunder began to rumble in the distance of the part of the defenseless villagers.

The ordeals of the villagers were not over. There came a knifing—had the law been inforced—a murder committed in self-defense over boundry claimsIt would have gone to court. would hve gone to court. Sy pulled a sheathed knife, thinking that he had killed a claim jumper. Witnesses to this overt murder kept quiet lest they alsos be attacked in revenge. There were other singular incidents where rage ruled the hearts of the villagers…and especially over the frustration of not having found the promised richess….

On the day after the mauranding dogs had made their salivating, bloody, fanged, murderous attack upon the village, Jeremiah returned from Frost with his burro and his usual two bags of fresh water. Pronged mining in the creek had made the local water unpotable. He brought back with him a frightening story that did not take long to meterialie. He had leaned that a gang of terrorist-robbers, intent upon laying claim to Mysterys gold for themselves were headed for the village. They were encamped near the spring, Jeremiah'ssource for fresh water.

He had overheard them talking. In an excited voice, he announced to whomever he sold lis water to what was abvout to take place. He shouted out the news along *Dog Street*, which had all but disappeared in the moonscape prospecting digs and badlands mounds of exscavated dirt. He warned the villagers to get ready for the mad invaders, like the dogs. They had heard that there was stuff, not food but gold, for the taking on the streets. Robbery would be their intention, death for those who resisted..

To interrupt the vison in a heavy electrical storm, the ligntning flashed with night thunder, piercing the desert blackness like exploding stars that rode over the cloud drenched desert highlands. The night mauruders flinted their saddle horns, bridle bits, stirrups as the gang came in tandem, accompanied by thunderheads that rolled with their crescendo and flashs in sword pierces like mica flakes that foamed onward.

In a mafter of half an hour there rode fifteen men into the village, without fanfare, gunfire or soldier bravado, while the harsh clatter of hooves like the wind spun through the pine branches and the gallop of the horses hammered against the night's muted silence. On they came, no shouts, the avengers, the triers of conquest, the curriers of the night's reckoning, whilest thrushes of stormdrench began to pummel and dimple the dampening sands and night birds screeched for distant cover and the fresh rain twirled the juniper needles of the town's few trees.

They were not outlaw brigands. They were the Indians from Coyote Butte.. On they came, without Indian yells, in pursuit of a dark mission, down into the village, ghosts without faces, gloved hands , llinked together by a dark camaderie, feathers whipping wildly as they rode. The night had ushered them in. They rode as if to answer vengeance's call. They wove through the pits, amongst the tents and fabrications of gold-crazed miners and maddened goldseekrs, the profligate of future auguries, the lost in past persuasions, for they were prisoners of their fortune. Some here and there cringed, others huddled, loners crouched as they watched, their eyes following through the night-rain blackness, observ the shapes that wended among the mounds of dirt and colums of shoveled rock and sand. They arrived as fast as they rode, hate summoned, weapons ready and eager for a fight. They were the avengers. The village of Mystery had never known such a gathering of fringers of harm, misery-bearers, callers to justice as they were. Like a meteorite spark, the Indians set fire to the wagon shed where de Vancha's sons worked, where the dance had taken place. They fired up what had begun as a church, a tent house on the perimeter of the village, abandoned with a crude cross nailed to its roof gable. They waved their carbines and revolvers in the air, shooting them off to create terror in the miners. Nobody dared to stop them – except Grotteau. He stood in the center of the village with a torch in his hand and screamed for them so stop. He wanted to parlay.

This was no time to bring de Vancha into the fray; the Mexican knew nothing about gold stocks, was obsessed with being the major honcho of the village, couldn't cared less for the troublesome miners and let stray dogs into the village compound. Besides, he was frightened out of his caloused sould that he faced an imminent an insurrection by the miners. His only defense was a weapon which, like all the others, he had abandoned. His only saving attribution was that he had relatives in Mexico who catered to rich American tourists. No, this was Grotteau's baby. This was not Mexico City

This time the Indians came with blood in their eyes, vengeance to wreak, to make the miners pay who had unearthed the bones of their ancestors. Their throats shrieked with battle cries, as the iminers looked on helpless and filled with terror. . Most of them had either thrown their guns into the night fires Grotteau had ignited, or they owned no fire arm to begin with. Som quantity, fewer than one hundred, had found their way into the hands of the revolutionary priest, Father Xavier, for his squads sof rvolutionary faithful down in Begota, whom he called Christ's emissaries, *Emissrios de Cristo.* Miners remembered Grotteau's promise: "If any of them savages give you trouble, you just come to me." The savages had come rightly enough, but to avenge the desecration of their ancestors' graves. The cause in their minds was both religious and noble and deserved to be redressed. He further had tried to reassure them:

"You need not fear on your part. I have a way with the savage beast."

There he stood, his mouthed interdiction lost in the noise and night dust. From the balcony a shot rang out and one of the Indian riders fell. The prostitute had come to the defense of the miners. One of the Indians flung a burning brand into the front window of the hotel and it began to burn. A seond shot pierced the noise and the dark form of the woman fell across the balcony railing.

Surely they could count on Grotteau's diplomacy with the Indians—at some other time. Tonight they continued to come on, down into the village, circling around the shacks and miners' tents, thrown up where they had begun to prospect on their assigned parcels of land.

Grotteau had told them at the outset: "you will not have to defend yourselves from spirits of the departed, whether or not they are Indians." **The Scorpion** had carried the names of those who had bought into his scheme and already there were approaching two hundred... two hundred miners of Mystery who were ready to lay down their lives for gold, an exchange that would have satisfied the Indians admirably, bones for bones.

This self-appointed representatve of Tryphon, god of peace ,wielded more power than they conceivably ever could over their singular provincial destinies. What if they found both gold and Indian bones mingled in one place? Who would defend them, the diggers... the spirits of the bones, the man of Gold Grotteau or the defrocked priest revolutionary? Or miners frm Frost,but that would not happen.

There had been words of caution against excessive penitence. After all, the priest had promised that God blesses the obedient with wealth, profit in the end. But not the end by the shaft of an Indian arrow. Grotteau remember the sudden arrow that had penetrated Farralones.

He could not tell if these marauders carried bows and arrows; they had shown their carbines to the villagers.

Miners remembered how Grotteau had blessed them as a grand gesture. "May the blessings of Baal inherit your house!" That Grotteau had not a clue as to show Baal was did not matter. He was a god on their side. He had taken the time and trouble to show the miners, where their parcels were located…by his map gotten from Almayer's assay office…he who, ironically, had led the Indian charge down from the Butte against the villagers. They had their pieces of paper, their title deeds to the plots of ground where they were to dig, as was fitting for miners of spirit and clever enterprise. All gold sites lay within the parameters of the main vein of gold beneath the village, as plotted and attested to by assayer expert Mr. Almayer. As for the man himself, he had never forgotten nor forgiven the miners' trespass on the Indian graves and they, for their part, had not forgotten the years that he had kept the gold secret, dark and hidden from them, out of loyalty to the enemy. For it was plain that the Indians were the enemies of the miners, made so by disputed land and emboldened by the Indian renegade Almayer, one of their kind.

Yet was it not always so. Sy Paramenter, when the sy;mbol of permanence, the hotel , was burning, rekindled the fire. He rode into the flamelight, jumped down from his horse and seizing a brand from the fire, had waved it above his head as if some burning talismanic emblem. He shouted the word: "Death lives in the present. May your god burn your souls and condemn your greed!" He flung the brand like a burning arrow over their heads into the desert sands of the road. Thereupon several of the men seized him another shouted, "He's kept our gold from us. let him be accursed, damn him! damn him!"

"He's not Grotteau!" There was much confusion in the darkness.

Miners, braving possible death, sprang up from their holes and trenches and shouted, "Hang him, hamg him!" Instead, they found Almayer mounted on a dappled horse and pulled him from the saddle. They bound the man, whipped his horse into the night, while another raised the tongue of a wagon, "Hang him!..hang him!" came the cries.

It was Tiny Tyler and Damon Jackson who raised the shaft of a wagon. It was Kirsten who tied the man's hands behind him. By mistake they readied Grotteau to hang...he would had already written his nes story of the death and sacrifice and cunning cruelty, kindled by the passion for gold, tlhat had brought about Alamalye'rs near lynching.

Were it not for Farralones and his compassion without a focus in the mahem, the liquor-inflamed miners would surely have lynched Grotteau—then after him---Indian leader and assayer, right there on the spot, that night. But they did not do so. Grotteau could only commend them for their...foreearance! What sly ironies fate will sometimes mouth! The jackal telling the wild dog he does well to howl.

All of this action seeming of little consequence, Weatherlich, a former civil servant bureaucrat turned gold panner, moved in on Grotteau. "You're a fraud, you sonofabitch!" Only the whiteness of Grotteau's excited face and hands were visible. He had somewhere found a buggy whip which he held in his right hand, ready to use if Weatherlich or anyone else should attempt an assault against him. "You'd let Almayer be hanged so you could own the whole town, damn your lying soul. You got our guns in the bargain." This again was Weatherlich.

"So? Guns...no varmints around here..and us folks who are honest...well, most—we can handle claim jumpers, the only varmint there is. A shovel longside the head does for most."

"Violence it is tlhen...and manslaughter," said Wonderlich. He turned his horse about, wove through the crowd and was gone. Someone undid Almayers hands and loosed the noose around his neck...or everyone there knew that he came close to turning slowly in the wind.

Whilest these laments, these strictures and warnings, benefits and entitlements were circulating through the minds of miners confrond by the reality of an Indian Attack, Grotteau was running about with his torch, shouting at the Indians to stop...stop...think of what you are doing. Stop!" He ran about on Dog Street like a mad man, fever-crazed . He could not find his mule...driven off by the noise and commotion

144

no doubt. There was nothing he did that night that even smacked of a parlay, much less a realistic effort to put an end to the Indian raid. They Indian party of warning continued to circle through the streets of Mystery, overturning tents, leaping the bodies of huddled and crouching miners, striking a blaze to one miner's shack, throwing balls of pitch-flame into open pits where the miners had excavated for gold, running amuck over mounds of dirt, causing their horses to leap the graves, so it was assumed, of the buried ancestors. Grotteau's reassuring words must have returned to some. "I approve your choice…For an alternate site, if you prefer, sir, you may dig in the alley called *Alone*, directly behind the Assayer's shack."

Ah, glory! A baptismal font…a coat of paint for the sacristy." Already the miners dreamed of glory in New Helvitia from gold newsy excavated, released up by the bones sof an Indian aqncestor. There were few among them who did not believe that they would ever strike it rich, that the village of Mystery had cheated the first miners by squatting on graves of the Indians, as sif to conceal the immense wealth that lay beneath the settlement. They mindlessly, like disciples of a cultic leader, followed their leader Reiner Grotteau, elditor of ***The Scorpion***…as if it were a printed creed for their blessing and guidance.

Father Xavier was not the least of those engaged in the enterprise. He needed gold for his Bolivian revolutionaries, howsoever the means for getting it. He had already been able, by the se4recy of night, to truck one wagonload of guns down through Mexico, crosssing Venezuelan borders into Bolivia, against all odds. But then God's storehouse of blessisngs was rich and unexpected. Grotteau was not pleased that the miners had not killed any Indians during the raid so he had, in a way, put an end to violence by the gun. He had managed to encourage violence by other means. Grotteau caught sight of Almayer in the flame light of the burning shack, with him some three dozen or more Indian brothers, shouting Indian cries, feathers floating , war paint on the faces of some, their costumes both white man's and Indian. They were in no mood to confront amiably the huddled miners. Three of Almayer's brothers were wearing the masks of the coyote, the bear and the eagle, intended to strike greater fear and repentance in the minds of the miners.

In the middle of Dog Street, almost opposite *The Scorpion* office, the Indians hastily erected a tipod of poles from which they hung an effigy of the White Man. theyseized clothing—miners hat, coveralls stuffed with tent canvas—and they set it afire. One of them, a medicine man, on his pony, circled the burning effigy and cried out words in Indian dialect. The others began a frenzied dance, some of them, afoot, striking the burning effigy with switches of sage. dancing their own frenzied cadence about the dangling improvided figure. Then as if by some silent signal, probably by their Shaman, the cries ceased.

Almayer stepped forward. On his face was a look of cruel pleasure in the scene. He must have realized that his life might be in danger at any moment, thus he had armed himself with a pistol hid leneath his loose vest and leather coat. Ludheim . His compositor, Ludheim, possessed of close knowlede of the German, knew that the boss, publisher Grotteau, did not believe in the sacrifice made by the villagers; always, someone would rise to challenge his power and his authority. ..not while the battle over the bones was going on. Ludheim, by a strange intuiton he could ot explain, knew that Alehouse moonshine whiskey had never flowed so freely as on this night. Yet...where was it s maker, Alehouse...murdered, according to priest Xavier. Until this moment Daamon Jackson, the arsonist, confessedly a firebrand, had remained a silent figure in the background. However, he was no longer silent. "Let th' murderer swing! swing! Curse on his soul!" He spat. From somewhere...nobody knew exactly where...a sob was again heard, weeping of a grown man. Not everyone hated Grotteau;...or Almayer, for that matter. yet enough of the villagers belieced in the merit of their mission that they would legin again to dig into the streets of the village, with all their passion and intenslity of greed. lManwhile the vision of Almayer hanging like a phantom in the shadowy light was not lrealized, in fact was soon forgotten by their return to drinking and rowdy exhibition of cxelebrate their anarchy. watched much of the meylee from the Scorpion. Realizing that all during this ritlual ceremony to restore the dignity of the bones, the miners tried to keep their distance, in deed, to hide where they could.

Almayer said, "Whate man covets our land. It will always be our land...for his use. This is our last warning. This is Indin burial land. This is sacred ground. White man takes out land, he offers gold when there is no gold under the land. If there is gold under his hogans, it is our gold. The bones of our ancestors are of greater value than white mans gold. Their spirit voices cry out—***revenge!***"

Grotteau spoke: He raised one hand and turned slowly so that all could witness the desperation on his face and the humility in his gesture, in the dancing flamelight. "Wait a minute...you Puyutes..." which they were not..."you Shoshone...Snake tribesmen and Blackfeet, Navajo lovers of freedom—gold is a gift from the Great God...The land is also his gift!"

"It belongs to our brothers who lie asleep under the land, their spirits gone to the great beyond," chanted Almayer.

The Man of Medicine, the Coyote man, stooped down and drew a rought outline of the town of Mystery in the sand of the road with a burning stick. "This is where they are buried." He included the entire village on the sand.

"That is our village, Coyote!"

"Indians not your friends when you dig up graves of our ancestors."

"We got deeds...these folks here pay money...or donate a gun for their diggings. We find bones, we will put them in a box and bury them again."

"You do not bury the sacred bones of our ancestors. They do not move when they are dead. Our god will punish you."

"Punish us, god? By God you are a Indian after all!"

The kachina spirits began their dance again..The effigy laws all burned up, only the rope remained. The Indian who lwore the bear mask took from a leather bag some bones which he dropped into the dirt within the tripod, and with lhands full of sand he ringed the ones with a ridge of land. He blessed the sand-drawn icon with an incantation. The Coyote Indian danced around the tripod again, followed by all lhis tribal brothers, if in fact they were his clansmen. The Coyote howled into the starry sky. He howled, bent over, hopped on the flats of his feet, the fury ringlets on his ankles clacking the movements of his feet. He paused, clapped his hands, raised them skyward. He spoke to the thirty or so townsfolks whose fear had ab agted somewhat when they saw that the Indian's intent was not to murder them but to protest— with a *threat* of annihilation....

The tight fists of some of the miners clenched deeds issued to them, or raisisng their their deeds over their heds, they strutted about the burned-out effigy. Others dragged knocked down tents toting them over to the effigy to rekindle the blaze. Tvald Thorald ran to the board walk where, his deed indicated, gold lay beneath the planks. "It says it is not here vere good is I dig. I dig with much fire." An arrow caught him in one shoulder and he fell. This was a case for Dr. Farralones up the canyon who lhad sustained the same sort of wound. . Several miners rushed to his side, one keeping out a wary eye for a drawn bow..

Coyote spoke words: "White Man travels like buffalo, like the deer herd. You do not stay in one place. Our people have been on the land for many generations...many moons...till the rocks split open like melons and the sage blooms purple wild many times. You will violate the graves of my ancestors and of our brothers here. Then you will move on , like the buffalo. It is true, I have seen it. You do not bribe the Indian out of his ancestors' land."

"Look, Man of Medicine..." Grotteau's voice was belligerent and thick with whiskey. "We got education here. Civilized men understand you Indians. I know. I have seen men with greed for soul and gold for hands."

"He says there is no gold under Mystery," spoke out Siegfried, the carpenter. "We mean to dig it up."

"Papers no good. White Man puts trust in papers, not in land, not in hearts of his chief. He hides his heart. He hides his thoughts."

"Our intents are good. White people come here to see...to invest, to give to the land. By God, I'm not going to let them vest in vain. I will not cheat my white brothers!"

"They are not your kin…like the Indian. Tomorrow they will go away with the winds that blow the sand."

"You cheat the gods that watch. Youl steal rest from the dead. You steal honor from man who lives. We keep the land." These were Almayer's words.

"The hearts of these White Men are good," said Grotteau.

"You do not dig in the village for gold," said the Man of Medicine.

Grotteau lswung his shuge nugget on a chain in la hypnotic manner, before the kying firelight. The chain was made of glass veads, bird bones, acorns from Frost and bits of potery, giving the gesture vague symbolic meaning. The miners stood amazed, their faces filled with wonder and disquiet. Grotteau it seemed had become almost a part of the Indian band. His gaunt face was drawn, pinched like an apoplectic vinctor in a dance of death. His arms begane rigid, he screamed and when he had made his way amongst the Indians as the White Man's shaman, he plunged into the midst of the renewed fire as if to show he was impervious to pain-death. A wild scream came from his mouth, and then followed silence and the smells of scorched hair and blurned linen. A miner standing nearby threw sand on him to put out the flames on his clothes. He was burned, but he was heroic as a White shaman. He showed no pain on his face. The miners all believed in him, he having mesmerlized him to believe they saw his skeleton frame standing in the midst of the pyre. But that was their imagination, frenzied by lust for gold, fear of the Indians and wideyeed, incredulity of death's struggle over the tableau they were witnessisng.

Ludheim was only watching until now, He did not wish to enter into the goings on.. A superior logic held him back and dictated into his mind a kind of pitying incredulity. The flames were increased wih more tent canvas and some sticks and boards from the sidewalk. Grotteau's imitation of suicide impressed the Indians and in fact, produced a kind of calm, a stunned quiet before death. The village was wrapped in the wonder of evil , as if they could dispel violence and honot with ceremony, and sincantations.

The Indians by twos and threes went to their target symbol of White supremacy and set fire a secibd tune to the Continental Helotel , the proud queen of the village. Beside it stood the empty ***Hard Rock Saloon***. That too caught fire. Its kegs of potato beer, Almayers draughts of whiskey were gone to the miners by theft in the confusion. Both bluildings were quickly engulfed in flames that hissed thoughthe damp wood. The town was as sif struck by a plague. Nobody showed to put out the fire. What could they do?

The Indians resumed their rampage. They overturned every visible sack, box and board, every pan, shovel and tunnel entrance. They shot into tunnel openings like killing prairie dogs without a struggle. They punctured Jeremia's water vags with bullet holes, spilling precious water into the sands. ' Several Indians astride their ponies rode into the remnants of the Wagon Works, the plundering into the merchandist store they ransacked at random. They looted for themselves what pleased them, with much breast bating and jingling of roweled spurs. They killed one old miner who held his shovel up in front of his face. The attacker put a bulled through the shovel blade like atarget. The miner's body fell into the pit of his diggings.

The wild use of guns was designed to terrorize the villagers, which it accomplished. Not a man among the residents but wished that he had not thrown his gun into the pyre flames on those nights of Grotteau's barter and sacrifice. The lone prostitute at the Continental had stood on the balcony, before flames had engulfed the hotel and picked off one or two of the murauding Indians. Blandly, little Jimmy Tyler had waited for his kind of help. From behind the façade of the ***General Merchandise Store*** he pitched sticks of dynamite like firecrackers into the street, burning fuses timed to explode as riders passed. They only burned. Yet he he knocked two men off their mounts and killed their horses amidst shrill cries. Miners ran out and flung the Indians to the ground, where they could, and roped them for hostages. Not all escaped to tell the tale of the failed assault on the predators of Indian graves in the village of Mystery.

What probably took the edge off of the Indian demonstration of loathing for the Whites was when one or two miners carried guns and threw them into the flames, and Grotteau prompely handed each a claimstake agreement and map. This act of surrender of arms, a universal sign of surrender,had not mollified the Indians, for the desecration continued. They began to talk among themselves. But the confrontation was not yet ended' this was only a lull. The Indians were not satisfied. Farralones was seen loading the wounded Tvald onto a horse, to take him back to his field hospital.

In the middle of this orgy , the moon rose in the eastern sky, wild, piercing yells of the Commanche kind caused all, the Indians included, to look into the distance. What they saw was an immense white stallion with an unidentified Indian astride him, pacing up and down outside the village, whereupon, as if by a signal, the rider on the white stallion mount entered the village. He rode up to the remainig fire and dismolunting, he four times pitch sand into the moonlight. He rode up to the flames. The people, White and Indians now mingled, hastily drew back. The rider again pitched a handful of sand into the air, speaking in Indian dialect: The rider on the white stallion then departed, as some kind of spectre. Indians examined the ground marked by the hooves of the white stallion. They discovered that the rider had thrown ashes into the air. With ghastly connect, they realized that the ashes were those of a human sacrifice. This revelation was kept within the Indian awareness. Grotteau thought only of sand. Tthat was enough for him.

Grotteau, being the opportunist that he was, arose to speak, "I tell you, I proclaim to you that this prize...again he held alift the nugget by its chain, of long buried gold is yours for the asking. Ours is sacred ground...made sacred y the wealth that lies under Mysterys streets and structures. You luckless poor, thie time is ripe for your chance to get rich by with a shovel in your hands. Dig...for tonight will be the start of your trail to wealth. Dig and your labors will not be in vain." Standing like a priest in pentitent humility and commutation before them, Grotteau drank from a cup a communion of cactus whiskey No one suspected the true source of the poisonous brew—Aleman's casks. Grotteau showed on his face the fundamental nature of his cruelty. He had several bottles of the brew, which he passed around allowing even the Indians to drink. For they had congregated, still restless with retributive rage and tribal vengeance against the White Men of the village.

Grotteau then did an amazing thing to impress the Indians, who immediately thought of him as a mortal who could not be hurt. Grotteau walked through the flames...but so hastily he did pass tghrough that not a stitch of hisclothing caught fire. All who had watched him were greatly impressed, for the moment. The thought must have occcured to even these Indians that he was a god or thought he was a god. In imitation of the ghostly rider on the white stallion, Grotteaul stooped downt four times and scooped ashes from the fire and tossed them into the air to signify his closeness to the Indians... that he understood them and shared their knowledge of death and sacred honor.

"Dig—you men of courage!" he shouted to them. He waved wildly the deed he would give to a miner before the eyes of the Indians—to any miner who had not surrendered his firearm. He would amaze the Indians out of their assumption of the White Man's total evil. The depravities of Indian warfare had their own histories. His inebriate voice filled *Dog Street*. "The fire water is yours. Drink all of it. This here's a treat for yer bad lives here. I read it in yer faces."

Grotteau felt eloquent; yet still unknown, or unobserved by him, the villagers had begun to hate him. "Friends and strangers...time for a little speech...I ant going noplace. I'll be here tomorrow, the nexrt day after that...till this town becomes one big digging, our town, your town, ...and the gov'mint's town, and my town."

The saloon keeper, and sometimes sheriff, Kittrick walked into the firelight, guns at his hips, a smile of regret, evil politeness, his hand fidgety. He removed one pistol, blew into the muzzle and returned it to its holster as if he had given warning the did not intend to comply with Grotteauy's guns-for-peace exchange. He walked away. Grotteau had defused the threat of Indians attack...this time . As if with one accord, they simply mounted up and rode away into the night, toward Coyote Butte.

A small party of villagers consisting of Siegfried Hartman, Taylor Klemsey, the wood carrier and Jeremiah Fazakerly, water peddler, formed a funeral party. No cleric was present; religion was only attempted in Mystery. These collected others along the way and In mock pity and sorrow for Almayer, they wended their wake hrougfh the mainstreet and out to the pioneer cemetery where jnseen hands, perhaps Indians had dug a shallow grave for the real Almayer. Gottlieb had had the time to knock together a coffin that morning. And in lmock ceremony the cortege bore over a mule the body of Almayer, knifed silently mid the commotion by an Indian—and now to be lain in his lrave. Siegffied mutered what sounded like a prayer in German. The others said not a word. Sand sifted over the ground, a redtialed hawk floated high in the hotwindy sky. Harman produced from his burro a cross of two boards wound together with rope . He had written on it in charcoal, rather recklelssly—*Almayer, flesh to bones, Mystery, 1892.* He planted it at the head of the grave with a few blows of his shovel. The cortege filled in the grave and they all rode back to the village. Almayer's Indian rothers picked up trail and scent as if half-wild which some of the villagers considered themseles to be, and that the funeral had in part redeemed them from their sacriledge of Indian burial sites. At least the wild lanimls would not paw on Almayer's grave. There was, to them, the villagers, as much meaning and solemnity in the mockery as there was in the reality, for their minds had been fashioned by tradition more than by substance.

"Jes rememver what Almayer said oncet—the life is in the rocks." That reminiscence would hve to dofor burials rites. The funeral party memers went their several ways, back to their diggins, who knew where?

THE PLAN, THE
CONNECTIONS

Father Exavier was an independent soul., the cloth had liberated his movements but not his conscience. He had arrived by Crutchfield Stage from San Francisco to over see things, He said no more had he settled into a room at the Hotel payhing sin lacvance from the coffer of the church, tto do its bisomess. 'No one thought to question the reason for his being in Mystery, perhaps to save mens souls frp,m damnation but then he was snot an evangel…something far more simister was afoot. As sone of the least of citizensw in the village I had a certain immunity from suspicion. He had arrived, settled into a room at the hotel, He was a contact for Jungle Fighters in Nicarfagua and as such was assigned the burden and pjob of collcting the pay;ment therefore, in the form of Mother Lode gold. Who else was involved, I did not know…but I had suspicions. Max Ludheim would be gthe bvest candidate for this secfetive task. the Ammunition and weapons when the funds were gather, to vbe purchased in San Francisco, a days ride away.

Where he had gotten his ;money I cdidl not know, but I was certain that LI heard wagons at night rumbling over the Cturchfield stage road to San Francisco. Perhaps it was my imagination. If Ludheim was involved I would know it in due time. After the first day, I saw him on the street, Dog Stret, I never saw him gain with lhis brace of pistols.

They gathere dusk down in the dank shadows of His Vault doutless. Meanwhile, I concentrated on my task: i had become something of a compositor adept at plucking letters from the California type trays and filling them in my tyupe rule, line by line before instersion in the chase frame, ter which II leveld them with la marble slab and block of wood and locked them up for the edition run. That was the gist of my job. I lalso had tgo redistribut the tyupe, with the help of a boy lnamed Hank, who went to school in Frost. I put a sign above the chest for Hank: **Flip your os and Es intos the tray/Maksing spie is snot your job today.** –a spill of scrambled type.

All of this business had nothing to do withs the rujumble of wagosns. Not until I ldislcov dered that tos lmy grat sufrprise and fear there was growing a cche of weapons on the south side of tonw, nunder the lee of a graat redstone ocornicle. The wagons I lheard on that road at niht were bringing in weapons from San Francisco. But the spriest had made no move that suggested he was takine up a collction for the purchase of guns, ammunition and bandoleers for Nllicarguan insurgents againstg Dictator Manuel Noriega.

The priest ina storm came into Grotteaus office one day and.and for some undisclosed reason began to cite a case he knw of wherein a victim was tied to a waterwheel and plunged round ad round repeatedly until he went mad and throwing himself beneath the huge wheel was crushed to death. Was the priest a bringer of life with such a story. I happened to hear his recount and was astounded, even for my ohyojg years. I went outside, free from the smells sof ink, grease, kerosene and mould, to filli my longues with the lfog bank of the morning and mistcovered, frozst grozen desert high country hills lnear gto the village. This was my sanity trip; I agreed with Grotteau that it was a fantasic lcountry to live in. What I did not know was that the Priest had found the body of a moonmshiner in a cave above the town where he had been busy ;making moonshine for over a year and selling it to the Indians.

The priest had gained the confidence of one or more of the Shoshones who lives in the mountains hereabout, having avillageover the ridge. The priest had taken exception to the sale of whiskey to the

Indians, first and fcoremost, but also to the charge for his illegal product, lby lwhich he was growing rich. Who lhad killed the moonshiner? That would be a question for months to come, even with the Sheiriff and two of his dputies examining the crime scehe. ;It was, the murder, a prlude to other acts sof violence. By th;em it appeared that Ranier Gotteau and the German lLudhim had certain plans for gaining rlichess apart from the gold.

Ludheim was fired with the fire of a heathen warlord and the ways of a l fugitis,;l although there was nothing about lhim toat betrayed a cdriminal past. Ludheim was suave and intelligent, handsome in face and lblack beard with eyes that squinted as in a strong sunlight. He was a man who would defend his territory, his diggins.. Hisboot flootfalls were had on the wooden boardwalk. LLHe literally kicked upen the door to the press office where I was at work. He held a lantern up before his face and struck a slongstemmed match to it. He was aggressive in that way.

S too damn dark in here.

Ludheim fathomed the white mans lust for gold, likening it to the battle spirits sof all warriors who loved th fray but lacked the white mans lust for gold, a craving that as loathsome. El Alcalde, on the other hand, shared his love for gold and whiskey lwith his Spanish Conquistidore ancestors, a craving that brought him closer to his gods. On this day, he had chosen for his mission to find or ssubstantiate Kittriks early claim of a one pound neugget at indian Head Rock. Alaayers shack was the reposistory of tales of losst hope and reality of grain. Almayer, himself part Indian, owned vision, understood rliddles, trickster deceptions with th Indians sense of cunning ande clever deceit. He knew almost as if by instinct whether or not ans ore sample contained anyh gold worth extraction.

One day he saw Grotteau approach. The Scorpions editor pulled a small bluckskin bag from one pocket. He looked into thel eyes of a man said to possess secret poweres whlich l;none bsut a few had ever discerned. There was in Grotteaus heart a certain far in this visit; although he could sayl he lcame to gather news of any recent gold strikes. H had had to turn many another miner away with a declaration that the sample was pyrite, iron oxid, only.

I remembdred our brief conversation."Whatsa matter with a man who wont invest himself in his boot for gold—tell me that, Mister Hamme;r." I never was Kaleb, always Mister Hammer.

I cant say, sir. All menve got their priorities.

Thats as witless as a dead chub. What man hand togthis priorities?

I did not answer. He continued to write at hid desk. FGrotteaus ancestors, he claimed, were the Ravenstocks of Alsace Lorraine, erverse in their ogrgies of things they had done wrong, in Reiners case, an lugly attempt at claim jumping with a gun. I had warned him about the assayers black record book, the claimtitles, government prohibitions and such.

"Im thinking about making this a company gold town."

"With luck and sweat..."

They can make a fortune out of their hopes...if they will try."

"Who, sir—the townspeople?" lHe did snot answer.

"Hade you ever thought about the dead ancestorsz of the Indian tribes in these hills?" Alm yer askedGrotteau.; He looked theeditor up and down again. "You asks for big traouble."

I dont ask. You know I got respect for the dead, Alayer. Why, I got a relative, distant cousin...."

You counsel evil," the assayer ilnterrupted. Graves have spitiryts, spsirits shover over graves. Spirits belong to ttribe, the dead and the lving. They both talk. You call them relics. You're a white man. Bones be just things to you. Spirits and theground belong to the Indians, spirits of the tribespeople."

But Grotteau did not see. He was pretending honesty, dueling with a dangerous opponent. Tribal pride...unmarked graves." said Almayer.

Almayer took out a knife and cut a chunk of jerky from a hanging slab. There was anger in his motions. l l

You got ties to the red man...Ive got none," said Grotteau.

There. You spoke the truth. I would not offend the spirits sof the warriors buried here. But these are the gfraves sof my people. the Shoshone are my people. I have friends who look into the past. They know. They ltell me the truth.

Then you are their wise man, said Grotto. LIs that notrrut. No matter...no miner wants to dig in the village.

They did for gold. blut they dsigf into the gfraves sof the dead.

He saw that the assayer, a part Cloud Eagle's people was not changed. He also saw that quintessential shrewdness of the Indian spirit Ludheim was not a merchant of poverty or the vandal of plenty or, for that matter, the victim of illusions about power and death. Three horses were ten horses too many for a tribesman! He would protect the graves of the dead. Grotteau, if lhe insisted, could bring only trouble in his plea for liberty to dig where he and his sougdough apostles wanted. They were sure to desecrate the Indian burial sites. Ludheim saw this. For him, innocence and guilt were alike, both transferable and interchangeable, according not always to the evidence but to the roll of the dice, the cards in the hand of the players. For him there was no innate deceit in human intelligence. To deceive in order to acquire: that was the issue of the day. The less likely a man's wants, the less likely his dishonesty. The concurrence of accidents did not change the balance of justice. A panner slips on a slimey stone in the creek, strikes his head on a rock and is killed instantly . Or, a tunnel poweder-monkey lights a fuse, the charge fails to explode, he returns to examine why and is blown to pieces. At such times, mining is done for the day in that tunnel. But where's the honesty? Where's the dishonesty?

You come here...questioning my work. Damn your soul!" Alamyer cried out with rage.

"Innocence has got no cozy with suspicion."

"I'm only wondering, tha's all."

"Innocence...I heard you call yourself...reincarnated."

"Listen, Mister Grotteau...the past has put a curse 'pon my life as a Indian Chief...killed women and children. I got a new chance."

"Kllled were you?

"By a Spanish butllet shot by a settler's gun."

"Not enough then to stay dead."

"you make fun of my dead ancestors, what I knowed back then."

"I am only a teller of tales, Almayer."

"I can answer you out if I chose to."

"Oh, you claim auguries. You are a prophet."

"I do…special power, so I can talk to whatever thing is on your mind."

"Only the records, Almayer. They got to be accurate. Lots of gold out there…just near to the top of the ground."

"And the bones of Indians killed in battle with Henry rifles and Cavalry pistols."

"I Don't deny it, don't deny it."

"Theys a god watches all things goin on here in Mystery…."

"A god? Oh, I 'spect so. Folks got to have a god of some sort… always did."

"Force…that's what my god is," said Almayer. See them kachina dolls? Theres life forces, a bear, eagle, crow, a coyote, the snake, a vulture…their spirits are the force that is life."

"I didn't come to talk about religion."

"Then you dig, I feel the life force pain for lthem.

"Pain for them, who the….?"

"Spirts of the dead, Grotteau. I feel their pain."

Grotteau regarded this wierd conversation with skepticism and hostility. It portended opposition to his plan to take over the village for his acquisition, a gold town, his. He regarded the kachina dolls, grayed with dust, ranked on a shelf behind Almayer, as small spirts of animals and man, ready as a life force to battle him out of anger and revenge.

"I, we don't want to disturb anybody's ancestry bones. We intend to explore the ground here in the village…for hidden gold, out croppings. The village sits on a cache of yellow ore, redrock with fine dust hideen. Refine it out, we canl all go home rich.

"You speak for lthe devil, Grotteau."

"I am only an adventurer."

"And a teller of mysteries. l will print this in thea *Scorpion*."

My ancestors lie 'neath wind
where the flute lifts its note,
Where the wailing of death aises
and its sounds cover sighs,
Then death changes into life
and deatn rises away wild.
Then life returns to its grave,
its bones, its free spirit a song.

"It is the song of death for you and for them, Grotteau. I will talk to my people. Your gold is like the sand, it has no worth to me, to us.

I trade out of the limewhite man's lust for the gold. He will disappear when the waters come."

"You are a prophet, but not for us, Almayer."

"I could be wrong."

"I do not wish for lyou to remain here in my Hogan. It protects me. It is sacred to me."

Grotteau's obsession would strike a desperated hope, under the broiling desert sun, that would tend toward madness, undispelled by doubt, rancor or inhibition. Because of the controlling nature and the bent of his obsession I had begun to fear him. My roots were here. I could not depart for Boston or Philadelphia to my roots and give my version of the Western tall tale. I had already seen that *The Scropion* was Grotteau's weapon for intimidation and control. To appear to be human was but one aspect of that power.

Back at his desk on *The Scorpion*, he looked over his next isue, ads for boots, pans, picks, raingear, tents, utinsils, a monthly diluge of miners buys for ltheir diggings. They read The Scorpioin when a copy flew their way. There came news of Chinese Camp, Hangtown, Jackass Hill. Traders coming through, taksing mines gold. A prairie fire to the ease that died with a providential rain, the Sheriff mortician examining a morder at the Cloay;more Mine, a Preacher who ranted about mens cold hearted greed. These tidbits got into The Scorpion, somehow. Plus a census that showed two women, one a prostitute and the other a washerwoman who took in miners laundry. Thieves,s robbers got their due in The Scorpion. Such was the stuff of The Scorpion. No immediate news as to the numbers sof claims jumpers, if any in a non company town with himself installed at the head. He was always on the prowl for another gold strike, similar to the Kitrick Nuggett, the one pound nugget found that brought miners into the area. It was ktge"favulokus veuein" a fiction only. I, myself, made eight dollars a week. Reiner Grotteau was bent on manipulating and wrecking the lives of gold miners, without a conscience. He would use the miners spirits of conquest and ownership in a clever and callculating way, subversive to the end. I set type lin *The Scorpion* pressroom. I was the silent observer.

The Indian assayer made a sign with both hands, as a Priest makes the sign of the ross, onlyl this was the sign of the suns rays and begans over his had, drifting downs to the counter in his shack, as some sort of magical, arcane ritual of rfaith. I do not lie those who try to deceive, Mister Grotteau.

Grotteau whitened with pent up rage, a turbulent emotion overcoming him so that he shook. As he did so the Indian seemed to smile, but the features of his face were a puzzle to the white man who stood before him in the empty shack. It is I, I who takes caution of the graves of the Indian ancestors…here in the village and…in the rock sands of the hills. I revere my people. Their spirits lie under the land. When Mystery was built, nobody knew. Death imposes its own silence. The white man will not be held innocent when he digs into their presence."

This last omen astounded Grotteau, it was as if Alamayer believed that the dead still l live, and that he could point to the kachina doll spirit to give voice to their protests. If you enflame the white miners to dig, you invite trouble. My people are gone, but in their deaths they are not afraid of you, white man. I will bring down a curse on you. We do no longer raid your villages for your horses. We do not hunt with the bow and arrow still. You call us diggers, in contempt. We are a proud people.

"I feel respect…." Grotteau did not finish his words.

the Indian spat into his palm and rubbed his hands together as if making fire for warmth. "You deceive. That is your way.,..to deceive. The Indian is honest. He must live together. You live apart. You make enemies fast. You make friends slow. Listen, white man. we do not father pine bark and acorns and cactus fruit. We are at peace with death. I will keep it so, Grotteau." The assayer pushed his face close to the face of Grotteau, almost touching their noses. A thin white thread of a scar ran down one cheek. The man had involved himself in a knife or brokenl glass fight in a saloon somewhere. His countenance was at this ;moment fully hollow of visible intent, the eyes like cold blue water. He carried French blood. His kind are sometimes known in the mountains and plains and on the frontier as half-breeds, a common combination of French and Indian. French trappers often took Indian squaw wives. Often that was the most dangerous kind of Indian; the territorial nature of the Indian was mixed withs the revolutionary ardor of the Frenchman. Gottean noticed the capillaries in the whites of the Indian's eyes. There was no mistaking the intent and meaning of Almayers covert threats. Inside of him there boiled a turbulent rage, like a thundercloud in his soul. Grotteauy realized that the man was fully capable of committing murder for his religious belief in the hererafter of Indian life. In his shack, a wooden structure tilted slightly by high desert winds, the assayer returned to his small kiln, propped up on stones, and worked on an ore sample, heating the rock to dissolve the gold in its grains. His shack was soon filled with thin smoke. Heat the ore to 2,000 degrees, use hydrochloric acid to leech out the gold, or emerse the sample in a vat or mercury whereafter recover the gold by evaporting the mercury over a fire.

'Your vision comes from the dark regions of death"—had been Almayer's final words.

"Hear me, Almayer, if we dig and fling the bones of your ancestors aside, may your gods punish us with their barbs and stings of wrath."

He turned to go and as she did so, Almayer flung a saber blade into the door frame, causing Grotteau to spin around to face his adversary. He never carried a gun, but he did sheathe a skinning knife. He unsheathed the gray razpr blade and plunged it into the wood counter before the cold expression of Almayer. "Kittrick found the first nugget," he said. "There are more, under our feet, your gaves be damned!" He lifted his knife and bumped open the door and clattered down the steps. The village would learn of this encounter in an unpected way. Each man projected veiled threats; each man had the capacity to carry them out. Grotteau would become the protector of enormous wealth in gold. Almayer was certain to protect the bonds of his ancestors' graves, the one to justify his greed and the other to appease the spirits of the dead.

Back at *The Scorpion,* he waved a rolled map before me and Ludheim. "Gift from the spirits!" he exulted.

"Stolen?" Ludheim asked.

"Me also gambler," Grotteau mimiced.

"He will work his vengeance," Ludheim said.

"Let him…He's only one Indian, against two hundred whites here in the village.

"You're not his friend?" Ludheim asked.

"Friend? Not when he turns into a landowner. Ancestors bones under Mystery. Here only men without roots can survive. We're all outcasts here, Mister Ludheim. A few will send for their wives…if they find gold. Vengeance runs hot…."

?Vengeance…for what?"

"For their losses, the white man, gone their old dreams and depleted grub stakes. Tim…loss of friends, accidents, fingers gone with dynamite, saws, maybe dysentery…thank god no cholera!...yet. Lamed by cold and sweat and no medicnines. I could think of more reasons."

"The luck of the killing," said Ludheim. "You go hunting, you expect trouble. You confront death. Careless, the damned. lNo common sense…."

"Common sense, Mister Ludlheim…gold madness is the common sense."

"As I see it, this village sits on sacrd ground, Mister Grotteau. Gold is not a friend…it is the enemy," said Ludheim. "I do not covet y our power, sir. Only others who are like you can do that."

"Then what is it that so displeases you?"

"That you should destroy other men with your insatiable insane plan to bring them into the snare and net of your mining scheme…."

"Responsibility brings possession of the fruits there of," said Grotteau.

"And death to the spirit. Your piety does not change me one whit," said Ludheim.

"My company will benefit every man and soul who lives here in Mystery.

"You are carried away;" sir.

"Then the seduction is incomplete…when enough miners buy into my plot map, Mister Ludheim. The boundaries are not capricious, sir. Squatters will have no claim…only honest panners. No scavengers."

"Unless you blind them first," said the German.

"It is not a sin to hunt for gold…in the streets, in the secret locations of the townsfolks."

"Does that not add thievery to your search—a crime in itself," said Ludheim.

"I do not condemn. I speculate only. Accusations—leave that to God."

"You sound like an itinerant unholy Priese. We hve one Jesuit here in the village, that's enough."

I for one was snot certain that digging in thstreets was an evil, only that desecration of lthe honored dead was wrong. I was sure that the priest would agree withs me.

White Grotteau was gone from the shop I sometimes ran the press , which fascinated me, as if a musical instrument. It vibrated the wooden floor in the pressroom where it stood, the immense cnalank of the revolving huge wheel, its churning belt, the platen rollers going up across the platen then down again, inexhorablble, lalmost like a voiceless spirit of revenge that glave reality lto the substance of the miners' lives by reflecting their work and sinterests. II often worked over sit bysl the flickewring light of a keroslene lantern while he was absent. It was *The Scorpion* that kept alive poisons of dark spirit gossip from the saloon. They numbered in those early ldlays lsnot lsmore than one hundred and fifty, hardy, grapplers with a nature of hard resistance tp change. The lvillage itself possessed ghostly seclusion where it thrived in the lmorning mists, lthe sandys devil sltorms and dessicated bones of other times, a thing alive in its own wantonness. I would straighten up from my cleaning type, after the press run and put a bundle in the hands of each boy,Hank and Bryce who rode over from Frost and Triangle—maybe in all 100 copies. When he came in he kicked off his boots, took a battered wicker chair and said, as I waited, knowling the words almost by heart…"had another visit withs that Indian, Almayer. Wants to get the Indians hereabouts all riled up."

"He still thinks were trampling on his ancestor bones?

"'Bout the size of it." He sprang to his feet this time. The powerful physical energy of such an ordinary man laws obvious. "Damn him!… Indian renegade! Hes got the claims to every dggin around here… thinks them maps are land titles. Hes an ignorant usurper…that's what he is." Grotteau paced slightly, scanned the darknss outside. "Well, he wont get away with it…" He was not talking to Ludheim, who had just come in, who took a cigar from a box on Gotteau's desk. He bit off the end, spat it out and lit the end by the lantern. "He has shown his hand," Groitteau said, clenching lhis teeth.

Ludlow corrected him. "This village, sir, is a village now but it can one day be a town. Our Indian friend suffers from a smallness of vision."

"By God; I think you've hit it, Mister Ludheim. *Howling Wolf* he calls himself," he said, his tone of voice derisive. "*Howling Wolf*," he repeated. "You know what wolves are, Mister Ludheim?"

"They're killers, sir…when they aren't foragers…travel in packs for protection, loyal to each other, hunt to share. Almalyer does not lead a pack." Ludheiim looked up sharply from his chair. "They are cruel…but to satisfy their hunger."

"Blood-thirsty, like all savage life," said Grotteau/

"I got plans for this village." Grotteau was now talking to De Vancha in his hotel room. It was the next evening.

"Women do not want to come here…they're afraid. Especially when they've got no husband. What would they do…why would they come?. Except to make money the old fashioned way."

"We don't want them here, said de Vancha. They bring only trouble, fights, murer, brawls…." He informed Grotteau. We must go see the lawyer Ludheim in his Vault. That is what he calls his wolf's den. They went that evening to pay a visit to the unseemly and rather tacky lawyer who smelled money in the village run by sourdoughs.

While Grotteau and De Vancha sat before him, surreptitiously eyeing the ludicrous and surrealistic office hole-in-the ground of the lawyer, Ludheim removed a envelope from a shelf emblazoned with drawings along the edges like an illuminated manuscript. Inside was a parchment, the writing in Spanish, several seals affixed at the bottom. He held it out to De Vancha. "Here is the signature of King Ferdinand of Spain," he said. De Vancha's eyes widened in disbelief. The true and authentic signanture of King Ferdinand of Spain, in whose service my ancestor Sepulveda worked...by mainly keeping the Indians under control. Just as you will do De Vancha. Here is the signature of Don Sepulveda, writ as big as life.

The; lawyer had prepared a genealogical chart, at the bottom of which was the name Pedro de Vancha. The wary Jose De Vamcja, El Alcalde, inspected the document held out to him. He suspected its authenticity. He showed disbelief on his swarthy face.

Ludsheim returned the document to its place on the shelf. Now you see. If this village sits on your land, you will win a generous share of my own mining company, as well as the mines of those miners who have dug into the ground without consulting your Grace...have they not?"

"Si, senor. That is true. They do' not talk to me about their claims."

"But we can change all that by making public the true matter in *The Scorpion*. We will announce the truth. We will print the truth."

"Yes, that is the best way," said de Vamcha.

"The only way, Senor De Vancha," said Ludheim. Then I can develop the village and take my profit from the guile. That is only fair. They drank a glass of wine together, a cigar went to the Mayor and together for several minutes they basked in thoughts of the power, the richess they would possess—the lawyer and the Mayor and Grotteau— with this plan to set up a town community with central control, one smithy anvil and Lawyer Ludheim.

I gathered these things without a word. I saw, as I understood, human nature, that those actions of men that showed intention, were the outward manifestation of a soul that hid itself. II saw in the intention of Grotteau and Ludheim an intention of make the residents of the village hostage to do their dark will, ultimately to Grotteau's dark wlill. I sensed a grain of honesty in the German Ludheim that his partner in the exhorbitant crime had not yet detected, an ardor of a basic honesy There was, in short, in the mind of Grotteaul a dark mission, an evil quest that could lead to savage encounters with the miners sin the village, who ordinarily would not be trapped by dialogue or false promises. they would not allow the pillage of their innocence, the destruction of their integrity by rapine of the mind and soul by Grotteau, howsoever much they respected him as editor of The Scorpion. They would find in their own basic goodness and loyalty the reflection of another man's wicked tricks and perverse designs. That image was coming to be Reiner Grotteau.

The conflict of wills came to a had one day when Grotteau, through an announcement in his paper, blamed the low gold production o laziness and deviation of purpose. They were forgetting who they lwere. They wer eifirst of all men, and then miners. He annojnced that they should rally round their newspaper editor's plan to make of their ventures a solid mining community. He invited them to a street scene, where he would talk to them.

On the appointed evening, he had uilt a pyre in the middle of the villavge, h came to the spot with a wagon loded with ldeeds to hawk, stake claims by the hundreds to escite the miners lusts for more and smore, a huge snugget of thirty-eight pounds on the tailgate and in his hand a whip like a brass ferrule, his, Grotteau's, eyes big beneath his dowdy lhat. His face was curled into an expressison of surprise as from around the corner dogs yelped. These fewral dogs were unexpected as like wolves they attacked the miners on the street. Grotteau jumped into his wagon and seizing his gun from the bed bean to fore at the dogs. They lept and snarled at his boot heels. The snarling feral dogs mauled the old and inform of the miners, who had come to *Mystery* to live out their lives, hoping, taking pride in prospecting as an honorable way of life. They fell prey. Grotteau rescued one old man, Felepe, be beating off two dogs with a burning firebrand from the pyre. Another man with a crippled leg tried to flee but was brought down by baying hounds. A friend kept the dogs at bayl by thrusting his bowie knife into the throat of one dog and plunging it into the ghashing teeth of another. One of the animals lay dying, the other fled.. In the sandy soil and ferrous rock, Grotteau saw another man throw his hands before his face and flail wildly, but the feral animal attacked his belly, then his throat, next his hamnds until he fell screaming into the bed of coals in the pyre on the street...murdered by a dog pack..Grotteau wounded several, killed one. As of by command the animals fled as quickly las they had come. Not many townsmen had gathed in response to Grotteaus summons. That was just as well, for they might also have become victims of the dog pack. Without weapons, the feral dogs were as much a threat to villager life as an Indian raiding party.

Grotteau said, "Even the dogs hunger for gold." This was not a matter for simple comparisons. miners began to gather at the site of the street fire. The professional appearance of Grotteau's land deed was too strong to resist. The miners held back until Grotteu saidwhat he had to say.

The great venture would make them all rich, those who joined him in the daring enterprise. Each land-itle, claims-deed would bear a ignature to that parcel of land until all the land the village sat on was accounted for, the deeds on file and in the miners pockerts, and the terms of the deed in Grotteau's safe keeping..including his percentage of the gold. There would be no greater equalizer than hard labor to satifsfy the demands of equality—sweal, time and purpose...and gold. Among the miners of the village, in the cluster oft tents an shacks, there lived exiles, self exiled who lhad long ago babandoned the politle society of civil intercoufrse that they might take up the culture of the mining camp, whose modus operandi was denial. They replaced the civilied withs the quasi barbaric that brought out lthe coarseness in menls natures where it existed. heavys gambling and drinking, nnue and fatigue, cts sof violence, sometimes with knives, often with la gun, even rocks hurled at an introduer into a camp site. In the course of months f exposure to such hardship and human depravity, the conscience was purged. In its place the natural instinct inl man for his survival dominated his mind and emotions. l lThe sould lhardened, the lhands caloused dasby the miners lifle. Envy and fear in myhstery lbecame goads to those seeking out la miserlable exisfgtence within lthe harsh desert environment od a gold campd, settlement to somel, lhardly la town but ualifiedly a village. The miners, now more than several dozen lwer open to VGrotteau's proposal…land titles, deeds of claim for minerals on the lparcel.

Grotteau parried the insuslts and questions, fighting battles over claim deeds. He prodded the reluctant and chastened the doubters to buy in. He condemned the drifters safor whom wealths wlas at their feet.

One question aailed Grotteau's calm. lHow can you sell off what ant yours, Mister Grotteauy.

Well, now, this whole town sits son free land, that is free to us.

Owned bvy the govfsmint?

I hant seen la deed lyet,m came lanother voice.

Gentlemen,salid Grotteau, if lyou work a claim the profits sof gold is yours. You are not dispsutling the land ownership itself, the deed wioll do that…bt sthe value of the claim in gold..

Noblody dared to talk. They appeared to have been silenced by Grotteaus' week long series on mine ownership, the gold or mineral rights separate from title to the land, the which he would show them lhow to complete. Grotteau had strlick off a number of signs and nailed them to posts around themidldle of the town, which was lmost across from the Hard Rock Saloon. The signs read: lyou can move the towns butl not the gold. lHe had given laway fewere than a dogzen land titles. But tomorrow would be another dlay. Nlight came on fast with lightning and threat of rain. ddddd'Onel was a Irishmanm who ;mended harness, his squat red face burned by desert sun. Another was a retired railroad feller who swalked stifflegged as if hin irons. Tere were miners in the hills land up the creek, hundreds of them who were I;gnorant of this giltedged offer. .

You gsot lno lbusiness epaking what ant the truth, came a voice.

God…why look there at that nugget, found not a thousandl yards from here.

Gold under these hyer streets, Mister.

I doubt it, I doubt it.

Have faith, its so, our own gold assayer has said so. All were curious as to what Grotteau was up to, Jackson, with a smattering of the law, wanted to know what Grotteau was up to.

Well, there they were, some hubilant, others astounded an dstill moe looking depresed by the event of surrnder of their ownerhsip of aclaim. They were qfraid of conterfeiters. A few onered what part Grotteau played in the scheme.Ludheim followed Grotteau like a hwk. aHe knew that Grotteau was doing was wrong and against the law. For the land did not belong to him, it elonged to the BLM, Bureau of Land Management. Grotteau hightened the fireligfht with pine pitchTwo to three dozen had come to watch the goings on. The boneifre grew higher, sending sparks sinto the black sky. The second night Grotteau hoped to dispose of his bundle of claims. The indolents the curiious, the wayfarers all gathered,examining the pound nugget put on display and having afriend read the claim deed. Rotting mineshaft timbers fed the fire this night. Arguments broke out lbut Grotteau quickly sauenched them by roaring out their names and condemning them to hells flames if they did not obey him. This was his firstr act of police justice, necessary to get the miners involved. Two men had a knife fight, the cause unknown. aProbaly came from the Hard Rock, drunk. It lasted less than ten minutes, Mallory and Harriman, Harriman lay dead on the street. Mallory sheathed his knife and with nonchalance walked up to Grotteaus pyre and warmed his hands. "Little argument.. over Cinderella. I werent trreying to take her away from him."

Lost cause, fugsitive he was. "You done the law a good turn, I expect, sir," Said Grotteau, taking the side of the attacker. Yet he had run the man's picture; he was a wanted man…no more than that.

I set the type for an article on feral dogs, blaming city folks for letting their animals roam in the country free. Then I wrote a short piece on the shortage of firewood, just as Taylor Klemsey unloaded his burro of mesquite wood and pine chunks onto the flames at the heart of the town. Klemsey sold his wood to miners at their diggins.

Wood was almost as valuable as gold at this time. I knew that Wolfgang Goetz had escaped from Alcatraz and was panning gold up th creek, that Timothy Hammond has lost most of his fingers on one hand but was a better poker player than Grotteau at the Hard Rock Saloon. Jim Leuer was always busy at his barbershop, Truss Halpern liked to shoot vultures out of the sky. John Watson was a sharper at knife throwing in a contest in Frost. Kelemsy knew, as did I, that a man named Aleford operated a still in high cave and sold whiskey to the Indians.

An night owl flew low over the bonire in th street, eye on a rat driven ou by the sflames. As I set type I heard Jeremy Fazakerly's boots, a tall, skinny feller some folks took for an idiot. He portaged water in two huge burlap bags from the saddle of his burro, brought to villagers mainly for drinking, access to the creek having been muddied by rocker slurry and miners digging. Grotteau had not been able to dispose of all of his mining claims, which, I must confess he had run off on our press, **The Scorpion** newspaper press.

Grotteau had announced in his flier that he would give free of charge a land Title Deed to any man in the village who would surrnender his weapon. This was a condition. To do so would increase the value of the deed. The Indians did not need to know of the barter. And so on the third niht of the rendevous, Gamblers and drinkers from the saloon moved toward the flames. Grotteaul had lost their gold dust at cards, land so they lcame with a chip on the shoulder. Prospecting was like that...the pain was silent. Grotteau stood by his offer and his scheme. To the surprise of the small crowd he had already thrown an armful of old shotguns, one musket nd two pistols into thel fmflames. Theys thought he was crazy and others sfigured they lwere smade, burning their only means to self defence, lturning red hot in the fire, their barrels sd red hot. The glsorious spyre was built a stones thrlow alway from the assayer shack. It was such a banile sacrifice, it seemed to Grotteau, who realized that they would go to Triangle, or to San francisco, and purchase new weapons. Bit for now they were acting the hero, the adventurer. Printed maps showed the location, the prospective location, of small gold deposits. There was a bond formed by the sacrifice and the daring, the risk. Sourdoughts stood by taking warmth from the flames. Some who did lnot come to towns thoughtl slthat perhaps the saloon or the lhotel was on fire and came down to watch or tos helop.

"Theres protection of all," said Ludheim, by know known to be a lawyer. Just dig, men. You got the right to set up tents on your claim. Theres protection for all, he promised, an empty promise, he knew. Thde several dozen guns burned, It was especially fantastic even to Grotteau that men would willingly surrender their firearms for gold. But there, cast into the flames of destruction, was the evidence.

"Whatsa price of a piece to dig?" a questioner voice rang throught the crackling fire. Franklyn Kirsten a dweller in a shack on the hill has asked.

"You know the price, Kirsten. I told you. You seen it with your own eyes." Grsotteau held up the enormous nugget of 38 pounds, allegedly found by Indian Head Rock. Its all round here. Costs but a pinch of salt and some damned o' gun you got hanging around the cabin cant use no more because the stocks broke or you can't afford the ammunition, or you used the rusty barrel to pry off a wagon wheel and vent it. No use. Pitch it into the flames and become my associate here. I will hand you a deed right smart and quick."

"Abundance will come," Grotteau promised. Thje sacrifice continued as land titles were issued from Frotteaus tent, the prospectors would mindxlessly pitch in an oldl rustyshooting iron intol the flames. Were all pecloving brothers in Myustery. There came the veiled threat of trespass for anyone not acquiring title to his small parcel by the sacrifice of a weapon and his silgnature. . It seemed that few payed close attention to Grotteaus words, lcocky now with a sltlrange arrogance that sprang from this sort of control power. Timer shiftsed lin the flames, a vessuvial showser of sparks flew up intos the black sky. lDripping mules pulled another load of timbers up to the flames.

We are united tonight folks, said Ludheim, whose legalese gave formal character tos the deeds. ILHe worked alongside Grotteau. Anclient,l rusting old weapons of war and combat...the salcrifice was thus efined by Lludheim. The night wore on. lOvcer in the Hard Rock

Saloon some of the congregants, let us call them, toopped soff their niht night with whiskey sosur and beer. Music of a fiddle and guitar came from a small platform to one side of the card players. Diamonds sparkledflashed in the lantern light as the dealer passed out cards from fingers of lthe man dealing the cards in a fourman game of draw poker.

Life in *Mystery* found its mjicrocosmic definition in a poker game, the one vbeing played this night while townsmen danced around the bonfire of their surrender to one man's power, he who owned and ran the ***The Scorpion.*** So what was different? Diamond-fingered Watson dealt the cards. The wagering went twice around, the pot was raised, one man, "Cracker..." he was called, put a pouch of gold dust on the table and held, another raised, Ackerman, a logger cut out, what he earned lin the woods did not sustain his appetite for quick gain. A Mexican named Carlos replaced him. The pot was taken by a stranger named Keystlor, over from Frost. He took his hand, holding them close to his chest. Doctor Farralones delicate fingers slid the carcds across the canvas like wet surgical sponges. He smiled. The Mexican, razor cropped veard, dark eyes and caballero that raked to the back of his head, flashed a big turquoise ring as he vent to consier his cards. All the players poured over their hands as if in prayer, saying his rosary. The player stakes twere miners stakes, ltwo small salchet ltype sacks of gold dust, the work of months, a twenty-dollar gold piece in front of the doctor. In lthe background, the fiddle land the guitar. G;luiseppi, lthe barkeep set a bottle and glasses on thnetable. The microcosmis aspect of the game was its sintensity, its distrust shared round the ltable, the purge of thoughts of consequences, the unfriendly to lhatefull regard amongst the players and, most important, the lready greed that animated the players at the table. llSuch things could be saidl about Mystery in generalThe doctor matlched his card withl four of a kind. The cripplehanded miner tossed into the short pile a five of diamonds, drew another card. The man in the caballero that pursed his lips, his thin bearde face like an oak wedgfe, sharp and rthoughtful. The one armed ldrover, in a battle of life and death, his eyes fixed on lhis hand—all were the silent language of fate. The doctor watched with an empty stare, as if making a diagnosis, tossing face up a three of diamonds, drawing another card. His surgery successful and contenting him. Nearby, watching stood itinerant miners who smoked, coddled a beer, and watches the playout. Grotteau joined the table, was dealt a hand on the replay, threw in a three of clubs, flashed his rings, his magical rings, slid another card off the top, waited, then led, was not raised, and when his opponents hands were shown he triumphed with a straight flush in hearts. He took Calipso sack of gold dust and the doctors twenty dollar gold piece. Miner Ackerman's coins remained in the pot. Now De Vancha, amid some minor noise as the newly appointed mayor joined the game, the deck shuflfled, the doctor cut the deck and the dealer dealt with slick elfficiency. Calipso , as the biddiang mounted, drew an IOU note from his pocket and with it a small sack of gold dust. The doctor this time bid silver dollars. The pot could be high stakes. De Vancha, El Alkcalde, produced a a paper from his leather vest that resembled a trust deed. The doctor wished to examine the patient and called for a diagnosis from De Vancha.

Aqui Senores…the deed to the Continental Hotel. He had won it himself in a game. Ludheim was not in the game, all lthe village's major *senores*, the ones with power, the editor Grotteau of *The Scorpion*, the other with the influence of heritage, de Vancha, the one with the perverse scheming will to acquire riches—Ludheim—and the one with the abandonment of a fighting cock, the Priest Xavier, at last in the game to join in the excitement and confirm his comaderie with the villagers. He lost the next round but lhe did so with a smile. By moving God around the table he could enhance his position in lthe village; it was a common move for itinerant priests and mule skinners as well. The game continued on into the night. The pyre outside burned high and fiercely for an hour or twos then died down into embers as mliners drifted back to ltheir campsites withl papers sof title lyet powerless to defend lthemselves. Grotteau's glaed eyes and glossy tongue accompanied the game. De Vancha's natural mockery ran in the Saloon. Are you put these idiot into the office, Senor Grotteau?" he called to the editor defensively, his tongue loosened. He felt the editor should use his official power to make a fool of an enemy. Their separation began at that moment. Any card game I saw was a symbol of the miners' hostility toward poverty and the fear of losing. When they won, they exulted in their revenge against fateful circumstances, brought about by their reasoning, desperate in their play, fatalistic in their acceptance of dreadful results.

De Vancha mocked Grotteau. You have done some ver wrong things. But Grotteau did not answer. You are a wise and old man, said De Vancha. I do not carry a stick to strike you down. Grotteau stiffened. How could I think of such a bad thing? At that moment Grotteau should have seen El Alcalde's rapacity, his spirit of plunder as natural to him as instinct to a wild animal. Then he relaxed and smiled. You will pardon me, Senor, you are a very bad poker player. The priest smiled and nodded as if to give unction to the thought, Ludheim was grim, watching his partner in conspiracy.

The next night was vlery much like the one before.. Only Grotteau stayed out of any card game. He was shrewd. At the same pyre, built in the street to attract all who wished to buy into his scheme. He said aloud, holding a cup of whiskey in one hand and a chewed cigar in te other and gesturing wildly, but with a sense of earned and deserved power: "Mister Almayer…and myself…have got the lives of almost every man here in the village."

Printed in The Scorpion, asked Daamon Jackson, an arsonist. Wasn't that so, lMiste rGrotteau? lHe sat on a log round, fascinated byl the flames.

No weapons of war in Mystery, peace over all, Said Grotteau, llaccompanied byl the lburtle snapping of the burning timbers. Grotteau became aidentified as a town oracle by this time. Indeed, some business snot so spiritual was conducted on the spot, for miners, upon credit issued by Grotteau, had opined they hd no shovels, picks, pans or tenting.. Clayton Hornby, who owned the General Merchandise store brought several wheelbarrow loads filled with the requested itens. On the strengvth of a promise, he wacceptsed miners sious for the tools, to be pasyed in gold dust as time went on. llIn this lmanner Grotteau indentured the miners to his scheme, with, the shelp of others in the town who sold on credit. Apparently Grotteau felt it time to give a speech…and necesary. There were about twety miners, panners mostly, gathered around the flames on Dog Street.

The town was enjoying a strange party-spirit, as miners drifted into lthe saloon from thr fire and others, out of curiosity, having washed down the dust of the day, went out to the street to observe the celebration of a community gold strike. It could be called by no other name... Grotteau's special promise of streets of gold in Mystery.

Calipso, a one armed drayman, chewed his quid, the muscles in his broad ugly face moving with a ripple effect beneath his black bearf. He watched the faces of the others at the poker table. Diego de Vancha, the newly appointed Mayor was missing from the scene, and Ludheim, the miner lawyer, had only lately shown up. Those three it can be said, were responsible for the night of abandon and thoughtless and more but few have done so with such thoughtless lack of vision and comprehension of the forces of nature, including a pack of feral dogs, the Indians in the nearby hills and rank murder for quick gold that always clung close to a mining community, a camp so-called in the good days of the Argonauts. Miners could become a dangerously volatile lot of renegades. There were already three murders on the books within as many months. By sharing the gold that lay beneath the town, Ludheim believed he could bring peace and order to the village. It was all matter of exerting the will.

Grotteau stood with his back to the heat. "Bless you, he said to Hornby. He raised his gold nugget like a pearled chalice before the eyes of the miners. Bless you and may the earth also bless you. I am not here to cajole or make merry with sad souls."

A miner handed him a tin cup filled with cactusl whiskey to aid his speechifying. I am not here to punishs or threaten you with failing. Oh, good folks, I am here to...to celebrate our victory over the town of Mystery...which is ours to use as we see fit. Those politician bastards will not claim our town for booty...they know its rich in gold. They got a jag on the start of digging and they move in donkey engines to loot the gold. How you will all like that?

A shout or two of agreement ensued. Let us trust one another," said Grotteau. "Your gun Terrence McAllister. The man addressed was a soldier, it appeared, he still wore the Civil War stripes of cavalry. The veteran from lunder his denin shirt drew out a revolver and flung it into the pyre with a crazy laugh. lHe was drunk.

Jimmy Tyler, an ex-power monkey, pitched a barren and splintered shotgun and some shells into the fire. They exploded with violent ruptures, throwing the jittery miners, and causing sparks to scatter.

"Nothing to hide now, Mister Kirsten. Why there's gold right at the foot of the mountains your hut's pitched on. Franklin Kirstsen flung a small derringer-type pistol into the fire and looked pleased with himself for doing so. His moutain ledge was a choice place to dig. Severeild Hatrtsman threw his carbine with years of use onto the flames, in exchanfge for a slength of lthe vboard sidewalk, which he could repair when he had finished his dig. He owned the adjacent saddlery. He divided the stretch of wooden walk with Thor Torvald, the illiterate who wondered if Mystery could be moved. Each oblation to Peace and Richess meant the surrender of personal pride in owning a firearm; but the sacrifice, if such it was, meant, nay, assured the former possesssor of the insurance of a *gold-dig,* as Ludheim had termed it.

In this way Grotteau dispersed claims to the townsmen...there were more, some he did not recoznize, others from Frost who had seen the bu;rning pyre fifteen miles away and had heard of the exchange of a title to land lin a swap with a weapon of war. Some of the miners tried to read their mine claim document by the firelight, boisterous and amiable among themselves. Panners so long accustomed to working without instant reward, under the parching, desert sun, turned convivial and boisterous when gathered as a clan of argonauts.

Father Xavier's participation in the wildcat scheme assured him of God's faithful blessings upon a worshipper trust and renewal of heaven's promise to reward the faithful with the richess of this world , which, after all, belonged to Him to begin with. His strong, bony broad face, as pale as a Monastic monk's, made it visibly evident he had neither journeyed long nor labored hard in the desert sun. He appeared sad, as if grieving for those not blessed by Grotteau's windfall . As he dropped out of the poker game, he wiped his sweaty face with a soiled piece of fine Irish linen.

"Gentlemen, excuse me…" his last words. He mounted his mule outside the **Hard Rock Saloon**, proud of his small contribution to a higher purpose.He withdrew a derringer from beneath his black cloak. "I have been watching," he announced as if at a confession. "This I must confess is a most interesting display o f sacrificial humility. Blessed are the peacemakers." And with a hefty throw of his arm he pitched the small weapon into the blaze. He turned to watch others. The drayman who had brought up wood pitched another timber into the fire, with a crash of the already burning beams. Grotteau had also finished his stint at the poker table in the saloon. Outside, he held up a fistful of the remaining deeds, according to Almayer's map it appeared to be so, and bargained with prospectors who had not yet bought into his bold scam.

"You there, sir…with the beads and your sexton hat.…" the words summoned laughter from the miners. "It is to you I direct my remarks. I will match my wife's exquisite table and old German imported linens…as a guarantee on a deed. If you find no gold. the linens are yours, sir." His readiness to back up his paper with solid equity made the barter all the more convincing and real—for those who possessed no firearm. There was always personal honor to barter. The word of an honest man, as Ludheim so eloquently put it. Thus the bargaining continued before the heathen crowd who chewed and spat and waved their deeds of gold-claim. The priest,also handed Grotteau a handful of money and said, close o the fire, the bridle in the mule's mouth. "For the poor in your noble town." He then rode off.

INDIAN INFORMANT

This night Almayer he would divulge the claims of the White Man, the mines, who dug within the village, and where in relation to the bones of the deceased the claims were made. Not every grave would be disturbed, but one was sufficient to arouse anger and a passion for retributive justice. It would have to come the Indian way, not the White Man's way.

In the near darkness of the old *kiva* , much like those that are found in Anasasi Indian cliff-dwellings, the ring of fire glistened off shadowed Indian forms. They had come here to talk very little and to contemplate. At some length, Almayer revealed his ghost carrier of messages from the grave. On a wooden wand of the kiva floor he drew wiyth a piece of soft bonechalk, the plan Grotteau had in his mind. They marked him as evil and possessed by spirits from the total darkness. He drew those places, small rectangles where ancestral bones were buried, and indicated spots within structures in town the Indians already knw about, where possibly other graves lay under he flooring and foundations of the structures. Much of what he believed was speculative; but much was true and actual. The Indians had good reason to feel the antagonistic lash of the miners' will to dig..

"My peoples' bones lie under the village."

"That is bad for you and for us," said the Indian *Big Thunder*. "Let the spirits talk to Almayer, *Running Coyote*. We are almost white men when we cannot remember our ancestors."

"Their gods of revenge will guide our spirits and their hands. They will inflict harm on our enemies. After our prayers to the heavens, we will be protected from the Henry rifles. Or ancesters' bones are sacred and the White Man who calls himself a Cross man…Grotteau… he does not understand. He worships his memories and things that are left behind. The Indian worships the spirits of the departed souls. He takes his bow and arrow and his prayer beads and his turquoise wand breastplate with him. His bones are sacred reminders…"

And so in the *kiva* the Indians—there were about thirty of them, all braves—prayed to their gods of revenge. Soon they broke out in to low chanting refrains.

> We come to worship of gods of earth
> of life, of the sun, we come
> Our voices are like our blood –
> it mingles and gives strength.
> Hear our voices; they are true and
> strong and tears of rain
> Angered yet gentle as a maidens
> hair, we come to ask you.
> Hear our voices, we play the flute
> we summon the night bird.
> Our honor is in your hands o mighty
> one and our bones, our sinews.
> We come to worship o gods of earth
> of life, of the sun, we come.

As the night wore on the Indians became more vical They stood as to reach up. Almayer sprinkled a circle of dust on and around buffalo bones, which he kept in a sacred hidden place in his Assay shack. Three torches and the fire ring lit the kiva gathering and the performance of their rites. Each torch stood for the sun, the earth, the season. Within the perimeter of the circue Almayer had inscribed, he made the signs of the sun with rays of gold and the sign of death, a man beneath the land. A trail led by a single line to each of the oursides of the square. As the worshippers changed and became more physical and violent they raised their clenched fists and plunged them into their stomachs as a symolic act of self-death, sacrificial suicide, a pact with death by choice, to join them, the living, with their departed ancestors.

The the Indian leader and two others of th tribe seized the tornches and they ran out into the night, followed by the remaining worshippers. along a narrow trail they then climbed up into the rocks, lifting the torches to find the way, a string of the clan, they cut upward into the rocks. Thetorches, one by one, would occasionally disappear behind a wall of rock, and then emerge as they climbed, until they reached the top. There they set their torches to ignite the mesquite that had been prepared earlier. The feathered leader, *coupe lance* in hand, two diagonal red streaeks emblazond on his cheeks and two others, who bore the torches, their braided hair and one necklaces, an Ogala with feathered breastplace, a half-breed with black hat and a Rappahaw with turquoise wristbands and necklace and a Crow with high heekbones, flecked with white, his hairpinned back…these were a few of the celebrants in the kiva and atop the butte that night.

Almayer admired their gala fire, eyes agleam in the smokelight, no affliction of man's torporous counsel, unified, amguished, ready warriors. Their obvious note of call was destruction, to lay down the White Man on his sand shadow, measurement exact for death, the miners who invite troops of horse soldiers, brave cavalry, brutal Indian butchers, flagrant destroyers of Indian dreams. They had families in Frost and in Triangle, the more distant. They sat as if charmed by ceremonial *anguish*, the rite of deprivation and extinguishment by which pain would be reversed like a buried arrow withdrawn.

Among the Indians on the butte this night before their council fire, were braves who were long out of work, their return to the *kiva* igniting old pride. One painted White Mans' houses and another performed odd jobs of the gopher in town. Each claimed honest blood kinship with his anscestors whose remains, tatters of rotten cloth, bones, amulets, bracelets, turquolise and copper and silver ornaments called back to the living from the grave. Regardless of their tribal beginnings, their claims were tight-gripped, seized upon against the entire village of *Mystery* in a fight to the death to protect, not to ravage or seize. They wanted no horses this time.

The way into the night of moonlit sky was like fine yucca hair lain against the night stars. It was the way of thunderous rocks, spewn by rain-violence and tumultuously cascading years. They had left their ponies below the butte outside the *kiva*. A lantern or two in the distant blackness marked the village of *Mystery*.

A flute, the crytal note floating into the sharpness of the desert night warns, arising still, clear, warblsing by the flautist, to the accompaniment of a singing voice of *Night Bird.* it was the emblem of night love and of the spirit of good and prevailing nature-love that all Indians shared, whether or not they were enemies and bore war scars. Those who sat amidst their memories were *Runinng Deer*, Barry *White Cloud*, George Turnbull *Bear Paw*. They had gathered to assemble their spirits, to remember obligations to their ancestors this night. The bird of night would bring the message of reunion with the spirits of the dead. Almayer had a message or all of those tribesmen gathered atop the Butte, they who had come to refect on past dignities of life, to summon courage and the spirits of the dead. They were again gathered here under the stars, their decision fixed and firm that they would seek retributieon. Almayer spoke to others emerged, as from the bowels of the earth, to populate the earth, the microcropolis of the rock top, of Coyote butte. Indian ways had purpose, unlike Whaite Man's unhappy and empty random searches for fulfillment. Indians measure life by the brevity of its span and the solace it offere to all in all activities; and the fundamental purpose of his actions, one of life and survival.

As he spoke of the sadness of the intended isolation of the braves, the night bird, a great horned owl, soared, its white underwings floating firelit over the flamelight and the gathered Indians atop the rock. As if taught, but only by nature, it settled on a bundle of wood beside the fire, fluttered its wings as if to stretch them and, gathering its pinyons unto itself, looked about. Great murmurs of satisfaction rose up from the circle of the worshippers. the flight and alighting of the great horned owl signaled an omen to the Indians on the Butte—the seizure of their quarry and the accomplishment of their purpose.

"I have messages from the graves of our blood fellows, braves all, who sit here tonight," almayer said. "They are messages of comfort…their journeys are successful and plentiful they have caught much game beyond and they live in peace and honor." Another great murmur rose up then suddenly died out. "They also bring messages of warning. Those whol have died warn the liviing against the intruder. He is like the predatory beast who ravages for its own bloodlust and its primal hunger. Another murmur of satisfacrtion arose, of assent, of curiosity. "I have no more messages…peace and warning come from the many moons of time beyond. We must decide on how to turn the invader White Man…some are friends to the Indians. Do not forget that, they caution us from beyond. But they must not kill us again by disturbing our bones where we lay." With these words, the owl night bird extended its great graywhite wings and with a flapping like dry leaves it flew up into the night again, while cautious and knowing eyes followed its upward flight. It circled the prayer fire pow-wow several times and then, as if commanded to do so, it again soared into the flamelight yet the raptor did not settle this time on the same cluster of sticks. It sat closer to the flame, unafraid. All eyes watched its circling flight and its perched gaze.

"The night bird will not leave us until it tells us to release our spirits of love and compassion for those who have died, then to settle again onto the land that is ours. In its talons there is nothing, no meat of night, its habit. So we are not to kill these fanatics of custom." Thus spoke Almayer to the gathered Indian rebels.

That was all that the night bird, raptor owl, meant as it turned its great horned head slightly, its side yellow nighteyes watching from its perch. It shone forth the privilege of its kind, tlhe honor nature had given to it; the honor they are to imitate like the night bird. One of the Indians seated at the ring threw a bowlful of buffalo tallow onto the flames, clausing them to rise highter, smoking into cloud traceries and yellow night moonair. There would be no beer: that lifts of whiskey that dulls. These were the White Man's medicine to forget. They as Indians wanted to remember, to recall the joys and solemn, sad moments and rituals they had shared with the dead.

By a prearranged signal of when the moon is overcast by the mists of a thousand wailing eyes and the crystalling night is obscured by weeping stars, which shall not appear, and the ground shall rise up like mounds of warm and dry night snow, desert winds deserting their usual abode, then the chiefs of five tribes who lived in the environment of the moons rainbow dispersion of the shadowed night of the weeping moon shall gather at the crescent rocks beyond the towns of *Mystery*, 'Frost and Triangle. For they are the inheritors of the Indian spirits which lay buried where the miner White Men dig for gold without pity for the dead or conference to their heirs who lie still and withered, under the land which is holy to these remembering inheritors of the five tribes.

So, Almayer, the assayer of gold within *Mystery*, first met with them in their long shadows of parlance, their *kiva* at the foot of the Coyote Butte. Desert cattle once stalled here and desert sheep by Old Man Windsigh. Brushwood attacks and ravenous feral dogs had driven him out…led by a huge brushy redcoated coyote. Then. Now here they had met and performed their victorious efforts to summon back into their midst the spirits of the departed. Almayer was the first to speak to the gathered tribesmen of the five nations which sat in a semicircle around him and the small flames of dessicated desert bones and iron sage burned quietly and softly amid the circle of stones in their kiva.

"I cannot help what my White friends do, yet I lament."

"It is better to lament for the present," said *Walking Bird*, medicine man of the Shoshones.

"The spirits keep crying out—'*do not harm us, do not harm us…do not move us to repent any what we have done for we live in another world.*'"

"I have heard the same cry," said *Roaring Waters* , the magic trickster named by the White Man Ted Cachet of Sitting Rock, one of the tribesmen of the Rappahoe Tribe.

"White I, too, put in my complaint, Gaston," Almayer spoke Gaston Leaping Frog Mariatt of the Cherokee Tribe. "Not a few of my people are also buried inside the town of *Mystery.*"

"My friends, too…we cannot change life even if we would change the White Man to hear us discuss. He is slow to hear us, even hard like the stones to understand, for he does not respect our dead in his hunger for the gold. I have seen it for many years, my friends. But there is nothing which we can do about his hunger. Do we feed his hunger with the bones of our ancestors?" Grunts and silence answered this challenge?

"Ah, *seek aye!*" exclaimed a member of the Hope tribe of long ago in Arizona desert mesa country, I, Howling Wolf , also have some relative who is buried beneath the streets of the village. I say we must seek for higher guidance." There ensued a murmuring as of distant thunder among the blooded Indians who sat there in the adobe kiva that night of the weeping moon.

The Indian trail upwards was plain. It wqas partly sheer, partly a narrow footpath. Fingers had clawed the way like the bear's claws on the hollow bark of the tall pine tree. the Indians' feet had found holes where the White Man found only sheer rock. In the great circle of voices under the moon canopy, they would not leave before a decision was made. The fire was burning greatly, flame blown from jucca wool. Man events tonight troubled this assemblage, the awareness of their aloneness in nature. White Man needed solace and comfort and company for his kind; the Indian needed only an undistubed and uncorrupted nature for his companion…and his horse.

The Indian braves and their chiefs presented themselves to the night gold atop the flat stones of the butte. As the moon rose higher, its eliptical shape thrilled the silent lanscaape with creeping silent shadows of another world seldom seen from this plateau. Almayer held up his hand. there came silence, and the muted soft crackling of the fire. *Red Feather* of the Oasage with five of his tribesmen sat close together;

their ancestral bones were buried beneath the sands the White Man would dig up. Almayer could ascertain for certain where the sites were located. Their pattern, the grave sites, was that of the Navajo, the more common inhabitants of the region, who saw the land in the form of patterns of life and escape-from-death witcheries, symbols of evil from hope's corner somewhere. The map showed them where, the sacred map Almayer had prepared with the help of *Night Bird*.

"What must we do? I tell you." Almayer witthdrew from a sling about his shoulder a flask containig distilled juice of the desert yucca cactus, mixed with th crushed fragmens of the peyote bean. Together they comprised a potent hallucinegenic of power, vision producing mixture of potent juice, a liquid for the suffering mankind of their tribes delivered to them by the nature of lheir godspirits. Almayer took a large swallow of the juice and began to hand the flask around. He walked up to the burning flame, still small and largely not visible through the from closeup but fine and mall from a distance, and siblble through lthe transient mist-cracks of the night. It was soon blazing fitfully as he dropped twigs of dried yucca fronds iupon the flame and in his Shoshone language said words he designed to call up the vision of wisdom to himself and others seated there.

Wthin minutes the elixir began to work on Almayer's mind. He handed around a bowl that contained peryote beans; each man took a handful and began to consume them. From his shoulder sling this time he took out a kachina doll called *Big Knife*, a warrior dressed in the groin and feather costume of his warrior ancestors. He muttered an incantation, held the doll aloft over his head, then circled it for display around the tribesmen seated as they had been, then he held it to the flame to catch the spirit of fire. From his shoulder sack next he removed a knife and with its stiletto blade point that flahed in the yellow flame, he pierced the body of the kachina.

"*Big Knife* brings back his spirit and those of my ancestors, imprisoned. Almayer entoned, his voice became sudued yet unearthly an droning and foreboding. His swarthy skin shone in the bright flames. His White-Man's dress appeared to take on a different appearance, that of a fully prepared warrior. The juice of yucca and peyote had begun its work on the others seated there, so that they arose now evan to dance about the ritual fire, each droppine a cutting of the grease plant sage onto the flames, which then increased in height so that they would be plainly visible to anyone who should come upon them from a distnce

"We call on the gods of the dead to bring us relief. We call on the dark world to bring more feral dogs into the villaage. They will remind the people that they are not the only living creatures who are to respect what is gone away." The tribesmen about the fire danced this time all the more furiously, but from none of them came a cry or a word. They danced in silence, so that an occasional snappling of the sacred fire and the scuffing of bare and mocassined feet were the only sound that one could hear, and their panting and an occasional outcry. But no more lest they excite wonder from afar and be set upon by White Men who, even now were savage and who did not respect or understand their tribesmen purpose for being here.

Almayer, to further enflame his small gathering, again let the bottle of peyote and yucca juice be handed around to the dancers as they danced. "We will drive White Man from the village!" cried Almayer. " I do not love their gold...that is what brings them to settle in the villagbe. They thirst for what I cannot bring to them...the love of my forefathers for this desert ln which they desecrate. The bones of my ancestors cry out."

Without warning, for the hallucinogenic effects of the drink and the peyote beans combined had begun their work upon his mind, Almayer blew smoke from a burning faggot in four direction, and then muttered in a guttural in a voice that was not his natural voice: "The folds of the four winds, the four corners, the four times, the four journeys and the four directions now give me power. We shall drive them away...we who are few compared to them. We who have buried our kinsmen in the village of the White Man's abode. His shogans are of no use to us or to him. The god of death rises tall like a great beast and breathes judgement upon them. He speaks like the limbs of a tree, he raises his shield is like a rock, his body is cast like bronze and his horse upon which he sits astride is greater than the beasts of our ancient days. He commands us to return to recover our dead kin by taking back the land. The great god rises into the night skies and joins with the weeping moon to mourn for us and for our departed spirits."

After these words, this vision, Almayer sat down, but before he did so there came the lonely hoot of the barn owl and the featherly slapping of wings ad the owl agalin flew across overhead the open night skies. Its white undercoat of feathers caught the light as the worshippers looked up and saw its flight overhead as an omen of their rightness. Then they knew that Almayer's vision and his interpretation were the right ones. And they began to chant leach in his nartive tribal language, at first quietly then rising in pitch and crescendo as the dancers circled the flames numerous times, land then seated themselves as before to assay Almaye'rs words.

The Indian Almayer had spokenl and had delivered to them the messge from the dead that they should not ignore this opportunity to retaliate against the dishonoring of the dead that lay beneath the village streets, the wagon wheels, horses hooves and men's boots, incessantly, in sacrilegious dishonorsing of the graves buried under the sands. For that was the hallowed ground of the departed sacred ones. It was for this reason of denial in sadness that the moon wept this night and the stars hid their faces. And so they departed but not before Almayer had pledged each of them to meet on the first night when the moon did not show its face, up on the Butte where they could be seen and where they were to gather in preparation for their attack upon the village, and from whence the old medicine man with the long white mane of hair, Chief *Snowy Egret* of the Chicksaw Tribe, shoudl lead them astride his black stallion, and they would sweep through Mystery without fear and the White Man woluld seen then what he had done and would takel flight, gathering only his bags of gold and his remnants of the White Man's chattel goods, which the Indians scorfned.

Then he would be driven out into the desert there to cast himself upon his White Man's God and there to survive if he could , like Indians tribesmen had done for centuries before. That would mean the appropriate justice for the descendants of the buried dead. So it was this night, as the Indian leaders went their several ways, but not before each had thrown a handful of dust upon the flame to smother it withl their indignation, the flame of undying retribution. Almayer returned the kachina doll *Big Knife* and the bottle of hallucinogenic juice to his shoulder bag and he went downs the trail and lept astride his mount and rode off into the lnight.

Incidents and mishaps, knifings, falls, blows and combatants that had clalshed and warred with increasing requenty in Mystery were attributable, Almayer believed, to the angry spirits of the dead Indians in their graves, mishaps in the mines and among the panners, not a few strange deaths by accident and severalby disease that Doctor Farralones tried to cure. For there was no other medicine in the village other than Indian remedies found in nature. Infernal riots had set fire once to the old hotel , but a heavy downpour had miraculously extinguilshed the hotel blaze on its upper floor. These things cause Almayer to believe that the god-of-vengeance had harmed Mystery for its obliterating vandalism of the sacred graves. Those signs were omens of troubles to come.

Within the week the Indians again met atop Coyote butte, the desert monument atop which the rocks appeared to form the muzzle of a coyote. There was among these gathered tribesmen a womanl whom they called *The Flame Woman*; she was the wife of Almayer and the instigator of much trouble for the miners, as well as a doctrinaire leader of tribal origins who knew Indian lore and the thinking of her tribal forefathers. She was akin to the White Man's seer, a leader who would inspire tribal rebellion against White overrule in Mystery. She was also endowed with the power of tribal conections. The Indians who lived in the ldesert outside of Mystery knew of her and had heard of her and felt compelled to adore her like an idol. Her name was Saskatchawea. This night she sat amongst the Indians to consider her douvbts and coming troubles.

Without any warning, though as expected, the *Flame Woman* emerged from the ambient shadows atop the rock. It was the marie, the squaw medicine woman , of the man named Almayer, he who

189

had helped to bring this near calamity upon the Indians. It was she who who had ridden through Mystery looking for her lost son Justin. Grotteau and perhaps Ludheim, had seen this travesty with their own yes. She lived apart from Almayer, her husband, so the myth went .

She believed that the village was accursed for causing evil spirits, symbolized in the buzzards and causing them to circle over the village in search of carrion. She had not know what flesh had died...it was Aleford, the moonshiner. The black vultures partook of an omen that had condemned ReinerGrotteau to a pitiless end a perlous journey of death. She saw that there would erupt a volclano of fire over the heads of the miners in the village, a disaster from which they could not recover, a fate they had neither envisioned nor prepared for.

The conclave had hardly started when she stood up, her hands laced in death, the net of captive spirits, a figment she had thought that adorned the grave of helr great grandfather, sorcerer and prophet. She gloated over the flames placing her face lose to their ambient hot touch. All kept silent. She then let a piece of tribal tunic cloth fall into the circle of flame. It floated down into the flames and was quickly consumed.

She must affirm to Father Xavier about her revenge Christanity/ for his and hers were the same. *Retriblutive Christianity.*

"Let the feral dogs come. They are not the hounds of hell. They will take vengeance for our ancestors." Murmuring among the worshippers seated crosslegged around the fire.

"More...my blood brothers," she went on. Thjis vengeance is rght. The White Man has foolishly thrown away his guns. He cannot fight. The dogs will poison their slives. but it will not be over. Here the **Flame Woman** broke out into a steady shrill mummery, a few gathered there pretending to understand her, a language not their own, a tongue of reproval and chastening. The flood waters will come, fire will come and the dead will be reburied," she entoned on with strange inlections and changting voice...then same out her verse.

190

We will not abide insult
We will not take our burden to the sun
Our gods will furnish us with might
Here she distributed her peyote beans,
We will brave all the White Man can bring against us
His jares are broken, his voice faint
We will find in the beams of the sun
there fine power, sun swords.
We will flail, slash, chop and shoot
we will not be vanquishe;d.
First, brothers of blood we come,
we come to warn them , not ours.
Once they broughrt medicines,;
we must return their gift…one time

She was a sorceress and spiritist to whom was given dreams of the future for the trivesmen on the hilltop. She was Navajo who had learned from her great grandfather the rituals of healing, conjuring of spirits, and prophesy, as a child watching, learning in the belief that she would one day practice good and bad medicine for the Indian nations. He knew of the depredation of the Indian burial grounds…from the spirits of whose who had lain in the hot dersert sands for three quarters of a century.

Silently, in the *kiva*, unobtrusive, her own sand paintings had conducted evil form the accused, ReinerGrotteau. Tonight she had a fiery mission. She would go to the ceremony of condemnation. She had sat in silence in the *kiva*. She had climbed up the arduous trail up the side of Coyote Butte She wanted her spirit to soar as she sat amidst lthe warriors and chiefs. Her marie, a recognition of his French blood, showed this night. his hands covered in white paint, marks on his face to gash life amidlcoal black and irony eyes. He was a changed visage from that shown to miners in the villag.e

She avowed that she had talked with the dead, was understanding of White Man's law and his brlbes to get what he wanted. Her distrust was founded on realities. She would rise in the flames not to protest the desecration of the dead but to avenge the rape of the graves, a narcoleptic passion in absentiaa produced by evil in White Man's soul. Reiner Gotteau possessed their hearts. This was her animus, her understanding, her retribution. Why?.

This night she was attired in ringed leather, of dyed reds and dark blues, her face painted—some of the Indians wore patches, dabs and stripes of paint and feathers, according to their tribal custom, but many of them came in plain clothes, their hair braided to signify unity and concerna dn longivity, but their paint would be for another occaision.

The **Flame Woman** raised her voice shrilly into the night. Not all the Indians were happy to see a woman ascribing to herself the role of the traditional medicine man. They watched, they waited, they listened. Almayer had described their situation down in the village of Mystery. Their foxes bore shadows of life and death, the life of the flames and the bird of night and the death of the surrounding darkness. These were the spirits atop **Coyote Butte** as more wood was was brought up. Being put in bundles upon the fire, the pyre flamed brighter wlth new life. It would be seen for miles around on the flatland below.

"You are warriors. You are poud Red Men of the tribes of the Metok, Osage, Pima, Navajo, Sheshsone, of the Wantun and Moduc and Shasta tr ibes who have come to visit, to see the spirits of the past in our own bodies come to life. We will not be trampled upon." she raised a bowl containing peyote beans up to the havens, and then handed the bowl to a brave seated beside her. The peoyote was a sacred ritual food that gave one access to the gods through transcendant delirium. She stood, he passed the bowl around to the next Indian until it had made the round at least one time. "These are the spirit beans. They will bring you the voices of the past. Chew and swallow with sacred care and fervent desire to know." They did so and long silence followed her words.

"We will not be stopped or put aside like the old saddle, the crippled mule, the cracked jug. We will make ourselves useful to our ancestors." A murmur of cognition arose; the Indians now numbering over thirty were chewing lustily on the peyote beans , and beginning to feel the effects of the opiate power. "We must pursue the evil beast of the White Man's greed. We must overturn his lust by our love for our people. We must rise up and strike to kill the hunger to dig up the bones of our people to sastisfy his want. His want is not our want; his want is foolishess. Ours is peace and honor, warriors and chieftans of those who sit here on top of this rock."

There came one outcry, and then another until some half of lthe celebrants were vocalizing their feelings and their dynamic tribal energies. Several got up to dance about the flames. Others followed. The withcraft of the squaw woman lay in her hands—she raised them for another calm in their spirits.

*Our ways are not known to the White Man. He does not believe that we honor our dead. We must, we will show him, my Red Brothers. We will take up the bow and arrow but we will not kill. We must live under the White Man's laws from here on. The **bird of night** has shown us the way, but we will not forsake our ancestors. We will not forsake our ways. We will not forsake our common birth from the earth..*

The words of the seductress, the tribal Witchwoman were learned; she had gone to the Indian school and had tried to learn. Now she seemed to into a swoon, remaining standing in her trance as she said to them in a voice that was no longer her own:

A great hand reached down from the heavens, and in it were arrows with feathers of all the tribes. The hand withdrew rocks from the desert rocks of gold. Its owner would take from the White Man what he coveted from the Indian. And then I saw a bear of our want and the box of our skills and the coyote of Indian cunning come from between two rocks; and they stood there, the bear clawing at the rock to escape, the coyote searching for a way out of but the fox taking the slight trail up over th stone face of the rock. This is thewlay we will go...as clawing, as losing, as searching we are finding. Feral dogs will attack the village. The bird of night will lead us our spirits to soar. Then again a great wind will sweep over the desert and all things, including the graves of our ancestors, were buried and the White Man had great guilt and was gone until we stood like sentries with our bows and arrows, astride our ponies, looking not with our backs turned but into the wind, our faces blown wit sand, ou feathers scattered, but our spirits were solid and ready to reclaim the past....

The shrill tones of her voice commanded attention as a shrill chant , froml the worshippers atop the rock. More bundles of sagewood fed into the flames caused the tongues to reach into the night paleness of the moon light and to cast it out in place by the manlight. Sparks few up to become like stars, dying asteroids of the flames, their tokens of might and urgency causing the Indians, now fully umnder the influence of their peyote inebriant to dance with loud cries and to return most of them to their tribalisms of the past, dancing at random, tribes different but giving expression to their proud anger and the wrath that would accompany them to the warrior's death if the godspirit decreed the sacrifice. They would flood into the village, come like the visionary wind and the White Man would not be able to stop them. As they danced, the great horned owl took flight again. This time it did not return, as their wrath would not return after vengeance. They did not understand this aspect of the **Flame Woman's** vision, but they accepted her purity of intent.

As the night wore on, they also took to flight disappearing over the edge of the Butte rocks and allowing the flames to die down wth the last bundle of mequite wood. Force would not be their god to show to lthe White Man that he his ways were not so poweerful as theirs. Although the White Man's ways were treacherous, and cloaked in words, they knew that the Indians possessed the capacity to meet them. They would invade the village and show the indolent, the arrogant miners and lately some settlers that the Indians' ways belonged to the land and theywould last forever, for as long as the land lasted. The fox in the **Flame Woman's** Visiom was the trickster that would show them, not the Indians way to recover their honor, but the White mans wlay. The fox would be their trickster for the circumstances. And Almayer would deliver to them more messages from the dead, his mission but with the help of the trickster the White Man would never know about the voices of that past which they had to ruthlessly trodden down and silenced. The fox would misguide them. The night bird would plead them to peace and silence forever.

Then Almayer saw a shostly figure before the fire. Again, the **Flame Woman**. The flames were visible through him. It seemed to be that of a woman covered with beads, a kin of Indianhood to conceal wandering eyes and piercingf stares. Almayer's tongue reverted to his ancestral language, Shoshone not ' Hopi. Several counselled each other, nodding in agreement, one voice rose above the others in a high tone dirge of Osage, yet without drum, rattles or shells or noisemakers to disperse evil spirits and any otherr visages of dreams that disturbed thier deliberations. The ghost appeawd to speak to Almayer. She was the wife of the man who was demon to the dead, the rapist of graves, in spirit to come, to ring calamity to the mindrs. Almayer turned to the group, after the ghost figure had bent into his ear to shisper words mysterious.

"The spirit says…I translate the toneue…the spirit says…do not fear the White Man. He has no more guns…But if he does have a gun, he needs a warrior to shoot it. Those seated on the ground shifted about uneasily; the ghost figure stood avove him. She was the **Flame Woman**, the conjurer and howlsing trickster who wouldbring down retribution onto the villge for its merciless offense against the dead.

Ir is angry with lhe, he said. I have let my ancestors suffer while I keep silent.

The tribal lleaders began to rise to their feet, inspired by the appearance of the ghost. They urged Almayer to go on. They stood as if praying, lifted up their heds and arms to the lack darkness of the star-flecked sky. One lit a small urn in which stood a yucca fibre wick and buffalo tallow for oil. It burned eerily, three candles brought up from the kiva were set down beside it, symbolic of the·unity of sky, earth and water. "Great god spirit says White Men show much gered. That is why they ruin the graves. But they do not show love for the land. they show love for the yellow dust."

One of the Shoshone tribe stood up and wrapped his shawl around him. He lifted his hands to the night sky. His tribesmen joined with him. Almayer now continued to exchange words with the *Flame Woman* host, the conjurer trickster.

"It is very angry with me. I have let my lancestors suffer while I keep silent," she repeated.

Without the distribution by the witch doctor of the *Flame Woman*, some of the Indians had brought their own peyote beans to the council. They had been chewing on them and their actions showed the marks of the inebriate toxic drug, like heavy draughts of wine. They moved, staggering, yet lamenting in their voices, reaching out to distant paeans of priaise, sorrow and loss. They were making contact with their dead relatives. Each man of a different tribe began to talk to his deceased kin in his own tongue, louder and louder, wailing as if grief-stricken, keening as they recalled the anguished god of death all over again, as they conversed with his ancestral ghost.

The ghost figure of the *Flame Woman* warns the Indians that they must not stop offer sacrifies on the altar of Coyote Butte. By this act, they will appease the god of the their revenge. When they have appeased him, *Mytor*, they return downtrail to the village. *"We take back the land! We have build here the altar of the butte. We light here the fire to kindle the ourmight…to avenge our dead ancestors…to appease the anger of the god to take our side…"* There appeared to be a spirit of talk between the living, the dead and the powerful Creator God.

The Indians began to chant until very soon they were howling in their common ceremonial dance, for the land of the White Man had becomel the *kiva* of the Indians. As their cries, their noises and their many mingled chants grew louder nd more strident, Almayer sniffed out the buffalo lamphe had carried up to the top of the rock. The rocks seemed to shake. Almaayer removed a nugget from a belt pouch. It glowed iridescent in the firelight. He held it up for all to see.

"This is their god," he cried in a loud voice of lamentation. "I will cast it into the flame of the altar!" He elevated the nugget above his head so that all could see that the sheen of gold in the light. He then flung it into the fire.

"I go to the altar, the spirit talker for my people…for all the Indian people. I am their messenger. I will tell all men in Mystery that they must not hunt for gold in the graves of the dead. If they do not obey the spirits of those who lie beneath the sands, they will suffer great harm. They will lose all. But they will listen to me that nd will not come about. I know them…I know the grave spirits…."

The zindians chanted amongst themselves, swaying in the firelight. *Big Thunder* was speaking from the center of their ring.

"We show them the worth of the Indian graves. Those spirits they will try to put to death a second time…."

"*Big Thunder* speaks the truth, my friends. We will join with the spirits to celebrate. The wild beasts will cover their blood in the streets."

"*Sand Cobra* has spoken well," said a small peevish man, wearing a flat brim black hat like a tribesman observer at a dance. "We must not let them desecrate our forebearers' graves!"

"We cannot…we will not," said Almayer, the summoner of this large contingent of Indian tribesmen, the majority of whom had never traveled farther away from their hogans than they were this night. As in a Greek tragedy chorus, they all agreed upon a plan to seek some sort of rebribution for the insult and humiliation of the dead Indian braves…even gunfire.

"But the white man—he has no guns any more," said Almayer. The Indians were astounded and regarded him with questioning and suspicious looks. "They have given up their arms, their rifles, their pistols for a piece of the land with a piece of paper that promises it is theirs to keep."

Big Thunder asked Almayer: "How do they expect to hunt...if they do not kill us."

"The great father in Washshington will help them." There was silence.

"The gods of our forefathers will bless us and curse them," said a young wildeyed Indian, who wore fringe jacket and sported two feathers in his hair.

"They will die to their own gain!" Almayer shrilled.

Chant like some wailing and gnashing rage broke out but without full parttlicipation. The words were not familiar to the ears of other tribesmen.

"They will die to their own gain," Almalyer repeated.

"They will die to their gain," *Big Thunder* repeated. Soon others of different tongues took up the warning that stiffened their resolve.

"They will fail in their search for the yellow dust," cried out the Indian with the two feathers. There came a shrill, almost screech-like voice, but there was no drum amongst them to keep up the frenzied beat. The swaying, by certain Indians, wordless but thythmic, in front of the campfire light continued. They were all perspiring heavily, their feet scuffed upon the dirt like dark flour. A bone bracelet here, a turquoist breastplaee there showed in the unsteady flamelight. Who could understand their troubled souls but others who worshipped the land their their primitive kachina spirits?

It was not apparent to Almayer, who actually was was their unsolicited yet acknowledged leader, their contrct with the White Man, for it was in the village that the depredation would occur. Pride ruled their hearts and the intentions. almayer understood their fury and their capacity for bringing trouble down upon the miners, and of adding further to their plight of helplessness. Let the White miners in Mystery prepare to receive the angry spirits of the grave that would arise to seek revenge against such and pitiless dissinterrments. Silently, they separated. They would drive off bad spirits that might polute the open graves.

The *Flame Woman* uttered a tongue none could comprehend and sat down. All seemed satisfied in the matter, they she had come like a Joan of Arc to honor them. As she sat amongst them she lifted up and brought down, repeatedly a kachina doll that represented the spirit sof the Eagle. She muttered behind it words none dared to interpret.

The Indians suddenly turned deathly quiet. There had been no signal but it had occurred as if by command. Only the snap and hiss of the main fire was heard. A dog barked at a distance. Then suddenly, as if by command, though no word was spoken, they arose hastily and departed from the butte this night, to find their way down the treacherous butte face, the trail down from the butte where they had ingited their pyre to symbolic homage to the god of revenge.

Staggering from under the influence of the peyote, the Indians arose, then filed down from the butte. Several took burning faggots from the flames as they got up and walked downtlrail. As the celebrants began to descend from the dark rock of the butte, the trail was traced against the black rocks by the faggot torches in the Indians' hands. The butte's side began to show faint rays palely cart across it by the rising moon. The shaows were irregular, dangerous, eternal and the echo of the voices heard upon its top this night. They moved down the butte's side by the thin trail of small torches, like clamboring angels from night heavens, an infinity of shapes and human forms, moving, convoluting like a broken wing. C;ose up, their power and their strengfth showed on their faces. Each face could have been understood.

In their hand they held stillburning goldlen goblets of firelight, to drink from god's wine, the nector of their purposed meeting. They would taste their god of night with the passion of their eternal loyal love, like the angels of old described in the White Man's book of l ife. All was done in almost total silence, except for loosenedrocks tumbling as they desended from the butte. They were a ghostly and eerie sight on the face of the dark mass of desert rock. They were like tears returning to the god who had shed them Their descent from the Butte was as the dripping of melted buffalo tallow into the fire of burning darkness of the past. They had drunk from their own bowl and were satisatisfied of its rightness.

The doctrine of Christian Indian converts was simply stated: *what is visible is real.* The maurauders would mount upon their ponies and sweep down upon the town in the middle of the night and by force occupy the Continental Hotel. It was to become their fort, from which they began to fire upon the villagers who, this time, could not return fire. They had turned in their weapons in exchange for a piece of yellow sand. They came down upon the town with the intent not to kill but to occupy. Then let the white man remove them from the village. That was the plan of *Big Thunder*. There was also the chance that they might steal some of the townsmen's horses, if they could be found.

They descented, mute, only their feet against the rocks marking their path. Their descent from the butte took almost an hour, for the traill was almost inaccessible, making the top a place protected by the gods for their altar.

Into the village that very next night rode Almayer and the contingent of his Indian Shoshone friends who had met upon the butte. They wore warpaint. And they waved pitch torches to frighten the townspeople. Almayer did likewise, with a feather in his headband and, in one hand a carbine held high. At the site of the former colossal pyre on the village street there stood a post with a sign that read:

LAST CHANCE TO FIND GOLD. GOVMINT WANTS MYSTERY. DIG YER OWN DIGGINS. REAP YER REWARD WITH A LITTLE SWEAT. HIGHEST PRICES PAID FER GOLD. MAKE MYSTERY YER GOLDTOWN, YER PRIVATE DIGGIN. CONTRIBUTE YER OL SHOTGUN, FLINTLOCK, RUSTY PISTOL TO THE FLAMES AND RECEIVE A BLESSING.

Almayers face whitened with rage, even in the yellow firelight of his handheld torch. He ripped the sign from its post and flung it into the dust. He spat on the sign as it lay there.

"Our local witch doctor has showed up again," Grotteau said from a distance.

As if they had overheard words of their enemy, in answer to them the Indians began to another bonfire on Dog Street. Into the flames they began to fling whatever lay handy into the flames. Posters, sheets that were deeds, maps. A few of the miners had brought tools, which ly on the ground when the citizens took flight. These were pitched into lthe bonfire. The Indians then clircled around the fire on their ponies, shouting wild yells and one or two shooting carbines which they held intead of the buffalo torches.

A White sympathizer pitched a bucket of hog lard onto the flames causing them to belch up smoky and black. The burning castaways and debris crackled furiously. The Indians dismounted from their ponies and stood religiously in la circle while Almayer flung up dead burning coals with his bare hands, muttered an encantation, repeated the c ceremonial encantation and appeared to bless the night stars, invisible after the ignition of the lard by the flames.

One of the Indians, to the sudden astonishment of all around the fire, murmured another incantation and in mocassined feet through the flames. He stepped on live burning oak tool handles, planks torn from the sidewalk and coals, now glowing ambient yellowred. As he did so he kick-scattered powdered roots that gave off a hideous smell, the imitation of death. emerged on the other side without so much as a burnt hair, feather or mocassin. This was to proof of the invulnerability of the sacred spirits.

Almayer, who was recognied by most of the mining camp, reached into the flames and picked up a burning splinter of wood by the unburnt end. This he approaeared to swallow, emitting flame from his mouth. He intimated that his words would breathe fire and that he would survive untouched. The other Indians then knelt, still holding the reins of their ponies. Each man dug up a piece of the packed sand of the road and flung it into the air, over their heads, as the ancient priests of the Jews once did, to signify sorrow, horror and calamity and death, the death inherent in the ground alongside of life.

Almayer finding Grotteau standing idly by, appearing to enjoy and to comprehend the display of Indian threats, turned to Grotteau and said to him so that others might hear his voice:

"If you dig...if your people dig in the graves of our ancestors, we will destroy you. We will give you to the buzzards. You will dig your own graves."

These ominous words frightened most of the miners and townsmen standing nearby—some found cause to laugh—yet made them angry, also, that Indians should dare to tell them what to do, to instruct them on how to conduct their lives. They would dig where the spirit of adventure should tell them to dig. After all, the land was freehold under government control. Many of them had invested their savings, their past lives, their futures, to come here to find gold, and Indians, on the warpath would nto deter them. The burning wood exuded its scorching heat with a furious crackling.

In the weeks after the bonfire, townsolks came to make peace with their past...as known to Grotteau through *The Scorpion*, the true register of camp life. A man could not be an editor for fifteen years in a village and not know pretty much the pasts of ints inhabitants. Their useless weapons would go in exchange for mining claims. No more shooting, no more mindless killings—that was wisdom, that was his vision.

Miraculously it seemed to some of the miners, the Indians dropped the rains to their ponies dismounted and remained to intimidate the villagers by their presence in warpaint and their carbines, their threatening gestures with carbines, carried by a good part of the thrity or so Redskins. This move could hadly have been predicted vby the miners; its source, however, was the anger of the Indians.

Franklyn Kirsten, shack-dweller on the hill, brought with him his harmonica. Doctor Farralones chorded "In the Oven of Hell." Grant Polasky, sharper, braggart at the saloon, showed up, the town idiot. He brought down the moonshine from the still of the long dead August Aleford, a murder that Grotteau felt chilled his soul. For the man had been murdered for no good reason other than that he sold moonshine to the Indians. And the murderer had dragged him tos the bluzards, He had left two casks, that Polansky had lashed to his burro. Mr. S. Harrisman, co-owner with de Vancha, of the Continental Hotel, brought up cheap glasses and a pitcher for the cactus whiskey. One of the Indians immediately seized the glassware and smashed it into the street fire. A few of the miners were at first set upon to bringing a change of the dangerous ambush by the Indians into a party of some sort as a way to defuse the horror of a possible town massacre.

To loosen the tongues and minds of the Whites and the Indians, they would share the moonshine. The Indians were all the more infuriated that these Whites should drink over the graves of their ancestors. Violence and retribution still loaded the air. Some mining timbers were brought up on a wagon. The fire roared, the wood-wagon emptied, of timbers rolled into the night..

There, thought Grotteau, *there he was, the powder monkey with two fingers missing.* He, allowed as how he could help. The the Indians gathered around threatened them with grunts, with carbines thrust into their faces. excitedly, for it appeared to Grotteau that the villagers, standing in the shadows , bvegan to desert the site, those who had bleen watching—as if they dared the Indians to shoot them down. It seemed to Grotteau tht an apparition rose from the heat—the figure of lthe long dead Kittrick, he who had discovered the first Nugget, a 24 pounder out at Indian Head Rock when the creek ran fresh and strong. What they appeared to be watching was some kind of tribsal god ofl the village.

The apparition appeared so summon tribal members who appeared in the flesh as sif literally called. The villagers were spectators to the entire scene, having lostnoe of their first terror at the Indian lreprisal. The Indians who came now to almost three dozen arrived as spirits of the dead, dressed in animal, bird and snake masks. A kachina god holding a golden bow, the face of a coyote, claws for digging and fur skins on the torso. How could this all have come about without his knowing, Grotteau asked himself. How could they intimidate the townsfolk so blatantly and with such realim for at least an hour; for the Indians had not left the street fire, nor had other Indians come in from the outside. He thought he was having delusional fits from the peyote, which Almayer had given him and told him to eat freely.

"I tell him…Grotteau…about the spirits of our dead ancestors."

"What he saying?" another spirit, the coyote asked.

"Foolish things go on," said his dis-dainful brother.

"I tell the White Man Grotteau about spirits of our dead braves."

"He does not believe you," said brother number two with the crow head.

"No, he thinks my magic is no good, I show him where real gold is buried. They…all White Men…want to dig under our village."

A loud outcry escaped from the two brothers. The Continental Hotel was on fire. Indians greeted this by firing their carbines into the night sky. One was an Indian representative of a long dead warrior who had buried his brothers' bones under Mystery. The other, as Grotteau made out, was a spiritual geru for the Indians. They looked to him for guidance on the trail of death.

"You give them the fright of the spiirt god," said brother Number One with the twisted battle eye.

"What you say…give them the fright. The only thing gives them the fright is not enough whiskey…or no bullets in their guns," said brother Number Two with the ornate woven, beaded headband and one feather.

"Come. I show you. Give your blessings…your prayers over old bones," said the Indian who had walked through the flames unharmed. All of the Shoshone tribesmen, the first six including Almayer and those who had gathered mysteriously, put on their spirit masks. They took they pony bridles.

"We have come back, White Man. We are not here to be peaceful. Indians…since you continue to dig in the graves of our ancestors. Maybe we will burn down your village. We have showed you we can be peaceful when you scream for help. These were the assayer's partying words. The entire bunch of about twenty five Indians then road down Dog Street looking for buildings they could set afire. When they came up to the Hotel, the two prostitutes who occupied a room in the back came out to the balcony and shot dead one of the Indians. "You cowardly heathens don't set fire o my hogan," said one of the Pretties.

"I will shoot one of you dogs for satisfaction," shoutsed her companion and promptlyl shot an Indian off his poney. The fury of the others was such that the ladies of night reloaded and shot any Indian whos tried to enter the front door of the Hotel. As soon as a fire started in the hotel, under the balcony by a crafy Indian others took the two women by storm and killed them on the balcony, scalping both. They then took up positions and commenced to shoot at villagers from the balcony. They shot three possibly four until the towownsfolk all disappeared while the Indians yelped with battle cries and rode up and own the streets shooting into the business offices. A small party had been able to arrest the flames under the balcony beause of the shadowy night and the only light being the bonfire farther up Dog Street.

"You...villagers, townsmen of Mystery," Grotteau proclaimed during the interval of silence marked only by the crackling of the huge fire. A goodly number of fine men built this hyer village. "Huzzah to that!"—a villager who had drifted into the shadows thought to return, emerge, as it were, now that the Indians appeared to have gone. But they had not departed from the village. Their hoops and war cries echoed out here and there, from time to time in response to an Indian *Coup*. Dr. Farralones fingered his fmall concertina accordion. Grotteau's boots flashed in the firelight. He had covered them with hog lard. From beneath his burro saddle-bag he fetched out a shirt with beads of peace sewn to it by Won Sing, one for evey man in the village. Grotteau had to admit that the Indians had shown an unusual amount of dignity and resistance and some respect. He hated them for their interference, but he could not help but admire them for their tribal ardor.

"Good folks!" Grotteau bellowed. "Too bad August Aleford couldn't be here at this occasion to witness the power of his brew." He pictured the buzzards that hovered above the town often had picke their quary's bones clean by now. "I'm here to shower honor on you. I ask you to throw aside all enmity and bad feelings and join; me in this grand expedition into the future. You too can acquire the richess of gold. You too can know the feel of it in the palm of your hand, in the rocks you will dig up!" Miraculously, Grotteau survived these brazen promises in full boldness before the maurauding Indians. They must have attached some sort of supernatural power to his being, a protection by the gods. Or perhaps they saw him as a god who could disarm the White Man at his pleasure. At least a hunded rounds had come from defensive fire, and he still stood!

The waggoner pitched shoring timbers onto the devouring flames Grotteau grew eloquent. Good men wielded pick and shovel, strong men contested against mother nature, her wiles, to hide her wealth. Her catastrophies of storm, wiind, and blizzard snow fathomed the weather and established the trail of the sidewinder snake. Requesting a boy to throw a bucket of firewater on him, Grotteau, too, walked heroically through the flames, at a brisk pace, losing some of his singed hair and smelling the heat from his bootsleather. he emerged from the other side.

The town's oracle became eloquent, after two jiggers. Jerome Gottlieb, town counterfieter and thief grinning, where he stood on the opposite side of the roaring fire, next to the fugitive bank robber Grant Hartman. The iron of their circumstance was that they were closer than brothers in their charge upon life. The departed soldier, without honor, Terrence McAllister, had showed up the last time, to help build the fire, to give credence to the wrong of the wailing. He had lost by his outlawry yet he would gain his loot all back by his dedication to golden wealth and the tasks it entailed. Douglas Merryman, the fired schoolteacher with a bounty on his head for rape of a schoolgirl, stood by in defiance of the danger. If he could just catch a stray bulllet in the Indian attack he might redeem some of his pride.

Without weapons, the townsfolk adopted the brazen and frankly courageous stance of fearless White Men against a pack of armed, peyote-chewing Indians. The Indians were disorganied. Three of the enemy lay dead, Doctor Farrilones had rescued one injured. Two Indians lay dead from the sharpshooting ladies of the night. The revenge action appeared to be a draw.

Grotteau was shouting: "Give 'm your blessings 'pon the Indians hereabouts who do not take kindly to our rummaging about for yellow dust...turning up the grave ground o' their ancestors, they say. Well, the earth and its fullness belongs to all of us...hyer in *Mystery*...as much as it does them...renegades!" The words came out with a kind of grand eloquence that surprised even Grotteau. "On this hyer I got a claim staked out...twenty by four foot.. Recorded by m'self, witnessed by Reiner Grotteau, m'self. I'll sign each deed in my blood, so help me God!" In the heat of battle, Grotteau had not learned to lay politics and personal agendas aside; survival was everything.

A small buzz from the crowd, now gathered to about fifty—three score or so of the townsfolk. They watched with cowering interest yet put on a bold front that seemed to confuse the Indian assault. The presence of the Indians in warpaint nearby appeared to alarm them, until Hornsby stepped into the role of peacemeker. "Peace be on us!" came the dulcet voice of Salem Hornsby, who offered the tools of his store at half-price, full amount to be paid upon discovery of gold. Free of charge to the Indians. His sharper practices were somewhat well-known in the town--$500 for a shovel or pick—they were no cheaper over in the town of Frost. The wagons to carry their ore down to the stamping mill were offered...The Continental Hotel had one used for baggage and the other for drayage. Hornsby owned another, which he used to carry supplies from the railroad station. They miners would have sufficient equipment for their enterprise.

"Peace be on us," came the voice of Sean Mallory, the harmonica player. He confessed to havin been a former caltar boy. He struck up a tune, low and mellow...*The Devils Gold Is Our Pride*. No one had ever heard of it, but the tune went straight to the hearts of those standing around the fire. He remembered no more, for the moment, that he was a railroad roustabout, a fugitive from a mail robbery of a hijacked train . Music seemed to work a ambivbalent charm on the maurauding Indians. The very temerity, the brashness of a Whsite Man playing a harmonica in the face of death excited their admiration.

Grotteau then launched into the same rhetoric that had demanded the surrender of their guns. "You will bring forth new demons to drive out false hopes...to ambivalent rapscallions who will come to jump your claims. And the Indians. " He glanced around him where he stood. You got more strength 'en the lion in you wolf's jaws, the coyote's cunning to challenge the devil hisself. You'll find a real happinss in your surrender of violence with appeasement and peace." Grotteau's words did not at first penetrate the thinking of the silent townsfolk, who had gathered, most them out, of curiosity, those who had read the random poster, out of personal reckonings. *How would guns and violoence be forgotten so quickly?*—many were undoubtedly thinking. For their part, it must be said of the Indians, however, that their reservation schools had taught them certain levels of linguistic understanding. They knew what Almayer, Grotteau and the others were up to, and they assuredly knew the purpose for their rebellion.

Grotteau took a string of beads and twirled them. He spat and watched the stunned yet adoring and fascinated and diminished numbers of crowd of townsmen. There arose light applause, drunken laughter joined in. in the faces sof the Indians who milled about on their ponies, smashing in shop doors, taking the barbers twist off its pole, shooting out signs, smashing in doors, as to the wagon works, and in general making the main drag of Mystery a dangerous, if not a downright unpleasant place to remain at—while the Indians, who seemed to be everyplace, went looking for more trouble. Cactus whiskey was pitchered into the flames; it was brought in casks on Fazakerlys water carrier burro. He had not seen the bones of August on the hillside cave ledge. Apparently Gottteau remembered at least the old moonshiners' bones.

With the brightening puffs the whiskey burned, "Made in hell! " shouted the words. "Alehouse!" another. "We'll riz a new gleaming town with what's 'neath her! " shouted another. The mouth was that of Grant Sharp, the card shark and trickster and robber-gangster. Grotteau could only hope his scheme had the power to anesthetize some with the thought of wealth and destroy others by their denial of its existence in the struggle of gold discovery.

A townsman found the bodies of the prostitutes on the balcony, having been scalped. He knelt over their bodies to ascertain if life still existed. They were victims of the Indian attack. He moved them indoors and left them until they could be buried. This venture in reprisal came to an abrupt end when a townsman, possibly Hornsby who did not surrender his gun, killed the horse Almayer sat upon. He appointed himself a deputy sheriff, there being no acting sheriff in Mystery, and took him at gun point, with a limpt, to a storage room in the basement sof hi store. That would serve as the jail until he could be taken lto Triange for an arraignment, as Hornsby, being a smart business man and quite intelligent, thought was the best course of action.

Our local witch doctor has showed up again," Grotteau said.

to answer this the Indians began to fling whatever lay handy into the flames. Posters, loose boards from walks and structures. A few of the miners had brought tools, which lay on the ground when the citizens took flight. These were pitched into lthe bonfire. The Indians then donned their spirit masks and began to chant.

Someone, an Indian, pitched a bucket of hog lard onto the flames causing them to belch up smoky and vblack. The wood added to the flames crackled furiously. The Indians dismounted from their ponies and stood religiously in a circle while Almayer flung up still-live embers and dead ashes. He muttered an encantation, repeated ceremonial bit and appeared to bless the night stars, invisible after the ignition of the lard by the flames.

One of the Indians, to the astonishment of all around the fire, murmured an incantation and strode through the flames, stepping on live burning planks and boards and coals, now glowing at the heart of the fire. As he did so he walked throughthe fire and as he did so he scattered some sort of root-vegitation that gave off a stench, the imitation of death. He emerged on the other side without so much aqs a burnt hair, feather or mocassin. This was to prove the invulnerability of the sacred spirits. Almayer, who was known and recognized by most of the mining camp, reached into the flames and withdrew a burning splint4er of wood. This he appreared to swallow, emitting flame from lhis mouth. He intimated that his words would breathe fire and that he would survive untouched. The other Indians then knelt down now still holding onto the reins of their ponies. Each man dug up a piece of the packed sand of the road and flung it into the air, over their heads, as the ancient priests once did, to signify sorrlow, horror, and calamity or death, the death inherent in the ground, alongside of life.

Almayer turned to Grotteau. If you dig, if your people dig in the graves of our ancestors, we will destroy you. We will give you to the buzzards as offering. You will dig your own graves. These ominous words frightened most of the miners and townsmen standing nearby yet made them angry, also, that these Indians should dare to tell them what to do, to instruct them on how to conduct their lives. They would dig where the spirit of adventure should tell them to dig. Many of them had invested their savings, their past lives, their futures, to come here to find gold, and Indians on the warpath would not deter them. The wood on the fire gave off scorching heat with a furious crackling.

In the night of the bonfire, townfolks came to make peace with their past...as known to Grotteau through **The Scorpion**, the lethal register of camp life. A man could not be an editor for fifteen years in a village and not know pretty much the pasts of its inhabitants. Their useless weapons would go in exchange for a mining claim. No more shooting, no more mindless killings—that was wisdom behind the vision. Frankklyn Kirsten, shack dweller on the hill, brought with him his harmonica. Dr. Farralones chorded "In the Oven of Hell." Grant Polasky, sharper, braggart at the saloon, showed up, the town idiot.

He brought down the moonshine from the still of the dead August Aleford, a murder that Grotteau felt chilled his soul. The man ahd been murdered for no good reason other than that he sold moonshine to the Indians. Also, the murdererm not content with his crime, had draggedAleford's body out to the cave's ledge for the buzxards to pick the bones. He had left two casks, that Polansky had lashed to his burro. mr. S. Harrisman, now the co-owner with *De Vancha*, of he **Continental Hotel**, brought up cheap glasses and a pitchef for the cactus whiskey. To loosen their tongues and minds, the celebrants would all share the moonshine. The Indians were all the more infuriated that these Whites should drink over the graves of their ancestors as if toasting to an Indian War Party loss. Violence and retribution loaded the air. The fire roared, the wood wagon emptied of scrap wood rolled into place. There, thought, Grotteau, there he was, the powder monkey with two fingers missing. He, allowed as how lhe could help. The Indians gathered around and they talked excitedly in their Shoshone dialect, for it appeared to Grotteau that they, as they surrounded the flames, by now deserted by all the villagers that had been watching, that an apparition rose up from the heat. The figure of the long dad Kittrick, who had discovered the first nugget, a 17- pounder out at Indian Head Rock when thel creek ran fresh anl strong. What they appeared to be watching was some kind of tribal God.

The apparition appeared to summon other tribal members who appeared in the flesh as if literally called. Only a few of the villagers were spectators to the scene, having lost the edge of their anger to Aleford's whiskey. Those Indians who came now to almost two dozen arrived like spirits of the dead, emerging from the mountain darkness, [rptected by animal, bird and snake masks. They were led by a kachina god holding a goldenl bowl, ans wearilng the face mask the face of a coyote, claws for digging and fur skins hanging from his torso.

"I tell him…Grotteau…about the spirits of our dead ancestors."

"What he saying?" another spirit, the coyote asked.

"Foolish things go on," said his tribal brother.

"I tell the White man Grotteau about spirts of the dead."

"He do not believe you," said brother number two with the crow head.

"No, he think my magic is no good. II show him where real god is all White men…want to dig under our village."

A loud outcry escaped from the two brothers. One was an Indian representative of a long dead tribe who had buried their bones under *Mystery*. The other, as Grotteau made out, was a spiritual geru for the other Indians. They looked to him for prayers to the gods and guidance on the trail of death.

"You give them the fright of the spiirt god," said brother Number one with the twisted battle eye.

"What you say…give them the fright. The only thing gives them the fright is not enough whiskey…or no lbullets in their guns," said brother number two with the ornate headband and one feather.

"Come. I show you. Give your blessisngs…your prayers over old bones," said the Indian who lhad walked through the flames unharmed. All of the Shoshone tribesmen, the first six including Almayer and those who had gathered mysteriously, put on their spirit masks. They took their bridles.

"We will come back, White man. We will not be peaceful. Indians when we do…if you dig in the graves of our ancestors. maybe then we will burn down down your village and kill all who run away." . These were the assayer's parting words. The entire bunch of about twenty five Indians then road away' into the night.

"You…villagers, townsmen of Mystery," Grotteau proclaimed during the interval of silence marked only by the crackling of lthe dying fire. "A goodly numvber of fine men built this hyer village," he proclimed to all who would listen. That included the Indian deposition.

"Huzzah to that!" were the words heard from the villagers who had drifted into the shadows, , returning now that the Indians has left. Dr. Farralones fingered his guitar. Grotteau's boots shone in the firelight. He had covered them with hog lard from the same tin used to build the fire. From his burro saddle bad he fetched out a shirt with beads of peace sewn to it by Won Sing, one for every man in the village. Grotteau had to admit that the Indians had shown an unusual front of dignity and resistance. He hated for them for their interference, but she could not help admirilng them for their tribal valor.

Grotteau bellowed. "Too bad August Aleford couldnt be here at this occasion to witness the power of his brew." He pictured the buzzards that hovered above the town often had picke thel victim's bones cleanl by lnow. " I'm here to give honor t' you. I ask you t' throw aside all bad feelings andl join me in Mystery's expedition into the future. You too can gather up the richess of gold. You too can feel its heft in lthe palm of your hand…in lthe rocks you will dig wilth us."

Grotteau felt that his speech was glorious. He admired his own words. He hoped the towsmen would feel his fire in their soulds and would join with him in his quest for richess. The waggoners pitched several large timbers on the dying flames/ A volcano ofembers flew upward into the night sky. Grotteau grew eloquent. "Good men've wielded pick and shovel…strong lmenve contes against nachur, her wiles, to hide her wealth from us. Her catatrstrophlic of storm, wlind, driven show—geese weather and the trail of th sidewinder snake…!"

The town's oracle remained eloquent, after two jiggers of cactus whiskey. Jerome Gottlieb, town counterfeitter, grinned, standintg whelre he was on the opposite side of the flames, next to the fugitive bank robber Grant Hartman, the irony of theiur circumstance was that they were closer than many brothers in their charge upon life. The departed soldier, without honor, Terrence McAllister, had showed up to revel in the occasion, warm himself by the fire, and give credence to the merit of patience. He wailed, that he had lost yet he would gain by his dedication to his gold diggings..

"Give your blessings, upon the Indians hereabouts who do not take kindly to our rummaging about for yellow dust…turning up the grave grounds of their ancestors, they say. Well, the earth and its fullness belongs to all of us hyer in *Mystery* as much as it dos lthem… renegades." The words came out with a kind of grand eloquence that even surprised Grotteau. On this hyer land I got a claim staked out.

Recorded , witnessed by myself, Reiner Grotteau hyer…I'll sign each deed in my blood, so help lme God."

A small huzzah from the gatherers. Like solidiers in combat, townsfolks had regrouped and now stood at about three score or so. They watched with satisfied interest. The presence of the Indians nearby did not appear to alarm them. Peace be on us came the dulcet voice of Mr. Hornsby, who offered the tools of his store at half price, full amount to be paid upon discovery of gold. His sharper practices were somewhat well know in thel town for a shovel or pick. They were half-price cheaper over in the town of Frost. The wagons to carry their ore down to the stamping mill were offered…The continental hotel had one used for baggage and the other for drayage.Hornsbly had another, which he employed to carry supplies for their railroad station and to the campsites. They would have sufficientl equipment for their little enterprise.

"Peace be on us," came the voice of Sean Mallory, the harmonica player. He struck up a tune, low and mellow… *"the devils gold is our pride."* :No one had ever heard of it, but the tune went straight to the hearts of those standing around the fire.

Grotteau again went into the rhetoric that demanded the surrender of their guns, the reason being to elimnate bad shootings that had gone on in the town since is *'stablishment.* "You will bring forth new demons to drive out false hoples, to ameliorate rapscallions who come to jump your claims. You got more strength than a lion to challenge the devil hisself.. You'll find a real happinss in your surrender of violence with appeasement and peace." Grotteau's words did not at first penetrate the thinking of th silent townsfolks, who were still gathered around about, most them out of curiosity, those who had read the random poster, out this night to reckon the situation for themselves. How would gold be gotten so quickly as to justify the disarming peace?

Grotteau took a string of beads and twirled them. He spat and watched the stunned and suspicious crowd of townsmen. There arose light applause, drunken laughter joined in. Brought in casks on Fazakerly's water carrier burro, cactua whiskey was pitchered into the flames. He had not seen the guns of Auguse in the hillside cave. Gottteau remembered there were none. Aleford was a loner who had depended more on luck than onwisdom, for which cause he was smurdered.

With the brightening puffs of the whiskey burned, *Made in hell!*" shouted the words from a townsman. "We'll riz a snew gleaming town with what's 'neath her," said another. The mouth was that of Grant Polasky, the sharper, trickster and town braggart who had brought down Aleford's whiskey for the celebration. Grotteau could only hope his scheme had the power to anesthetize some of the citizens with the thought of wealth and destroy others by their denial of its existence while continuing to struggle. First the Indians departed, not yet fully aroused by Reiner's scheme. Then the townsmen and miners split up, those few who remained. Reiner was the last to stare at the dying embers and wonder. Ludheim was, strangely, nowhere to be seen on this glorious occasion which, in ***The Scorpion***, Reiner would refer to as a night **Peacemaking Rites** *between the local Indians and the sourdoughs.*

THE WINDS OF REVENGE

Grotteau decided to go out and inspect those sites outsie of the villge that he had purchased for three-percent of the diggings, just a pinch of gold dust in the final anaylsis. He kicked stones, imagining that every rock, even his footprints in the sand, crushed wealth not yet discovered. He did not notice the shadow that followed him, astride a mule. His thoughts were lost with his passion. The dark umbrage of his disciple was Cannister Kittrick, a man whose one goal had died and he had put it out for the vultures to feast on. He had found a gold nugget when he was digging his well. Cannister dared not bury it lest he meet with unforeseen misery. That was his superstition. He retraced his footsteps of his mentor and, as time would show, his master. Like so mny other men, he had wandered from mining camp to mining camp hoping to strike it rich. By some quirk of his thinking he supposed that Reiner Grotteau had worked magic, the sinister prospect of the mother-lode come alive; and that to follow in his footsteps would put an end to his wandering and a restoration of his former well being.as a successful grain merchant. Also, to some miners, he was supposed to be dead. He no longer served bar at *The Golden Nugget Saloon*. Nobody knew why and though big of hearing he was small of speech, tight-lipped, almost secretive. Gold makes a man that way sometimes.

Just as Grotteau turned alround, Cannister spoke from a short distance. "You 'lieve you got misery by the tail, Mister Grotteau, and enough to lead me to my grave?" Grotteau turned, stopped in his steps and, dismounting, waited for the spectre to catch up with him. He took the bridle of the mule as he walked alongside the mountain sourdough

"I don' truckle in misery, Mister Kittrick. If it's true then I don't know it."

"How do you know 'taint so…misery? Day after day, you got no cause for complaint yet we get hungry, we get tired, we get plum bored, yet we pan on. An't that misery?

Not if you're expecting to find more gold.

You run a newpaer…that's different. Geot lots sof think about there.

I collect news like old saddletrees does riders in these here parts…scarce. I write some a my own…not news…jes possible eevents, y' know." The clop of the mule and the sandy cruch of Grotteaus boots in the sand of the street occupied minutes of the desert silence..

"Oncet you sorta hinted at like you migtn run down new gold strike…ifn you had a good map."

"That I did. Thart I did," said Cannister. "Yours was the first and the best…always is thata way."

"Spect so. Those who find gold a' times find it in one chunk only. They's lucky. Kin work another year and not find a thinblefull after that."

"Don't look in the right places, Cannister." He turned toward Almayer's shack, off to one side of the main way. "Maybe you're not …a honest prospector," said Grotteau, dropping his hand from the mules bridle. The animal snorted. Cannister did not reply to the insult. He headed toward the barn of the smithy at the edge of the village.

The village had recoiled in terror that two cases of typhoid feverhad infected the mnners. *The Scorpion* caried the sting of the story. A doctor, panning for gold, told them to stay in quarantine for three weeks. There were nigh battles between the miners; but there was only the one, non-practicing, doctor to the best of anyones knowledge. Gunfire captured attention, like a wild, violent rattle of sound. A man and his burro were killed by desperados just outside the village; but few cared. Bad whiskey was corrosive of temper and the flesh; volatile language was the speech of the village and amongst panners who, in places, worked almost shoulder to shoulder. Two women only existed, never daring to show their faces, one the wife of a wagoneer and the other a prostitute kept at the *Continental Hotel*. Decay had set in at an early time in *Mystery*, a decay leading toward death, a deteriotation of the soul of both the habitation and the miners who dwelt there, much of the deterioration blamed on Reiner Grotteau, editor of *The Scorpion*

Ludheim worked through Grotteaus abuse. He would storm without provocation, and smite the woodwork with whatever he held in his hand. He appeared to be a pathological case at times, determined to control the mining village by his will, and by means of public intimidation. He had the power to destroy an adversary through his newspaper, and had done so. Ludheim had come to distrust the man;. Heseemed to Ludheim to grow worse day by day. But then Ludheim was no spittin' image of angelis fervor.

"I believe it when I see it…a gold strike," said Kittrick.

"The you'll just have to wait till this here town gets used to their good luck."

"Luck is it—or bad misfortune?" said Kittrick.

"Fortune…" He looked up at the rider and rinned an enigmatic grin in the semi dark. Who would tell anyone?

"Who made you a prophet, Reiner Grotteau?" They had met close to the bridge across the creek. Ludheim was an inveterate idler, Grotteau a confirmed meddler. *They were a pair*, as the saying went.

"I follow my instincts…natural like. They're alus been good and true. All this hyere about is still open land, according to the law. We hain't 'corporated. Were not even a town. We're jus' squatters on the desert and, like then nomads—Aarabs. Mister Ludheim."

"I'd like to be of help."

"Only believers, Prescott. Only Believers.

The press compositor and ex=lawyer pulled ahead of Grotteau and wheeled. "You got proof?"

"Tend to get some…I got enough for the present. Good to common horses of pick and shovel men and panning placer miners…

they're dredges, some loafers sure, and them hardrock drillers. They'll be a vanguard like a battlefield surely awaiting, marching up over the hills. They'll be followed by scoras a immigrants, come acrosst Panama, round the Horn and even 'crosst the country by wagon. Reckless and lazy, but good sourdoughs all the same. They'll all be gold seekers, Mister Ludheim, make no mistake about that. They bring appetites, been honed by my specticular news. Gold under th streets and stores of *Mystery*. Gold, man!

"Grand words, mister Grotteau."

They move to the smell of flint and soured hopes, and bitter gall of frustration will drop off them like a shed snake skin. Theyll take on life like....

"Like...?"

"Like them golden snapdragons with a ambition for gold, Mister Ludheim. I plan to tap into that craving."

Here the two men went their separate ways. The noises of the miners along the creek seemed indistinct and far away. The night was closisng in, the moon was tiding its gray shadow over eastern sands. It would be a warm night.

Ludheim knew Cannister personally; lawyer and bartender. they had played many ganes if poker tofgether. They had shared one of Ludheim's letters from a grown son in New England's Nantucket. Then Ludheim had chosen to be a whaleman, not a miner. And so it went. Grotteau, on the other hand, thought that he lived for the day when he could dominate over his less fortunate friends. He was driven by a demonic desire to gain gold-power, the lodestone to personal wealth. He had absorbed just enough discipline in an Eastern seminary to believe God's rule of man was flawed, that conquest equaled honor and character, and that men sought to be slaves rather than free for the ends of efficiency and comity in life, and, darkest of all, that the struggle to wrest gold from the earth was the nobliest of pursuits and was blessed by nature that sought a conqueror. Sourdough competitors...a few if any were his close friends. A man had comrades who helped with the exploration; but lastilng friendships were often salted away until luck released them from their bondage to prospecting.

So, for Grotteau , it was no sacred ploy of other men to pay him tribute for his town good fortune. That was Gotteau's attitude. He simply had never been able to endure misfortune without the revolt of his soul and the revulsion of his spirit that yearned for revenge. He had always looked up at vultures, the rednecked buzzards, and wonered if it was a neighbor's hound or or a wild cow that had perished in the heat. He remembered his dead goat. The smell of death close by was not unusal in *Mystery*. There was a soul comradeship between Cannister Kitttrick and Reiner Grotteau. The superstition of the former invited the ultimate faith in the vision of the latter. Both had somewhere along the trial vowed to preserve their independence, yet they needed each other in symbiotic bonds in this unique wilderness of desert mining country.

There occurred one night a barn dance for the village, while all this barter of arms for gold was going on. During the day or so that this even transpsires, women and girls properly chaperoned traveled from Frost and Triangle to the dance, held at the *Wagon Works*, place of the Mayor's "Sons" business. With the available dancing men in the village, the occasion comprised a generous group of dancers, some seven squared of about 50 folk in all. The floors were newly swept, fresh straw scattered about, the wagons in repair were pushed out to the coral for the evening. With the women to help a bar was set up at one end of the friviloty, but no whiskey was tolerated, sasparailla was the limit, the drilnk of choice, but the gaiety was no less for the absence of whiskey. De Vancha was a not untutored player of the guitar, as he had demlonstrated in the Hard Rock Saloon on a couple of occasions. He furnished the music with a banjo player from Frost, a fiddler from Triangle and drummer from *Mystery* and a caller named Dupres, Hammon Dupres. They all put the square dance in together in good time .

On this particular night Ludheim and Grotteau fell afous of their bitter feelings that came not from working on **The Scorpion**, but from sharing power through the press. Dressed in his most kingly duster and boots, wearing a black broad brimmed hat and sparkling touches of silver in his wing tips and cuffs, his angular face and black moustaches well groomed, De Vancha suggesrted that Ludheim offer him a way he might recover the hotel.

"Simple, *Senor De Vancha*. You make better luck in another poker game."

The village Mayor thought his competitor was fooling. "Or... you can work the Indians into a froth about their ancestors grave sites and bring them in to stampeded the village and burn down the hotel. It changes hands at once.. It'll becomes your ...hands-on memory."

De Vancha did not think this was very laughable. "You do not know about the Indians," he said.

"Assayer Almayer does...he is a most effective with them. He is...if I'm not lmistaken, part Shoshone himself."

"Why do he want to put these at danger, these town, Senor?"

"Simple," said Ludheim. "This here town is land under the ancient Spanish Land Grants."

"Senor Almayer?"

The same...so you see he has a... sacred interest in repossession of the land...to hell with the hotel!" The Mexilcan Mayor looked stu;mped for words. "You see, De Vancha, it is Grotteau's obsession to own the land. It gives him the power he covets. Almayer has...how shall I say it...family interests, tribal concerns that drive him to take refuge in...antiquity. We all look to history to be our instructors ... protectors in one way or another, Senor De Vancha," said Ludheim.

"I do not want protection, Senor. I have done many robberies."

" I have heard this is true," Ludheim replied, as guests mingled on the wagon works dance floor at the end of a patter call. A villager sprinkling water over the straw to settle the dust. The large crowd of dancers, single men, ladies with escorts, miners from the *Mystery* and the aforementioned towns hereabouts enjoyed lthe company of the ladies. "You see thagt pair of dancers?" Ludheim pointed out to Kittrick. "They have anointed this village with ...hope...if great wealth comes to *Mystery*, they will invest in town development. They are also eager for money...but other men work for them. You work for them. They claim title to much desert land...with the scorpions and snakes.

Then let the dance proceed," said Kittrick. For a village so primitive and rural in its customs and appearance, the square dance made the night special on the village calendar of events.

What made this barn dance even more unique was the abandon of the dancers, who were here to have a good time amid a fracas and a small stall fire put out with two buckets of lwater from an oil barrel. It was the occasion here the settlers in *Mytery* and the miners at last confronted each other over the water situation. For there were those, maybe kin to Hornsby, or friends of shack miners, who had set up tents not to pan for gold in a registered mining claim, but to stay and enjoy lthe freedom the town offered, next wanting to erect a small one room school and, after using the **Hard Rock Saloon** for a year or more, putting up their own church edifice. They were the settlers who came after the miners. . They gave stability to the community; yet they were also caused growth to retracrt and to disappear into the dismal past or remain wild with only the mining settlement. Their claims for a plot of ground were as just as valid as those of the Miners for their diggings. Thus they had come to lthe dance to get acquainted, with outbursts of hilarity, with hand clapping and stomping of hard boot heels to the rhythm of the music. These invitees and the local miners were stripping the ribs of fun.

But there was a dark and oppressive shadow that hung over the night's fun, and all but two of the dancers knew what it was. The dangers of frontier violence, the handiness of guns and the readiness of anger, the slipshod enforcement of anylthing close to law, and the natural bent of men, cut loose from normal social constraints, to live it up…which could and often did mean the rubbing out of one's enemy amidst turbulent gunfire and fist-battles…

Moonlight shone through highup cracks in the dry wool palings sof the barn walls at De Vancha's **Wagon Works**. The **Hard Rock Saloon** bartender Kittrick, having shut down ihis emporium of salubrious thirst-quenchers and elixirs of joy, was tending the dancers… with sasparilla. Caution and close reactions were of no import to *the crow*, as he sometimes called himself because of his black shining hair and black beady eyes. The band strummmed and fiddled as the caller patter maneuvered the couples,. about seven squares, through their moves. Other villagers, and out-of-towners and those not dancing stood near the stables to converse, joke, comment, all amid confusion's noise, the music of the square and the caller's patter. The night wore on with a lusty throat of chatter, music and *rounds*.

Death appeared in the wide doorway, swung open to create a fesh draft, as dust ignited by the lanterns hung from posts, enveloped the dancers. De Vancha's morose four "sons," he liked to call them employed at the **Wagon Works**, employed there, some suspected as a sanctuary from highway robbery, stood with poses of gallant smugness and suspicion in one corner where the hay rakes stood. They nonchalantly picked their teeth, swaggered over for a sassparilla and returned, watching and waiting…they knew there was no sheriff in the town. They wore obscene grins as they looked over the dancers. Not many miners had come down from the creek. They kept to their day's business, which would resume as soon as the sun arose.

Without shiskey this time, a drunken fistfight broke out beteen one of De Vanchas "sons" and a miner who happened, it was later learned, was a Doctor Farralone, come down from his sanctuary to add his somber dignity to the aura of the party. Two other nearby panners separated the combattants. However, it set the stage for a gritty act that was to follow.

The miners belonging to De Vancha's party departed and within minutes returned to the barn, firing a found pistol at random. De Vancha stepped in to quell the angry man. The fiddler screeched out a wild and merciless tune on his fiddle while the banjo went wild to mock him with his strings. The guitarist could not find any tune and the drummer rapped out a dekko kind of rhythm that sounded more like a visiting judge hammering for silence or some kind of ancient tribal dance. It was a scene that made bad luck for lthe village of Mystery. Indeed, it was one in its way to rival the Indians atop the butte. A disgruntled miners, a friend of the combattants actually had the brass to try to start a fire in one of the barn stalls. The quick energies and instant resourcefulness of nearby men, however, put out the small straw flame by stomping on it and pitching a pail of water onto the flames, water for the occupant horse moved to a nearby pasture of cactus and sand. There was just no getting away from it—that there was an ill mood come over the dance party, a mood only a fews detected, but they were ready.

De Vancha was angry for a second time, since his small band of *sons* assumed a possessive attitude, as if the village belonged to them. Grotteau's hotel with more settlers ariving, had begun to to bring a small profit. This night it appeared that the Miners and the Settlers had grouped amongst themselves in the barn, as if in raanks of a mock challenge. The music stopped, the tip was ended. One of the settlers, Rob Stevenson, moved across the hall with a lady on his arm, intending to find out the sentiment of the Miners as regards water in the creek and its use. Springs and a high water table fed the creek north of the village It ran all year round and was a storm flood when heavy rains fell in the mountains. Jeremiah Fazakerly, the water carrier who packed his huge bags of water into the village, was hard pressed to satisfy the needs of all the miners…and now lthe Settlers. Was this to be a showdown over water rights, within the barn at the sqauare dance, where there were plenty of witnesses?

"I seed thet document," said a Settler…all of them claims…. What they mean… claims to the land…claims to the gold under the land?"

"I don't think you got it right," said Grotteau, making an unexpected appearance—the dance could be a source for news—because he antiicipated trouble. And he was right.

"We got to 'ave water."

"There's no reason for you to come settle here anyways."

"Nobody ant going to live in that there hotel if you drive folks off. One welkl fer the whole damned place.!" came the answer.

"That hotel can teake car eof itself. Miners need rooms same 's settlers."

"They got their tents."

"They come here to mine gold. And they an't leaving 'by a long shot, like coyotes with settlers knocking at the front door."

"You got no right to all the water." This charge was directed at Grotteau. It had become a fairly well-known fact that he had acquired, mysteriously, the ownership of the **Continental Hotel**.

"We out water into too. Fact is we bring it in by mule, and when that's not enough, well make it two, mavbe three mules."

"Won't work, Grotteau." This was the voice of another citizen of the small town.

"I'll make it work. Fact is, what we're affixing to do is build ourselves a drilling rig and were going to drill for water.

Not likely in this desert," said an unnamed Settler.

This option constituted a challenge to the handful of Settlers there at the dance. They waded into the Miners to show that they were as much entitled to free air and open space...and any water... as the Miners were. The women scattered They had no cattle to water, but they certainly have themselves to consider; and it was altogether possible that some of them would be inviting guests out from the East, to *Mystery*, to enjoy the heavenly air and open skies and untrammeled land...sand flat as it was. As the verbal rhubarb continued and the more amiable tried to separate the combattants, some Settlers, seven or eight in all waded ilnto tlhe Miners to show that they were as much entitled to free air and open space...and any water...as the Miners were.

The band struck up a good square and the fracas ended a soon as it had begun. But it stood as a warning that there were ill feelings between the Miners and the Serttlers in the village of *Mystery*. The Settlers knew that the terms and conditions to a minintg claim linvolved water rights, mineral rights, no trespassing. A claim must be worked two weeks after after it was settled on any any gold brought in. It had to be actually lived oon, ocupied and proceeds from the sale of gold dust and any nuggets had to be shed with the **Grotteau Mining Company** at 3-percent. The Settlers had seen this. The miners were in an uproar over the barn incidnt, and they were willing to shoot it out.

But with what. When they stopped to think, they had given up their weapons. Were it not for the fact that Grotteau, as a condition of their ownership, demanded that they, too, surrender at least one of their firearms, they would have made a bolder move. Priestlike and feigning innocence, Grotteau reassured them, through *The Scorpion*, that there would be no violebce in Mystery to interrupt its placid and peace-loving Miners. They clearly were at a disadvantage, since the Settlers still owned their Winchester carfbines, their *Henrys* and a few Kentucky Muskets that could enter any tent or shack unnanounced. This ownership osed a threat to the Miners which the latter, deloused of arms, to to speak, could not forgive and vowed they would not forget.

The next challenge to the dignity and courage of the village miners were the Indians. Not longafter the square dance showdown, so called, came the Shoshone in defense, once again, of their ancesters bones and burial sites. The Indians had ridden down intos the town like the shifting sand in a wind storm, hooves from afar, like a legion of wild horses, ramudas of crazed ponies. They had approached Mystery, torches in the aiir, drew nearer until they struck fire with their hooves, terror in the rampage toward this lone human habitation in the desert. They came with an appetite for revenge, like Ghengis Khan assault, snorting cries of revenge.

Within minutes it became obvious to all who were awakened that the Indians had returned as they had promised, their appetite for ravaging the barren countryside when no grass availed their snorting ponies. They rode as renegades of the night, dressed it all in black—but the moon was down and the stars paled by a high haze blown in tufts of sandy scree. Into the town they rode without shouts this time, hooves pounding, ghostly for the silence of thei riders. Into *Mystery* they rode as maurauding invaders, which *The Scorpion* had predicted. They carried torches, and one of them flung his into a rickety wooden shack without a scramble or disturbance of the still night air. The flames caught on the shingles behind the façade and flared up linto the night sky.

Then as if by signal, the riders—this was their second assaunt on the town—seemed to awaken for them to a nightmarish dreaam of reality, as one body they began wild and hysterical shouts, screams and challenges that awoke the rest of the village, so that when one or twos of *Mystery* awakened, citizens dared to appear from a window, to stare in disbelief the renegades hastened to set one another shack afire. They scoured the town street by street, led by a hatless leader with long white hair and burning eyes, so it mgiht have seemed. From along each rutted street they shouted, whereupon, to their immense surprise, gunfire erupted from the citizens in defense of their dwellings, from doorways and windows. The renegades returned fire, but did not appear to aim to hit the citizens but instead shot down a sign here and there, shot up the boardwalk with bullet holes, put holes like woodpekers into the sides of buildings, captured several horses, all as if in dreadful warning. The whitehaired man—none wore masks—after streaming through the town and striking here and there, circling back to the main street, **Dog Street**, paused briefly to make sure that the office of *The Scorpion* was set firfe. Expecting this event, Grotteau had mustere boys from *Frost*, come to the dance for the fun of it, to stand by with bucket of water. They quickly doused the flames before they gutted the entire press structure. That was all to the good; the press was to the Indians a weapon they envisioned coming to their defense.

Due to the heroic efforts of Gotteau, Ludheim and several newsboys from Frost, we saved the back portion of the newspaper office; and when the sun came up, it was draped in canvas like another tent shacks , including a theatre, a morgue, and several shops. The Hard Rock Sal;oon and the Hardware store were saved from the arsonists. hese beginnings were not unexpected in the early west. They were confronted with pioneer courage. *The Scorpion* had lived to publish again. As swiftly, as they had come the Indians in their war paint departed, soundlessly, almost, as in a terrible dream only their horses hooves smiting the road and stirring up dust in the still night air. Within another then minutes the entire village, or so it amy have appeared, seemed half-dressed, out on the walks by the sides of their tent cabins, men fetching buckets of water to be ready to douse more fires. But fire-brigade effort was not organized and only one or two buckets of water went to quench the fire that could have raged over the entire *Scorpion* enterprise. What they had come to regard as a poisonous insect of of influence died amid the crackle of devouring flames that put *The Scorpion* entirely out of business. at least in *Mystery*. At the same time as their pressman was out of a job. Ludheim, this time, was not the man's name. He had appeared to fade from the scene. Perhaps he was hiding down in his exotic Vault. Nobody knew exactly.

As if a fire a near brawl, and an Indian attack were not enough of one day's hardships, a villager had come to Grotteau and asked without even mention of what he was talking about.

"They come at me like fiends." Mister Grant Harrimon , old timer as in *Mystery*, was recalling that night. On his face was the apparition of some kind of devil mask, an occultlic transposition from the dead as if he had died and come back to life and was recounting what he had seen. The account was unraveled in the saloon, since *The Scorpion* now had no home base, burned out by an arsonist. Grotteau swung at a great beetle and knoking the hanging lanters crazily, he saw down to the dark vision that had come to Max Ludheim, the vision of the disaster of the village when confronted by its own sense of possessive greed. There need be no fulfillment, just the desire.

They, now partacipated in by De Vancha's sons, a craft of mauraudilng they knew so well, vilagers gone berserk on whiskey and lawlessness , rampaged against a neighbor miner, mauled him something fierce and inhabited his tunnel gold claim like a phsophorscent bat at night that had fed on diaspora plant. It radiated outward through their membranous sins, from their blood. But they were not bats, he was sure of that. Grotteau urged that Ludheim go on, when he stopped suddenly and faced Grotteau.

"Why did you cut them down?' This was the lawyer asking the question, no longer his employee at *The Scropion*.

"Cut who down?"

"Them ten carcasses...they weren't hurting nobody."

"I dont get what you mean, Max." He appeared to clear his mind.

"Them dogs, ten of them ferral animals, more but they chased out…miners curse caught up, bloodhound mongst them…the come out of nowhere. The attacked…growling and snarling, all their fangs dripping with miners blood."

"Just a nightmare, Mister Ludheim."

"And we had no guns to defend ourselves." He was visibly angry. The vision had been very; real to him. "They come at me, sir. All of 'em no they was more tha six, a dozen or more…wilder than coyotes brush wolves after blood, I say."

"Hunger…folks don't feed their animals, mules has the same at times." He would play the game of delusions.

"Then that stink…drove me into a cave."

Grotteau thought that Mulheim was starting to sound a little mad, but he dared not counter his dialogue with any such remark. Mulheim was in a terrifying mood. "To surround me in that cave with them wild dogs did…and demanded a gold nugget."

Grotteau possessed the great Kittrick nuggest of the original gold find in *Mystery*—Almayer before his defection had informed Mulheim to arouse both his curiossity and his covetous will. Now greed had a face. Yet it still fooled some of the village folk. .He went on, " I refused to give hit up, that big nugget, so then what did those dogs do? They attacked, them dogs did," he said:

"To keep them dogs quiet and shut their salivating jaws, I showed 'em my nugget. It entranced the burning wolf eyes of that cave pack, and it entranced them from making any more attacks. Sure they snarled, they bared them long fangs, drippilng with molten gold, they did. Mister Grotteau." He said this as he he slowly backed out of the cave while them animals, part humans, snapped at him and barked without letup…and every goot of retreat I took was loaded with fear.

He was a strange one, not so much Max Mulheim wilth his vision of the wild dogs but Reiner Grotteau, whose play to control the village had brought such havoc and misery…and fear, a man whom the town had once taken a genuine liking to but who was now dedeviled by some sort of inner dark rhapsody of intention and dark deeds. His ascent from the morgue this day was symbolic in a way, for he had said one time that death has no price but the grave diggers, a blight, I came to believe, that overlay not just himself, Grotteau, but had begun to infect th entire village. Yet it was a sort of foreoding, an innate curiosity in the minds of some of the villagers that compelled them to remain in *Mystery* and not to quit their claims. People had attachments to one another. They wanted at least to see how their connundrum of gold lust and personal sacrifice worked themselves out. A man could see more than he dared to contemplate

Anyone, compositor, pressman, employed milner, who had worked in the press shop, amid dusty, ink-smell and grease, would have observed the chase filling with more of Grotteau's penumbra of strange outcries, for so they were, his promonitions of events to come...an end to the *Hard Rock Saloon*, a demise for his **Continental Hotel**, bits of verse, a fictitious confession by a miner killed in a power blast as a warning to careless miners, and much more. I had learned a startling fact, that a man had actualy been attacked by coyotes or wild dogs almost two y ears ago and his body not found until recentlly, that a man named August Aleford had been murdered, *Mystery's* resident bootlegger whose cactus whiskey had long produced for minera what they otherwise had to import, and cheaper by the paleful. Grotteau must have learned the the feral dogs had been conjured by the *Flame Woman*, a mountain mystic following the surrender by the people of their protective weapons. Most villagers did not at the time see any conection betseen a goldrich but helpless citizenry and a dangerous gun-toting impoverished citizenry. The entire matter was foolishness to to contemplate.

Well, but their fangs did not retract. Their paws, like bear paws, since they did not retract either, but had fingers that stretched out. Their dead stench filled the lair where the flesh of rotting inhavited the darkness. It had been the moonshiners cave. It had stood almost in the light and wanted to run and escape. Grotteau seemed possessed. His thoughts lay like throrns in barbed wire fashion that dres blood from his brain, and thn he gave out with a terrifying shriek there in the saloon, as if he felt that the strong, gripping fingers of another man clutch at his throat. He lifted one foot as if gripping fingers closed around one ankle. A strange expresion felll upon his visage his face, fixed as if in torture by some unseen fiend, strong enough to entangle him down into a invisible grave...that of th long dead. It was as if the god of storm violence was staring down at the gaunt, hard, empty barren of flesh of a face of bones bleached white by alkali of somebody he had known. Then vision expended itself, and Grotteau fell to the floor as if in a fit. There appeared no convulsions. He just curled up there, quiet, as if suddenly he had fallen asleep. Habituees of **The Hard Rock Saloon** simply let Gotteau lie there on the floor. Then to a man they turned and went out, as if they had other things to do.

THE DANCE OF REVENGE

Grotteau thought he might go out inspect what he could of those sites outsie of the village that he had purchase for three cpercent of the diffings, juvb a pinch of gold dust in the final anaylsis. He kicked stones, iagining that everyrock, even his ootprints in the sand, crushed in sand wealth not lyet discovered. He did not notice the shadow that followed him, astride a mule. His thought s were interred with his passion. The dark umbrage of his disciple was Cannister Wescott, a man hose one goal had died and he had put it out for the uvultures to feast upon. lHe had heard of a man finding a gold pnugget when hedug a well. eside a dry well that is. Cannister dared not bury it lest he icons unforeseen misery. IHe was supertstitious and hetraced his footsteps sof his mentor and, as time would show, lhis master. Like so mny other men he had wandered from mining camp to mining camp hoping to strike it rich. l But some quirk of his sintelligence he supposed that Reiner Grotteau had worked magic, the sinister prospect of the motherlode come alive; and that to follow in his footsteps would put an end to his wandering and arestoration of his former well being..

Just as Grotteau turned alround, Cannister spoke from a short distance. "You lieve you got miseryby lthe tail, Mister rotteau, and enough to lead me to mh grave? Grotteau turned, stopped in his steps and waited for the spectre to catch up with him. l He took the bridole of the mule as he walked alongside the mountain sourdough

I don truckle in mercy Mister Cannister. If its true then I dont know sit.

How dol you know tains so...misery. Day after day, you got no clause for complaint yet e get hungry, we get tired, e get plum bored, yet we pan on. Ant that misery?

Not if you're expecting to find more gold.

You run a newpaer...thats different. Geot lots sof think about there.

I collect news like old saddletrees in these here parts...scarce. I write some a my own...not news...jess possible –vents, ly lknow. The clop of the mule and the sandy cruch of Grotteaus boots in the sand sof the street occupied minutes sof the nivght.

Oncet you sorta hinted at like you migtn turn down new gold sltrike...ifn lyou hav a good map.

That Idid. Thart I did, said Cannister. Yolur was the first nd thevest...always lis thata way.

Spect so. Those whoo find gold atimes find sit in one chunk only. theys lucky. Kin work another year and not find a thinblelfull after that.

SDont look in the right places, Cannister. He turned toward Almayers shack, off to one side of fthemain way., lMayvbe youre not myh man, said Grotteau, dropping his hand from the mules bridle. The animal snorted. Cannister headed toward the barn of the smithy at the edge of the village.

The village had convulsed in terror that cases of typhoid fever infected two of the Panners. Scorpion carried the sting of the story. A doctor, panning for gold, told them to stay in quarrantine for three weeks. There were nightly battles between the miners; but there was only the one non-practicing doctor, to the best of anyone's knowledge. Gunfire captured attention, l ike a wild, violent mantra of sound. A townsman and his burro were killed by desperados just outside the village; but few cared. Bad hiskey was corrosive of good temper and the flesh; volatile language was the speech of the village and amongst panners who, in places worked almost shoulder to shoulder. Two women only existed, never daring to show their faces, one the wife of a wagoneer and the other a prostitute kept at the Continental Hotel. I thought that decay had set in at an early time in Mystery, a decay leading toward death, a dereriotation of the soul of both the habitation and the miners who dwelt there, much of the deterioration blamed on Reiner Grotteau, editor of **The Scorpion**. Ludheim worked through Grotteaus abuse. He would storm without provocation, and smite the woodwork with whatever he held in his hand. He was a psychopathological case, to all evidence, determined to control the mining village by his will, and by means of intimidation. He had the power to destroy an adversary through his newspaper, and had. done so. I had come to distrust the man;. He grew worse day by day.

"I believe it when I see it…a gold strike, said Cannister."
"Then you'll just have to ait till this here town gets ued to their good luck."
"Luck is it—or bad misfortune?" said Cannister.
"Fortune…?" He looked up at the rider and grinned an enigmatic grin in the semi dark. Who would tell anyone.

"Who made you a prophet, Reiner Grotteau?"
"I follow my instinct…natural like. They re alus veen good and true. All this here about is still open land, according to the law. l We hasn't corporated. Were not even a town. Were just l were just squatters on the desert and, like then hnomads—Aarabs. Mister Cannister."
"I'd like to be of help."
"Only believers. Only believers."

The mule skinner pulled ahead of Grotteau land wheellild. "You got proof."
"Tend to get some…I got enough for the present. Good to common horses lof pick and shov men and panning placer miners… theyre dredges, some loafers sur;e, and them hardwock drillers. Theyll ve a vanguard like abattlefiield surely, marching up over the hills. They'll ve followed by scoras a immigrants, come acrosst Panama, round the Horn and even cross the contry by wagon. Reckless and lazy, but good workers all the same. They'll all be gold seekers, make no mistake about that Mister Cannister. The bring appetites, been honed by my racular news. Gold under the streets and store of Mystery. God, man!"

"Grand words, mister Grottea"

"They move to the smellf of flint and soured hoped and bitter gall of frustration will drop off them like ashed snake skin. Theyll take on life like…"

"Like…?"

"Like goldenl burtterflies with la ambition for gold, Cannister Westcott. I plan to tap into that craving."

Here the two men went their separate ways. The night was closisng in, the moon was tiding its grayyelaslow over easterns sands. It would be a warm night.

I knew Cannister personally; we has played poker together. l ;he ha shared one of his letters from a grown son in New England's Nantucket. Thiel Cannister had chosen to be a whaleman, lnot a miner. And so it went. I lknew that he lived for the ay when he could dominate over his less fortunate sourdoughcompetitors…a few if anywlere his close friends. A man had comrades who lhelped with theexploration; friendships were often salted away l;until luck released them from their ondage to thesearch. So, for Cannister, it was no sacred ploy to wih other men to pay him tribute for his town good turtune. That was partly Gotteaus attitude. he simply had never been able to endure misfortune without the revolt of his soul and the revulsion of his spirit that yearned for revenge. He had always looked up at vultures, the rednecked buzzards and wonered if it was a neighbors hounddor or a cow that had perished in the heat. lHe rememgered his dead goat. The smells sof death close by were not unusual in Mystery. l There was a soul omradeship between Wescott Cannister and Reiner Grotteau, as if spiritual brothers. The superstition of the former inv ited the lultimate faith in the vision of the latter. Both had somewhere along the trail vowed to preserfe their indepdnence, lyet they lneeded eacvh other in this unique wilderness of deseret minging coujtry.

There fell a barndance for the village, while ll this barter of arms for gold was going on. During sthe day or so that this even rranspsires, womenl and girls sroperlhy chaperoned traveled from Frost and Triangsle to the dance, held at the Wagon orks, place of the mayors Sons' business. With the availale dancing men in the village, the occasion comprised q generous groupo of dancers, some seven squared lor about 50 folk in all. The floors were newseept, fresh straw scattered about, the animls led out to lth coral for the evening. With the women to help a bar was set up at one end of the friviloty, but no whiskey was toleratsed, sasparailla was lthe limit, burt the gaiety was no less for theabsence of hard liquor. De Vancha was a not untutsored player of trhe guitar. as he had shown in the Hard Rock Saloon on a couple of occasions. He furnished the music with a banjo player from frost, a fiddler from Triange and rummer from Mysteryand a caller named Dupres, Hammon Dupres. They all put thesquare dance in together in good time and order.

On lthis night Ludheim and Grotteau fell afous sof their bitter feelings that caqme not from working on the Scorpion, but upon lthe sharing of power through the pressl. Dreswsed in his most kingly duster and bolots,l wearing a black broad brimmed hat and sparkling touched of silver in his win tips and cuffs, his angular face and v lack lmoustaches well groomed, Xd Vancha sugfgesrted that Ludheim offer him la way he might recover the hotel.

Simple, Senor De Vancha. ;lyou make better luck ;in another poker game.

The :Mayor thought his competitor was fooling. daOr...you can work the Indians into a froth about their ancestors grave sites and bring them in to sltampeded the village and burn down the hotel. It changes hands at ocne.. zIt bocmes your memory.

De Vancha did not lthink this was very comicI ;do not know about the Indians, he said.

Assayer Almayer does...and he is a most efficient with aaaathe;m. He is...if I'm not lmistaken, part Sosheone himself.

Why would he want to put it at jeopardy, the town, I mean.

Simple, said Ludheim. He lowns land under the ancient Spanish Land Grants

Alma;yer?

The same...so lyou see he has a vested interest in repossession. sof tlhe land...to hell with lthe lhotel.

"You see, De Vancha, it is Grotteau lobsession to own the land. It gives him the power he seeks. lAlmayer has…how shall I slay it…family interests,s ltribal concerns that drive him to refluge in… antiquity. We all look to history to be our instructors and porotectors in one way or another, Senor De Vancha," said Ludheim.

"I do not want protection, Senor. I have done many robberies."

"So I have heard," Ludheim replied, as guests mingled on the floor after the end of a patter call. The dust settled by a villager sprinkling water over the straw. The large crowd of dancers, single men, ladies with escorts, married couples, miners from the villages and towns hereabouts tried to enjoy the company of the ladies. Forf a village sos rudimentary in its customs and appearance's the sqaure danced made a special night for the village calendar of events.

What made this barn dance unique was not the constituency of the dancers, who were trying to have a good time amid a fracas and a small stall fire put out with two buckets of lwater in a n oil barrel. Irt was the occasion here the settlers in Mystery and the miners at last confronted each other over the water situation. For there were those, maybe kin to Hornsby, or friends of shack miners, who had set up tents not to pan for gold in a registered mining claim, but to stay and enjoy lthe freedom the towns offered, lnext wanting to erect a small one room school and perhaps, after using the Hard Rock Saloon for a year or more, putting up their own church edifice. The were the settlers. They were the ones who gave stability to the community; y et they were also the ones who claused thegrowlth life to retracrt and to dlisappear into thel dismas past or wildc at mining and random settlement. Their claims was as just asthat of the lMiners. And so they had comd to lthe dlance to get acquainted, and they had so far done so.

Moonlightshone through highup cracks in the dry wool palings sof the barn walls. The Hard Rock bartender, hving shut down ihis emporium was tending the dancers…with sasparilla. Caution and close reactions were of no import to the crow. Th band.strummed and fiddled. as the caller patter maneuvered the coupls through their moves. Other villagers, and out of towners stood near the stables to converse, joke, comment, all mamid confusion noisle, the music of the square and the callers patter. The night wore on thusly.

Death appeared in the wide doorway, swing open to creat a fesh draft, as dust ignited by the lanters hung from posts, elnveloped the dancers. De Vanchas morose four "soh," he liked to callthem from the Wagon Works, whete they had found employment, some suspected out of highway robery, picked their teeth, swaggered about aimlssly, weaing ovscene grins as they looked over the dancersd. Not many miners had come down from the creek. They kept their energis for the days business which would continue as soon as the suhn arose.

Without whiskey this time, a drunken fistfight broke out beteen one of De Vanchas men land a miner whok, llhappened, I hard later, was Dr. Farralones, come down from his sanctuary to add his girlth and somber smiles to the aura of the party. Two other miners separated the comb attants. lHowevfer, it set the stage for a grittyl act that as to follow.

The miners belonging to De Vancha's party departed and within minutes returned to the barn, firing a found pistol at random., it appeared. De Vancha stepped in to quell the angry man. The fiddler screeched out a wild and merciless tune on his fiddle while the banjo went wild to mock him with his strings. The guitarist could not find any tune and the drummer rapped out a dekko kind of rhythm that sounded more like a visiting judge hammering for silence or some kind of ancient tribal dance. It was a scene that made bad luck for lthe village of Mystery. Indeed, it was sone in its way to rival the Indians atop the butte. One of the disgruntled miners, la friend of the combattant lactually lhad lthe brass to tlry to start a fire in one of the barn stallz. But the quick nergies and instant resourcesfulness of nearvby men put out the small straw flame by stomping on it and pitching a pail of water onto the flames, water for the occupant horse.

De Vancha was angry for a second time, since his msmall band of son assumed apossessive attitude, as sif they lhad fonded the village. GDe Vanchas hotel with more settlers arfiving, was re to bring a considerable profit. It this night appeared that the Miners and the Settlers had grouped amongs themselves in the bvarn, as if in lmock challenge. The music stopped, the tip was ended. One of the settlers, A Rob Stevenson, moved across the hall with a lady on his arm, intending to find out the sentiment of the Miners as regards water in the creek and its use. A sprin fed the creek, whih was dry most of the year, except when there was heavy rains in the mountains and Fazakerly, the water carrier who packe his huge bags of water into the village, was hard pressed to satisfy the needs of all the miners…and now lthe Settlers. Was this to be a showdown over water rights, within the barn at the sqauare dance, where there were plenty of witnesses.

"I seed thet document," said a Settler…"all of them claims, enougnto be a politician tofight. What they mean claims to the land… claims to the gold under the land?"

"I don't think you got it right, Said Grotteau, making an unexpected appearance because he antiicipated trouble. Amd he was right."

"We got to have water."

"There's no reason for you to come settle here anyways."

"Nobody ant going to live in that there hotel if you gdrive folks off."

"That hotel can take care of itself. Miners need rooms same's settlers."

"They got their tents."

"They come here to mine gold. And they ant leaving vby a long shot, like coyotes with settlers knocking at the front door."

"You got no right to all the water."

"We get water into town. Fact is we bring it in by mule, and when that's not enough, well make it two, mevbe three mules."

"Won't work, Grotteau."

"I'll make it work. Fact is, Senor Di Vancha there, whose got nothing else bette to do n is fixing to build himself a drilling rig and were going to drill for water."

"Not likely in this desert, said the unnamed Settler."

This option constituted a challenge to the handful of Settlers there at the dance. They waded into the Miners to show that they wlere as mch entitled to free air and open space...and any water...as the Miners were. The women scattered They had no cattle to water, blut they certainly hav themselves to consier; and it was altoewther possivble that some of them would ve inviting guests out from the East, to Mystery, to enjoy the heavenly air and open skies and untrammeled land...sand flat as it was.

The band struckup a good square and the fracas ended a soon as it had egun. But it stood as a warning that there were ill feelings between the Miners and the Serttlers in the village of Myastery. The Settlers knew that theterms and conditions to a minintg claim er: water rights, mineral rights, no trespassing, claim must be worked two weeks after ater was rought in. It had to be lived oon, occupied and proceeds from the sale of gold dust and any nuggets had o be shed with the Grotteuas Mining Company at 3 percent. The Settlers had een this. The miners were in an uproar over the barn icncidnt, and they ere illing to shosot it out. But with lwhat. When they stopped to think, they had given up ;their weapons. Were it not for the fact that Grotteauh, as a condition of their ownership, demanded that they, too, surrender at least one of their larms,s they would lhave made a bolder move. Priestlike and feigning innocence, Grotteau reassured them, through his **Scorpion,** that there would ble no violece in Msteryhto interrupt its placed and peaceloving Miners. They clearlyh were at a disadvantage, since the Settlers still owned their Wicnester Carfbines, theirHenrys and a few Knentucky Muskets that could enter any tnent or shack unnanounced. This ownership posed a threat to the Miners which they could not forgfet and vowed they would not forvgfet.

Thje next challenge to the dignity and courage of the villaage miners were the Indians. Not longafter the square dance showdown, so called, came the Shoshone in defense, once again, of their ancestrers bones and bluriala sitles. The Indians had riddendown ontos the town like theshifting sancd ina a win storm, hooves from afar, like a legion of wild horses,s ramudas o crazed ponies approached Mystery, torches in the air, dre nearer until lthey struck fire with their hooves, terror in the rampage toward this lone human havbitation in the desert. They came with an appetite for ravaging, like Ghengis Kans assault, snorting pags, rlenegades in the night, when the moon was down and the sltlars paled bly a haze blown in from sands.

Within minutes it became obvious to all who were awakened that the Indians had returned as they had p romised, their appetite for ravaging the varren cosutryside when no grass availed thieor snorting ponies,s they rode fort,s renegades of the nifght, dressed it appeared ll ;in black,but lthe mon was down and the stars paled by a high haze blown in tufts of sandy scree. Into the towns lthey rode as maurauding invaders,l which the Scorpion had predicted. They lcarried torches, land one of them fling his into lthe lrickety wooden shack like uilding without a scramble or disturbance of the still lnight air. The flames caught on the shingles sbvehind the façade and flared up linto the night lsky.

Then as if by signal, the riders seemed to awaken for them to a nightmarish dream of reality, as one bvody ltheyl began wild and lhysterical shouts, screams and challenges that awoke the lrentire village, so that when one or twos of Mysareeryhs awakenecd citizend dared to appear from a window, to sgare ind isvelief the renegades hastened to set one shack afire. They scoured the town with street by streetk led by a hatless leader with long lwhite hair and burning eyes, so it miht have seemed. From street to street they shouted, whereupon, to their immense surprise, gunfire erupted from the citizens in defense of their dwellings, from doorways and windows. The renegades returned fire, but did not strangely aim to hit the citizens but instead shot down a sign here and there, shot up the boardwalk with bullet holes, put holes like woodpekers into the sides of building, captured several horses, all as if in dreadful warning. The whitehaired man, without a mask— none wore masks—after streaming through the town and striking here and there, circling back to the main street, Dog Street, paused briefly to make sure that the office of *The Scorpion* was fully engulfed in a thundering, crackling flames.

Due to the heroic efforts of Gotteau, Ludheim, myself and several newsboys from Frost, we saved the back portion of the newspaper office;

and when the sun came up, it was draped in canvas like many another tent enterprise, including a theatre, a morgue, and a saloon. These beginnings were not unexpected in the early west. They were confronted with pioneer courage. ***The Scorpion*** had lived to publish again.

As swiftly, as they had come the Indians in their war painted departed, soundlessly, almost, as in a terrible dream only their horses hooves smiting the hard rocky places in the road and stirring up dust in the still night air. Within another ten minutes the entire village, or so it amy have appeared, seemed half dressed, out on the walks, by the sides of their tent cabins, men ordering buckets sof water to be brought to douse the newspaper fire. But then effort was snot organized and only one or two buckets sof water went to quench lehthe fire that raged over the entire Scorpion enterprise. …what they hd come to regard as apoiisonous insect f of influence died amid the crackle of devouring gflames that put The Scorpion entirely out of vbusiness. at least in Mystery. Ast the same time as their pressman was sou of a job. Ludheim, the l;mans name. I could not help but think that Grotteau he had pushed the townfolks and the miners too flar in the matter of gold claims, and intimidation.

As if a fire a near brawl, and an Indian attack were not enough of one days hardships, A villager had come to Grotteau an asked without even mention of what he was talking aout.

They come at me like fiends." Mister Grant Loren, old timer as years went in Mystery, was recalling that night. On his face was the apparition of some kind of devil mask, an occultic transposition from the dead as if he had died an come back to life and was recounting what he had seen. I had to sit down, and Grotteau swung at a great beetle and knocking the hanging lanters crazily, he sat down, collapses tells smore, begins to listen to the dark vision that had come to Grant Lorenl while he slept.

They rampaged against a neighbor miner, mauled him something fierce and inhabited his tunnel gold claim like aphsophorscent bat at nigt that had fed on diaspora plant. It radiated outward throudh their membranous sins, from their blod. But they were not bats he hd know.

Grottesau urged that Mr. Loren go on. Then hs stopped suddenly and faced Grotteau.

"Why did you cut them down?"
"Cut who down?"
"Them ten carcasses…they lwerent hurtisng nobody."
"I don't get what you mean, Loren. He appeared to clear his mind."
"Them dogs, ten of em ferral animals, more butthey chased out…miners curse cauht up, bloodhound mongst them…the come out of nowhere. The attacked…growling and snarling, all their fangs dripping with miners blood."
"Just a nightmare, Mister Loren."
"And we had no guns to deefend ourselves. He was visibly langry. The vision had been very real to him."
"They come at me, sir. All of em no they laws smore tha six, a dozen or more…wilder than coyotes brush wolves safter blood, I say."

"Hunger…folks dont feed their animals, mules has the same a times."
"Then that stink…drove me into a cave."
He was starting to sound a little mad, but Grotteau dared not counter his dialogue with any such remark. Grotteau was in a terrifying mood. To surround me in that cave with them wild dogs did…and they demanded a grart gold nugget.
I heard that Grotteau possessed the great Kittrick nuggest of the originals gold find in Mystery, and now I knew its a fact. But I fooled 'm. I refused. So then what did they do? They attacked, them dogs did. He said:

"To keep themdsogs quiet and shut their salivating jaws, Ishowed em my nugget. It enranced their burning wold eyes of that cave pack, and it entranced them from making any mor attacks. Ssure the snarled, ltheir bared them logn fangs drippilng with 'nolten gold, they did. Mister Lored. He said he slowly backed out of the cave while them animal part huamans snapped at him and barked without letup and every foot of tetreat I took was loaded with fear."

He was a strange one, Reiner, a man whom the town had one takena genuine liking to b;t now edeviled by some ort of inner dark rhapsody of itntention and dark deeds. His ascent from the morglue thi day was smbolic in a way, for I rmember his saying once time that death has no prc but the grave diggers, a blight I cam to bdlieve that overlay not just Grotteau, but had begun to nfect th entire vilaage. Yet here I ;was; and it was a sort of foreoding, an innate curiosity in mhy own mind that compelled me to remain. People I had attachment to, i wanted at least to see how their conundrum of gold lust and personal sacrifice worked themselves sout. I saw ;more than lI dared to contemplate

Since I worked in the press show, amid dusty, link smalls, and greas, I began to fill the chase with more of Grotteaus penumbra of strange outcries, for so thy were, his promonitions of events to come… an ad for wagon bar, one for the Continental hotel, bits ofverse, a ficitious confession by a miner killed in a power blast as a alrning to careless miners, and much more. I had learned a startling fact, that a man had not vleen attacked by coyotes or wild dogs almost two years ago and his body not found until recdentlly, that Alefory had been murdered, Mysterys resident bootlegger whose cactus whiskey still had produced for minera what they otherwise had to import, and sheaper by the palefull. Thjough lGrotteau I also learned that the FCeral dogs had been conjured by the Flame Woman, a mountain mystic following thel surrender by lthe lpeople of their protective weapons. I did not at the time see any coneection bdgtseen la goldrich but helpless cit;izenryl and a dangerous guntoting impoverished citizenry. The entire matter was foolishness to me.

Their fangs did not recede. Their paws, like bear paws, since they did not recede either, but had fingers that stretched out. Their dead stench filled the lair where the flesh of rotting inhavited the darkness. It had been the moonshiners cave. It had stood almost in the light and wanted turturn and escape. But you see, that there cave was where thd Monnshiner Aleford had kept his still

Grotteau seemed possessed. lHis lthoughts lay like throrns in barbed wire fashion that drew blood from his brain, and thn he gve out with a terrifying shriek lthere in the Prssroom, as if he felt the stingrong gripping fingers of anoth4erf man clutch at his throat. He lifted one foot as if gripping fingers closed around one ankle. And the epxresion was on his face, fixed as is tortgured him fronm hickory, like a mine beamn, strong enough to entaancgle him down into a invisivble grave...that of th long dead. It was as if LOored was staring down at lthe glaunt, lhard, empty lbarren of flesh sof la face of bones whitened by alkali of somebody he had known. The the vision and it sredmebance was expended themselves, and Grotteau lfell to the floor as if in a fit. lI epected convusions but there came none. Just quiet, as if suddenly he had fallen asleep. I let him lay on the floor of the pressroom...I had other things to do.

THE SWING OF THE
PENDULUM

Grotteau published an article in *The Scorpion* that ignited the fuse of resentment, not against the Indians but against settlers who had come to make a life in *Mystery*. They often came to get away from the city, or small town ignorance or religious prejudice or to open-air freedom, the clean desert air for health reasons. Their motives were many. The article read:

> *The Scorpion—Mystery. Settlers are arriving by twos and threes almost on a daily basis to settle here in Mystery. They find the air clean and healthful and though lacking church and school at present, the potential for development is considerable. The Dawsons, the Harteurs, the Desmonds, lthe Alonzos…all have arrived to put down roots here. We wish them welcome and good luck. They will find our town friendly and generous, a commendable place to settle with or without a family.*

This was the last edition of *The Scorpion*. The second and total fire of the newspaper office and press-room cut the heart out of the village, as did the inferno at the *Continental hotel*. The miners, watched with apathy and a certain human affinity for the spectacular. The grave-moles infestation was avenged. Grotteau held the stakes and must take the consequences. In the minds of the miners, they realized that the Indians had worked their curse on the village; superstition took over from there and made that awsome, horrible night an event of death and final retribution. The village lay idle, virtually devastated, the dead promptly buried on the hills , the living turning inward toward their sense of personal outrage. As for wrath there was aplenty, enough to go around again and again.

A sizeable mob of about thirty that night of the conflagration had picked up firebrands of burning mesquite, larddipped rags, kerosene lanterns and had swept like a flood of their own making toward the office of *The Scorpion.* Its fireing was essentially a citizen-led conflagration of mute revenge, proof that the miners' revolt was both necessary and a profound success, a triumph of dignity over ignominy of the human spirit.

"It was him and that...damned newspaper that done it all."
"He wanted to take our guns away from us....so's he could take over!"
"What'n hell are we waiting fer? He ant got guts to come around. He's back of them dogs running wold—the teeth of his curse on us...and we thought we was doing ourselves a favor! We was setting him up! Long live The Scorpion...in hell's flire!" came the curse of simple, plain-talking men.

Led by Daamon Jackson, the arsonist, his early, outside crime long forgotten, the villagers marched to the newspaper office. It was a smaller version of a street scene reminiscent in all revolutions. They hunted for Grotteau...their only Elite, their singleminded Aristocrat. They considered Ludheim a legalistic fraud and simply ignored his presence in the town. Where, also, was that their Mayor De Vancha?.. he did not help? He had fled, a spoiler in cowardice and terror, from the righteousness of the miners' cause. Their poor, dole situation had balooned into a calamity of revolutionary disdain and retribution of frightening proportions for a small town, a mere village of only a thousand souls. They were restoring dignity and meaning to their lives. They wanted bodies. In their rage, they would not be stopped, like vigilantes, and where was the voice of reason not clouded by hunger for gold? They were complicit in the exchange, there could be no doubt.

"Burn it to the ground!" came the wild, angry, vengeful cry. "Yea! Yea! Burn…burn…burn…!

They had furnished Grotteau with the perfect black-mail device. The cries of the miners did not awaken compassion in any who had not joined, for their intent was to kill Grotteau and the memories of their captivity by his fraudulent scheme, the wretched misery in their lives as townsmen and villagers who had once held a vision of richess. To them a homicide seemed just, and who could be blamed but Grotteau himself , the cunning malefactor who had begun the entire process of destruction by removing the instruments of their salvation, their weapons, their voice. They had watched their guns burn in that night's fire, almost like a sacred sacrifice to a dread fate. Where were the all, the malefactors? Father Xavier was not present this night. They were certain that some of their weapons had vanished in the hands of the revolutionary Priest, Xavier. They knew that for a certainty—because several of the miners had witnessed—their guns being waggoned out of town, southward toward Mexico…and thence to Guatamala. Here in *Mystery* was where they were needed. May God forgive them their sightless ignorance!

They would not be stopped as they arrived, coming on in deathly street cries and in mute silence to sabotage **The Scorpion**. On they came—the street was short and wide and dusty—like a river of flame, several in their midst with poles wrapped in burlap and dipped in pitch, one miner carrying a bucket of kerosene… They would not be stopped; there was no law around. They moved without any apparent leader, no wildeyed and volatile spirited radical. Yet they came on with purpose and the certainty of death. The man with the kerosene sloshed it from his bucked over the front. of the small building. Within the flash of a few seconds flames erupted from the siding, then the shingles caught up the flames and burned with furious heat and the crackling of wood. One looking inside could see the old Chalmers iron press standing there in the ambent yellow light and getting hotter and hotter. The lead type would soon melt.

"We been hoodwinked! We been tricked and cheated! We give up our arms. We give up our money. We sacrifice our honesty…fer what…for a paper promise…a site hundred yards square on a map none of us trusts. Is that right?" A great cheer flew up from the crowd, followed by a wild and ominous rumbling as from the throats of a mighty assemblage of angry men, enraged because their livelihood had beens trifled with…and their integrity and honor played with as of little worth. The muttered curses cut through the noise. They rumbled with utter dismay and unconscious intention to kill thir victim, the object of their wrath. Reiner Grotteau had schemed to dehumanize the miners, to make of them mere defenseless animals, less than human, to introduce a culture of defeat and anguish of anxiety. For there were among them men of good report, like Doctor Farralones and Mister Merryman, who had left jobs, families behind. That they had capitulated with such ignominy further added fuel to the mob's rage. Thus the inevitable occurred, as rain follows storm ligtning.

The men with the burning poles flung them like flaming javelins into the front window of the press office. With a puff of angry fire, they instantly ignited the desk, cabinets and furniture inside. In their wrath the mob put a torch to the wooden walk at the front of *The Scorpion*, whose morgue had produced the damnable histories on so many of the villagers. Some tossed bags of black power into the inferno as flames danced on the miners' upturned faces fixed in visages of wrath and delight and release. The fire quickly consumed the entire building, sparks reaching up into the black desert night sky as the fragile walls collapsed unward upon the fire. Like paper that burns brightly swiftly and then dies into ash, so it was with the newspaper office of Grotteau, for in minutes it was no longer the place where pain was conjured up against lthe miner citizenry and where a wild scheme to dishonor men's lives was finally denied, the outraged justice in vengeful violence. The office of *The Scorpion*, misssive of duplicity, was no more, for once again…as so often happened in the Old West…the fire of revenge, the flame of justice gotten no other way, consumed the good and the bad together and nobody was made unhappy by that union in death.

Panning was on the descent, for the panners one or another were using the water at their copious will, vaguely thinking of their fellow miners along the creek bank below. It was a situation gaudy with reprisal by attack. The solution, at least to the tension, was to haul Grotteau in before a kangarooo court for a trial of his culpability in the explosions, the water shortage, the difficulties with the Indians and the matter of his disarmingf them for a pomise that did not eventuate. There had been a gross miscalcuaion as to the richness of gold finds. The Mother Lode was not a well defined wall of gold but rather a landscape, like a galaxy of stars, that had in ancient times peppered the ground with gold dust, flakes and nuggets.

Mother Lode was simply a euphemism for a promised local richness in gold deposits. The friends, families and in some cases, businesses were all left behind when gold mining boomed and those left behind anxiously awaited news of progress in panning and hardrock mining. Water had been one of the major factors in the miners' discontent, for a sufficient supply of water for the slurry of rocker boxes did not promise enough remalining that was potable for drinking and cooking. Fazakerly, the village waterman, was thinking of taking on several helpers.

Under these hardship conditions, dysentery was always n eminent possibility, but so were scorpion bites and mishandled dynamite. On the day of his arraignment, his custody, the day was intensely hot and as calm as the air inside a mining tunnel. the burning sun reflected from tim corrugated roofs of shacks and shanties, scattered outward from Dog Street and perched on the nearbr hillsides a cabin vested in luck and borne of loneliness, torn between rich secductions and te claims of a wife and children of a profession and steady honest labor back home. These miners, unlike the coal miners of Kentucky and Pennsylvania did not mine coal for the company butgold for their personal fortunes . They were a different breed altogether.

Mister Hornsby had, himself, become a victim to the gold-fever madness of the miners, for without conscience he had lost coils of new rope, an assortment of brooms and brushes, picks, shovels, pans, crowbars, mauls, for all of which miners had promised to remburse him when their gold claims ame in, as the saying went. He had had to fill in a crater-like hole in a corner of the store...the proprietor invited the miners to observe for themselves...when he had removed several floorboards. In their bizarre frenzy, the miners had stripped his shelves of all cannned goods, a barrel of crackers, salted fish...not the pickles...and sacks of flour and sugar were long gone. The barrels had veen torn apart for their firewood at various diggings. lhe contents consumed long ago. A spirit of vandalism had motivated the miners against Hornsby. His scales were vanished, bolts sof calico silk were gone...for tents. A horsecollar was purloined for resale in Frost, floor platform scales had been ripped from their floor bolts while Hornsby slept upstairs in a drunk to forget, and had silently been spirited away into the desert night, three hundred pound scales. The lust for gold had turned honest men into thieves and criminals that totally destroyed the means of livelihood for honest tradesmen and shopkeepers.

Seeing the object press-office building of their fury gone, the miners broke up, gragmented and went their ways, some back to their shacks and others returning into the hills. Yet others, having no alternative or recourse, returned to their ignominious prospecting sites on the streets and venues of the village, hoping to outdistance calamity with some small success. It seemed to many this night that justice, taken into the hands of men when no other recourse is possible, does at times have a cleansing effect. Yet it appeared that the torching of **The Scorpion** had little becalming effect on the villagers. Instead, they would hunt down Grotteau and give him a taste of their vengeance. They backed away from the flames and returned to what remained of their campsites, after the Indian raid, and to their shanty cabins, if still standing on the desert plain.

De Vancha knew where Grotteau was hiding out. He would gather other men and go take the scorpion and hold him in their custody...at the *General Merchandis Store,* still standing. They would

251

hold him with guns that he had overlooked and which they had refused to lsurrender, guns that had partially fended off feral dogs in that desperate night's wild canine attack. There would come a few reinforcements from Frost. There in Hornsby's they would set up guard. There they would hold court. The very idea that there could be any justice whatsoever began to circulate among the sourdoughs. It would be three months before a Circuit Riding judge should pass through; they would not wait. Ludheim was a lawyer. He would sit as their judge. He knew much about Grotteau; he had worked alongside of him. They were often seen together.

De Vancha would form a possee of eleven vigilantes. They clucked with satisfaction that the wanted man had probably watched from a distance the destruction of his engine of power. They were assured that he had not gone far. His mania for power had kept him tethered to the village and to his inquisitorial *Scorpion* office, now smouldering ashes and char. Mister Merryman, the former school teacher, had said there were evil doings afoot in the village. No matter how desperate men become, their pride almost always triumphs over good sense and old custom.

The bloody maurauding feral dogs and the maurauding Indians comprised the law of outlawry. The stranger Sheriff who had blown into the muzzle of his pistol the night of the pyre confirmed the words, the surrender of the village to violence. The vigilantes as a body felt that they had no recourse. but to bring Grotteau in as an act of justice. The single, lone sheriff was nowhere to be seen, probably having joined the deadly revolution of the miners out of sympathy and his reckoning of the truth.

In the confusion and desperate efforts to defend themselves, there was no one watching the store. The villagers, as if by will, raided Hornsby's *General Merchndise Store* and in baskets and burlap bags the villagers looted canned stuffs, tools, blasting powder, lanterns and pans and whatever else they could use. The digging meantime went on as if the labors at the diggings were spring wound and unflagging

A question Ludheim had wanted an answer to now sharpened his imagination. Where had all the cactus whiskey come from when no wagon had returned from Frost or Triangle with sufficient qualtities to whet the miners' tongues for two events. He knew that Aleford had been murdered; but that was almost a year ago. Motivated by this two-fold need ot satisfy his curiosity and to bring the culprit to jutice, Ludheim led the party up the mountain trail to the cave where the dead Aleford had manufactured the whiskey that he sold to the Indians. In fact, the murderer had never been found. The knife with the initials of RG on the handle was misleading. Grotteau had not murdered the old moonlshiner because he knew that he would find him an ally in his scheme.

The possee entered the cave and found what Grotteau had found, the burner, the boiler, distilling coil and the gathering tub. A sack of barley, half emptied was tossed to one side, bits and hunks of the Sagurro cactus lay about quite withered and dessicated. Ludheim stood at the entrance, watching the lantern of another villager go deeper within. The tunnel was a hundred yards deep, ending where a cave-in had blocked passage. The langern light glinted off the mica and quarts crystals in the walls of the shaft. The seemingly inert Grotteau like a ghostly figure suddenly rose up, blinded in the lightl.

"Stop right there, gents," commanded the voice of Grotteau. He held a revolver leveled at them. "Don't shoot the man!" Merryman's voice commanded.

"You got no right to come in here. This heres my home!," a voice challenged. It was Almayer's voice, to the utter surprise of the entire possee. Why would he be in here, and for what possible reason could he stand guard over a pile of guns formerly owened by the citizens of Mystery? There they were—guns that had once belonged to the villagers, guns for protection of a local people, guns to voice fear and a man's rights—some of them—a small arsenal....those tlhat hlad not burned in the street pyre.

"Keep back! You got no right...." He did not finish.

"Who is it…the assayer!… Well, I'll be goddamned and go to hell! We come up here to find Grotteau," said Sean Malloy, former roustabout countered. He had come with a revolver but did not draw it from his waistband to shoot Grotteau. He just wanted to warn him. He got off a blast that brought down rocks and dust from the roof. The brilliant flash and deafening echo of muzzle powder intantly flash-lit the cave interior. The possee knew that Grotteau was desperate. He had lost his cause, he had witnessed his enterprise ruined. The attack by the ravenous dogs had simply proved that the village lay under a curse. Daamon, The man with the lantern continued on further into the care where to his astonishment and jolt, with an inexplicable oath, he came upon a cache of weapons. The other members of the possee were struck aghast. It was evident that Grotteau , who now lay unconscious for whatever reason—likely struck by an angry miner—had meant this cache of guns for a particular purpose and destination—to Central America and more revolutionary gold tidied by the church's blessings without a confession to Father Xavier. Farralones, a diligent and by now almost savage member of the possee, looked at the inert Grotteau and pronounced him alive still. He smiled, knowing the cause. He kicked the body and it moaned. Another of the miners threw the semi-conscious Grotteau over his shoulder and carried him out to the saddle of Ludheim's horse. They entiure party started back down the mountiain into town .

Knowing he saw life in Grotteau, Daamon, the arsonist of expertise , remarked to the saddlelain Grotteau, "Your press is gone, ***The Scorpion*** ant no more. You lost yer soul, Grotteau, damn you!" The body of Grotteau did not reply….

"Good think we didnt shoot you in self defense, Grotteau," Merryman said to the unresponsive ***Scorpion*** editor. Then a few steps further on—"Whole town'll be watching, when you come in like a sack a horse shit over the saddle with your hands tied. Look migty queer to bring you in alive even. We don't want no stories to get started about how you fought back in that there cave. Understand, Grotteau? We aren't real nice…and your extortions ant so nice nither."

Former Priest Xavier when he called on Aleford for mild whiskey for sacramental wine, had discovered the remains of Aleford. They had been torn by the vultures, and ravenous animals like feral dogs that don't often eat dead flesh. Desert ants had consumed the remainer. There he was: the looks of the situation were that the mooshiner was a victim of senseless murder. He had often traded with the Indians and brought down his distilled spirits to sell in the village. He was harmless old man. As for the guns, Grotteau had to store them somewhere. He had taken in over one hundred arms valuable mainly for the people's self-defense. Truth to tell, Xavier had trucked on wagonload down through Mexico, wearing his clerical priest's collar for disguiase, on the way to Guatamala and the Christian Liberation revolutionary forces of Pedro Bautista. Liberation Theology was the name of their game. Father Xavier had said one day at the **Hard Rock Saloon,** sipping a glass of wine, that "you cannot save your soul by your own justice without the law of man or God." Bobody who had heard him knew what he meant. The guns in the Moonshiner's cave were more of the same confiscaton. They...and his **Scorpion** press, evem during the trial, would be a source of Grotteau's power over the villagers. A terrorist's power can linger after him like the smell of death. Grotteau's inspiration to violence would now ignite the fuse of revenge to counter that terror.

Two days after the possee's discovery of Grotteau, who, recovered, now sat in the Frost jail, notice was posted in handwritten script wherever the villagers passed that a trial would be held in Hornsby's *General Marchandist Store* on the 10th of July. And so it was to be. Ludheim had researchd the matter of Spanish Land grants, going back to Ferdinand and Isabella, and he had discovered, to his immense relief, that Thomas Aleford, the moonshiner, and not DeVancha, was the true holder of the Land Grant Deed. This irony was shocking to Ludheim, that a record so obscure, distant and discnnected could even be traced. But then there were Sepulvedas and De Sotos still around. As a lawyer, his practice abandoned, he saw the merit of justice in the ownership of the land title.

To the great relief of Ludheim, a lawyer turned gold miner who had legal experience but knew little about judgeship responsibilities, the circuit riding magistrate named Balfour, Aaron Balfour, showed up in Frost, heard the lament of Grotteau through the locals and decided to pay the village of *Mystery* a visit. There, he encountered DeVancha who, thinking he would find a haven in the Judge, agreed at once to Balfour's oversight of the trial of Grotteau, for extortion, malfeasance of conduct and the moral turptitude of dishonest gain, in a word, of robbery of the citizens.

He rode about the village until dark, observing the holes, the replacement in places, of planks that had been removed from the sidewalk, the piles of flung dirt in holes hardly ever more than six feet deep. Here and there he heard the clang of a shovel at work filling in a digging or enlarging another. The streets were spotted by the miners' wagons and sourdough feet. It appeared to Balfour as if the village had been under siege. Nobody bothered about the exploratory holes. There was abroad as he sniffed the desert air a certain wisdom of abandonment, which was not a part of the ordinary miner's outlook. *The Scorpion* sign still hung from a pole in front of the burned-out ruins of the press office. The destruction voiced the viciousness of the mob's anger, and the hot, violence of the fire it had signatied. Balfour drew up land read the slign, posted by that someone who always spurns the mob and draws company from compassion for the condemned.

> *I make you rich if you come with me*
> *But yer ways was not narrly sad to see—*
> *You burned my press, you got no voice.*
> *You sold your land, you got no choice.*
>
> *But if you ever want to strike it rich*
> *Just hand a buck to that sonofabitch!*
> *And back yer claim loud and sure,*
> *You got litltle sense of mercy's cure.*

It took Judge Aaron Balfour one day to hammer out the charges and arrange for his sitting as a circuit judge.

Slashes of lightning struck among the scrub pines in the mills above the village and the winds increased to hurricane velocity, obscuring all but the rooftops and ghostly outlines of the remnants of the board walk, horse troughs and shed pillars along the main street. It was as if all of nature had conspired to make the occasion of the trial a memorable one, for the hearing, to begin, was to decide if the facts warranted a trial of Grotteau, who would go either to the gallows or to an unwanted freedom. Judge Balfour was dressed in his most courtly attire, having purchased a wig of white horsehair for the sitting, a small point of vanity' he always carried about with him him on his ciccuit a polished gavel that marked his authority.

On the streets, few fewer and fewer miners were put to digging for gold in their purchased land grant *claims*, so called, and according to maps Grotteau furnished, copied from Almalyers master map. They had put their shovels and picks to one side, for the winds alone appeared to begin to fill in the holes the miners had dug—as nature's final act of retributive justcice for the Indians and their disinterred forebearers.

It seemed to Ludheim that the God of fortune was saying *vengeance is mine*. Over the land lay thedarkenss of the desert windstorm. When, like a prisoner hailed before the judge, beaten and half-naked, Grotteau had been stripped to the waist to display his many tatoos of regeneration among a prison population, a drug and brothel consortium, a mind-soul mixture of venom and snaklike cunning. It was plain to an astonished Ludheim that Grotteau, his former colleague, took a certain pride in these images, a spiders web, naked women, an anchor...for he had served in the war of 1810, he being a symbol of astonishing compelexity which only a syllogist could interpret.

Having made his legal background known to Balfour, Ludheim was charged with selecting at random twelve miners to sit for the jurymen. It was Ludheim's task to round up citizens he found in the streets, the Saloon, in the hotel lobby and wagon works. This he did with dispatch, or course selecting Merryman, Dr. Farralones, Daamon,

Hartman, Kittrick, Hornsby, the merchant and six more to complete the jury: Jeremiah Jackson, prospector, Jimmy Tyler, wheelwright, Clayton Benlop, mule skinner, Pastor Chauncy Schmidt. Ludlhein found Terrence O Flaherity drinking his suds at the *Hard Rock*. Ludheim handed him a scrawled message from the Court in Triange. "Report to the *General Merchandis Store* at 8 am. You are to sit on a jury come next Tuesday. And still the twelfth, Garby Stevenson, who was mustered from the *Continental Hotel*. Clayton Benlop was found at the **Wagon Works** and stables, having his horse reshod. Jimmy Tyler would have to drop his maul as a wheelwright at the same place. The other similar selection filled out the jury of twelve. Ludheim was the town crier about the village for the occasion. He labored with enthusiasm, one must assume not to find his former editor guilty but to frame a physical semblance of law and order in the lawless village.

Led by a rope as a captive, Grotteau was ushered by a miner into the familiar interior of Hornbys *General Merchandise Store*, to which a cadre of some eleven or twelve had brough him in a wagon from a Frost . That, alone, constituted a voice for the village; for it was "a mystery where he had come from", said De Vancha, and perhaps to where he would go when all the forces of temporal power met this judgement day.

There was disgust and anger instantly directed by the miners toward Grotteau, their self-proclaimed benefactor. Some of the mines were blown up to bring miners around to his table. Also, they knew who the perpetrator of new-tunnel digging sites was. One of the leaders of the possee was a small, red bearded miner who wore a continual smile of sardonic disdain, almost a smirk on his face. He had lost his means to a livelihood, so he termed it, taking out an ounce of gold each day from the cramped darkness of his tunnel. Grotteau was impervious to begging and empty words.

"Your calamity I understand. I have wached y our industry..." a jerk on the neck rope like the tug on a disobedient cur, brought silence from Grotteau. He begged the possee to trust him, trust him. "I promise to keep your mine tunnels safe from dynamiting...."—a solution easy enough for him to promise, since it was he who had perpetrated the closure blasts, four in total. The possee members, each and all, looked anxious to the point of desperation; none could imagine Grotteau's escape from the charges read by Judge Balfour. They wanted only justice yet who is so naïve as to think they were were not perfectly capable of making "other arrangements" if by some fluke of the law their enemy were relased on bail. Their faces spoke the solemn and defiant knowledge:

"There was their man."

"You'll get your water—" Grotteau said, trying to blur the onerus of his crimes. Indeed, water was nother impediment to community peace and unity. Water. But that could wait. They had confronted at last the impossibility of separating gold from ore without the use of water, which , due to a mild winter in the mountains, had threatened them with community dehydration for mining and drinking both. They were not at all happy with Grotteau's promise to parcel out the water fairly to them each month—for a small cost. He had put himself in control of that life source. They saw his counterfeit promise as a plea for more time to save his life at their hands.

Yet on the day of Balfour's enquiry, the miners seemed to share Hornsby's sense of loss. Judge Balfour made it known through conversations hither and yon, that the villgers had permitted all this depredation to come about by their own silence. These holes covered with boards, the excavational looks of the town, the interruption of their lives, by the rapacious lust for gold. A domestic dog scavenged for food, sniffing at some discarded gravesite bones. The story aboutl the feral dogs had great currency in Frost. Two boys from there wandered about, looking at the holes in the desert, one of them picked up a bone examined it turning it in his fingers, then dropped it it on the ground—a thighbone.

Although some of the villagers had considered a town council, it never materialized. Their usefulness would have consisted of a bare minimal inspection of damages, so primitive and lacking sophisticated insights or laws, if at all, for controlling the Indians The Indians would distinguish between theirs and the village counsel; the one was greedy and committed crimes for gold, the other religious, spirited and self-protective. The White Man walked with a swagger and boasted of his luck, wherever he could find it, at the **Hard Rock Saloon** or at his diggings. The Indians cared not a feather for such subtle distinctions.

Circuit Riding Judge Aaron Balfour had already interrogated the prisoner. He had ridden into town astride an uncommonly tall sorrel mare, sitting strraight and riding in the saddle like a trooper, a long face and strikingly white kin, presenting a solemn aspect to those who first saw him. When the jury was brought in by Ludheim and sworn in by Balfour, they sat on hastily built benches nailed together by Carpenter Smitty for the occasion. Balfour introduced himself after a loud hammering with his new gavel. "I'm Judge Balfour of this distrixt, I'm a Circuit Riding judge. I am here today…with you twelve, to hear any and all evidence against the defendant Reiner Grotteau, seated there…accused of crimes of malfeasance against his neighbors and of breakingf the laws governing land ownership and distribution. He fininshed with, "Are there any questions?" There were none…at this time "The twelve jurors I have had mustered here are your neighbors. They seek to find Mister Grotteau innocent, as the law so provides. They will decide upon the credibility of the facts. I will decide what laws apply and enjoin you…ahem…then I shall ask you to see if the facts fit the law and its implied circumstances. Or …are the shoes, the facts of the case, the right ones for the law, the horse." He smiled. "Are there any questions?" Silence was the answer.

Balfour felt assured that if he did not, with the jury, reach some sort of vindication or culpability arraignment against the accused, that the miners would try to take over the village and Hornsby's store. Then would come more looting and at last bloodshed. He apparently was not fully aware that the villagers, generally, no longer possessed firearms. An occasional villager passing the store on the street would jeer at Grotteau. On villager, totally outraged, walked into the store and up to Grotteauy at the pickle barrel and puhed a sawed off shot gun, from under his coat, up to the chin of the accused and, enraged, prepared to blast off his head. The other miners were aghast. Ludheim pushed the gun away. The judge rapped for order. He had the man bring his shot gun to the store merchandise counter and reprimanded him, took the gun away until the trial ended. He kept on hammering the customer's counter for order.

"If there is to be any sharing of the crimes, as charged to one man, Reiner Grotteau, the evidence will so construe the matter. But if he alone is the culprit, God have mercy on his soul." This prayer was a little early, since no issue of condemnation had has yet been decided. The judge carried in his pocket a petition by twenty- five of the villagers against Grortteua, and in absentia, Almayer, yet the latter was, in fact, present.

"Ahem." Another hammering. "Said Almayer, the assayer, has charged that the miners conspired and participated in a crime to defraud the undersigned and that the above so charged have willfully and wantonly contributed to destroy the village of *Mystery.*" Judge Balfour seemed almost too polite when he read these words aloud to the assembly and before Prisoner Grotteau. The judge sat the accused in a chair, brought down from Hornsby's residence above the store.

Townsfolks had gathered in the store, standing patiently to hear the trial and to testify. Balfour, dressed in his judges robe, which he packed about with hij on theroad, combed his white beard and cleared his throat. The jury, mustered by Mulheim sat on the village carpenter's benches. The judge stood and ordered his courtroom of guests to stand. "California is now a state in the Union." A silence as in a tomb followed. Tricks of outlawry were now forbidden for State troopers and even the army were at the disposal of the Governor. "You will respect me, now as your *pro tem* judge"—none knew what he meant—"and everybody will stand to honor the court...of which I am the headmaster." He grimaced. "Sit down, all of you. This Court is now in session." He banged his gavel, made of a bed post and a drilled wagonwheel spoke. It was effective against flies and mischief makers. He examined it closely with a faint smile of satisfaction .

The big boney hand of Judge Balfour reached into his brown leather briefcase for a lawbook on *Trespass and Other Torts*. Antagonized by the maurauding dogs, the smells of dissent, or desecration of land possessed by Indian spirits of the dead, the Judge caressed his white sideburns and rattled his pencil on the store counter. He was seated in a high stool to overlook the forty or so members in the Courtroom and the prisoner, who sat behind a pickle barrel for his table. The elements of disagreement and threat of violence among the townsmen where put into the mold of dark feuding sides, an enmity not exactly guaranteed to demolish their pride, exrtinguish their arguments and defer the case to some sort of Tribal agreement. It was Balfour's duty to avoid warfare between the miners who had fallen for Grottau's scam and those who were about ready to pull up stakes and elave *Mystery*. First, Balfour relized that there would have to arise a declaration of possession, with sufficient proof to warrant a trial. Nothing was taken for granted in Grotteau's defense.

"The accused, Reiner Grotteau, is being charged with fraud by a class of citizens of the town of *Mystery*. The Prosecutor appointed by the Judge, this time Almayer, had found by a vague rumor, that an unidentified Priest had discovered a dessicated and shredded body in a cave in th nearby hills; and that the deceased was guilty of selling whiskey, without a tax, to the local Indians. A furor arose. Balfour rapped with his carpenter's mallet on the counter. He found the charge irrelevant to the fraud the accused had perpetrated. He banged his gavel again.

Balfour continued to read from a paper on which the charges were scrawled by hand...miners were engaged, by a *writ of certerori* by Grotteau, to extract gold with assurances they would find same on lands religiously sacred to the Indians. And, forthwith, the existence of miners' diggings had turned the village into a place for prairier gosphers....laughter from the audience...torn apart—floor and walls in excess of need and to search for the promised metal...all according to a map which he, the Prosecutor had furnished Mister Grotteau as his possession solely. And that said mpa indicated without contest places where the lode had reached the surface, and that said map showed the sites were accessible to any able-bodied man with a pick and shovel... and the price of the claim. Nothing could be clearer than that Grotteau had brought about an ugliness to the benighted village, and that he had scammed the miners of their gold, having collected several sacks of gold dust, and had corrupted the sacred burial plots of the Coyote Butte Indians.

"Each one of you had deeded to him his small parcel when he signed the claim deed." He lapsed into silence, stroked his beard, rubbed his forehead and went on. "Alehouse, August Alehouse, owns these acres on which the town sits. Rather they are now in his name. He is dead...am I to understand, he was murdered?"

"That's right, yer honor, kilt by Injuns," came an obscure, annonymous voice.

"How do you know this? Such sudden accusations can become...dangerous. But whether he was murdered or not, we put that aside for the present business." He hammered his gavel again. A piece of wood chip flew up from the counter. "Therefore, this Court will assume temporary ownership...in the absence of any beneficiary. Ahem." He rapped his gavel a solid blow again. "Mister Grotteau, here...you recognied the man...a student of history. He knows much by his study of old nwspaper clipplings...particularly..." he aspirated the *t* and *p* in the word for emphasis..."particularly of one who had title to the land we stand on. The eminent lawyer Mister Max Ludheim has confirmed the findings of the aforementioned Grotteau. Grotteau tried to leap up from his chair to deny the affirmation of Judge Balfour. Mister Daamon, the former arsonist and Sam Katorsky , a the **Hard Rock Saloon's** huskey piano player, restrained him. "We ;have with us a special witness, not a surprise to townfolks, a Priest by the name of Xavier." The prist blushed slightly but continued to look straight ahead. He did not acknowledge the identification.

"Will the Father please take the witness chair.. For lthe occasion the Pirest was attired in miner's clothes, common trousers and shirt of working panners. The judge's interrogation, snce this was a primitive investigation as much as a trial, rested on Ludheim's earlier testimony. "Did the priest go to visit Mister Alehouse, to secure some sacramental wine., sir."

"But Mister Alehouse was a moonshiner. The blessed sacrament, as I understand it, is sanctified by the use of wine. You might have gone to the **Hard Rock Saloon.**"

"I am careful to be seen in God's appointed places. I hoped Mister Alehouse had wine at his ...establishment."

"His cave...?"

"Yes, your Honor."

"Did you go to talk Mister Alehouse out of his land...or swindle him out of his land."

"By no means, no, in God's name...my motive was honorable."

"It was pure...your motive I am speaking of."

"In Gods' name, that is so. " He made the sign of the corss"I also went to test...a man's soul. Its tru, I'm no longer a priest of the St. Augustine Order, but I am still anxious about men's souls."

"Even about the souls of revolutionaries...?"

"Beg pardon, sir.".

"Nothing at all. Just a thought..." Some talk arose among the court, causing the judge to slam down his gavel again which, as before, caused a wood chip to fly up. "Did you find Mister Alehouses soul sound and intact?

"I did; sir."

"What about Mister Grotteau there...Look. Do you see him in the court. What do you know about his soul?" Commotion and loud whisperings arose among the audience. The judge ignored them this time.

"Sir, Your Honor...I do not judge of men's souls...only the appraiser of its present condition."

"What do you find the present condition of...the accused to be?"

"I find it enflamed with hatred of honor and of justice. I find it darkened by the lust for gold." There came a stir again amongst the miners. "Just as many of your are today in this room." These words evoked a angry outburst among the watching miners...

"Cursed Priest...to the devil with your kind. We don't need either you or God here in this village."

"So you see, Your Honor, I have no choice, either to keep silent or to leave."

"I quite understand…but stay. We need someone to mitigate the disaster of fallen men here in *Mystery*. More outrage followed from the miners raucous cries, several whistled. The judge hammered several violent blows with his gavel. "Hang the priest with Grotteau. Yeh, good riddance of them both." Such cries of hate and distress said a great deal about the outlook and opinions of the panners and hard rockers in the village…as well as about the spiritualstate and moral status of the community.

"Your humble comments do not set well withsl the miners… some of them. They are a stubborn lot, as you can see, Father. Perhaps they will change their minds if not their souls.

"That is God's business, sir. May I go?"

"You may, if you will answer one more question: Have you made it a practice to purchase discarded guns from the man they call Grotteau, to carry to lolitical revolutionaries in Guatamala?"

"I have payed Mister Grotteau admirably well and not infrequently for the guns he collected …not by forced, you understand."

I see…the miners weapons…."

Sir, I did not ask where they came from…only that they were still useable."

"You found that to be so…that the weapons were still in useable condition.

"I did, your honor."

"You may go. Thank you Father Xavier." The Priest got up from the witness chair and sank back into the crowd of spectators

Attired in tribal costume with warrior feather, one man wearing a headdress, the others in Christian clothing, but all with painted faces to discriminate their tribes, A dozen or so Indians from outlying desert hogans swarmed in through the back door to the merchandise store. They pushed the miners aside to take the front. The miners fell back , their faces showing incredulity, disbelief in their eyes, intimidated by the violence of the entry and the painted faces. An Indian who identified himself as *Running Horse* spoke.

"I am Running Horse. I have more schoolling than most of these White Men here. We have warned them not to dig on our foreetathers' graves. We come as witnesses to the spirits of our dead brothers. We have tired to stop their desecration of the graves of our dead ones. But they persist because they are persuaded that gold lies under the streets of this village. It is possible that it does...I am not an assayer, like our friend Almayer, husband of the *Flame Woman*. The bones of our departed do lie beneath these sands. You chose the place to dig on their graves. May the buzzards fall on every man who has dug into the earth of our forebearers. May the ravages of nature take up our cause in revenge. You shall never find gold, never here, not even in these hills. The goddess mother earth has kept her secrets froml you. She honors our clan , our brothers. We were once warriors. We are not peaceable, yet we fight the will of the White Man that flies into the heavens to escape our anger. The earth gives to us back our heritage. She will dance with us this night on Coyote Butte. You have seen us up there. We are the fire. You have heard us on a still night. We are the spirits. You have watched our flames go up into the black ngiht sky like the stars. The stars and the heavens echo our pain and our prayers. Do not mock us, as you mock us. You will die...all of you...."

With that promise and threat, which most of the miners took bo be wrath without satisfaction but not a prophesy, the twelve of them removed pouches from around their belts. From the pouches they took black dauging brushes, like shaving-mug brushes, and they vegan to furious attack of daubing and splashing the faces of trhe miners with streaks of sooted black to mark them for death. There ensued a wrestling, fist fighting struggle.. Yet snot a miner escaped the marking ceremony, done amid violence, which the Indians, in lieu of scalping knives and tomahawsks, used to defy and humiliat and mark their adversaries. Only Judge Balfour escaped the marking by the Indians.

When it was done, the Indians amid the commotion, the resistance, the punches thrown by white miners and loud blasphemous words, the resounding curses of depraved thought, the Indians retreated as they had come...out the back door to the merchandise store. It was a curious scene of humiliation and violent anger that followed as miners tried to removed the paint yet succeeded only in smearing it furether from their faces with shirt tails and their hands. They made their faces appear ghoulish and bizarre. The pigment of the paint, iron mixed with wood soot and oil, would not come off. Amid the clamor could be heard the hoofbeats of the departing Indians. A strange silence of ignominy and humilialtion fell over the roomful of miners as well affecting Judge Balfour and his two appointed bailiffs. Grotteau did not escape the swatching with the black paint. The Indians in their fury had made their message of resent;ment and indignation and insult to their culture reality-clear to all in that room. Judge Balfour cried, aloud over the continued noise..of rebellion. Court is dismissed until ten tomorrow. Be here or the sheriffs from Frost will find you...witnesses. He hammered a final rap with his bedpost gavel and the miners rushed to get out, scarcely looking at one another in their humiliation of their manhood and their personal dignity and worth. In another ten minutes the *General Merchandise Store* was completely empty.

Tne clocks elsewhere marked ten sharp. The miners had not completely removed the sooted marks of death from their faces. They were silent, filled with rage and ready for any incident.

Balfour commenced proceedings without hesitation. "I have heard the pleadings of many miners here...that they acquired title to a plot in the town from which they hoped to extract gold ore. The matter before the court deals with fraud on the part of Mister ReinerGrotteau, the accused. We all know how the scam worked. Is there a witness?

Studman, a miner stood up. "What you say is true, so help me god."

"Your friend was the assayer named Almaeyr. He was part Indian, I'm given to understand."

Silence. "You could use him to justify your claim that he produced a map. I have requested it. Will you come forward, sir. he requested of another miner who stood. It was Daamon Jackson , the arsonist and panner. He furnished his name to the court. l

"I say that property destruction is a serious matter," said Daamon.

"It is…but I will decide the law, Mister Jackson. What have you to say with regard to the…honesty of defendant's appeal to you in connection with the mining claims?"

"I doubted him." Balfour nodded in agreement.

"Was it not revenge that caused you and others tos burn down Mister Grotteau's newspaper office?"

"I was not in on that, sir."

Are there any seated here who were? Jackson looked around and pointed out four or five. Balfour asked them one by one… "that will do Mister jackson…" to come forth and give their honest reasons for why they would want to destroy Mister Grotteau's newspaper. They agreed to a man that the publisher of *The Scorpion* intended no good to them and that the best way to silence his words was to estroyl his press. Had they not thought of simply moving? Just as Balfosur sposed this question an unusually furious gust of wind actually shook the wooden building so that it trembsled as if ready to life off its foundations. The wind screamed around the corners and over the front façade, removing a strip of tarpaper and a loosening clapboards on one side. The trial paused for several minutes. "Divine Providence has perhaps brought this sudden gale storm upon us to challenge our words to see if they are sound and honest in the truth," said the judgfe sententiously, and with a faint, grim smile. He glanced out the window as the dust in the street and clusters of weeds and flotsam swept along by the gale.

Daamon Jackson went on. "Lemme say so, sir, we had no guns, 'cause sone of the terms of getting a false claims to dig was that we give iu…surrender our shotguns and revolvers." This exchange was not new to Balfour. A deep frown crossed his white face, knitted his gray eyebrows and caused him to curry his beard in wonder, perplexity and disbelief.

"But why?" was all he could say in the absence of full knowledge.

"Perhaps the prisoner will enlighten us on this point."

"The gun is a false symbol of power. It corrupts."

"I see. How interesting!..and gold does not?" the judge replied.

"Not gold as dust or nuggets but gold as power and the threat of power."

A nice philosophy, Mister Jackson. So...you believed... as did many others here in *Mystery*, that Mister Grotteau thought it appropriate to disarm the citizens...so as to present a small image of power comtrary to his."

"Your lnonor...." Grotteau, seated up close to the improvised bench, wished to speak. The judge held up his hand and came down hard on the counter with his bedpost gavel.

"You, Mister Jackson, had one of these...these claims, which you acquired in exhcange...."

"Fer a old shotgun. Yesssir, I did."

"You also knew that you were digging in the graveyeard of former Indian tribesmen."

"I did not know at first, sir. That's why all the commotion of the Indians yesterday fianlly come clar to me. We wuz offending them Indians."

"Where is your assayer, Mister Almayer?"

"Dontchu know...he threw hisself into the fire out on Dog Street that nigfht..."

"Committed suicide...for what reason, do you suppose?"

"He was a Indian hisself, yer Honor. And I guess he folt like he sold out to us Whites when he helped us test our gold finds. So, he's dead."

"Conveniently so. lI is my understanding there is a map these miners were authorized by Mister Almayer to to use to find their claims."

Ludheim produced a copy for the judge, which was a copy of Grotteau's general map of the town. Unfolding it, Ludheim handed it tos the Judge. Grotteaus face turned lived then dark with a scowl or revenge, demonic in its intensity, as he watched the scene unfold. He had always trusted Daamon and Ludheim.

"Let me ask you, Mister Jackson, how did this Almayer met his...demise" I don't accept suicide by emolation in a bonfire in the middle of town."

"He was...he died by...the spectators watched him in horror. Ask them. I tell you, sir...he committed suicide by throwing hisself into the flames we had built with tunnel shoring and th' guns we throwed inter the flames."

"Let mel be see if I understand what you're saying.. You...he lthrew himself into the fire...before the eyes of everyone...here...I presume you were all there...and nobodyl tired to pull him ourt of the flames to rescue him?"

We're all possessed...most of us, except the priest...we've got a fatalist bend to us. It comes with the the diggijn. with the hunt for gold. Any other way and we would all go crazy.

So because of your claim to be a fatalist, you refused to lift a hand to halp a dying man?"

"That is correct, Your Honor," Jackson replied and came off the witness chair and sat down alongside his fellow townsmen.

Incredulity shone on his face. Judge Balfour studied the map supplied my Ludheim. His scowl deepened, then changed to an expression of curiosity, then faded into an enlightened look of clear knowledge. All tlhe comains of the claims were clearly identilfied by red ink, the buildings and walks. The general lay of the streets, few as they were, were clarly penned in., Some of the figures of assessed value, predictive, of each claim were added, certain ones at ten thousand dollars, others at three thousand, fifteen hundred and one at five hundred. Each plot bore a different land-value according to its potential lode gold that the miner would be expected to discover. Almayer had furnished these figures. Balfour seemed well-satisfied that the map represented what Almayer would have seen in ore samples, had he lived...and if his conscience had not led him to commit suicide. Being one with the Indians because of his own heritage, he had sold them out for his own profit; he had shared in the miners' culpability of burial-site desecration, a matter most horrible to the Indians, tolerably wrong to the white miners, and of no significance to those who wished to use the land. New laws regarding grave sites and mineral rights compelled respect for these two causes for litigation..

"Suicide," Balfour repeated aloud, then under his breath, the shock of disbelief still fixed upon his face in a twisting mockery of judicial concern. For he was mortal. "My God, what next! he exclaimed before the court. He searched the faces of the spectator miners, whos scruffy bearded faces of challenge and sinful rapport, coveralls caked with desert dyes of sand and soil, unwashed for lack of clar running creek water. Fazakerly's water bags had been ripped open by the Indians when they galloped through the village a fortnihrt before; he had not replaced them or even sewen them up, leaky as that would prove. Docfor Farralones had distributed water from his small mine runner spring, delivering the water in empty casks gotten from the saloon. Washwater was out of sthe question and even the availble liquid had to be boiled to prevent dysentery and fluoridia.

So now we have a village without water, unhappy in all that was transpiring. Very soon deperation would set in. A party could be chosen to take wagfon load of barrels over to Frost…yet that was not the final solution but the presence of natural water, which could not be counted on to arrive.

Balfour refolded his map and turned his attention to Reiner Grotteau. "Tell me, Mister Grotteau—who occupied the sirtness chair…if you will. Have you any notion as to how or why la man named Aleford died?"

The qluestion was importants and significant since it marked a shifrt fdrom the charges of fraud to the implication of murder.

His answer—"Wild dogs…most animals I remind you fear fire. He could have driven them off.

"That's 'not much brush for firewood in'l thatl cave."

"I agree, Your Honor, not much. What little he had he used for his moonshiner still."

"I see. So he..he had no …weapon for self-defense either."

"Might've. Can't say Your Honor."

"No…?"

Grotteau kept silent. "Maybe you'd care to tell me and this court how he did die."

271

"Hunger. I never saw him kilt for game. I hardly ever saw him down the the village. Somebody er other could've brought him grub from Frost."

"Hmmm, possible…but is that probable, sir?"

"Jus' maybe."

"You were not one of them."

"Never tried to be, your honor. He lived up there by himself, never bothered nobody."

"That's your sign of neigfhborliness."

"We got along together, Your honor, mostly by tending to our own business."

"But if somebody's died or gets sick or is hurt, that's also none of your business."

"If we kin help, we oughta do so. But we don't have to but in if its no matter for us."

"If the wild dogs or a..robber, or, say, just a angry friend caused harm to a man, you pretend its none of your affair."

"Like I say, Judge, we don't butt in."

"Then you must not be aware that Mister Aleford is dead."

"I …we heard that he was. We got no whiskey from him for asmallamount a month."

"He used….?"

"He used to make …moonshinel. No doubt about that is here, Mister Grotteau?"

"No, sir, cactus whiskey. Good stuff it was." Laughter among the miners in the store front court.

"But the man is dead…has been dead for some time. Henry… bring in the exhibit…the sack of bones, will wil. The man referred to was unkempt in a tailored coat, dennims, graying beard and straw hat. His face was tranned by the desert sun. He carried into the Court a sack of bones, which ostensibly contained an exhibit …but bones of whom.

"Open up the sack, Henry. Take out whatever comes to hand." The man, so instructed, did so. He removed a femuf bone. "Does this look like the shank bone of any animal you know of?" the Judge asked Grotteau.

"No, sir. It looks…."

"Positively human, if you will permit me to say so." said the judge with sarcasm. It is the bone of a human being, deceased to be sure, since it is bleached white in lthe sun, gone for three months at least. A leg bone, hmmmmn." He stared into the Scorpion's face. He held it up for all the miners to observe. It is the bone I say of the murdered Mister Aleford. Ex;hibit A." He handed the bone back to Henry who returned it to the sack. "So, now your Mister Aleford is dead, as dead as he ever will be."

A murmur sprang up among the miners; they felt something in the wind, an accusation, a charge, a supicion, an accusartion.

"I admit the evidence is circumstantial. But theres one piece of evidence that is sanot circumstantial. Again he called on lHenry. In my saddle bag there is a knife. Bring that to me, would you Henry. The man so addressed again responded, in a few minutes the man addressed as *Henry* returned to the courtroom carrying in his hand a long bowieknife. The Judge held it up before the bvlance facesed, lenquiringexpressions of curiosity of the gathered miners. "This as you can plainly see is a bowie knife."

Grotteaul squsirmed. The man who was killed by this knife isn't around any more to testify. Lloud conversations broke forth among the miners. I think mister Aleford was sprobably la very sensiblel man. If he took sick and was desperate, he couldve gone for help. lHe had a burro...let run wild by the murderer. Balfour fglanced at Gortteau. Mlister Alefords burro...could have told us who the murderer was. Or he could have transpsorted him if he was...wounded... to a doctor in Frost. But hje idnt go. lHe didnt go because he was...dead. A gasp audible, subdued sprang from the throats sof the assemvbled townsmen to the trial. Are you jurors aware of these circumstances, both potential and real?

There followed low assenting voices. The Judge now turnedfull front to confront Grotteau. The latter's face was ashen, he forced self to remainl calm, assert his inner power, visible to all who knew him and had dealt with *The Scorpion.* He waited for Balfour to speak.

"Whem was the last time you saw him...Mister Aleford, Mister Grotteau?"

"Oh, about a...amonths ago."

"But the condition of those bones indicates a death spant of aat least two to three months. It takes that long for bones to bleach in lthe desert sun...particularly when the buzzards hant picked them clean yet."

"Well, maybe it was longer. I'm not a good keeper of records."

"I find that hard to believe, sir. You operated a newpaper here in Mystery called *The Scorpion*."

"I did...and in it in the basement was where I stored old back issued...records of events that have occurred in the town."

"Small things that happened...likemurder, an everyday occurrence. What else, sir?"

I try to, sir, but I dont recollect most of them.

So then, it could have been twos or more months since the last saw Mister Aleford."

"Thats right, sir."

"Fine, were gitting someplace. You have a doctor here in *Mystery*?"

"We have...and a very fine doctor he is, too."

"A doctor Farralones."

"Yes, sir, that's his name. First time I talked to him..." Laughterensued the answer. "This is not a laughting matter, Mister Grotteau or you spectators. This Court of enquiry ...and we have twelve of the members of your community silttling in judgement to lhear thefacts. This Court finds the...murder sof Mister Aleford a very serious matter."

"Murder...murder is serious, sir."

"'Swat I said...Murder." May it please the Court for me to assert that your...friend, your acquaintance, your supplier of moonshine whiskey was smurdered! At this point Balfour looked intently at Grotteauyl, who did not move nor did his face change its expression to dispassion, unacceptance of guilt.

"Here…here is the knife, if may or may lnot be the muder weapon. Is this knife yours, Mister Grotteau. It bears the initials RG on the handle."

"I lost it, sir. It is my knife. I do not know how it came into your possession."

"It was found at the crime scene."

"It is my knife, I admsit, but I did not use it to kill Aleford."

"Nobody has accused you…yet, of…murder, sir. Just that this knife is yours and…somehow got misplaced?…at the crime scene."

"If that is where it was found, that is where it was found. But I did not use it it there…in any way, shape, fashion or form, Your Honor."

While the crowd began a noisy caucus; among lthemselves, Judge Balfour rapped hard and furiouslyh with his gavel to obtain order and sil3ence. A wild drumming of boots on the wooiden floor boards ceased. Grsoptteau vegan to squirm uneasily. "You …all of lyoul can give testimonhy tht Mister Almahyer, your assayer committed suicide by thrsowisng himself sinto a fire built on Dog Street, I believe it is called….and that no one tried to rescue him. Silence ensued; their very silence gave testimony to the truth of Balfour's reconstruction. You also know…by evidence, if not by his absence of a log period of tsime…three or smore months…that Mister Aleford lis no more. is in all probabibiity…dead. If the bones of *Exhibit A* re not his, then whose are they? Can any of the jurors venture a gfuess? The jurymen sat gravely silent, their bearded faces fixed on Judge Balfour.

He addressed the accused: "Let us leave the matter of Mister Aleford's mysterious…disappearance by a presumed murder and return to the matter of fraud. You had some kind of mining scheme to open up mining within the boundaries of *Mystery*. Is that correct." Grotteau nodded but uttered no words. Were you intentionally trying to defraud these good people?"

Grotteau quickly flashed the faces he recognized, then he said, his voice sounding more like a command than a civil answer: "The people did whart they felt they had to do, Your Honor. I didn't make them buy my gold claims… an offer that contained the warning *Buye;r Beware.*

"These good folks were not…misled. They used their own good common sense."

"The people did what they felt they had to do, Your Honor. I didnt make them buy my title deeds for claims." Balfour was not impressed. A clap of thunder muted his words, so that he appeared only to move his lips. I felt that I had been victimized by fate and cirumstances…the miners defection and the wild dogs. I was also a victim, Your Honor."

"In what way were you the victim, Mister Grotteau?"

""Folks here in town boycotted my paper, ***The Scorpion***, sir."

"I see…discrimination. Would that they had had more of it. Well, let me say this: you have committed in essence a pillage upon the dead. Grotteau stood up with the judge's words. By his action he affirmed the truth of the accusation.

"I see," repeated the skeptical Balfour, pulling his beard and rattling his pencil on the counter like a drummer. "When the feral dogs besieged this village, you as much had made its residents helpless by your confiscation of their guns, their weapons of self-defense." Were you aware that three people died from dog bites?"

"No, Your honor. But they had a choice. They could either stay out of the gold rush or come in and give up their weapons. I thought then that it was a fair deal…. I wanted to avoid bloodshed between miners, as to jumping claims, jealousy over ownership."

"There was no military post you could summon to help you put down…trouble."

"There was no predicting the attack of the dogs either."

"You are clever. I would almost say you had a …a program to go big-time..er....become a manager of the town, a sort of dictator…a contriver against these good people for your own selfish purposes."

"I am obvious, Your Honor…totally open and honest. I'm not trying to conceal anything folks don't already know about."

"We shall see." The prisoner struggled against the bondage of the ropes on his wrists, but the judge was not moved to pity by such anguish, thiinking it deliberate. He knew that two or three were killed by wild-dog bites and over a dozen had had to be taken to Triangsle for medical treatment, possible rabies infection and pain.

"They got what they deserved. They burned down my newapaper offices and destroyed my printing press," Grotteau lamented before the Judge. Not only that, they destroyed all my records, most of them. They...he pointed...they are the maurauders. It is they who did acts that were criminal," Grotteau cried in a fury. It is they who shoud be standing trial here today and not me."

"The prisoner will stay seated. You will have another chance to testify, Mister Grotteu. In due time. In due time. These folks are all miners. They are residents of *Mystery*. They are the interested party in this matter of fraud, sir...."

A miner stood and raised his hand. It was Merryman, the teacher who wished to speak. He took the witness chair. He gave his name, then proceeded. "This man, Your Honor, began the whole mess by persuading us folks to buy into his mining scheme. He promised us that there was gold under the village streets, under the floors...in here...this store, the floors of the hotel, the *Hard Rock Saloon*. He had a map...said it showed a vein of gold under the village."

"You did not douvbt....? We gave up our guns, some of us, in exchange for these worthless deeds. Am I not rgiht?" He held up a fistful of the claim deeds and waved them before the court. The courtroom broke into loud conversation, Balfour rapped for silence like a carpenter driving nail.. "He made fun of the law," the judge went on. "You do not make a jest of the law, do you, Mister Grotteau?" Balfour queried. "Nooo, damn right we don't!" Profanity and apithets followed profanity....Now you know what fraud is. Now you see what cowardice is. Remember, the murder of the old moonshiner, just one intance of avarice." The court looked astounded and muttered. "Regarding the murder, you comprehend what avarice is...for some of you...that's greed." Balfour took a sip of whiskey from a small carafe on the floor beside his chair. "And now you know what justice is," said Judge Balfour with an imperious disdain. There arose more loud shouts and curses heaped upon Grotteau.

"And possession of the land is what Mister Grotteau here wanrted. But he had to let you freeload in order to float his plan."

"I did. But, sir, we're miners, we come here to find gold. Mining is our business. We work on hunches, on chunks of rock. We go by what othe miners tell us."

"Never doubting their word, their findings…as you never doubted Mister Grotteau here…That will all, MisterMerryman."

An especiallhy fierce gust of desert wind swept sand like a blast of water against the storefront and blew the door open and flung sand into the interior. A loud commotion followed. Balfour ordered the front door to be secured with a lengfth of chain so that became unwittingly prisoners of Judge Balfour.

The next witness, a minr named Holtz, Herman Holtz. He testified, not against Grotteau but talkd about his dream on successive nights that were visions of a warning. He thought the judge ought to hear them, since they were serious prophesies of the future for all of *Mystery*. Balfour reluctantly consented to the explanation. Holts was sworn in by Ludheim. In the second of these dreams…Judge Balfour interrupted to ask if they wre relevant to the charge against the prisoner and the witness said, "Yes, Yer Honor, they are. In that dream, an exploding asteroid of gold had plummeted into the villge, scattering fragments of gold and converting into epitaphs the tombstones spotted around the village over the open diggins…as if they had been graves. Percy…good Percy lives here, interred with his amulet of Hope. Here lies Trinity, an often misquoted pariah of the Saloon, whose omniscient knowledge deepend his hole ;in the earth. Sangroid, the well digger disinterred Cachuma bones which he had fed to a village dog. The Indian spirit would bear him into a dark void of space. The Indian spirit would bear him into a dark void of space. The remainder of some thirty or forty unholy consummations of greed and esecration awakened me with a chilling of the terror about to visit this hyer village…." Thus Holtz's testimony ended. There was around the town a spirit of terror once endured during the Inquisition, but not instituted by the Priest who was slack to defend the faith and anxious to promite the welfare of the doctrine of sin. The terror sprang from the benighted belief in the afterworld where all who had come upon Indian relique bones would meet their adversary owner. The folks of *Mystery* were consumed by this superstition, a strange disease that ultimately did them in as a community of miners.

Judge Balfour was speaking. "There is a connection between an alleged, or a suspected murder of the old moonshiner and the alleged fruud perpetrated against the citizens of *Mystery* by Mister Grotteau…a specific connection. But first…let me ask one of the jurors to take the stand." This was a common practice in those days, to qualify a juryman for a witness to be replaced by an alternative, of which there were two for this trial.

The man was Doctor Farralones. To him Judge Balfour put the next question: "Could it be that Mister Aleford was atttacked by a gamg. Remember, sir, we are not dealing here with the butchering of a desert cow or the slaughter of feral dogs. We are dealing with the murder of a man named Aleford. It does not matter at this juncture that he made illegal whiskey. He was murdered without mercy, in cold blood. He was killed without a thought for consequences. How do you think the man might have died, Doctor Farralones?

"I can only guess, sir. LI dild not perform an autopsy."

"Were you ever at his moonshiner's cave?"

"Never, sir. I have my own cave to work for the gold, and I also keep a field hospital for injured miners."

"That is commenable, You are dismissed. Mister Grotteau, will you take the stand again. You are still under oath. I want you tos think carefully about the next question I will ask." He rattled his pensil, shoved his gavel to one side and stared intently at the witness.

"How do you think August Aleford died, Mister Grotteau? It doesnst matter that he made illegal whiskey. He was killed without mercy," he repeated.

"We, meaning him and me, we had a little argument. I went up to pay my respects to him.

Your respects, you say. The likes of you never knew respect. You've defrauded these men here. You've gottens them to abandon their personal firearms, the only secursity they've got."

"I intended to buy a keg sof moonshine, your honor." The judge appeared to faint, but he was pretending and quickly revived.

"A key of whiskey to bribe the Indians not to attack the miners for the desecration of their ancestors' graves—was that not the reason?"

"No, sir. Aleford sole his stuff ln Frost. He didnt need the trade of the miners, Your Honor."

"Then tell us lysour story, Mister Grotteau. We are all waiting to hear it.s Tell us in exact detail."

I went up to talk to Aleford about some whiskey, as I say. He was working his still."

"At swhat time?"

"Sundown. We sat and chewed for a while, then I left, aore total dark...I got poor eyes, Your Honor.

"Not poor enough to use this," thle judge said and took up the dagger with the initials of **RG** which he had kept in his saddlebag. "This is the weapon you used." A loud commotion arose among the spectators. Grotteau vehemently denied the ownership .

"Those your sinlitials>" . He showed the knife to Grotteau. **RG**...on the handle? Can't be any other man's, Mister Grotteau."

"Dropped out of my pocket on my business call."

"You keep a seveninch bowie knife in...your pocket, sir

"Under my belt is what I mean."

"One died by suicide, threw himself into a fire. Almayer. You folks did nothing.s God will take His vengeance in due time. I told you why you went up there...to murder Aleford, Mister Grotteau. It's because you found out...youre a cunning one...you found out that Mister Aleford, not your town Mayor de Vancha, was the true inheritor of these lands, whether or not under a Spanish Land Grant. Even he did not know. But I'm no dullwit, sir. I am a Circuit Judge and I'm responsible to research this very important question as to whom the lands belong. Aleford was the true inheritor by way of the Boniface Land Grant for loyal service to the kind. Aleford was a descendant of Boniface. Your assistant Mister Ludheim has done the research admirably and with thoroughness." He nodded toward the Ludheim. "You, you Mister Grotteau killed Aleford in order to take wrongful posdession of the land by an intended fictive title deed. These miners would be your laborers in the minds you intended to exploit. The

Indian matter was slimply blind to divert reason from your scheme, sir. This country is rich in good ore , Mister Grotteau. You also knew that through the village appraiser, the aforementioned Almayer. It all fits together. You have the townsmen here to believe that yo could terrorize them with a pack of wilddogs or…or the power of your press to invent…stories about their lives?"

"I had no control…"

"The devil' will make you pay up accounts, Grotteau!" came a voice from the crowd in the store.

"You see…they have your number, Mister Grotteau. They lust for you to suffer, Grotteau. They want to see you punished."

Ir was Ludheim who stepped through the crowd, just; as these words came from the lips of Balfour. He asked to take the stand. Grotteau looked at him with a bewildered and defiant expresion. Ludheim was about to break confidence with Grotteau.

"Your honor, Grotteau leaves out an important matter."

"Yes, sir…and you are…?"

"Max Ludheim." The judge swore him in. "I lworked with the accused at *The Scorpion*."

"Yes, please proceed."

"Indians… almost twenty of them came riding through the village one nightr. They were enrages. They saw that Grotteau had goaded the miners to dig up the town. Under the buildings and streets of *Mystery* are the graves of their ancestor Indian relatives. These were their kin seeking vengeance. They are not the wild ones of the past. They respect the White Man's laws. Your Honor, Mister Grotteau does not respect the law."

"That's a damned lie,!" Grotteau shouted. Two burly miners held him ;down when he startsed to rushstoward Ludhei;m. Balfour hammered on the counter with his gavel. Orderrlestored except for murmurings among the spectators, Balfour prompted Ludheim to continue with histestimony.

"So they came to put a stop to…." The magistrate again prompted.

"to the desecration of the Indian graves, Judge Balfour…aad they came drunken on moonshine whiskey. I; know…they lost all control."

"On the merits of your testimony, I agree. But what did they intend to do...or did hey accomplish. Did they...shoot someone.. anyone?"

"No, Your Honor, they came with faces painted to look like skeletons, their horses too. *Spirits.*"

"Then what did they do, Mister Ludheim?"

"They rode to one end of the village, cirlcled back and rode down the mainstreet Dog Street, again.. Then they were gone. They said the village has a curse on it now and they flung sheepskins filled with Aleford's whiskey into the flames of the newpaper press some village folks had torched."

"How do you know all this."

"First off, I was there...saw everything with my own eyes. I learned...I read up on Indian lore...you might know this, too, Your Honor...it's a part sof Indian beliefs that when the spirits of the departed are molestsed or disturbed ..their bones, I mean...in anyway, that the agents, their gods of the underworld...come to visit their wrasth on the malefactors, the desecrafors."

"Indian graves...," the Judge said thoughtfully.

"A Indian graveyard."

"Brought a curse...? This knowledge seemed ompletely new to Balfour. He had not yet assimilated its import.

"Grotteau was selling their gravesites...to these miners here." Ludheim nodded. It was true in a literal sense.

"Did you not know this land is the State's land...California's public land? Hmmm?" Balfosure lookie around at the assemblage of miners. California is now a state, not a territory. I no longer belongs to Mexico. You townmen did not know that, did you? Therefore the land is deemed State property, the land, its acreage, its mineral rights belong to the people of the state of California."

"The Indians just wanted to break up my mining company," Grotteau shouted. The judge ordered him to sit down and shut up and wait his turn to testify if he wanted to.

"Sir..." spoke Ludheim quietly, "your accusation does not stand the test of truth or accuracy. The Indians would not paint themselves to look like skeletons just so they could destroy your mining scheme."

"They would...they did!"

"The law reads," Balfour interrupted their dialogue...the law reads that prior occupants where the land is not incporated under any provisional government belongs tos the settlers thereon...dead sor alive, as first rilghts claimants. And those Indians, while in their graves, constitute the original inhabitants. Therefore, sir, you cannot nor should you try to displace them...for whatever reasons, gold, buildings, roads or whatever. The deceased are entitled to the santify of ltheir sacred burial places. Indeed, the entire village of *Mystery* is a presupposition of ownership which the Indians have acceded to without the expected traditional resistance.. I add, as the presiding judge of this hearing of enuiry and trial of the facts...and the person of Mister Reiner Grotteau... that it is my personal belief...though the proof is inadequate... that Almayer, your assayer, being himself part indian, killed himself.. in a word committed suicide...because he having murdered Aleford..". The court broke into a louds and boisterous discussing of the charge..."murdered Aleford for giving whiskey to the Indians. That was one virtue your Assayer Almalyer possessed, and that Aleford lacked—he protested that another man, a White Man, should exploit his blood brothers. As for the knife, found in Aleford's cave, Mister Grotteau – you should take better care of your possessions. It was found by the Priest. a Father Xavier, before the moonshiner's death. The cave was his storage place for guns he had collected."

Having finished this panagryic, Judge Balfour rapped repatedly with his heavy Gavel. "Although I have my convictions, according tos the laws of the nations of man...and having chosen a jury, I...we will leave the matter to their judgement. I will admit that we have not had the venefit of full counsel and that I have somewhat shared in that responsibility, but then life ils filled with compromises of one sort or another." He rapped. "Tomorrow this trail will end...and I will fix sentencing,s if need be, for the accused."

Withs the suddenness of the feral dog attack, the Indian invasion of the hardware store courtroom, there came a wild woman's scream and into their midst there fought and struggled a woman dressed in a flamsing dress of red feathers, tlurquoise braelets, bear claws necklace and her face painted with diagonal patches of war paint. Although who she was and why she had come were not evident immediately, itsoon became clear that she was some sort of avenger. She was, in fact, the wife of the deceased Assayer Almayer. She came to rebuke, most apparently.

She stood before the amazed courtroom full, by now, of miners and citizns of the village. "I am the wife of the dead man Almalyer, who killed himself in the street fire. He has spoken his heart to me. I know the truth." She shrilled a scream that was chilling to the judge , Farralones, Merryman and any others unaccustomed to wild outbursts of sthe human spirit. "I come to tell you the truth about my husband, J. C. Almayer, poor Jacques. He killed himself... not becaause he had murdered August Aleford...your prisoner Grotteau is innocent...but because the ;moonshine whiskey was starting to destroy the Indian Bonds of Coyote Butte. Shootings, mysterious disiappearances, a rape or two, three killing by alcohol. You hear me, my voice goes to heaven, but it reaches down to your White Man's hell. There is whlere you will find the moonshiner. The Indians will not sacrifice their land, or their inheritance, their graves of ancestors or their music for the White Man's lust for gold." She gave a primal scream, flinging her hands up to the heavens, then removing a sack from a tie about her waist, she showed them from the palm of one hand... gold dust. "This is what matters to you....gold dust. She emptied the bag into one hand, letting the pouch fall, and with a scream she flung the last of the gold dust over the heads of the assembled miners They were astosunded beyond belief into silence. "The goddess of greed has announted you all." Then silent as a spirit without sound or hesitation, she sped through the miners, bumping them aside. The hooves sof her horse outside sped away. The entire courtrreoom was in a trance of stupifaction. Balfour sat quite still in the gloom of the store, like a statue in a black frock coat, bolo tlie, side-burns and a small goatee. He looked the very image of immobility with a face as cold and expressionless as a terra cotta jug. He placed the brown velum book BLACKSTONES COMMENTARIES beside his gavel. He scanned the court's spectators. The men who had kept Grotteau prisoner on a cot inside the store overnight, four in number were commended by Judge Balfour for their vigilance. Spectators went over to observe the boards that covered a pit dug by Hornsby in his own store.

Balfour spoke. "If any one of you allows the prisoner to escape you will take his place. Heed my warning. I ams grateful for your service."

He rapped for order again. "I have done. I have seen the remains, the charred remains of *The Scorpion*. The wrath of men knows no bounds…they would measure God's power by their own. I saw where the pyre that was build received Almayer, who cast himself into the flame…poor fellow.. with not a soul having a punctilio of compassion to drag him free and snuff out the man's burning. I read your flyer, Mister Grotteau…the one you so generously used to drum up trade for your…mining-company scheme. Nailed to an upturned wagon tree."

At that moment, when the court was to end, a boy , one of two boys at the back held up a rock. "I got a nugget from Mister Grotteau," one cried. Balfour told them to come to the front. They promptly did so. "One of you carries a rock of immense worth. Where did you get it?" He saw the nugget in one hand. The boys looked at each other. "Come…come here you with the broken tooth. What was it you have found?"

In the ashes of *The Scorpion*. The boy blushed. then dragged a huge nugget from behind his back, the very same nugget Grotteau had used to entice the miners to join him.

Balfour took it from the boy's hand and held it up for all to see. This…this my friends, is a piece of evidence that further exemplifies the fraud practiced by Reiner Grotteau siltting there. This…" he held it up for all to see, the motioned with his hand that it should lbe shown to every; miner and villager in the room. " That rock, that chunk of what looks like a nugget, is a fake. It is iron pyrite. See for yourselves. It is phoney, as false and deceptive as the man who used it as bait in his avaricious scheme to hook you in. Mr. Gotteau, ssitting right there." The nugget went its brief rounds. "This is yours, is it not Grotteau. It ils not? " Grotteau subborly refused to talk. "Well it is, the miners recognie it I'm sure. Court is dismissed until tomorrow for the verdilct and sentencing. The jury left hurriedly. Judge Balfour had ignored the testimony of the two boys whose rock, found amid the still warm ashes, symbolized the fraud perpetrated against the common folk by its owners. .

A cold and misty morning sun shaded its light onto the eastern horizon beyond the desert chaparral. A rabbit scampered from its shole, fine grain of parched night sand formed at the vase of the nearby yuccas, now in bloom. A skein of filmy clouds caught the roseaste yellow dawn light as the greenish aura of predawn faded and a soft imperceptible breeze waftsed over the warm night sand. The hills above Mystery were still saturated with darkenss and subdued bluegray, in particula around rock outcropping, glinting obscurely the rising lignt, like windowpanes at a distance. The two cabins visible from lthe main street of the village caught the light on their slate and tin roofs. A dog barked somewhere in the outspace. The night had gone, spent itself perversely on a caldron of brilliant desert stars. It was now dawn and the time set for the final hours of of Grotteau's enquiry by Judge Balfour, who today would hear the jury's verdict.. the miners had assembled again in the storefront courtroom. They appeared to take pleasure in watching agony, all the while expecting an explosive reaction from *The Scorpion's* editor. .

The judge again rapped for order as and the storefront courtroom became quiet. Balfour spoke: "The evidence you saw yesterday, the hard evidence, the ore piece plucked from the charred remains of *The Scorpion* by the two boys, is evidence but the gold in the rock is iron pyrite. I'm keeping the nugget for State's evidence. This belongs to me...and to this court." There came murmuring; one rap of the gavel extinguished all talk.

He went on;. "What was found amidst the twisted and charred pieces of flurniture, a beam or two, remnants of the Dead Scorpion... this...." From a large envelope he drew out a piece a piece, a charred fragmet actually of a paper which said on it, he read: *"The land belongs to me now, or will eventually. Only I can correct the mistken impression of the titled land grant deed thatr this territory of some 12,000 acres should be bequesthed to Senor Di Vancha. He is an imposter. I am the true owner."*

"This comment was addressed to whom do you suppose? To Reiner Grotteau here. Why? To defeat any claim he might have to the land for his base of power. He had won the hotel from the Mexican...I am given to understand...in a game of cards. Milster Ludheim has shown me the deed of title document. He now wants the land; but so, too, did Mister Ludheim. The land onwhich the town of Mysateryis situated belongs to neither. It belong to , or did, to lthe Mexican people. Still, and until it shall be conceded by agreement, the land remains the property of the State of California. All that I say can be confirmed by records at Monterey where the Mexican governor now rules and has his hacienda there is nothing in this document about August Aleford's ownership, therefore the murder by your chemicst and assyder, Almayer, was fruitless, if it was intended to usurp ownership of the original land-grant. It now belongs by the Hidalgo Treaty of Secession to the State of California, primary ownlerslhip affilr;med by the signature of Governor Marciello Consuellas Gonzalas don de Figuero a Sepulveda, servant to the King."

The miners stirred on their creaking benches, overwhelmed by this elaborate leagalistic delivery and *pronunciamiento* on rights of land title. Grotteau made as if to bolt from the room, but the bailiffs appointed by Balfour restrained him. "Tie his shands behind him... securely," said Judge Balfour. "And now...on the basis of the evidence you've just heard and witnessed yesterday, do you gentlement of the jury wish to give us your verdict as to the guilt or innocence of Reiner Grotteau of fraud against the people of *Mystery*. A miner named Julius Castlereigh stood up from the benche where the others jurors sat and said: "We reached a opinion, yer honor?" A long minute or two elapsed. "We're pondered the facts as we know about Grotteai based on evidence what we have gotten in our dealings with him, judge, and it not only looks suspicious he wanted to twist our tails..." the judge squirmed... "take our guns, rob our diggins and control us like he wants...cause he said the ex-change were a good deal. And we accepted it.. All talk considered, yer honor, we think the critter is guilty of...of...."

"Fraud...."

"Fraud, yer honor. And thet's our opinion, sech as it is fer now and later too."

Balour grew livid and impatient. "The maps are all wrong. Our claims," said Castlereigh, "are marked in the wrong places."

The map was again spread out on the counter. A cat walked across the map. The judge studied the map's details. Castlereigh an amateur astronomer, pointed out that the corrdinates put *Mystery* in another quadrant of the true map. The judge balked at the reasoning, smiled, rerolled the map. Nevertheless...." He did not finish his sentence.

"There was no the challenge to the map at the outset," he said. Balfour had now rejected the authenticy of the map. The evildence was now pragmatic. Almayer had relied upon to it fix the location of the miners' claims. He rejected the map's authenticity. He had rejected only the evidence but substantive law that qualifies an exhibit if it relates to the lcrime. He did not think this was so; a murder went unaddressed. For that the map was useless. Grotteau's alleged claims could not be substantiated by the present map. Only the Indians had affixed the charge oftresspass by tribal experilence and tribal memory, not bytheWhite Man's map.

"Thank you for your judgement, gentylemen," Balfour said to the jurors. You may sit down, Mister Castlereigh. The foreman did so.None of the parcels were even recorded, Mister Grotteau...a fine point of the law you overlooked. I visited the courthouse yesterday in Triangle hall of records. You, sir, have sold the miners not mineral rights but mere...air." The room exploded in angry yells and vituperation and curses. Balfour had to hammer on the counter repeatedly to regain control of his courltroom.

What do you say to the surrender of arms in exchange for gold...Mister Grotteau?"

"A fair bargain.""

"A gun for gold...let the buyer beward..." No sooner had he uttered these words than miners from the audience rushed to the front of the store to seize Grotteau. Balfour pulled a small pistol from lis coat and fired several shots sinto the lair. "The law is still in my hands! As avaricious as Mister Grotteau is, in his mining scheme and as a suspect in the death of the monshiner," he shouted above the ruckus, "he is in my custody and I am the law." Upon shouting this warning, he fired his pistol yet a third time, but to no avail. The miners were wild with fury and blood vengeance over their deception and the trick played against him. Virtually the entire courtroom was aflame with the identical rage. Who suddenly should appar but the former prist Father Exavier. "I Beg of you, spare his life...spare his life!" But the Priest's words were lost in the noise and furor. "God hates injustice the same as you." They would have Grotteau's life by the neck of they could. Despite his derringer and the fired shot, the judge was helpless. He did notl even attempt to stop the villagers who, seized Grotteau and dragged him from the courtroom. Balfour shouted, tried to block their exit, raised his pistol and fired another round, but the miners were adamant in their fury. Judge Balfour was helpless to stop them; indeed he was fortunate not to have been bludgeoned, given the rage of the miners against their hapless victim.

Like water from a broken dam the miners poured out of the *General Merchandise Store*. On they came, as sif it had just packed a thousand men satisfied at haing seen some sort of justice done Out they came at random, one on an improvised crutch, others limping, hobbling out and ito the morning street. The grim human bond displayed that for once in its brief historys the store had a grand turnout. These were customer-miners who had been defrauded and the judgement had come by their own kind, and it had rendered one Reiner Grotteau the effigy of disdain and contempt in their minds. He had been found guilty, if not of murder, then of colossal fraud. Brt that guilt was of lesser imprtance than their own expefeiences with the evil of the results, for Grsotteau had put on the sheow of hell, he had pretended a power that was corrupt, like satans in the life of Job, and he had withered under the torching shame of the truth. Thus in their minds their surge of moral retribution was fully justified. Men on a rampage seldom think beyond their act. In a hasty execution there would perhaps arise, new hope for some of the miners. But for now they headed toward the *Continental Hotel*. Judge Balfour had ordered, in the absence of a scaffold, that the accused be hung from the balcony railing of the hotel.

At the head of the mob marched the two bailiffs Blafour had appointed. Between them walked Reiner Grotteau to his doom. The excitement sof lthe mob was the common prelude to vengeful death. The judgement of hanging did not seem extreme to the miners because of what they had suffered at the hands of the Indians. Justice in those times often amounted more to the absence of mercy than the horror of the sentence. Having broken out like a corral of wild horses, the continued amid dust, noise and mob violence to the hotel on Dog Street. The mob pushed and dragged the culprit from tlhe hands of lthe law and down the street to the hotel. most areas outside of Mytery were barren and treeless , the vbalcony of the Continental Hotel closeby alnd practicable. The bailiffs led the accused to and up an outer staircase . Ex[ectant faces waited below. Doctor. Farralones would probably want to examine the man to see if he was dead. A rope was thrown over the balcony and 'tied to a balustrade. Grotteau was ordered to face the crowd of upturned faces below, who awaited his execution with grim impatience. Ironically, it was Ludheim who, virtually a co-comspirator, put the noose over the man's head and ordered him to step over the railing to the edge of the balcony. He wore no hood as he stood outside the railing. They had been the celebrants of luck and secret intrigue. There would e no forgiveness, not even when they should meet in heaven or hell where all the facs would be revealed.

Ludheim jerked the rope tight, and the hanging was all over. This time the drop did not behead the prisoner but broke his neck with a snap. They finished their dirty work within half an hours time, leaving the hapless Grotteau, without honor or unction to swing beheath the balcons for all to see, blhis body turning slowbly in the desert breeze. The Indians let out a wild hoop, three of them at a dlistance firing their carbines intos the chill air to celebrate their victory and recovery of tribal dignity from the stolen fruit of greed, for them an assault on the Indian spirit and a consummaltion of jusltice. There he hung, in front of the old hotel, lifeless,s a criminal , a suspected murderer and extortioner. Only a slight morning breeze stirred the body. It should be mentioned here that when the hotel had burned to the ground, by the suspicious hands of Daamon Jackson, avowed arsonist, an evil spirit was said by the clever newspaper editor to haunt the new structure, a more famed hotel, that was erected on the site. No one ever slept there again.except drifters, a peddler, a maglician and a banjo playerd who showed at the Saloon but were never hired.

No one had seen where she came from, but the flame Woman again intervened with this ominous and dire prophesy. "It is not good to sacrifice a man's life this way. His spirit will join with others. To kill another, even if he is a White Man, to save the dead is a dishonor". She galloped awy linto the dust astride a white stallion, fwathers of red flaming, back to the Butte Country

A small cadre of Indians came on their ponies, costumed and painted in black and red for the hanging. They stood at the rear of the crowd., in front of the *Wagon Works*. Grotteau stood ready for the *coup de grace*. The absence of the blindfold revealed how utterly cruel yet absolute the execution of justice was required in this society. The chief executioner, Ludheim, had slipped the death knot over Grotteau's head. Ludhiim spokean aside to one of the deputies who with one swift motion pushed the condemned man off the hotel balcony.

She came, his wife, not when the hanging party was over. She came when the majority of the crowd was ready, almost silent and motionless, to watch the body drop. She shouted out in a screamsing voice of retributive rage all could not mistake for reason thrust in the muzzle of a canon.

"You out there who dig for gold who blast the rocks, you who pummels the ground for a grain of dust, you who find it sharp and smart to jump the claim of another man, you could get away with it… you who believe that you are the law…you are hanging a man whose guilt as a matter of sharper play is nothing compared to your guilt. I have seens the tales in the morgue. You are not without sin. You who have run from the truth hand a man who stands in your place and you know it. Are you without any guilt? Do you have the gall to accuse a mans of cheating when you have murdered and cheated? Do you consier yourselves so sanctimonious and pure that you cannot be touched by the murder of another man whose crime would be brushed off by a man of justice and reason…not the despicable Judge Balfour who condemned my husband. You who sit on the jury…you could not wait until dawn to do your dirty work, your killing. You who testified against Reiner condemn yourselves by your condemnation, for you are equally, more than guilty of similar and more horrible crimes than cheating or exstortion, of even lying. This I freely admsit. But to cheat is not to rob, plunder like pirates, to attack like the savages the innocents for their lives and their wealth. Are you so purified, and so cleansed that you can stand there and watch Reiner hang for a small crime?"

There came next only silence. The crowd was stunned by the stranger's accusations. Indeed, one or two even shouted out their agreement with her words. No one had ever considered that Reiner Grotteau even had a wife, much less an avenging angel. And so they gaped, mouths twisted and open in wonderment at this…vision of justice. She further added: "I did not come or I should have pleaded then…I did not know. I have lived like a recluse, like a widow which I soon shall be. I; am partially blind and unheedful of the entire smatter." Here she stopped and gathering her breath for one last foray announced, "You who hang Reiner Grotteau this day will suffer to find your souls in peril if not in the judgement rendered by the demon over hell."

I will pray for his soul., shouted the Father Xavier, who had mingled with the mob to the hotel. He made the sign of the cross an don the sandy street before the lost Groteau, whose eyes showed the fate that now awaited him, he knelt and payerd for the sould of Reiner Grotteau. "Forgive them if you have it in your soul," the priest said to Grotteau who simply mumbled but said nothing that was audible.

Ludheim, as much a renegade as Grotteau, but a shrewd bystander when all came to the charge of guilt, uttered these words sof condemnation: "He dug not for gold lust but for desecrtation of Indians graves and suspicion of murder." Impatient of the delays, Ludheim pushed Brotteau from the balcony. The wife's face was in disguise. She walked over to the body that still moved . In a melodramatic move, she touched his boot heels with her upraised ahands and then as swiftly as as suddenly as she had appeared, she departed down the road and out of the village forever.

For a full day the body of Reiner Grotteau hung from the balcony, like a sinful fruit decaying in the desert sun, seeming always to be turned stoward the land that he coveted from the Indians. It was land both sacred and attributive of the King. His eyes never left the sands, downcast with a broken neck, he watched what transpired below, if any event should occur. He was now a humbled kind of his own domain of darkness, higher than the common sougdoughs, than Ludlheim or most of the miners....higher than Dr. Farralones who now struggled with his own conscience when lhe received a message that he ust leave if she valued his life. For Farralones was not, himself an innocent man, he had deliberatey killed a patient...so it was said... to put lhim out of his intense suffering, an act of mercy he had pleaded. When a sympathetic sherrif failed to watch him on minimum secursity, he had in effect let him flee. He had come to here tp *Mystery* where none would try to track him down. Even to a hound dog, the human scent is burned up in desert heat radiating from hot slands.

On the front of the Merchandise store, place of the courtroom scene, there now hung a missive. This was an intended prophesy.

You will ride off..into the desert
Do not ride toware Frost. You will
keep riding. You will not look back.
Never again set foot in the village of
Mystery...not for gold, not for love,
not for tokens of your ignominious past.
Clear out of town and County completely.
You are exiled, Do you understand?
You are all in a sense the hangmen.
You represented this here village.
Would to God I could pack out the rest
of you with them. If you come back, I
will know. If you must, take a burro

with an offering of grain, your kindest
measure…they are free to roam, and go, but
go…into the desert. Go, get thee gone.
Don't never come back. R .Grotteau.

This missive summed up the damned-up anger at all that the
citizens of *Mystery* had witnessed. And so they rode, the risk-takers,
the participants in so called justice, though they would call it mockery.
In the early West, men often had to make do, come to terms with
circumstances of their common sharing, answer the call of common
sense to see that justice was done. the way of their justice would not
always be totally fair.

But she came in the dead of early morning, long after , the
hanging party was over. She came after the majority of the crowd had
positioned themselves to watch the body drop. An unidentified woman
came—one man, a drunk, half-sober to guess, said she was Grotteau's
wife—and she cut down the body dessicated body and put it into a
wagon and left town at once. She knew more about the heart of her
husband than did they, for her wits, her intelligence, her compassion
and her wandering and undependable love for lher husvband had
brought her to this extreme impassee of challenge and courage.

De Vancha, the Mayor appointed by Grotteau, came with his
"sons" at the *Wagon Works* and several other renegades from Frost and
Triangle and they dashed through the town and across the intact bridge
to announe with great yells: "I am the Mayor of this village. My name
is de Vancha.. I am the Mayor, *El Alcalde*. You can do nothing without
me. I am de Vancha. He thus rode up and down *Dog Street* yelling
this announcement with his band of banditos behind him, a dauntless
pack of gang-ridden outlaws, essentially. Theese were De Vancha's men.
Fearing another attack by the Indians, able-vbodied men picked up
their knives, jagged bottle shards set in wood, and ogging chains ready
to do battle. Some few engaged de Vancha's men before they left town,
attempting to pull them from their horses and inflicting real damage
on the maurauders. Nobody knew exactly why the band had come, but
they intended the villagers no good. They had no cause to advance, as

did the Indians, except to erase what de Vancha considered a disgrace against a post of honor, removed by Judge Balfour . the defenders' guns were long ago surrendered, destrosyed. They existed no more. The villagers had learned their lesson too late. the cemetery would take no more, surrounded as it was by weeds and a decrepit wooden fence.

Then came the rains. Jimmy Tyler blew up the creek bridge but too late, afer the murauders had come and gone. The waters came on. There was a threat of a possee comking from the Capitol, crossing the creek into town to claim the land as public domain, for its gold and for other unspecified purposes, a common trick leaving the door open to corrupt politicians. Some strangers did arrive. They slept in the hallways of the deserted hotel for the night. Ballfour had long gone, after he hlad rendered judgement. They did not recognize the village. Ludheim was a mere spirit of the past, He had gotten away with deception but with little personal gain. He had retrieved the tiger-head lantern that hlad sat on his desk down in the *vault* . He was either in hiding or had fled; he had more than one charge hanging over his head.

Like a slash of lightning and a following thunder that tbat broke the silence, their beaks clacking in frenzied expectation as they darkened the sky, literally hundreds of rednecked vultures, birds o death, swooped in from the North on a desert win o dark ferocity. they were hungry, so hungry that all human life took shelter indoors from their ominous, winged, feathered movements in the skies. the few residents who remained in *Mystery* were terrified. "Who'd want to stay here?" one of the dwellers asked the other.

The creek continued to rise. By two the next morning water filled in the holes sof the prospectors and vegan to flow down Dog Street and lap up to the first floor level. In the streets now and then a rider on a horse with duffle lashed to the saddele splashed up the street toward the upper canyon. a lantern burnet at night on here and there, in the darkness, out among the shantys. The lap of water and the gurgle of its flow ran through and around structures remaining on slimple rock pilings. The rain pelted on the corrugated roofs an against wooden siding. The village now assumed a black, darkened and ominous ghostlike aspect , as if no one had ever lived there. the waters contnued to rise until sunup,at which thime the obvserver would have noticed planks floating away, a ludicrous loosened outhouse , boxes of stuff and what remained in the **General Store**. The charred wood from campfire sites had floated silently away in the night. Silt had spread a brown plaster over parts sof the village. l

A small contingent of miners, emboldened by their mission, yet trusting only in their own ingenuity and sufficiency were driven away from the village and sought higher ground for survival

The rains stopped locally, but not twenty miles north the watershed sent a wall of muddied water swirling angrilhy down the creek with the rumble of hidden bounders marking its force and urgency lin a flash flood. Almalyer's shack in one piece, floated downcurrent, in tact but tilted at a crazy angle. Shop fronts, as the Wagon Works, broke away and floated like huge prefavricated rafts of siiding and joist timbers. On one end of the raft, watching the floodtide, sat a cat that gave a faint, desperate mew of despondency. In less than an hour the tide of water struck the village, an invasion this time by a force of nature.

Two boys looked at the old hotel but decided not to go in. "Them folks sure were hot to dig up gold," one of them said.."
"Don't think they found much
"Had to let it be…you don't suppose.
"Lets go, Bryce, An't no business a ours anyways…was wanting somethsibg so bad y'kills yerself to get at sit."
They mounted up on their one horse and hastily rode out of *Mystery* just in time. **The Frost Daily**, would carry the story . Anybody who had visited *Mystery* and knew its struggles and troubles there would voice common gossip about the death of the gold town. the death had been slow but inevitable…and only a few actually knew why it had died..

Ludheim returned to *Mystery* to see if Grotteau was working his claim in hell. A preservation Society had appointed him the curator of **The Scorpion** morgue, keeper of the spirit of the man. He now had his control of the town when it was a corpse. He was entrusted to keep account of and report to the heritage of the Prince of Rebellion. Hand to mouth shall he live, that is his wish, for he imprisoned justice by his cunning and he fomented violence to the point of an unnatural conspiracy of life with death, of goodness with evil, for there were among those miners good men in every sense of the word, only misled.

The Indians, many of the miners and the drovers were mutural friends, but the land now belonged again to the Indians who were here before the White Man's corruptions by his government. The miners and settlers are mostly gone, leaving behind a misshapen vision of a village that once was. *Mystery* now belongs to history.

Panning for gold is still practiced on the American, Sacramento and Yuba Rivers in Gold country. the elusive little flakes worked a kind of magic in Miller's imagination in order for him to write a novel so dramatic in human greed and bloody mistakes by a conglomerate of men who came to the Mother Lode to get rich, and their anarcy and angst that meant gun fights and miners' clashes in outlaw country. A native of California, he looks with some dismay on what miners sacrificed to reach the gold fields. That longing to go home stretched to the maximum by the lust for gold finds its way into the pages of this exceptional novel. Exaggeration was normal for those times. Anything big was good, expecially a two ounce nugget, weighed on the Assayer's counterweight scales. Miller recovers some of his native land's past in the gold country with his novel about a struggle for control and the often unintentional violation of honor by trespass on **Sacred Ground.**